I0657305

CONTROL POINT

GEORGE E. LARAMORE

Copyright © 2012 by Dr. George E. Laramore
All rights reserved.
ISBN: 0615647960
ISBN-13: 9780615647968
Library of Congress Control Number: 2012911115
George E. Laramore

This is a work of fiction. Characters, names, places, and events are either products of the author's imagination or are used fictitiously. Any resemblance to actual persons, living or dead, events, or locales is coincidental.

ACKNOWLEDGEMENTS

I would like to thank my wife, Shelley, for all her support during the writing of this novel and for insightful conversations during our evening walks.

CHAPTER 1

IT WAS LATE OCTOBER and the dreary Seattle winter rainy weather was just beginning. Dean Alfred Schmitt sat back in his chair at State University and contemplated his upcoming meeting with Malcolm Colridge, the head of the Blackmont Finance Group. Three years earlier, in his role as leader of the School of Medicine, the dean had convinced the University Board of Regents to endorse the construction of a new research facility in downtown Seattle, and an elaborate funding proposal had been developed. It would shift most of the financial risk in the project to outside investors through the sale of three tranches of debenture notes. The final phase of the bond sale, underwritten by Blackmont, was about to take place. Citing concern about the overall health of the financial market in light of the recent subprime mortgage debacle, Colridge had asked for the meeting with the dean prior to the issuance of the notes. This was potentially a lucrative arrangement for the dean. For steering the underwriting deal to Blackmont, a substantial amount of money would be going into his personal account.

Schmitt reflected upon his career: B.A. at Northwestern, then Harvard Medical School followed by an internship and residency in Internal Medicine. He had picked internal medicine not from any desire to take care of the "whole patient," a formula that was becoming

1

fashionable today, but rather because it was the best pathway towards academic success and the control that went with it. Schmitt had entered academic medicine at New York University and then risen through the ranks to the exalted position of chairman of internal medicine before being recruited by State University eight years earlier as dean of medicine. After coming to Seattle, he met and married Paige Black, the recently divorced daughter of a Seattle "old money" family. Unfortunately. the new Mrs. Schmitt proved to be an independent sort who was not amused by her husband's dalliances, and filed for divorce when she learned about them. Besides the alimony, which she didn't need, she was demanding exorbitant child support for their two young children. The costly legal battle was drawing to a close, and Schmitt's financial position was becoming increasingly precarious. The deal with Blackmont, which would be dated to occur after the divorce was finalized, would give him a new start.

What the hell thought the Dean, *the overall profits coming to Blackmont would be well over 100 million dollars and his cut was an insignificant amount to them.* This money would allow him to continue the lavish lifestyle to which he had become accustomed as he met and mingled with wealthy major donors to the medical school. *Now to allay Colridge's concerns and push the deal through.*

Margo, the dean's long-suffering secretary stuck her head in the door and announced, "Mr. Colridge is here for his 3 o'clock appointment."

"That's fine" said the dean, "please show him in. Also, would you bring in a fresh pot of coffee and a couple of cups?" Unlike many of the younger secretaries, or 'administrative assistants' as they liked to be called, Margo did not feel that bringing in coffee was a demeaning act. She and smiled and nodded.

Colridge entered the office in his usual rush. The purpose of the coffee was to slow him down and give the dean a chance to talk in a more relaxed setting. Too bad this was a state school with strong rules about alcohol on school property. Otherwise the dean would have offered Colridge something stronger. "I have real concerns about this bond deal," began Colridge. "It depends so much on the research dollars being brought in by the people in the buildings, and I've been reading about government research funding being cut over the next few years."

The dean started at Colridge's abruptness. Then he laughed and began a variant of the same lecture he gave to donors when talking about the elaborate research enterprise of State University. "Over half of the research activities in the new complex are targeted towards cancer," he began. "Pardon the pun but 'Cancer is a growth industry.' It has been that way ever since the National Cancer Act of 1971. The Nixon administration set out to cure cancer by treating it as a type of engineering problem, which could be solved if only you threw enough money at it. The National Cancer Institute's budget became a separate line item in the federal budget and Congress funded it generously. Between 1998 and 2003 the funding for the National Cancer Institute, or NCI, literally doubled. There was so much money floating around that there was an exponential growth in the cancer research enterprise. Right now, almost five billion dollars per year from the NCI alone go into searching for the cure. This is almost 17 percent of the total National Institute of Health budget and that doesn't even count the money that the private sector is pouring in."

"Yes, yes," replied Colridge, "I know all this. But this is past tense – what happens in the future determines whether or not you will be able to afford this new research complex of yours. Show me those projections again."

The dean wheeled his chair around, reached into his briefcase and pulled out a USB drive with the most recent version of his presentation on it. He plugged the drive into his computer and immediately got the error message —"drive unrecognized by the operating system." He uttered a curse word under his breath and once again wished that he could have an Apple system in his office rather than the PC that stood on his desk. However, since several of State's major donors had made their fortunes writing software for PCs, this would not do. He could just imagine the reaction of the head of the Board of Regents were she to see a Mac in his office. He sighed, shut down his computer and rebooted with the USB drive in place. After typing in his password – needlessly complex, he thought, in terms of the alphanumeric combination of upper and lower case characters plus symbols mandated by network security – his computer started up. To make things worse, the password had to be changed every three months to keep the hackers at bay. This made the task of remembering the password a major problem; the dean was running out of mnemonic phrases to help him remember. He would have to start writing the password on a corner of his desktop calendar the way many of his colleagues did. The initial screen showed an aerial view of the medical school with the Olympic Mountains in the background. This time the USB drive showed up on the desktop, and the dean opened it to his Powerpoint presentation.

He beckoned Colridge over as he started through the presentation. The two men were a study in contrast. Schmitt was just over six feet tall, a former college running back, he was starting to show the signs of a paunch in spite of frequent visits to the gym. His thick, black hair had touches of gray at the temples. His tailored Armani suit was blue with light pinstripes. Colridge was short, wiry and going bald from the back of the head forward. He tended to fidget nervously, and the dean had often wondered if he had an overactive thyroid gland. He was wearing a well-cut, blue blazer and grey worsted slacks. The dean scrolled through the presentation with Colridge hovering over his shoulder until he found the slide showing the NCI budget over the past twenty-five years.

"See the continuous increase in funding," he pointed out to Colridge, "and there is no sign of its slackening. State University researchers have been getting an ever increasing percentage of these dollars. Right now, we are within a stone's throw of overtaking Harvard in terms of total federal funding dollars. Indirect costs, the amount of money that is given to the University for administering and supporting this research is 56 percent of the money that is awarded. That figure is for the main campus. We've negotiated a higher rate, 66 percent, for grants in which the research will be done at the new complex. The School of Medicine received about $750 million dollars in direct NIH awards last year, about half being related to cancer research. This means about $210 million dollars each year going to cancer research overhead, which will easily support the bond payments on the new research facility."

Colridge was not so easily mollified. "Yes, but isn't it true that over the past year, the NIH budget has flattened? Also, what would happen to all this research funding if someone were to find a cure for cancer? One of our board members, Samuelson talked about a new vaccine that will prevent cancer from occurring. If that works, there go all your research dollars."

Margo entered the office carrying a tray containing coffee and fixings. She placed it on a small table in the corner of the office and left.

The dean chortled. "Finding a cure for cancer in the sense you are using the word is highly unlikely. Statistically zero in fact." The dean motioned Colridge over to the comfortable leather chairs arranged around the table. "Would you like a cup of coffee?" he asked as he reached for the carafe. "You take it with cream and sugar as I recall." Colridge accepted the cup and the dean leaned back in his chair.

"Cancer is not a single disease, but rather a spectrum of diseases. About all the different cancers really have in common is unrestrained growth. This is triggered by changes in the programming of the cell, which is sometimes caused by outside agents such as tobacco tars, pesticides, radiation, viruses, or anything else. Treating cancer involves taking care of it after it has already developed, either by cutting it out surgically, burning it out with radiotherapy, or poisoning it with chemotherapy. Although science has a better understanding of the human genome than it did in 1971, when the National Cancer Act was passed, we are nowhere close to attacking it at its fundamentals."

"Yes, but what about this new vaccine for cervical cancer?" Colridge persisted.

The dean took a sip of his coffee and continued. "I assume that you are talking about the recently announced vaccine targeting the Human Papilloma Virus? Yes, this is promising, but in the United States, there are only about 10,000 new cases of cervical cancers per year out of about 1.5 million new cancer cases. Even if the vaccine prevented all new cases, which is highly unlikely, this is less than 0.7 percent of all new cancer cases – truly an insignificant number. Why, we already know how to prevent about 20 times that number of cancers by just getting people to stop smoking. Fat chance of that happening! The overall cancer death rate has not changed since the 1950s. If you stop and think about it, a real cure for cancer would be disruptive to the economy. Look at all the pharmaceutical companies that would go bankrupt, the radiotherapy equipment manufacturers, not to mention the various clinical research organizations. They make their living carrying out clinical trials that compare one form of treatment with another. Success is scored as a few percentage points gain in some clinical parameter. Hospitals would also lose one of their most profitable service lines. If anyone were to actually find a cancer cure, rather than hailing him as a hero, the establishment would be more likely to put out a contract on him."

"This makes me feel a little better, but my investors will still want the university to assume more of the financial risk for the project. Otherwise, they won't underwrite the senior level bonds, much less the subordinate bonds. This means that our separate side deal for your own account is off too."

The dean grew visibly flustered, but forced himself to calm down. He walked over to another corner of his office, where a model display of the planned research park was set up. There were three major buildings set at the eastern side of Lake Union which would total one million square feet of research space. At a construction cost of $500 a square foot, this was the biggest project that the school had ever taken on. The buildings were clustered around a central fountain with a surrounding green area. The dean eyed the top floor of the building nearest the lake where he had mentally designated space for one of his offices – after all, one had to be accessible to the troops, and a certain level of ambiance was expected for those at the top. He motioned for Colridge to approach the display.

"This new complex will provide one million square feet of new research space and will generate approximately $400 million dollars in grant funding each year. The indirect costs on this will more than cover the financing of the project."

Colridge remained adamant. "The subprime mortgage fiasco almost tanked the entire financial market, and investors want more security or higher interest rates for assuming the risk. If research funding dries up, this will be so much empty space. What can you pledge for security to guarantee the cash flow?"

The dean thought a moment. "Well, our clinical enterprise generates even more cash flow than our research – over $1.5 billion dollars a year counting hospital revenues. What if we structure the deal so that these clinical dollars underwrite any revenue losses on the research end?"

"What sort of paperwork would we need to make this happen?" asked Colridge. "It seems like it takes forever to get any sort of formal signoff accomplished at State University."

"You're telling me" responded the dean. "However, as dean, I oversee both the research and clinical funds flow and I'll talk with the school's legal advisor, Alice Maxim, about how to make this happen. Would that satisfy your investors?"

Colridge smiled, put down his coffee cup and walked to the door. "I think so. Give me a call when everything is ready to go. In the meantime, I'll call a meeting of our investment group to get their approval. One thing I've learned is to give them plenty of time to think about things since they don't deal well with surprises. Of course, our 'private placement transfer' to your personal account will take place as soon as the first traunche of senior bonds is sold."

The dean saw Colridge to the door and, as he left, told Margo to arrange a meeting with Maxim for sometime late the next day. Drinks and dinner afterwards should assuage any concerns she might have about his proposal.

CHAPTER 2

AT THE SAME TIME that Schmitt and Maxim were having dinner, Gabrielle Jones, or Gaby as her friends called her, was being admitted to the medical oncology ward at State University Medical Center. This was her second admission to the medical center for the treatment of her ovarian cancer. As she worked her way through the prolonged admission process, she recalled how her cancer had been diagnosed. Her belly had been slowly enlarging and she began to have trouble taking a deep breath. Dr. Kim, her family doctor, had gently probed her belly and then had asked the nurse to prepare her for a pelvic examination. Following the exam, he told Gaby that there were some things he wanted to check, and ordered a CT scan. It took two days to get the study scheduled at the new imaging center in Sequim, but then the scan confirmed his suspicions about what he had found during the examination. There was a 14-centimeter mass replacing the left ovary and a substantial amount of fluid in the abdomen – ascites he had called it. Further studies showed that there were small tumor nodules scattered throughout her belly and Doctor Kim told her that surgery was not possible. He then referred her to cancer doctors at State University, where fluid had been suctioned out of her belly and sent for analysis.

She saw Dr. Greerson, reported to be one of the best gynecologic oncologists in the country. She liked Greerson in spite of his somewhat brusque manner. He spoke 'straight from the shoulder,' as her husband used to say.

"Gaby," he began, after he reviewed her records and examined her, "this is a bad situation. You have an adenocarcinoma of the ovary. It has spread all through your belly and all of it can't be taken out surgically. However, taking out as much as possible is still the best thing to do and we can follow up with other treatments."

"But why did I get this?" asked Gaby. I've never smoked or drank. Oh, perhaps a glass of wine from time to time, but that's all."

Greerson sighed. "Nobody really knows what causes ovarian cancers. They don't come from smoking or drinking. They run in some families, but you don't have a family history for that. There are some genetic studies that we might want to talk about later. The important thing for you to realize is that there was nothing you did to cause this, and all we can do is to move forward and treat it in the best way possible."

Gaby had the surgery and while a great deal of tumor was removed, there was considerable disease left behind. She was in the hospital for about a week, visited frequently by her granddaughter, Meredith Jones, who was then a third year medical student. Gaby was very proud of Meredith whom she and her husband had raised since the girl was seven years old. Her parents had been killed in an automobile accident. Meredith had proven to be a very good student, and following high school, had received an academic scholarship to State University. She had been attracted to medicine both because of the research but also for the opportunity to help others. "To make a difference," Meredith had said. They had moved to Sequim, Washington, upon the retirement of her husband, Walter, and had purchased a small home overlooking the Strait of Juan de

Fuca. Meredith had been ten at the time and quickly adapted to the rural life, which was a far cry from her prior days in Detroit. She never tired of prowling through the tidal pools to see what strange sea life could be found.

Following Gaby's diagnosis, Meredith read voraciously about ovarian cancer and talked to many of her clinical professors about the disease. She and Gaby often discussed treatment options. They agreed that chemotherapy should be tried, and Greerson had arranged for her to be seen by the medical oncology service at the Cancer Center. Dr. Olson was the senior doctor who saw her, although there were a lot of students and residents following her around the hospital ward and doing most of the routine work. During rounds they all wore white lab coats and looked over Olson's shoulder when she examined Gaby. They took copious notes in little note pads that they carried in their coats. Gaby was flattered by all the attention.

"Based upon randomized trials," Olson began after reviewing her case, "chemotherapy, using an agent called cis-platin, has been shown to be effective in treating your kind of ovarian cancer. We will start with that and then switch to other things if we need to." Olson then went on to explain all of the possible side effects, which sounded pretty scary to Gaby. However, with Meredith to guide her, she agreed to undergo the treatment.

It took a while to get the treatment started. Gaby's insurance company, a Medicare managed care organization, initially refused to pay for it because of her age. "Seventy-one wasn't all that old," she had thought. It took letters from both Greerson and Olson as well as multiple phone calls from Meredith before the company finally acquiesced. The chemo treatment was difficult and had caused her to become very nauseated in spite of the preventative medications that she was given. Meredith had later told her that the nausea medicine probably should have been started sooner, and so this time Gaby watched carefully to make sure that an IV bag containing Odansetron was hung an hour before the cis-platin was started. She was also going to make sure the she had some Odansetron pills to take home with her after her discharge. She had been flabbergasted at the cost of this medication when she got it after her first course of chemotherapy; $12 per pill was outrageous. Good thing that she had insurance, even though it was the managed care version of Medicare. She was only too aware of the costs of cancer treatment since her husband had died eight years earlier from prostate cancer. At that time neither of them was covered by Medicare.

"Hi Gaby", said Laura as she breezed in. Laura was the nurse on the cancer floor who would be taking care of her. "I see that you are going to be staying with us for a couple of days. Did everything go OK with your admission?"

"Yes, that nice young Doctor Erickson took care of getting me settled in."

"He is not only good," replied Laura, "he is also cute. He is going to be a really good doctor once he finishes his training. He always puts the patient first. Will we be seeing your granddaughter during this visit? Let's see, she's a third year medical student now, isn't she?"

"Meredith is doing her surgery rotation now, and probably won't be in to see me until quite a bit later – you know how long a surgeon's hours are. She will have more time after she finishes her third year rotations and can start her electives. I think she is planning to try her hand at some research next year."

"Here's the dinner menu. Just check off what you want and you can eat while you wait for her."

CHAPTER 3

A TALL, ATHLETIC, YOUNG woman with reddish hair, Meredith Jones was scrubbed into a case that entailed a partial resection of the pancreas for cancer. It was a Whipple procedure that involved taking out the gallbladder, the common bile duct, part of the duodenum, and the distal part of the stomach, and the surgery had started at 8 that morning. It was now 5 PM. Meredith had joined the case around 11:30 AM after completing teaching rounds with those members of the team not directly involved in the case. The chief surgeon, Dr. Mikani, had been scrubbed in from the beginning, although he had scrubbed out for a brief break and some lunch around 1 PM. *Guess surgeons are self-selected for their bladder capacity*, thought Meredith. As a third year medical student, Meredith's role consisted of holding clamps and identifying various structures pointed out by Mikani. At least by now, she had learned to scrub in a manner that satisfied the OR surgical nurse.

"Jones, what is the name of this operation and when was it first performed?"

"This is called a Whipple after the surgeon who developed it," replied Meredith. "I don't know when it was first done, but in the late 1800s I would guess."

Dr. Mikani harrumphed. "Does anyone actually know when Dr. Whipple first did this surgery?"

The fourth year resident, James Morgan, who had heard this question before, promptly interjected, "Dr. Alan Whipple first described this procedure in 1935. He was at New York Hospital, which later became Memorial Sloan-Kettering Cancer Center." Morgan was technically very good and was planning on a private surgical practice when he completed training.

"Very good," replied Mikani. "Jones, what is this structure and how would you find it on an x-ray?"

Meredith thought back to the anatomy chapter she had read the night before and said, "That is the superior mesenteric artery and it overlies the first lumbar vertebra. Then a small artery or 'pumper' was cut and this occupied the full attention of Mikani and the OR staff for a while. Mikani called for a clamp and attached it to the artery. Morgan then 'buzzed' the clamp with a Bovie, and a small amount of smoke curled up, resulting in a slightly acrid odor that Meredith could smell through her mask. The team settled into their work again with each performing his or her particular part of the procedure. Classical music, as favored by Mikani, played in the background.

Mikani returned to his clinical teaching as the case proceeded. "Jones, what is this patient's prognosis? Remember that the frozen section showed that the tumor has spread to two nodes along the greater curvature of the stomach."

"Not good. Probably around 15-20 percent three-year survival at best. Do you think you will be able to get out all the gross tumor in the pancreas itself?"

"Gross tumor, yes, but there will be at least microscopic disease at the posterior margin. Morgan, is there anything that we can do to improve things for the patient?"

Morgan quickly reviewed the results of the GI Study Group trial of chemotherapy and radiotherapy with the caveat that this trial was for patients with negative surgical margins. Then he mentioned the studies from Japan and the United States on intraoperative radiotherapy.

"Intraoperative radiotherapy," asked Mikani, "what is that?" He already knew the answer but wanted to see what his residents knew.

"We arrange to transport the patient down to the basement of the medical center where radiation is blasted into the tumor bed before we close him up. It makes logical sense, but there aren't any really good, controlled studies that prove its effectiveness."

"Unfortunately," said the anesthesiologist, "we can't do that because of the lateness of the hour. Remember the notice from the OR Committee the last time we tried to start the intraoperative part of a case after 5:30 in the afternoon?"

"How could I forget" chuckled Mikani. "I had a long talk with George Lattimer, the chairman of Radiation Oncology, after I got that letter. While I was initially steamed at his department for keeping 'bankers hours,' I found out that it wasn't their fault. Their doctors are willing to stay as long as necessary to treat the patient. However, the hospital doesn't want to pay the overtime for the technologists who actually run the machine. We used to keep them around until 8 or 9 o'clock at night and then end up not using intraop radiotherapy. The hospital got stuck with the cost without any compensating revenue."

"Yes, medicine is a business," said the anesthesiologist. "I'm not sure it's what I would pick as a career if I were starting out today. Recall what our medical center CFO said when asked about cutbacks at the last medical staff meetings? One of the younger docs from Emergency Medicine challenged the new policy of preferentially trying to recruit paying patients into the medical center as opposed to those on DSHS medicaid and asked how this fit in with our mission of providing patient care to everyone. 'No money, no mission' was our CFO's response."

Mikani rolled his eyes above his mask. "The role of a medical center administrator is a tough one these days. Insurance companies are squeezing both the hospitals and the docs. The feds keep cutting back reimbursements under the rubric of pay-for-performance. They say that this is to improve patient care, but it really gives them an excuse to hold back payments. Right now there are only three really profitable service lines for hospitals: cancer, stroke, and heart. If one of them were to go away, the hospitals couldn't make it in the current funding climate. State Medical Center is locked in a battle with Nordic Hospital, our cross-town rival in all three areas. Boganstein, the Chair of Neurosurgery, about had a stroke himself when they beat us to the punch in forming a neurosciences institute and advertising it to the public."

The case continued until 8:30 in the evening before the patient's incision was closed and he was taken to recovery. Orders were written and the team departed to make final rounds on the other patients in their service. Afterwards, they were going for beer and pizza at the Northlake Tavern, a local watering hole frequented by the medical staff. They asked Meredith to join them since this was her last day on the surgical service, but she declined saying that she wanted to look in on her grandmother and then needed to get home and take her dog for a walk before going to bed. She was tired since morning patient rounds came all too early on the surgical service.

CHAPTER 4

MEREDITH TOOK THE STAIRS up to the cancer floor rather than using the elevators. Given the amount of time she spent in the hospital while doing surgery, she took every opportunity to squeeze in a little exercise. She ran up the stairs two at a time, pushed open the door, and walked down the hall to the nursing station. Recognizing the nurse behind the desk, Meredith greeted her a little breathlessly. "Hello, Laura. I remember you from when my grandmother had her surgery a month ago. You were on the surgical unit at that time. What are you doing on the cancer care ward?"

"The hospital is always switching us around depending on their staffing needs. I actually like this better than surgery as you get a better chance to get to know the patients. I guess you are here to see your grandmother?"

Meredith sighed, "Yes I am. Do you think it would be OK if I took a quick look at her chart before going in to see her?"

"Well ...," started Laura, "that might well be outside the HIPPA guidelines that the hospital is always talking about. But since you are on the medical staff and involved with patient care, and since there is no one around, I guess that would be OK", she said with a wink. "Also, as I recall from her last admission, your grandmother has given written authorization for you to see all of her medical records."

Meredith quickly retrieved her grandmother's chart, went over to a corner of the nursing station, and started reading rapidly. The intern's admission note was only partially legible, but she was able to make out the main conclusion, while he could not palpate any large abdominal masses, he thought that there was some return of the fluid in the abdomen. Fortunately, the chest x ray continued to be negative. Meredith put the chart back in the rack, and putting a smile on her face, walked down the hall to her grandmother's room. She quickly peered around the door to make sure that Gaby was awake and then entered the room.

"Hey, Granner, how's it going? Everyone here taking good care of you?"

Meredith leaned over and kissed her grandmother on the forehead, then quickly looked at the IV pole to see what fluids were running in. There were two bags hanging; one contained the cis-platin and the other a saline solution. The cis-platin bag was about halfway finished.

Gaby's face lit up when she saw her granddaughter. "Oh my, yes. Everyone here is wonderful to me. If I don't have any problems, I get to go home tomorrow afternoon. The American Cancer Society volunteer driver will be picking me up at noon, so you won't have to worry about my getting home. I know that your surgical rotation keeps you really busy, but I am so glad that you could come in to see me tonight."

To Meredith, Gaby seemed as cheerful as ever – unlike many of the patients who were on her team's surgical service. In fairness though, she had to admit that many of her patients were in a great deal more pain than Gaby was in. She did think that Gaby looked like she had lost some weight and was a little more drawn about the face than before all this started. Meredith sat down and she and Gaby talked for about a half hour. Gaby caught Meredith up on what was going on in Sequim, told her that the hospital in Port Angeles still hadn't found a replacement for the medical oncologist that had left during the past summer, and talked about the upcoming fundraising dinner for the local medical park. In turn Meredith told her about her surgical rotation; how it was finishing up tomorrow, and she was really looking forward to her next rotation – Radiology which would have much better hours. She also talked again about her plans for a research elective at the beginning of her fourth year. She wanted to do something in the area of cancer and was looking for a project that would involve more than just analyzing clinical outcome data. Prior to starting medical school, Meredith had obtained a master's degree in computer science; she seemed to have a flair for programming. Ideally, she wanted a research project that would involve computer analysis, as this would keep her skills sharp. She had asked some of her professors to recommend a good person to work for, and the name of Jack Olivetti had come up twice. According to her professors, Olivetti was trying to gain insights into biological systems by applying mathematical modeling. This weekend she would look up some of his work on PUBMED and see exactly what he was doing. She had until the end of the school year to set something up, but didn't want to wait until the last minute, like so many of her classmates did. She also thought she would sit in on one or two of his lectures to get a firsthand impression of what it would be like to work with him.

After a while Gaby's head started to nod; Meredith kissed her goodbye and left. She went down the stairs to the bus stop where she caught the number 48 which headed north out of the university district. It let her off two blocks from her apartment. She used the large key on her ring to let herself into the apartment building and then the smaller key to enter her apartment on the second floor. Her basset hound, Sam, greeted her at the door and danced around her feet as she entered the apartment. After she fed him, she put on his leash and took him for a short walk in the continuing drizzle. Then she went to bed. Before dozing off, she thought about her upcoming Radiology rotation and wondered about the new people she would meet.

CHAPTER 5

IT WAS JUST AFTER the Christmas holiday, and Colridge was in his office preparing for the first Blackmont Financial Group board meeting of the New Year. Many of his staff were still on vacation, which made this a good time to work without interuption. Colridge had set the board meeting agenda over the holidays and had spent a considerable amount of time mulling over where to position the discussion on the bonds for the State University research complex on East Lake Union. The timing of the discussion was critical in determining the receptivity of the Board to the venture. Colridge decided that he would first present the profit and loss figures for the last quarter and then have the discussion of the two financial ventures the group was currently considering. One of the choices was to take a position in a new casino operation sited on one of the Indian reservations near Seattle; the other was to underwrite the bonds for State's research complex. Since the board members had other obligations, the meeting wouldn't be starting until 5:30 PM.

The members started arriving around 5:15; old Fritz Helmuth came in first as usual. Fritz prided himself on unctuality and tended to over allow for delays due to traffic. The other members trickled in. The newest member of the board, Adam Martileni, was the last to arrive. They helped themselves to coffee, water, or something stronger according to their preference. A light dinner would be served at 6:30, and Colridge hoped to be mostly through the discussion by that point. The board members quickly reviewed the pro forma on the casino operation and approved it unanimously. Based upon conservative projections of patronage developed by marketing, the revenue stream should clearly support the operation. The university research complex was a different matter. The pro forma itself looked good, but then Matt Roudine challenged the numbers in the projection. Roudine held up that morning's *Wall Street Journal* with its article on decreased federal government funding for research. "How sure was Colridge that the figures would hold up?" he asked.

Helmuth chimed in, "Don't forget what von Eschenbach, the former head of the NCI, said about eliminating all pain and suffering from cancer by 2015. What would the need be for all that cancer research be if that really happened?"

Colridge coughed discreetly. "I don't think that is likely to happen. Look how quickly the NCI distanced itself from von Eschenbach's remark. Curing cancer is not an engineering project like building the atomic bomb or putting a man on the moon. The experts I've talked to say that there just isn't enough known about the problem to solve it. State University is one of the top research universities in terms of government and private research funding, and this is going to continue. Besides, Dean Schmitt is willing to guarantee the research revenue stream with money from his clinical operations." Colridge then passed around copies of the letter of agreement produced by Schmitt and Maxim.

The board members looked at the letter and Roudine asked, "Can he really do this?"

Colridge replied, "As Dean of the School of Medicine Schmitt controls both the research and the clinical revenue. It all comes together in his office anyway."

Martileni spoke up for the first time. "How solid is this clinical revenue anyway?" he asked. "It seems to me that if someone really found a cure for cancer, the clinical revenue not only of State but of most major hospitals in the country would drop dramatically. Yes, the hospitals would certainly make some money providing the initial treatment, but this would certainly not make up for what they would lose from all of the surgeries, admissions, medications, and whatever else they do for the cancer patient today. There has got to be a lot of money in cancer. Just look at all of the advertisements that both State and Nordic are putting out on the radio, television, and the paper about why people should come to their particular cancer center."

The fifth member of Blackmont's advisory board, Jim Grener, chimed in. "Given the upcoming election with the Democrats poised to take control in Washington, I think health care expenditures will be going down anyway. The bond issue is for $500 million, but I wouldn't want to see Blackmont underwrite more than half of that. Don't forget that it will be at least three years before the research complex is completed and fully operational. The bond debt will need to be covered during that period. Let me put this in the form of a motion and we'll take a vote. It is getting late and we all have other things to do tonight."

Colridge protested. "State won't want to start construction unless they can be sure of having enough money to finish the project. If we don't take on the entire project, we will need to bring in some outside capital to provide State with a complete package. Otherwise, State will probably go with someone else."

Roudine persisted and called for a vote; Grener's proposal was approved. The meeting broke up. Martileni stayed behind, indicating that he wanted to talk privately with Colridge. He walked over to the buffet, poured himself a glass of red wine, and began to speak.

"Malcolm, I know some people who might be interested in taking the rest of the State bond issue. They have some money that they need to put to work, but would like to stay in the background. Let me give them a call and pitch the deal to them. If this works out, I would expect Blackmont to give me a small percentage for my effort. This would be in addition to the regular distribution to the board members, of course."

Colridge took a sip of his wine and looked over the glass at Martileni. He knew that Martileni was well connected and had heard rumors that some of his business associates were a bit shady – not the sort of people that one wanted to get in bed with. However, it wouldn't hurt to explore things further.

"Make your call and then let's get together over dinner later this week and talk about it. If the deal is sound, we can make it worth your time."

The two men nodded and left the room.

CHAPTER 6

JACK OLIVETTI WAS SPENDING another late night in his laboratory. As was often the case when he was engrossed in a knotty problem, he had totally lost track of the time. His cell phone beeped and he answered to find an irate Meg Jenkins. Without preamble Jenkings began the conversation by asking, "Where in the hell are you and don't you know how long I've had been waiting at the restaurant for you?"

Jack suddenly realized that it was Friday and that he had a dinner date with Meg that evening. He had just met Meg at a party over the holidays, and now it looked like this was another relationship that was going nowhere. Jack was tall, a little underweight, with dark curly hair. Women would give him a second look, but then soon realize that a committed relationship was not high on his list of priorities. To Jack, science came first. Meg continued to ream him out and then hung up in a huff. With a sigh Jack turned back to his lab notebook. The results on the latest set of mouse tumors were intriguing in that there were some long-term survivors but not many. It was as if the treatment had worked in a few cases, but not in others. This was surprising since all of the mouse tumors should have been identical, and the results of treatment should have been very similar.

Jack was an assistant professor in the Department of Medicine and had just received his second RO1 grant from the National Cancer Institute or NCI. This had taken a lot of pressure off him since with proven grant funding, the Appointments and Promotions Committee, or A&P Committee as it was generally called, would almost certainly approve his promotion to associate professor when it came up next year. State's policy of 'up or out' after six years as an assistant professor kept the junior faculty hustling for both research publications and grant support. While there were written departmental criteria for promotion, in practice a lot depended upon the support of the department chairman. Jack's chairman, Samuel Bremenoff, had been clear from the beginning about the importance of having a financially independent research program. The Department of Medicine would provide only temporary bridge funding at best if the research dollars dropped. There were funds in the new grant for another postdoc and a student helper, and Jack would need to start looking for these people soon. His program was growing, and he needed a bigger laboratory as well. Laboratory space was certainly in high demand at State University, but as an associate professor, his chances of scoring a bigger lab were good.

He started doodling on the large white board on the south wall of the laboratory. He headed two columns, respectively, 'similarities' and 'differences' and began to list the attributes of various cancers. The 'differences' column filled up much faster than the 'similarities' column. Cancers behaved differently according to where they arose, whether they spread through the lymphatic system or blood stream, how fast they grew, whether they were familial in origin, whether there were proven environmental associations such as smoking and lung cancer, particular mutated genes, and familial predisposition vs. spontaneous occurrences, and how they were affected by tumor microenvironmental factors such as inflammation and oxidative stress. Under the 'similarities' column, Jack listed abnormal DNA, unrestrained growth, and generally a small subpopulation of treatment-resistant stem cells.

Why do cancers not know when to stop growing? Jack asked himself. *The p53 gene is supposed to tell cells to stop dividing and to die if their DNA has been replicated incorrectly during cell division. In some cancers the p53 gene is defective, but not in all cancers. What causes the cancer cell to effectively become immortal? What if there were another gene, as yet undiscovered, that controlled for this? And if the gene were found, how would you go about either turning it off or inactivating the protein that it produced?*

State University had a strong genome sciences program, and in fact, this was the main reason Jack had come here after completing the MD-PhD program at Harvard and residency and fellowship at the University of California at San Francisco. Maps of the various genetic elements abounded in the literature, but in most cases people didn't know much about the proteins they produced, which actually regulated the cell. Jack's research involved screening cancer cells looking for classes of proteins that were different than in normal cells. The newest generation of protein chip arrays made it possible to screen for many thousands of proteins at a time, provided one knew what proteins to look for. Jack had gone down this route for a while but now thought that the key must be a protein not yet identified. Currently, he was working with two rapidly growing tumor cell lines, a Burkitt's lymphoma and a highly malignant brain tumor called a glioblastoma multiforme. About the only thing these two tumors had in common was rapid, unrestrained growth, which was what Jack was looking for.

Jack and his collaborators were slowly working their way through the genomes of these two tumor lines, hybridizing segments of their

DNA and looking for similarities. Then they would use a polymerase chain reaction to amplify the segment of interest and transcribe the DNA information to RNA. They would then see what proteins the RNA generated. A computer program rapidly sorted through the two DNA databases and flagged possible regions of interest. By now, Jack and his team had sorted through the known oncogenes and were working their way through the supposedly silent areas of the genome. Even with the mapping of the human genome, the function of only about 10 percent was known with the remainder being silent, or not producing a known protein. It was getting late, and Jack was getting tired, so he decided to copy the latest output to a USB thumb drive, take it home, and look at it in the morning after his usual Saturday run along the Burke Gilman trail. A former high school cross country runner, Jack had not been good enough to compete at the college level, and currently time did not permit him to run more than two or three times a week. This was probably a good thing since over the last couple of years he noticed his knees hurting if he ran more frequently, as he often did when on vacation.

Chapter 7

Jack's alarm went off at 6. He groped on his nightstand to find the shutoff button on the clock. Then he then got out of bed and made himself a cup of coffee before putting on his running gear. He looked out the window of his apartment and saw that last night's light drizzle had stopped. *No need for the Gortex jacket this morning,* he thought to himself. Even on weekends, Jack was an early riser and felt did his best thinking in the morning. Ideas often came to him when he was zoned out running; his mind would freely associate from one thought to another.

He watched the news on TV while he finished his coffee and then loped down the stairs. He stretched out his quads and hamstrings and started jogging the six blocks through the residential area before hitting the Burke Gilman trail and picking up his pace. He headed north and soon overtook a couple of young women, students most likely, who were listening to their iPods as they jogged. Jack had tried listening to music while running but found that not only did it interfere with the running experience, but it also made it difficult to hear overtaking traffic – either bicycles on the trail or cars on the roads. He began to sweat and to think about his research problem. *What was he missing? He had looked not only at the known oncogenes but also at the DNA segments located near them. How was the information transmitted to the gene controlling the cell growth and what if a completely unidentified gene was the key control element? If the signaling messenger was a protein, then the gene segment coding for it wouldn't have to be located anywhere near the growth gene since the protein it produced would be distributed throughout the cytoplasm. In fact, the control segment might be located on a completely different chromosome. Epigenetic regulation, it was termed. Still, if everything funneled down into a final common pathway, then this might be an approach that would be broadly applicable to all tumors.*

After about 30 minutes, Jack looked at his watch and turned around. He continued to mull over the problem. It looked like he would need to broaden the data base search to look for more widely ranging associations. This would take a lot of computing power – considerably more than he had access to in his laboratory. However, his new NCI grant had money in it for time on the Blue Waters system at the National Center for Supercomputing Applications at the University of Illinois. State University was connected to the Blue Waters system via the G2 eithernet backbone. The Blue Waters system was a joint collaboration between the University of Illinois and IBM and could do over one thousand trillion calculations per second. It was the first such system with large amounts of time available for civilian use. This made it possible to perform system modeling and data analysis that couldn't be done before. Jack would need to carefully define the search parameters to avoid burning up his allotted computer time in fruitless searches. He could set up the parameters on his laboratory computer and debug the search routine using a smaller data set. Then he could connect to the supercomputer and do the full blown search. He ran by the student gymnasium; and adjacent parking lot was empty, not surprising since the gym didn't open until 11 AM on Saturdays. He continued up the trail and turned off toward his apartment where he climbed the stairs and cooled down before heading into the shower. Afterwards, he planned to watch some of the bowl games on TV before heading to the medical school library to catch up on some journal articles.

CHAPTER 8

THE FOLLOWING WEEKEND, MALCOLM Colridge invited Adam Martileni to be his guest at a Sonics game. The tickets were great, at midcourt and three rows up. They actually belonged to Blackmont, which carried them as a business expense. It had taken a while to get season tickets this close to courtside, and with the likely move of the Sonics to Oklahoma the following year, Colridge wanted to see as many games as possible. The game was a close one with the Sonics leading by only two points at half time. By mutual consent, the two men had avoided talking about business although both knew that this was the reason Colridge had invited Martileni to the game. During half time, they ordered hot dogs and a couple of beers from the vendor, watched the cheerleaders perform, laughed at the antics of the team mascot, Sasquatch, and generally had a good time. The game went into overtime with the Sonics finally winning. Martileni had made an appreciable bet on the Sonics through a bookie in Los Vegas, and so was in an especially good mood.

After the game, the two men found their car in the garage reserved for season ticket holders. They exited the garage, wound their way to Mercer, and then turned north on Eastlake. "I thought we would stop at Serafina for dinner," said Colridge, who was driving that evening.

"Fine with me," replied Martileni. "Shouldn't be any problem getting a table at this hour and it is a good place to talk."

As Martileni had predicted, the restaurant wasn't that crowded and they were shown to a corner table. They reviewed the menu, ordered the chef's pasta special, along with antipasta and a bottle of Chianti. After the wine and appetizers had arrived, the men began to talk. "So, how much did you win on the game tonight?" asked Colridge.

"A cool grand. The Sonics were underdogs, but I thought that they would come through given the other team's injuries. Now tell me what you really want to talk about. I'm pretty sure that it's something besides basketball."

"Yes," replied Colridge. "I want to find out if you were serious about knowing people who would like to get in on the bond issue for State's research park on Lake Union. The overall financing would be one billion dollars, with half of that being in the form of senior bonds, which will be easily sold, leaving five hundred million to be financed through subordinate, higher risk bonds. Blackmont's board only wants to take on half of the subordinate debt, and the deal will collapse without someone else agreeing to take on the other half. Would your friends be up for that much?"

Martileni whistled softly. "Two hundred and fifty million dollars. That's a lot of money, but the answer is yes if the risk and reward are right."

Martileni and Colridge then got into the details of the offer, talking about cash flow, interest rates, and the dean's promise to backstop the research money with draws off the clinical revenue stream. Colridge then addressed the question that Martileni had raised at least indirectly during their private conversation after the last Board of Directors meeting. "In view of your invaluable assistance in brokering this deal, we can give you the opportunity to purchase a certain number of the bonds at very favorable terms – say a million dollars worth at ten cents on the dollar."

Martileni smiled, reached across the table, and shook Colridge's hand. "You've got a deal."

"Great. How soon can we get the money on board?"

"Probably in about two weeks if you need it that soon," replied Martileni.

"No, any time within the next month will be fine. Once we get it into an escrow account, we can move ahead with selling the rest of the bonds. How will the money arrive anyway?" Colridge asked that last question with some concern given what he had heard about Martileni's business connections.

As if reading Colridge's mind, Martileni chuckled and replied, "Don't worry, it won't be in the form of a truckload of small, unmarked bills. It will come in the form of a letter of credit from a Las Vegas bank. My business partners are all legit – at least they are these days. However, they still take losing money very seriously, so for the sake of us both, I hope there are no snags in this. Otherwise, our families may be collecting on our insurance policies earlier than expected."

Colridge laughed weakly at the last remark, and the two men made more small talk as they finished dinner. As he dropped Martileni off at his home on the Magnolia bluff, Colridge remarked that he would give the dean a call tomorrow and let him know that the deal was on. Project planning with the architects could proceed.

CHAPTER 9

THE DEAN WAS HAPPY to hear the good news from Colridge. He asked his secretary to set up a meeting with Peter Drisco, the founder and CEO of AVARTEC, a biotechnology company located in Seattle, not too far from State's new research complex. Once, when Schmitt and Drisco were having drinks together, Schmitt had asked where the company's name came from. Drisco laughed and said it was a combination of two words, avarice and technology, and the name summed up his business philosophy.

Drisco had started out as a molecular science researcher at State . He had discovered a way to inhibit tumors from growing blood vessels to supply their nutrients and parlayed this discovery into a new pharmaceutical agent, *INHIBIT*. With the blessing of State University, which mandated under the Bayh-Dole Act to commercialize its scientific discoveries, Drisco had organized a group of venture capitalists to provide substantial investment capital to commercialize his discovery. The new company was launched with great fanfare in the Puget Sound Business Journal. From a marketing point of view, the drug was ideal. It inhibited tumor growth, had a different toxicity spectrum than more traditional chemotherapeutic agents, and could be added to almost any chemotherapy regimen. Once it had been approved for any one particular tumor treatment, it could (and would) be used for other kinds of cancers as well. It promised to be bigger than *Avastin,* which generated an annual revenue stream of 3.5 billion dollars through its worldwide sales. *Avastin* only prolonged life expectancy by a few months on the average; *INHIBIT* promised to do better than this. As with most drugs, had taken many years and approximately $800 million dollars to bring *INHIBIT* to market. It took even more time and money to bring biological agents to market; over one billion dollars according to industry surveys. FDA approval had just been received, and the drug, which had been patented immediately after its discovery and prior to the completion of clinical trials, would be on patent for eleven more years. Drisco's legal team said that there were ways of extending the patent beyond that. If the drug was a success, the financial return on AVARTEC's investment would be enormous. Drisco and his investment group were about to become fantastically wealthy, with State getting a significant return as well. After some exchange of phone calls and E-mails, the meeting between the two men was set for the following Thursday at 4 PM.

Schmitt drove to the meeting and parked his car in the AVARTEC visitor's section. He walked to the front entry foyer, where he signed in at the security log. He received a visitor's badge incorporating radiofrequency indicator technology, or RFI as it was commonly known. This let the AVARTEC security team track the movements of employees and visitors as they moved throughout the research complex. Then he took the elevator up to the fifth floor and entered the administration area. "Hi Patti," he said to the receptionist. "I'm here for a 4 o'clock with Pete."

Patti smiled and asked him to have a seat. She said "Mr. Drisco is on a long distance phone call that is taking longer than expected.

He will be with you in a few minutes. Would you like some coffee or tea while you are waiting?"

"Yes, coffee, black, would be great. It has been a long day."

Just after the dean had taken the first sip of his coffee, the door to the inner office opened and Peter Drisco came out smiling. "Good to see you, Al. Sorry to keep you waiting. Bring your coffee into the office." The two men sat down in a pair of comfortable chairs facing each other across a small table with a glass top. The view from the west-facing window was magnificent with the sailboats on Lake Union in the foreground backed by Queen Anne Hill and the Olympic Mountains.

The dean began. "Let me start by telling you the good news. We have completed the financing arrangements for the new research complex. Once the complex is finished, we will have some additional research space that would be available for your company to lease. Having our researchers and yours in the same location would improve our two groups' ability to work together and would leverage your private research funding with ours, which is supported with federal dollars."

"With the FDA approval of *INHIBIT*," said Drisco, "we certainly anticipate needing more research space, as much of our current space will be turned over to manufacturing. But as I've said before, our goals are not necessarily the same as yours. Your researchers are looking to publish as soon as they discover something new, while our people are looking mainly for commercial applications and have to delay publication until after a patent application is filed. Things get a little murky when both groups are involved in a project and when funding sources are mixed."

"I've been thinking about this problem," replied Schmitt. "I think we can protect your company's interests by setting up shared resource space to be used by both groups and using material transfer agreements to establish ownership of intellectual property. In regard to the publication issue, we could set up a committee with representatives from both sides to review presentation abstracts and manuscripts prior to submission, with due consideration to the needs of both sides."

"What is the advantage to State in this arrangement? I don't believe your faculty would be enthusiastic about this arrangement, particularly the review process, which they would perceive as taking away their academic freedom."

"State Medical School would get a guaranteed revenue stream from the rent your company would pay for the research space. We would also get funds for equipment and your company's support for selected research projects. Of course, we would negotiate a favorable indirect cost rate for this private sector support to reduce your net cost."

Drisco thought a bit and said, "I think this could work. We certainly are going to be looking for research space, and the location of State's new complex would be convenient for us. Let me review the broad details of this proposal with my Board and get back to you. Our next Board meeting is coming up in a week and I will give you a call after that. If they are in agreement, we can have our two legal staffs get together to iron out the specific details. Is Alice Maxim still heading up this work on your side?"

"Yes," replied Schmitt. "You will find her very easy to work with. She can see the big picture and not get bogged down in all the minutia associated with a state institution."

CHAPTER 10

TIME'S ARROW MOVED INEXORABLY forward during the remainder of the academic calendar year.

The bond sale proceeded without incident, and contracts with the architects and the builders were concluded. It took about six months to complete the preliminary drawings and actually start construction. It was mid-July when the dean removed the official first shovel of dirt wearing the obligatory hard hat and fixed smile for the press photographers. Coverage was generally favorable, but the *Times* reporter, Pillipitch, took a cynical slant, as was his wont. His headline read *STATE U RESEARCH BEHEMOTH CONTINUES TO EXPAND*. Pillipitch talked about the continued growth of State's research enterprise and asked whether the focus on research detracted from the actual teaching of students, which, after all, was what the citizens of Washington wanted most from their university. Pillipitch was not a fan of the dean, he had publicly taken him and the School of Medicine Board of Directors to task for 'not minding the store' during the past federal investigation on clinical billing. He concluded by asking the question, "how big do we want research at State to be anyway?" The dean and the Board of Directors didn't particularly like that question as they felt that all growth in their research enterprise was good.

Meredith had completed her third year clerkships receiving excellent grades and recommendations. The faculty and staff had all commented on both her intellectual curiosity and commitment to her patients. She had received permission to take a year in the lab before starting her fourth year clinical work. If she liked the laboratory work, she was considering switching to the MD-PhD program for medical scientists. She had landed a position in Jack Olivetti's group. As the most junior member, she washed a lot of glassware and helped out with small, well-defined projects under the direction of the more experienced personnel as she was learning about the ongoing research program. She attended all of the lab group meetings, held at the end of the day unlike the early morning meeting times favored by the clinical groups. Meredith also made a point of reviewing the seminar and colloquium schedule for the week and asking Olivetti which ones he thought would be worth attending. She intended to take advantage of this year by really immersing herself in research to see how she liked it.

Olivetti's idea about looking for non-spatially correlated cellular growth control units seemed to be bearing fruit. He had gotten his computer search program running, and the Blue Water Computer had identified several possible candidates. His lab group had joined with others to obtain a "shared projects grant" from AVARTEC to purchase a next generation DNA sequencer from Illumina, and this promised to make analyzing the genomes from his tumor cell lines faster and less expensive. This was a necessary step to achieving the holy grail of cancer treatment – a truly individualized therapy. AVARTEC was actively working with State on several research projects. Of course, AVARTEC's main purpose was to develop marketable therapies rather than doing pure research, but Jack didn't have any problem with this. Industry support was increasingly important in these days of decreased federal funding. It just needed to be properly managed. Once the new research complex was completed, Jack and his colleagues thought that the collaboration between AVARTEC and State University would continue to increase.

Gabrielle Jones had undergone two additional admissions to State Medical Center for chemotherapy. Greerson had tried cis-platin one more time, which had shown some short term improvemen. Then he had switched to paclitaxel, which, he told her had originally been derived from yew bark. The paclitaxol hadn't caused her nearly the nausea as the cis-platin had but had dropped her blood counts precipitously. This had worried Meredith, who was concerned about Gaby picking up an infection. Fortunately, this did not occur, and Gaby came through this phase of her therapy without having to be readmitted to the hospital.

CHAPTER 11

JACK WAS CONDUCTING THE monthly meeting of his research group. To encourage attendance, he provided cookies and soft drinks from one of the project budgets. After everyone had settled in, he began the meeting by asking his postdoctoral student, Bryon Heymond, to review the results of the most recent set of mouse experiments for the group. Under a research contract, the group was studying a new compound from AVARTEC, termed *Compound 10*, which many thought would be the next generation of *INHIBIT*. The most recent experiment tested traditional combination chemotherapy in one group of mice compared to two other groups of mice – one of which received the same combination chemotherapy with the addition of the recently approved *INHIBIT* and the other of which received the combination chemotherapy with the addition of *Compound 10*.

Bryon opened his lab book, quickly summarized the latest set of results on the EMT6 mice, and concluded, "… and so the mouse group treated with the standard chemotherapy regimen of cytoxan, methotrexate, and fluorouracil, or CMF as our clinical colleagues term it, alone had a life expectancy of 36 weeks; adding *INHIBIT* increased the life expectancy to 50 weeks, and adding *Compound 10* to the CMF regimen extended the life expectancy to 60 weeks. The difference compared to the control group is significant at the p=0.04

level for the *INHIBIT* group and p=0.01 level for the *Compound 10* group."

"Excellent work and summary, Bryon. This will make AVARTEC happy. Was there any unexpected toxicity?"

"No, the usual hair loss and nausea, but this seemed about the same for each group."

"Let's plan on presenting this at the next ASCO meeting. Bryon, you will be first author on the paper, I will be the senior author, and we'll talk later about who else in the lab should be included. How about preparing an abstract for me to look at next week? If the abstract is accepted, we will follow it up with a paper to the Journal of Clinical Oncology."

Bryon was happy to do this. Having a first authorship on an ASCO presentation would be a big help in finding a permanent position after his postdoctoral appointment was finished. Olivetti was a great mentor and was more than fair in spreading the credit around to the more junior members of his research group.

Meredith had never heard of ASCO; so she turned to the young woman sitting next to her and asked, "ASCO, what is that?"

"ASCO means the American Society of Clinical Oncology. It's the largest society for medical oncologists and cancer researchers in the world."

Olivetti connected his Powerbook to the flat panel display mounted on the conference room wall, and genome sequences appeared on the display.

"Let me show you all the latest correlation results for the human Burkett's lymphoma and glioblastoma cell lines. Just got these back from the Blue Water computer at Illinois, so I really haven't had time to work up the graphical displays as yet. The sequences shown in yellow are common to both cell lines. If we eliminate those sequences whose function is known, we are left with the dozen or so shown on the next slide. What we need to do next is to amplify these genes and then transcribe them to the corresponding RNA sequences. After that, we can see what proteins they ultimately code for and hopefully identify the function of these proteins. What I'm looking for is a correlation in which the protein produced by one sequence directly regulates the activity of another sequence by binding to a promoter element for another sequence. We can screen for interactions to a first approximation by seeing whether the proteins will even bind to the sequence. Remember, we are looking for a common control point that confers immortality and limitless growth onto the cancer cell, but perhaps with tumor-specific regulation of the gene."

Meredith was following Jack's line of reasoning carefully and thought that she saw a potential problem. "What if the critical growth pathway you're looking for involves a higher order correlation?" she asked. "Say, of the twelve sequences you've identified, suppose one produces a protein that interacts with a genetic segment outside of these twelve, which then produces a protein that goes back and interacts with another of the twelve?"

Jack smiled. "Good observation. I've thought of that possibility, but I want to rule out the simpler two-way correlations first. I've also been talking with John Reherson's group in the physics department about using their time-dependent density functional calculations to model the protein's active sites once we know its structure. I want to see if there are any structural similarities that might help us identify the control element from the protein it produces. It would be interesting if this protein not only controlled other elements in the group but also some of the known control oncogenes such as the p53 sequence. We might see this if the protein has more than one catalytically active site. Reherson's wife died of breast cancer about a year ago, and he would like his research to help us better understand cancer. His group is busy with a lot of other projects, but he is willing to teach some of us how to use his computer code. Meredith, since you have a strong computer science background, would you be interested in working with me on this?"

Meredith happily accepted. The discussion continued, Bryon sai "This is really interesting work but how would you use it to disable the cancer cell?"

"What I want to do is build an antisense RNA strand that would bind to the messenger RNA coding for the control protein and disable it. We need to find both the immortality segment itself and the promoter elements that control it. Since the only way of getting the antisense segment into the tumor cell is to use an RNA adenovirus that is replicative competent, this limits the size of the segment that we can insert. This means that we will most likely need to attack the promoter element or elements rather than the immortality gene itself. Here, let me outline the procedure I have in mind."

Jack then stepped to the white board at the end of the conference area and wrote the following sequence of steps

PROPOSED PROCEDURE FOR ATTACKING TUMOR GROWTH CONTROL POINT

    I. *Determination of tumor control protein critical element*
- a. *Obtain tumor tissue*
- b. *Emulsify to obtain nuclear DNA*
- c. *Genetically sequence DNA*
- d. *Search for gene sequences specific for tumor cells*
- e. *Insert suspected sequences into E. Coli to produce corresponding proteins*
- f. *Identify proteins and determine their structure*
    - *f1. X-ray crystallographic analysis*

   f2. Computer modeling to determine changes in aqueous environment
  g. Identify active sites on proteins
II. *Preparation of treatment vector*
  a. Reverse engineer DNA sequences corresponding to active sites
  b. Develop antisense sequences that will disable active sites
  c. Produce RNA sequence corresponding to antisense element
  d. Incorporate RNA sequence into replicative competent retroviruse
  e. Allow virus to proliferate in viral culture medium
  f. Verify presence of tumor-disabling element in virus
  g. Inject virus into test subject

"Using a replicative competent virus sounds dangerous. What if the virus gets away from us?" asked Bryon.

"The virus needs to be able to replicate to make sure that it affects all the cells in the body. After all, cancer cells can be lurking anywhere. The body will eventually be able to eliminate the virus on its own, just as it recovers from the common cold. But by that time, the reverse transcribed antisense element will have been incorporated into the DNA of the cancer cells and will have turned off the critical genome element. Since only the cancer cells have the targeted genome element, this won't affect the normal cells. However, I've selected a virus that only infects the somatic cells and not the reproductive germ cells. I don't want to take any chances of DNA alterations propagating through future generations. That would be the height of irresponsibility, not to mention never getting Review Board approval for the study protocol."

"Won't that mean that the process isn't going to work on tumors that directly involve the reproductive germ cells?" asked Bryon.

"True, but we could always use a different virus in such situations – one that would infect the germ cells. I am going to leave that question to a later set of studies and not worry about it at this stage."

"Why do we need to know the protein that it causes to be expressed?" queried Meredith "If we can turn off the process at the gene itself, why worry about the protein messenger?"

"It may turn out that we don't need to know this, but in science, research paths are often tortuous. There may be other control elements as well. Nature has the habit of using the same code sequences in many organisms. Only small differences in the DNA determine whether you turn out human or a chimpanzee – about 1-2% in the active DNA is all the difference there is."

One of the lab techs started laughing and said, "In the case of some of my dates, I think it was probably less than that."

After the laughter died down, Jack continued his impromptu lecture.

"Remember that there is only a limited amount of RNA that the virus can carry with it due to its small size. We probably will need to specifically target the active portion of the messenger protein and block that part of the transcription process."

"How do we find out the protein structure?" asked another researcher.

"That's a more tedious process, replied Jack. We have to replicate the DNA coding sequence and insert it into tame E. Coli bacteria for which we know all of the genetic code. The bacteria reproduce and elaborate the protein. Then we filter it out and crystallize it. X-ray crystallography lets us identify the protein structure. In the last decade there has been a lot of progress in automating this process and we can use well-established techniques. However, this requires considerable computer processing time for large proteins, particularly since we are dealing with many very small crystals rather than a single large one. According to Reherson, the computer codes now keep track of the scattering phase shifts of the different reflections. The crystallized protein will most likely have a different quaternary structure than it would have in the cell, where it is surrounded by cytoplasmic fluid. The crystallography data will probably be pretty good in terms of the central portion of the protein which is hidden from the surrounding fluid, but we'll need the computational structure determination to get the outer part of the protein right. We can then correlate the results of the structural code with assemblies of the molecular elements obtained from the mass spectrometer."

Meredith asked, "Why don't we just use the computer calculation alone and not bother with the x-ray crystallography?"

"It's a question of computer processing power. If we can give the computer a good starting point for the large number of atoms that make up the central protein structure, then it won't take as long to self-consistently solve for the entire molecule. This will reduce the required time from months on a supercomputer to days or even hours."

This last statement led to other questions from the group. The discussion continued for a while longer, and then the lab meeting broke up. At its conclusion, Meredith made arrangements to meet with Jack the next day to find out more details about the project with Reherson. If she decided to pursue a Ph.D. as well as her M.D., this might make a good thesis project. She was also interested in learning more about the x-ray crystallography part of the project since this appeared to have wide application in biological research.

CHAPTER 12

DURING THE NEXT FEW months Meredith spent her mornings in Olivetti's laboratory learning molecular biology techniques and her afternoons with Reherson's physics group. The physicists were open and friendly. Like most scientists involved in basic research, they were excited that their work might have some practical application – particularly in a field as important as cancer therapy. Meredith was given a Linux workstation in a corner of the laboratory and shown how to log in and access the density functional code, or "DFC" as it was known within the group. Meredith had user privileges, which allowed her to access and run the code, but not make changes within it. The code was complex having evolved over several generations of graduate students and postdocs, but Reherson had insisted that the evolving changes be well documented. There was a fairly complete written description of the current working version for Meredith to study. Basically, the program modeled a part of the potential seen by the electrons in terms of a function of the electronic density. This enabled it to achieve the computational speed necessary to model fairly large molecules. Meredith's task involved modeling the protein molecules as well as the surrounding cellular cytoplasm. The cytoplasm influenced the protein's shape and hence its function. The first molecule she tried was benzene, a small, well-known molecule.

She picked it in order to make sure that she understood how to input data to the code and it gave back correct results in terms of structure and bonding properties. Confident, she then moved on to larger, but still well-understood organic molecules and at last felt ready to try an unknown protein.

She and Olivetti met a couple of times a week to review her progress. While Meredith had clearly become the group's expert on the code itself, Jack was able to make several helpful suggestions. These included: 1) initially simplifying the calculation by treating the surrounding medium as a dielectric, and 2) going back and refining the calculations at the end. Jack also suggested porting a copy of the code to the Blue Waters supercomputing system in preparation for work on really large molecules. Reherson was agreeable to this with the stipulation that his group would also have use of the ported code. Even with Reherson's help, it took several weeks to port the code.

"Meredith, are you about ready to try your hand at a real tumor?" asked Jack. "I would like to implant our glioblastoma or GBM cell line into nude mice, then excise the tumors and work through the process of trying to identify the growth control element and the transmission protein. If we can do that, we can try to tailor an antisense element to shut down the growth."

"I believe I understand the procedure well enough to give it a try," Meredith replied. "Let me help with the experiments on the mice as well to get some hands-on laboratory experience. We should probably take out some tumor samples early in order to do the gene sequencing and amplification process. This will give me time to get the calculations finished before the tumors kill the mice."

"Don't worry about that during this first set of experiments," said Jack. "We are just going to try and identify the control elements at first; we will worry about how to disable them later."

Things went very smoothly for a first set of experiments. GBM tumor cells were extracted from the growth medium, diluted to a standard concentration, and then injected into the flanks of immune-deficient nude mice. When the tumors had grown to about 2.5 centimeters in diameter, they were surgically removed, emulsified, and processed through the Illumina sequencer. Two candidates for the tumor growth control element were identified. They were amplified using a polymerase chain reaction, or PCR as it was more commonly known, and then the corresponding RNA homologs were constructed. The RNA was used to produce proteins which were crystallized for x-ray analysis. They were also run through the automated mass spectrometer to determine their structural units. The molecular data was then given to Meredith who set up the input file for the DFC code. Using a high speed internet connection, she ran the calculation on the Illinois system. This took ten hours of processor time and at the end, the results, in the form of a tabulation of atomic positions and energy levels as well as a graphical display of the structure, were returned to Meredith's work station. The entire process had taken three days. Once the output from the Blue Water system was obtained, Meredith and Jack sat down in front of the terminal to look at it.

"Look at this!" exclaimed Meredith excitedly. "I've identified three possible proteins for the growth element – call them A, B, and C. They appear to be similar but have a slightly different configuration meaning different binding properties. Going back to the initial sequencing, 'A' is about four times greater in abundance than 'B' and 'C' is present only in trace amounts. What do you think this means?"

"Hard to know," replied Jack. "Could be some sort of contamination or perhaps, there really are several different control elements. This is a human tumor cell line and so could well have some heterogeneity in it due to genetic mutations. The pocket structure of the proteins looks similar, which would seem to indicate some cross reactivity in terms of binding to other proteins. Let's redo the experiment using a monoclonal animal tumor in genetically identical mice."

"Which animal model do you want to use?"

"Let's go back to the old reliable 36B10 rat glioma tumor in Fisher rats. It's been around for a long time and its properties are well understood. The animals are available in the Vivarium and we have frozen cells in the freezer. We can be ready to assay the tumors in a couple of weeks."

Jack recruited other members of the group to help with the experiment. Things went as expected; tumors grew on the flanks of the rats in a few weeks. The process of excising the tumors, emulsifying the tissue, performing the genetic assay, amplifying the result, and determining the structure took several days and ate up more computer time from Jack's grant. The end result was a single candidate protein which had some striking similarities to the A,B, and C proteins identified in the previous experiment.

CHAPTER 13

AT THIS POINT WORK had to stop temporarily while Jack wrote a proposed treatment protocol for the animal studies, which had to be approved by the University Animal Use Committee. Meredith was frustrated by the delay, but Jack explained to her how incredibly lucky they had been to have gotten so far so quickly.

Jack explained, "Most of the time in science, experiments only show things that don't work. At least this time, we have some indication that we might be on the right track. We won't know for sure until we have completed the work on the animal models. Even if it works on rats and mice, there is no guarantee that the same approach will work on more heterogeneous, wild-type human tumors. Don't forget that we found not one but three possible control proteins in the human tumor. It might be that we need to shut down all three in order to stop all the tumor cells from growing, and that would be a more difficult job."

As Jack expected based upon his prior experience, the University Animal Use Committee raised several concerns about the protocol. These did not relate to the logic of the experiment but rather to the well being of the animals. The committee wanted assurances that animals in which tumors were not controlled would not be allowed to suffer but would be "euthanized in a timely manner using a neck breaking technique ..." according to the somewhat stilted language in the committee's letter. Jack reworked the protocol to address the issues raised by the committee. He explained to Meredith that while it might be obvious to the two of them that it would pointless to keep treatment failures alive for a prolonged time as well as an unnecessary expense, this needed to be spelled out in writing. The University had recently gotten some bad press relating to its research on animals and wanted to avoid any more problems. Jack's revisions did not reach the University Animal Use Committee in time for its next meeting so approval of the proposed experiment was delayed an additional two weeks.

Jack's detached approach contrasted with Meredith's greater sense of urgency. Gaby's situation made the search for a cancer cure a personal matter to her. She could not help but think that with almost six hundred thousand cancer deaths each year in the United States alone, a month's delay in finding a cure meant fifty thousand deaths that might have been prevented.

The protocol was finally approved for the treatment of ten animals and the experiment started. 36B10 tumor cells were removed from the freezer, thawed, and allowed to grow in culture. The culture medium was spun down in a centrifuge and the two scientists diluted them to a standard concentration.

"Let's start by injecting the tumor cells into the flank of three rats. Two weeks later we will inject the cells into the remaining seven rats. That will give us time to do the tissue assay from the tumors on the first three. We'll have the viral vector prepared to treat the last sevem before their tumors grow to the point of major suffering. Since both the rats and the injected tumors are genetically equivalent, what we learn from the first batch of tumors will apply to the second batch."

"I see that," said Meredith. "But if we were going to use this treatment on humans, wouldn't we have to do the assay on the actual tumor we wanted to treat?"

"Yes," said Jack in a somewhat distracted way. He was showing Meredith how to immobilize the rats prior to injecting them. "If this works, we also have to figure out a way of speeding up the process before human studies could begin. A human is much larger than a mouse, so considerably larger amounts of the treatment agent are going to be needed."

The first three rats were injected; the tumor nodules all "took" and started to grow. After two weeks the nodules were about a half centimeter in diameter. Jack took the rats out of their cage and showed Meredith how to break their necks in the prescribed manner. The tumor nodules were excised and emulsified. The cells were spun down and put through the genome sequencer. Jack and Meredith looked at the mapping data. They identified two possible candidates for the control segment based upon similarities to the elements identified in the early work on the GBM human tumor line. The RNA homolog was constructed and the corresponding proteins produced. Meredith put the proteins through a mass spectroscopy analyzer, and after obtaining their amino acid building blocks, began calculating their structural and electronic properties.

The supercomputer run took place Sunday night and the next day Meredith and Jack met in the lab at 7 AM, each carrying a double shot espresso drink from the coffee kiosk. Meredith pulled up the output file on the lab's new Mac which had four of the new, ultrafast Intel quad-core processors and a thiry-inch flat panel monitor. The graphics display was rendered blazingly fast and she soon had the structures of the two proteins rotating on opposite sides of the screen.

"What do you think? Is one a better candidate than the other or do you think we need to worry about both?" she asked.

Jack took a sip of his coffee and watched the rotating structures for a while. "I think the larger one on the left is the more likely candidate," he replied. "Look at this region of the molecule – see the shape and size of this indentation. It looks similar to the pockets we saw in the GBM case. Which DNA sequence gave rise to this one, and was it the more prevalent of the two?"

"Both DNA segments were about equally concentrated. But I see what you mean about the similarity in this segment of the protein," Meredith said. She used the computer mouse to move the cursor over part of the computer rendition.

"Let's target this one then. When Bryon gets in, I will have him construct the antisense element corresponding to it and start preparing the adenovirus vector."

Meredith and Jack excitedly interrupted each other as they tried to explain to Bryon what they wanted him to do. He soon caught their excitement, marshaled the lab techs, and started them working. It took three days to prepare adequate amounts of the genetically-altered virus and inject it into the tail veins of the remaining seven rats. The nodules on the rats now were readily apparent and Bryon documented their location and size. Then they waited.

CHAPTER 14

AVARTEC's MARKETING ARM WAS in full swing, with drug detail people touting the amazing results of a combination of *INHIBIT* and chemotherapy for all the common tumors. AVARTEC was planning a major exhibition at the upcoming ASCO meeting with three-dimensional virtual reality presentations of how *INHIBIT* worked and summaries of the latest human clinical trial data. As required by the agreement between State and AVARTEC, the abstract from Jack's group on *Compound 10* was being reviewed by a committee consisting of representatives from both institutions. Arthur Jenkins, the head of the review committee, was a senior administrator at AVARTEC. While pleased with the study results, he was concerned that publicizing *Compound 10* at this stage might detract from the marketing of *INHIBIT*, something he could not allow to happen.

Jenkins began the discussion. "The work out of Olivetti's lab looks nice, but I wonder if showing the data on *Compound 10* might be premature at this stage. After all, this is only one mouse study. It would be nice to have some confirmatory data before presenting it at ASCO. I think the part of the study showing a benefit from *INHIBIT* could certainly be presented and published now. What do you think about asking to have the abstract rewritten to show only these two arms of the study?"

Michael Phillips, a member of State's Department of Pharmacology, couldn't believe what he was hearing. "The data look sound to me and the *Compound 10* results are statistically significant. Yes, other studies might not show the same gain, but this information should be disseminated to the scientific community. Olivetti is a careful researcher and he would not have approved this abstract if he didn't believe that the data were sound."

"I'm not saying that the data are wrong, just that this might not be the best time to publish it. AVARTEC needs some additional time to get *Compound 10* further along in the patent process. Our partnership recognizes AVARTEC's economic issues as well as State's scientific research interests. Don't forget that *Compound 10* was made available to Olivetti for study through a Materials Transfer Agreement. AVARTEC retained certain rights, among them the right to review and approve conference presentations and journal publications making use of it."

Phillips acknowledged the truth of this statement half-heartedly. "Well, when do you think AVARTEC would approve release of this data – assuming they hold up, of course?"

"Perhaps at next year's ASCO meeting," replied Jenkins.

"So what you are really saying is that AVARTEC's interest in marketing *INHIBIT* trumps getting data out about something that might be better? After all, AVARTEC will also own the rights to *Compound 10*, which looks like it might be a better drug and help more patients."

"It's the phrase 'will own' that is key here," replied Jenkins. "AVARTEC needs some time to be sure that we have *Compound 10* locked up before turning the public's attention to it. It is not as if we are keeping a better drug off the market right now. It will take several more years of work to get permission to move *Compound 10* into human trials given the slow pace of working through the FDA."

"The FDA is certainly a dinosaur, even compared to other government agencies. I agree with that. However, the underlying issue is about academic freedom," said Phillips. I call for a vote on whether the abstract should be approved as written or whether the part describing the results with *Compound 10* should be eliminated."

The majority of the committee members had been carefully chosen by Drisco and the dean for their willingness to adhere to the party line so the outcome of the vote was a foregone conclusion. The tally was five to two in favor of having the abstract rewritten to describe only the improvement achieved with *INHIBIT*.

Phillips glumly acknowledged his defeat. "OK. I know when I'm licked, but I think this decision stinks. Let me talk to Olivetti before he gets the written report of this committee. That will soften the blow, give him time to make the changes in the abstract, and still meet the submission deadline. You should know that I am going to ask Bob Katterhagen, my department chairman, to bring up this matter at the next Medical School Executive Committee meeting for discussion. MSEC may want to make some changes in the terms of the Materials Transfer Agreement with AVARTEC when it next comes up for renewal."

After the meeting, Phillips stopped by Olivetti's laboratory where he spoke with Olivetti and Bryon Heymond. He gave them the bad news about the committee meeting. Bryon was particularly upset, but Jack was more sanguine.

"Well, I guess that without AVARTEC making *Compound 10* available, we wouldn't have been able to do the study. Can't argue with that. I just find it offensive to withhold data so that AVARTEC can make more money on *INHIBIT*. Particularly since *Compound 10* is just another step along the same pathway and it will eventually make AVARTEC more money anyway. You can bet that they already own the patent rights to *Compound 10*, so Jenkin's remark about needing more time for this is an outright lie. The clinical trials are almost sure to work since it has better activity and the same set of side effects as *INHIBIT*. Oh well, eventually we'll get to publish the complete paper."

"That's easy for you to say," Bryon replied. "You and others from your lab will get the credit for the work on *Compound 10*, but I will be out of here at another job when the final paper comes out."

"That's certainly true. What if I guarantee you an authorship slot on the publication when the work is released for publication? On the positive side, you will be getting two publications for your CV instead of one. You know what they say about 'weighing the CV instead of reading it' when promotion time comes around."

Bryon and Phillips laughed. Bryon was mollified. "Well, when you look at it like that, OK," he said. But imagine what AVARTEC's reaction would be if instead of *Compound 10*, we had come up with a totally new approach to treating cancer that would make *INHIBIT* and other drugs in their pipeline totally obsolete. It would not be pretty."

Jack thought about the work he and Meredith were doing on targeting the cellular growth control element. "Well, you never know what might happen someday. Mike, what can we do about getting the master agreement with AVARTEC reviewed? The way things stand now, even if materials transfer does not come into play, the fact that AVARTEC has provided equipment like the gene sequencer down the hall which my lab uses, could be construed as giving the review committee oversight on anything coming out of my lab."

Phillips said, "Well, the dean and AVARTEC are pretty tight, but the Medical School Executive Committee still has to approve the scope of agreements like this. At the review committee meeting,

I said that I was going to ask Bob Katterhagen, to bring up the disapproval at the next MSEC meeting. Bob can also ask questions about the strings that are currently attached to shared equipment use. This is a much more overarching and worrisome issue. According to some of Bob's remarks at our departmental faculty meetings, the dean keeps a tight rein on MSEC. Items that the Dean doesn't want discussed are voted on as part of a consent agenda. The chairs don't see them until the day of the meeting. No one has the time or the energy to print out the documents and review them before the start of the meeting. However, if one of the chairs wants to bring up an item for discussion, he or she can let the other chairs know in advance. That way they can be thinking about it ahead of time."

"Let me know what Katterhagen thinks, and in the meantime, I will talk to my own department chairman about what happened and my concerns for the future."

CHAPTER 15

IT WAS THE SECOND Friday of the month, and the School of
Medicine's Executive Committee was set to meet that afternoon. As
usual, that morning the agenda had been sent out by the dean's office
for the department chairs to review. Along with the other chairs, Bob
Katterhagen had downloaded the PDF files containing the agenda.
They listed the items to be discussed at the meeting. Katterhagen
noted that the discussion topic on whether to restructure the general
nature of the partnership agreement between the medical school
and industry was last on the agenda. At least it was on there. He
had asked for it to be included on fairly short notice. Prior to the
meeting he wanted to talk to some of his fellow chairs to let them
know his concerns. He retrieved his Blackberry, pulled up his contact
list, and scrolled down to the direct line of Samuel Bremenoff, the
Chairman of Internal Medicine. Internal Medicine was by far the
largest department in the medical school, so Sam had considerable
influence. Besides, this topic of discussion had been brought up
in part because of problems faced by Jack Olivetti who was one of
Sam's faculty, and it wouldn't hurt to be sure he was in agreement
with what Katterhagan was proposing. Katterhagen placed the call.

"Sam, good morning. This is Bob Katterhagen. Do you have a
few minutes to talk?"

"I always have time to talk with you, Bob, but I do have a meeting relating to department space allocations in about a half hour. As you know, assigning lab space to faculty is always a contentious issue, and I don't want to start off the meeting by being late."

"That's for sure," Katterhagen acknowledged. "Have you had a chance to look at the agenda for today's MSEC meeting yet?"

"Not yet. Let me pull it up now. I will put you on speaker phone while I do this."

Katterhagen heard a click and then the sound became a little more hollow. He heard some tapping in the background as Bremenoff turned on his desktop computer, opened his E-mail account, and downloaded the agenda file.

"OK, I've got it now. What do you want me to look at?"

"Take a look at the last item before we go into executive closed session for the faculty promotion vote. I asked that the way agreements are structured between State and private industry be put on the agenda for discussion. There really are some problems with the amount of control that certain industries have over our faculty's research and I believe that the structure of the basic agreement template needs to be revised. As things stand now, any commercial partner can prohibit our faculty from publishing or presenting data at meetings if it has had any involvement at all in the research project. This is slowing things down, and moreover, puts our faculty at risk for getting 'scooped' by their competitors."

"Does this have anything to do with the dispute between Jack Olivetti and AVARTEC? Olivetti told me last week that the AVARTEC review committee put a hold on some of the data in an abstract he was going to submit for an upcoming meeting. By the way, he was quite complimentary about Mike Phillips' effort to get this decision overturned."

"Yes, after all this happened, Phillips came to me and pointed out the serious problems we would have if this trend continued."

"It's a complex situation given that we depend so much on industry funding to support our research – particularly since NIH funding has started to decrease in absolute dollars. We both have faculty who are dependent upon industry money, and without it, we would have to terminate a lot of people who work in the labs."

"Don't forget though, industry needs us as much as we need them. The majority of the biotech companies don't have enough of their own research space, and depend upon our investigators to do most of the early-stage basic research. It is also more cost effective for them not to have to support a large, in-house basic research program. I don't have a problem with companies developing and marketing discoveries that are made in our labs if they have significantly supported it. But putting a 'hold' on our presenting research merely because some of it was performed using equipment that they provided is quite another matter."

"I agree," said Bremenoff. "Clearly we need to talk more about this and eventually make some changes that will put us in a better position. I am looking forward to the discussion this afternoon."

Katterhagen sighed, and the two said goodbye. It was characteristic of Bremenoff, thought Katterhagen, to want to study an issue for a long time before making a decision. Perhaps this was partially due to the personality types that gravitated to internal medicine. Katterhagen looked at his Blackberry again and scrolled down to Emanuel Romez, the Chairman of the Department of Surgery. Manny, as he was known to his friends, did not have any trouble making a decision based upon the best available data, and then acting upon it. He was one reason that things got accomplished at the MSEC meetings. Romez's secretary picked up the phone. She told Katterhagen that Romez was already in the operating room. She would have him call the pharmacology department chair back when the case was finished. Katterhagen thanked her and continued to work through the list of department chairs.

Chapter 16

It was shortly before 4:00, and the department chairs were filtering into the large conference room where the MSEC meetings were usually held. The various vice deans and associate deans were already there as was the dean himself. Everyone helped himself or herself to a soft drink, tea, or coffee, took a snack, and sat down at the long table, which dominated the room. The dean and chairs sat at the table along with some of the more senior vice deans. The rest took seats along the periphery of the room. As usual, the group from the dean's office tended to congregate on the dean's left. His secretary, Margo, who took minutes for the meeting, sat in the chair next to him, and Alice Maxim took the seat next to her. The meeting began with a review of the prior month's meeting. Robbie Lawrence, Vice Dean for Clinical Affairs, called attention to a few typos and name misspellings. Unlike the majority of the attendees, Lawrence made a point of actually reading the minutes. With Lawrence's corrections, the minutes were approved. The dean then led off with a series of general announcements about upcoming lectures and awards. Next he reported on the status of the ongoing searches for new chairmen for several departments. Chairs had recently resigned either because of a better offer from another institution, retirement, or disgust with all of the paperwork. Some wanted to go back to being just a professor.

The dean thought to himself, *four ongoing searches with little progress being made on any of them. And then when a good candidate is identified, he will want the moon in terms of salary and laboratory space in order to come.* Then he asked if there were any questions?

The various vice deans then gave brief reports followed by a short presentation by Martha Hodgin, Chief Development Officer, on the status of the ongoing fundraising program. Hodgin had a difficult job because the School of Medicine was expected to raise at least half of the three billion dollar goal for State. The university president had been continually on the dean's case about this. Hodgin closed by saying that fundraising would be a lot easier if she could tell the potential major donors that the leadership of the school was solidly behind it. She then asked all the chairmen and vice deans to pledge significant amounts. Most of the conference participants had already pledged but there were a few holdouts, who squirmed a bit in their chairs. They knew that there would be follow-up phone calls first from Hodgin and then from the dean with some not-so-subtle pressure being applied.

The first discussion topic was the ongoing construction project for the new research complex. The first building shell was nearing completion and the other two building foundations had been dug. The dean showed some slides recently taken at the project. Cement trucks were shown coming and going and construction cranes hauled up steel I-beams. He talked about 'naming opportunities' for donors who gave sufficiently large sums of money to the school. Maxim spoke about the financing of the project. She stressed the partnership with Blackmont in terms of raising capital and the need for continued high levels of research funding to support the cash flow for the project bonds. Of course, she failed to mention the bogus guarantee letter that she and the dean had cooked up for the

Blackmont board and the other investors. Finally, the Vice Dean for Research, Nancy Shalle, talked about how research space would be assigned in the first building to be completed. All of the department chairs perked up when this topic was presented. Their existing space was crowded, and new laboratory space was critical if they wanted to either hire new people or coax current people into staying.

Shalle began by saying, "We are going to continue our policy of assigning laboratory space on the basis of research themes or programs. There will be investigators from multiple departments in each program. The laboratory space itself will remain under the control of the dean's office. Space in building number one will be largely devoted to cancer research and so your research proposals must address this area. Send your proposals to me in two week. I then will develop groups and laboratory assignments based upon synergies between the proposals. I probably won't get this done before the next MSEC meeting but I should have the first iteration ready by the following one. I will also need a listing of the last three years of grant funding for investigators whose programs are being considered. Please include any grant proposals that either have been submitted or are far enough along to be submitted for the next funding cycle. Our office has records of the amount of the financial awards for the various grants, but I want to make sure that we don't miss any. For proposals under development, summarize the requested funding year by year. Any questions at this stage?"

Romez of surgery was the first to raise his hand. Shalle nodded her head to Romez who led off by asking, "Will some of the programs have a clinical focus such as 'outcomes research' or are you just looking for wet-lab-type basic science?"

"Buildings one and two will be primarily wet lab space with offices for the investigators. Outcomes people will have to wait until the final building phase, but there will be opportunity for backfilling of space vacated after some of the basic research groups move into their new space."

"How important will current funding be in assigning people to groups?" inquired Katterhagen. "Given the stagnant NIH funding picture, many of our senior investigators are seeing budget cuts when their grants are renewed. Our junior faculty often have to submit their proposals two or three times before receiving funding."

"Grant funding will be a very important criterion in assigning new lab space in building onw. The indirect costs of the grants are needed to pay the rent on the building. It is just a fact of life."

Maxim interjected, "What Shalle means is that the cash flow from the research project supports the bonds that were issued to build the research complex."

Bremenhoff spoke up. "So in essence what you are doing is pulling out the better-funded investigators from existing space which is already paid for, and putting them in the new building. That way the revenue steams associated with their grants are assigned to support the new project. If they remained in their old space, the indirect costs could be used to support other academic missions of the school."

"I don't like the way this discussion is going," interjected the dean. "What we have done is to make new and better research space available for your faculty. This will help them build their programs. Yes, the more productive investigators will be rewarded, but that is the nature of the system. The less productive investigators will also benefit in that additional lab space in the older facilities will be available to them after their colleagues move."

"It looks a little like a house of cards," Katterhagen persisted. "The whole thing will collapse if there is any lag in grant funding, and in spite of the best efforts of our faculty, this is something that we really cannot control."

"However, there is a way we can insure against this," said the dean. "This brings us to the next topic on the agenda – the nature of the relationship between State and industry – that some of you wanted to discuss. I have been in discussion with AVARTEC about offering them a long-term lease on some of the space in the new building. AVARTEC would also provide a substantial amount of lab equipment, which would be under a 'shared use' arrangement with our investigators – expensive items like genome sequencers and mass spectrometers, for example. The arrangement would encourage a more active collaboration between our faculty and AVARTEC investigators, which in turn would most likely lead to AVARTEC's supporting more of our research work. This would reduce our dependence on the NIH or other federal agencies."

Katterhagen looked over at Bremenhoff who was sitting on his right. Bremenhoff had a puzzled look on this face. Where was this discussion going?

Bremenhoff spoke worriedly. "What would the cost be to our faculty for using equipment provided by AVARTEC or any other company, for that matter? As many of the chairs know, Bob and I asked that this item be placed on the agenda because of some problems that one of my best researchers, Jack Olivetti, had with the AVARTEC review board. They refused to approve an abstract that he wanted to send out for the ASCO meeting. The quality of the data was never an issue; it was just that AVARTEC wanted to delay publication of some of the results for marketing reasons."

Katterhagen interjected himself into the discussion. "What Sam says is absolutely correct. One of my faculty, Mike Phillips, is on the approval committee. He came to me after the meeting in which Olivetti's abstract was disapproved for submission. This is a bad trend, and I think that we need to reassert control of the dissemination of our research. I would not be in favor of any new agreement with AVARTEC or any other company that has such a restriction. I think that we need to revisit our older agreements as well."

"Come on Bob, be reasonable," replied the dean. "Agreements with industry are about the only new growth area in research funding. Commercialization of research is not bad and its something the Bayh-Dole Act even requires for federal funding."

"Yes, but Bayh-Dole doesn't proscribe publication of research results, which is what happened to Olivetti. This was an end run around academic freedom which is what a great university such as State is all about."

"Academic freedom as you are using it is just another term for going broke," replied the dean. "But I agree that the issues are complex and need to be studied more before we make a decision. I will form a committee made up of some of the chairs as well as representatives from AVARTEC and some other companies with whom we have active collaborations. The committee will report back to MSEC. I will be in touch with some of you about serving on the committee."

"Bob and I would like to be on this committee," said Bremenhoff.

"Thanks for volunteering," replied the dean. "I want to think a little to make sure that the committee is balanced before I decide on who should be on it. I will get back to the two of you."

"Bet we never hear back from him," Katterhagen muttered to Bremenhoff. The group went into executive session to vote on the faculty who had been reviewed for promotion by the A&P Committee.

The chair of the A&P Committee this academic year was George Latimer, Chair of Radiation Oncology. Latimer noted that while there were no significant concerns with any of the candidates, the committee as usual had a difficult time understanding the nebulous criteria used by some departments in deciding whether someone should be promoted or not. He asked all the chairmen to review their department's criteria and to define them better. Privately, he doubted that this would happen since the majority of the chairman liked the flexibility of doing what they wanted with their faculty. The individuals participating in the executive session voted in a perfunctory manner and the meeting adjourned. Everyone was looking forward to the weekend.

CHAPTER 17

SATURDAY MORNING DAWNED BRIGHT and clear, which was very unusual for Seattle this late in the year. Meredith decided to take a break from her lab work and her studies and drive over to Sequim to visit Gaby. It was over a month since she had seen her although they spoke on the phone at least once a week. Meredith packed a small overnight bag and attached her bike rack to the back of her five-year old Passat. She was an avid biker and planned to take advantage of the weather to ride some of the country roads around Sequim that afternoon. Her basset hound, Sam, got more and more excited as she packed. He loved a car ride. Meredith loaded her road bike on the rack, told Sam to jump in, and drove off. She merged with the northbound traffic on I-5, took the Edmunds exit, and drove west to the terminal for the ferry to Kingston, joining the other cars in the ferry line. Given the time of year, the line was mercifully short. When the ferry arrived and had unloaded, the waiting cars drove on and parked according to the attendants directions. She remembered to disengage the motion detector on the car alarm. You could generally tell the newbies to the ferry. Their car alarms would go off when the boat started rocking during the crossing. Meredith walked up to the passenger deck to enjoy the view for the short ride across the sound to Kingston. The Olympic Mountains were ahead, the Cascades behind, and Mount Baker visible to the north. To Meredith's way of thinking, on a day such as this, there was no finer place in the whole world.

Arriving in Kingston, Meredith joined the line of departing cars and headed towards Sequim. The drive itself was uneventful. She listened to soft rock on the car radio, exiting the highway in Sequim and heading north to Gaby's. The house was situated on the water overlooking the Strait of Juan de Fucca and Dungeness Spit. The spit had given its name to the species of crabs that were caught there in great abundance. She pulled into the driveway, got out and stretched before heading up to the door. Sam had jumped out and was relieving himself against a large rhododendron that grew next to the driveway. Gaby was normally a fastidious gardener, but Meredith noticed that the plants had not been pruned, and there were still deadheads clinging to the rhododendrons. Although she had her own key, she knocked politely and waited until Gaby came to the door.

"Meredith, I'm so glad to see you. How was the drive over?" Gaby exclaimed as she hugged Meredith. Sam butted Gaby with his head as his way of asking to have his ears rubbed.

Gaby's demeanor was as cheerful as usual, butMeredith thought that physically she looked wan.

"Beautiful! The ferry ride over was especially nice. Not much traffic this time of year and no waiting in the ferry line. Guess people are doing other things now that the normal vacation period is over. How are you feeling now? It has been about a couple of months since I have made it over here."

"Yes, I know that you are really busy with your research projects, but you have been good at calling me almost every weekend. Take your bags up to your room; once you have unpacked, I will make us a pot of tea and we can sit and talk."

Meredith went up the stairway to her old room on the second floor of the house. She opened the window curtains and gazed out over the straits to the north. She saw seagulls whirling over the beach and could hear their screaming cries through her closed window. She took out the few items she had brought from her overnight case and put them away. She also brought out her medical kit. She thought that she would go back to the car and take out her cycling gear later. Right now she wanted to talk with Gaby.

Meredith went back downstairs and into the cheery kitchen where a kettle had just started to whistle. Gaby placed some loose tea into a strainer, put it into a chipped yellow teapot that had been Meredith's favorite when she was a little girl, and poured in the boiling water. The two women sat down at the table while the tea steeped. Meredith noticed that Gaby's movements were a little slower and more deliberate than usual – as if she were trying to avoid moving in ways that were painful. Her arms seemed thinner than before, but her abdomen remained full and round.

"Have you been losing some weight?" Meredith began.

"Don't I wish," replied Gaby. My weight may be down a pound or so, but my clothes are fitting more tightly than ever."

"When was the last time you saw Dr. Greerson?"

"It has been a couple of months. I had an appointment with him last week, but I couldn't make it because Mrs. Wilson, who was going to drive me to Seattle, got sick herself."

"Have you called and gotten another appointment?"

"Dr. Greerson is going to be away for the next three weeks. He is speaking at a meeting in Italy, and then, his nurse tells me that his wife is going to fly over and join him. They are going to take a vacation along the Amalfi coast. The poor man works so hard, it will be good for him to get away."

"Well, he must have someone covering his service while he is away. Perhaps that person could see you?"

"I'd rather wait for my own doctor, " Gaby said adamantly. "But if you're worried, why don't you take a look at me yourself while you're here."

Gaby poured the tea into the two cups she had removed from the cupboard. Meredith stirred in a spoonful of honey and sipped it appreciatively.

"OK. Let me get my kit after we finish this tea. I will look you over before I take my bike ride. No cooking tonight, let's just go down to the Crab House instead. It will be my treat."

Meredith and Gaby continued to talk and Gaby poured each another cup of tea. Then Meredith went upstairs and retrieved her small medical kit. She brought it downstairs, got out her stethoscope and sphygmomanometer and took Gaby's blood pressure. It seemed a little on the low side, 105/60, so she took it again and then a third time after asking Gaby to stand. There wasn't much change in the blood pressure or heart rate when Gaby stood up and so Meredith thought her fluid balance was probably OK.

"Great blood pressure – no heart problems with you."

"My heart will keep going long after the rest of me has quit," laughed Gaby.

Meredith listened to Gaby's lungs, pounded gently along her spine, and felt for enlarged lymph nodes in her neck and under her arms. Then she then asked Gaby to lie down on the living room couch where she examined her abdomen. It was somewhat swollen and tense but wasn't tender even when she probed more deeply. Meredith couldn't feel any lumps or masses, which was good. Looking for a fluid wave, she asked Gaby to place a hand and arm on top of her abdomen, and balloted gently on one side with her right hand while feeling on the other side with her left hand. She could feel the transmitted pulses, which indicated that fluid was present.

"Looks like you may have some fluid in your belly," said Meredith. "Do you have any trouble breathing – particularly when you bend over?"

"No, everything is fine."

"Well, if the amount of fluid continues to increase, it will cause problems. It might have to be taken out as it was before."

"Ouch," said Gaby. "If it has to be done, couldn't you just do it?"

"No, it needs to be done sterilely in the clinic. What I want you to do is to call and make an appointment just as soon as Dr. Greerson returns."

"OK," agreed Gaby. "Now why don't you go for your bike ride before we have dinner. It's starting to get dark earlier and I don't want you riding when people can't see you."

Meredith nodded, packed her equipment back in her medical bag and took it upstairs. She changed into her biking clothes, carrying her biking shoes down to the front porch before putting them on. She then removed her bicycle from the car rack, clipped into the pedals, and took off down the road. There wasn't much traffic which allowed Meredith to reflect upon Gaby's situation. While her grandmother was doing reasonably well at the moment, this wouldn't last indefinitely. The fluid accumulation in her abdomen was a sign that the tumor was continuing to progress in spite of aggressive treatment. Meredith mulled things over as she started up a steep hill. She shifted gears to keep her pedaling rate the same and started the climb.

"I wonder if there are any new clinical trials out there for ovarian cancer? When I get back to Seattle, I will search the NCI link on the internet. I'll look at the latest work in the gynecologic oncology journals. It is too damn bad that medical research moves so slowly when it comes to actually treating patients."

A car came up behind her and Meredith was careful to move to the far right of the road as it passed. After she crested the top of the hill, she shifted back to a higher gear, moved back to the center of her lane, and began to make some speed. She kept going this way for about two hours making a long loop on the back roads which returned her to Gaby's house. She was sweating hard and had the familiar sensations of fatigue and a feeling of accomplishment as she dismounted. She showered, changed into slacks and a sweater. Over dinner Meredith talked about her work in Olivetti's laboratory.

"We are trying a different approach from the usual chemotherapy or radiotherapy which hits normal tissues as well as the cancer. Each cancer cell just wants to keep on dividing, and we are trying to stop this. Our virus puts a blocking protein in all the cells but normal cells don't have this faulty governor so they won't be affected. We have only tried it on a few mice but it seems to work the way we expected. The mice seem to only have a mild case of the flu for a few days following the injection as the virus reproduces and infects the body's cells. There are still a lot of questions about which kind of cancers this would work on and how to best use it in connection with more standard therapies."

"Why would you want to use more standard therapies along with this virus if it works as well as you say? I know how sick I got with the chemotherapy and how sore I was after the surgery. I would take a case of the flu any time."

Meredith tried to explain how clinical trials worked – taking one small step at a time – but found herself agreeing with Gaby. Both were tired, so after enjoying a couple of glasses of wine with their food, they returned home and retired. Meredith allowed herself the luxury sleeping late. She didn't set her alarm and slept until about 10. Gaby had been up for a couple of hours and had coffee ready. After breakfast, Meredith repacked her things, loaded her car, whistled for Sam to jump in, and gave Gaby a hug.

"Now don't forget to make an appointment to see Greerson as soon as he gets back. If you have any trouble getting on his schedule, let me know and I will see what I can do. While I don't have any clout myself, my boss, Dr. Olivetti, does, and I am sure I can get him to make a phone call."

Meredith drove back to Seattle again enjoying the half hour ferry ride but also worrying about Gaby. As usual, Sam sprawled out on the passenger seat and slept most of the way.

CHAPTER 18

BRIGHT AND EARLY MONDAY morning Meredith was the first person in the laboratory. She quickly reviewed the most recent literature on ovarian cancer on the NCI Pubmed site, but found nothing that might be helpful to Gaby's situation. Then she went to the vivarium and retrieved the test mice. The previous week they were covered with tumor nodules, but now their skins appeared smooth and unblemished. At first she thought that the test mice must have been moved and that these were a different batch. She sought out old Halderman, who actually ran the vivarium.

"Did you move Olivetti's batch of test mice over the weekend, for some reason?"

"Nope," Halderman answered in his slow, Southern drawl. "They are in cages 17A and 17B the same as before. Been taking good care of them. When you first brought them back they seemed really pooped for a day but then became more lively and really scarfed up the food that I gave them yesterday."

"I can't believe it's the same mice. I don't see any nodules at all, and they are running around like they have never been injected with cancer cells. I need to take these back to the lab and examine them in detail. Would you help me load them into the travel cages?"

"Sure," replied Halderman.

He got out the flat traveling cages, put on his gloves, caught the seven test mice, and put them in the cages. Then Meredith put the cages on a trolley and wheeled them down to the elevator, and up to Olivetti's lab. When she got there, she unloaded the mice and began to look them over. Even on careful inspection, she found no trace of the tumor nodules. Olivetti arrived in the lab at about 8:30, and she told him the exciting news. He looked over each mouse carefully and then admitted that he didn't see or feel anything either.

"No way!" he exclaimed. "Even if the treatment worked, the tumor nodules couldn't have gone away that fast. Someone is playing a joke on me and has switched mice."

"That's what I thought at first, but look at this mouse with the crooked right front foot. I remember this little guy from before. There wouldn't be two mice like this in the vivarium. Besides, who would go to all the trouble to pull such a trick and how would they do it without Halderman catching them?"

"Hmmm. I suppose if blocking the gene somehow triggered cell apoptosis or spontaneous cell death, the tumors would lyse or breakdown and there wouldn't be anything left to see. I was just trying to stop the cells from dividing, you know – a reproductive form of cell death. Having the treatment directly trigger apoptosis or direct cell death would be a definite bonus. But before speculating further, let's really look hard at these mice. I will call down to the Nuclear Medicine lab and see if we can get some time on the animal PET scanner. After that, we are going to need to sacrifice a couple of them and do a detailed necropsy."

"I know about using PET scans on humans for making diagnoses but I didn't know that we had special scanners just for animals"

"Same thing really, but with the small sizes of mice and other test animals, we get better resolution with a small-bore scanner tailored to the size of their bodies. We use the same set of diagnostic compounds that we use for people – unless, of course, the radiology group is experimenting to develop something better. The imaging uses the same correlated gamma rays that are released as the emitted positron decays. The targeting comes from the particular way the compound concentrates in the tumor. We use F-18 deoxyglucose to look at metabolic activity, isotopes of nitrogen or oxygen to look at amino acid synthesis, F-18 labeled misonidazole to image hypoxic tissues – just about anything you want to look at. Since rapidly growing tumors have higher metabolic rates than most normal tissues, I want to use F-18 deoxyglucose to look for hidden tumor tissue."

Olivetti called down and arranged for some scanner time at the end of the day. Fortunately, enough F-18 deoxyglucose, or FDG as it was commonly termed, had been made in the morning isotope production run for the extra set of studies. Much less activity was required for small animals such as mice and rats than for humans. Olivetti recruited the lab techs to help with the project, and soon everything was in order. The rats were taken down to the PET suite where they were injected with the FDG and scanned. Olivetti went down to the PET suite himself and looked at the images as they were taken rather than waiting for them to be snet to his office computer. There were the usual areas of increased activity in the brain, bladder, and liver, but no specific hot regions indicating residual tumor. Two of the rats were selected for necropsy, and the other five returned to isolated cages in the vivarium. Their fecal waste and urine needed to be quarantined until the specific activity of the F-18 had decayed to allow for safe disposal. Olivetti wanted to watch the five remaining mice to see if there would be any tumor regrowth from occult tumor cells that could not be detected on the PET scan. He also wanted to see if there would be any long-term side effects from the treatment itself. By now, he was beginning to believe it really was the same set of test mice.

"How long will we need to isolate them?" asked Meredith.

"Leave that to Halderman," replied Jack. "He knows what the protocols are. F-18 has a half life of just under two hours and in a day its activity will be less than 0.02 percent of what we injected. After a couple of days, there is nothing to worry about. I want to start the necropsy studies first thing in the morning. We will need to take the usual low-level radioactive waste precautions with their tissues, so take a look at the written procedure tonight."

The next day, the two unlucky rats were killed by breaking their necks. Jack guided Meredith through the procedure and they carefully examined the lungs, livers, brains and other organs without finding any evidence of residual tumors. They also looked at multiple bone marrow preparations under the microscope without finding anything.

Finally, Jack looked up from the microscope and said, "We need to do the experiment again and this time monitor the animals much more closely. I also want to try a mouse tumor system as well as the rat model. We'll inoculate 20 rats with the same tumor type as before and 20 nude mice with the 4T1 tumor line. Since the animal tumors are identical and the animals are the same genetically, the only new part of the experiment will be to work out the blocking sequence for the 4T1 tumors. I want to go through the procedure starting from scratch for both sets of animals. We have learned a lot more about proper technique since we did the first set of experiments."

"What kind of tumor is 4T1?" asked Meredith.

"It's one of several adenocarcinoma breast cancer models," replied Jack.

The tumor cells were thawed and placed in a culture medium to grow. Three additional mice were then injected with an aliquot of the cells in order to grow tumor nodules. After a week, visible nodules appeared, were excised, and the tissues emulsified. They focused in on the DNA segment that they had previously identified as candidate "A", amplified it via a PCR reaction, and produced the corresponding RNA homolog, and protein. The protein was then crystallized and its amino acid elements determined with the mass spectrometer in the same manner as before. Meredith then started her electronic density calculations. Just over two weeks from when they began, she and Jack were again looking at a complicated, multicolored molecular image on the large monitor in the laboratory. The same characteristic pocket structure was noted in the molecule, but the 4T1 pocket differed from the active site for the 36B10 tumor.

"The same but yet different," said Jack. "I've an idea. Let's crosscheck the specific activity to see if the vector for one cancer affects the other type of cancer also. We will take the two groups of animals and leave five untreated in each group as controls, inject ten with the vector virus tailored for their specific tumor, and inject the other five mice with the viral vector tailored for the other group's tumor."

"Good idea," said Meredith. "But I've learned from Reherson's group that small structural changes can cause big changes in electronic properties, so don't be surprised if there isn't much cross reactivity."

Two sets of vector adenovirus cultures were prepared and the two sets of rats and mice selected and injected with their respective types of tumor cells. The animals were individually identified with ear tattoos. Meredith and Jack examined the animals twice daily, making a careful note of the location and growth rates of the various nodules. The glioma tumors grew more rapidly than the breast tumors. When the tumor nodules were about 0.5 cm in diameter, the animals were segregated into three test sets: in each group one set of ten animals was treated with the antisense vector specifically tailored for its particular tumor, another set of five animals treated with the antisense vector tailored for the other tumor type, and the final five animals served as untreated controls. Prior to injecting the vector-carrying adenovirus, Jack and Meredith imaged the animals in the animal PET scanner using FDG as a metabolic targeting agent. The nodules on the animals showed up bright red on a false color image indicating that they were much more active metabolically than the surrounding tissue. This would serve as an additional control on the experiment. After the viral vector was injected, they watched the animals even more closely and measured their tumors three times a day. Jack and Meredith made independent measurements and compared them later.

"Look at this plot of tumor nodule sizes with time," Meredith exclaimed. "There is a noticeable slowing of the growth curves starting two days after the viral injection for the animals treated with the vector specific for their own type of tumor. There is a little slowing of the growth for the animals injected with the vector for the other tumor type, and there is continued tumor progression in the untreated controls. This is true for both the 36B10 and the 4T1 tumors."

"You're right," said Jack. "The next couple of days are going to tell the story. If everything goes as before, then we should see the nodules start to shrink in the appropriately treated animals. How do they seem to you? While they seem to be drinking the water in their cages, they have hardly touched their food pellets."

"They do seem a little more sluggish and perhaps a little warmer to the touch than before. Here, let's measure their body temperature."

Meredith measured the temperatures of the animals and found them to be higher than normal by about $1°$ C.

"Wonder what this means? Do you think it could be a response to the proliferating virus that we injected?"

Jack and Meredith left the vivarium and soon became engrossed in other things. They reconvened eight hours later for the next set of measurements and found the animals were even more listless. This made it easy to catch and examine them. Even before all of the nodules were measured, Meredith turned to Jack and said, "It's working! The nodules are clearly smaller in the treated groups."

"I think you are right," said Jack. "But we need to clearly document everything, so continue measuring the nodules and record the data as before."

Sure enough, the growth curves for the animals injected with the correct viral vectors showed a definite downturn. The growth curves for the animals injected with the other viral vectors showed a slowing of the nodule growth, but no regression. The control animals showed unrestrained tumor growth. Subsequent measurements showed a continuation of the same trends. By day five after the viral vectors were injected, those animals that had received the one specifically engineered for their tumor were nodule free; the animals receiving the vector for the other tumor type had substantially larger nodules, and the untreated controls had the largest nodules of all. The animals without any palpable nodules were hungry and energetic while the other animals, although not as listless as before, seemed to be in considerable pain due to the size of their tumor growths.

"Let me set up PET scans on all of the animals just as soon as I can arrange it," said Jack. "It may take a day or so to get scanner time but the radiology group owes me a favor or two."

The next day at 7 AM, Jack and Meredith examined the animals again, confirming what they had noticed the preceding evening. They placed the animals into the flat transport cages, loaded the cages onto the trolley, and headed down to the research PET facility. In the facility, they retrieved the prepared FDG which was waiting in its shielded container. They explained the measurements they wanted to Barney, the technologist who would be operating the machine.

"I just run the machine and produce the images," Barney said. "You two will need to do all the animal handling. I don't like those rats and mice anyway – they bite you every chance they get."

Jack and Meredith quickly started their experiment by capturing the mice one by one and injecting an appropriately diluted aliquot of the FDG solution into their tail veins. After waiting an hour for the compound to distribute in the animals, they started scanning them in the order they had injected them. Meredith kept careful notes, correlating each animal with its set of PET images. They looked at some of the images as they were processed but mostly archived them in an electronic file for review back at their laboratory. Then they loaded the rats and mice back into the traveling crates and returned them to the vivarium where they were to be kept in isolation. Radiation precautions again were taken with their soiled litter bedding and fecal waste.

On the way back to the laboratory, Meredith and Jack stopped at the espresso stand in the medical center building. Jack got a double tall mocha, Meredith her usual cappuccino. Once in the laboratory, Jack checked his E-mail and returned phone calls while Meredith pulled up the images on the large screen monitor. After reviewing them, she quickly made a set of written notes summarizing her findings and then went to Jack's office.

She began talking excitedly as soon as she entered the office. "Jack, look at this! There is no sign of PET uptake in either set of animals that received the correct viral vector for their tumor – other than the usual normal tissue uptake in the brain, liver, and urinary system, of course. However, you can easily see the nodules in the other sets of animals. The untreated control animals have the most metabolically-active tumors. I haven't had time to run a specific activity analysis on them as yet, but I will start this right away."

Jack looked up from his computer and took the sheet of paper that Meredith handed him. "This is even better than I had hoped. Show me the images."

Jack followed Meredith to the large screen monitor and they reviewed the image sets one by one. He could find no flaw in Meredith's analysis or her conclusions.

"We need to get this written up right away," he exclaimed. "The ASCO meeting is coming up, and I want to see if I can get this work accepted for the special session on late breaking research. It really could be quite important."

Meredith was thinking of Gaby's situation. "Yes indeed. It could be very important. When do you think we can try this on people?"

Jack rubbed his eyes. "That will be quite a long way off. There are a lot of safety studies that need to be done. If those pan out, we need to set up an affiliation with a certified facility make viral material that we can actually inject in humans. Don't forget that animal model tumors are homogeneous unlike spontaneous natural tumors in humans. These which can exhibit much more complicated behavior."

"Well then, what about trying the treatment on a spontaneous animal tumor?"

"Great idea. I don't have ready access to animals with spontaneous tumors, but my colleagues at the Veterinary School at our sister institution in Pullman do. I'll give them a call and let them know what we are doing and see if they would like to get involved. If we can find an appropriate tumor, we can probably treat the animal on one of their research protocols and not have to write a separate research protocol for our Institutional Review Board. Since we are set up to make only limited amounts of the viral agent, and we will have to transport the animal to our lab for treatment, it will have to be a small animal such as a cat or dog and not one of their cattle or race horses. In the meantime, why don't you complete the detailed activity analysis?"

Meredith had mixed emotions. She was elated that the experiment had worked so well but frustrated about how long it would take before the treatment could be tried in humans. Jack just didn't understand what this could mean to cancer patients and their families, and she resolved to push it along as fast as she could, even if it meant cutting some bureaucratic corners.

CHAPTER 19

DURING THE FOLLOWING WEEK Meredith completed the remaining analysis of the PET data. None of the treated animals seemed to be exhibiting any untoward side effects. Jack was going to spend the coming weekend writing the abstract for the "breaking results" ASCO session and Meredith was going to catch up on her journal articles. Sunday morning, she got up at about 9 which was late for her, and took Sam for a walk. The basset hound was delighted with her attention. They went down the stairs and Meredith hesitated for a moment at her landlady's door. Mrs. Gleason, had an elderly pug named Butch, and Meredith sometimes took him on walks with Sam. Her landlady was having some hip problems and the elderly woman wasn't able to take him out for exercise anymore. Butch seemed happy for the fresh air and exercise; he and Sam got along well. Meredith knocked on the apartment door.

"Just a minute" came from inside, and Meredith heard some shuffling noises. The door opened slightly and Mrs. Gleason peeked through the crack.

"Why Meredith, how are you? Won't you come in?" Mrs. Gleason opened the door completely.

Meredith stepped into the small apartment noting the slightly musty smell. There was an overstuffed chair and couch next to which were two small tables with lamps and lace doilies on them. Along the side of the wall was an old bookcase holding a set of the Encyclopedia Britannica, many works of classical literature, and several modern paperback novels with garish covers.

"I'm taking Sam out for some exercise and thought I would stop and see if Butch wanted to come along."

Just then Butch hobbled out of the kitchen, where his dog bed was located. There was a large fresh bandage on his right rear leg, and the lower part of his left front leg had been recently shaved.

"Thank you dear," said Mrs. Gleason. "But I'm afraid that he isn't up to it right now."

"What happened to Butch?" asked Meredith as Butch and Sam sniffed noses.

"He has a cancer on his leg," replied Mrs. Gleason. "A few weeks ago he started limping and I noticed this growth on his back leg. His vet examined him and did some tests. He thought it was a bone cancer from the way it felt. He asked me if I wanted to try and treat him or just make him comfortable for a while. If the pain got too bad, he said he would put Butch down. Butch and I have been together for 14 years – since before my husband died – so I said that I wanted to try and treat him. The vet arranged for a biopsy to find out what kind of tumor it was, and it's something called an osteosarcoma. The vet says there is some chemotherapy that will slow down the growth but it will make Butch pretty sick. He also said that there is a clinic up in the northern part of Seattle where he could be given radiotherapy. I don't know what to do."

"In people, an osteosarcoma is a bad-acting tumor," said Meredith sadly. "It may be better in dogs, but I don't think so."

"The vet doesn't think so either. Anyway, Butch isn't up to walking right now, but thanks for stopping in."

Meredith and Sam started for the door. As they were leaving, Mrs. Gleason hesitantly asked, "Meredith, what do you think I should do with Butch? I don't want to see him suffer with the tumor and I don't want to make him sick with treatments that most likely won't do him any good."

"Mrs. Gleason, that's a very tough decision to make. We have cancer patients and their families who have to make it too. Right now, Butch doesn't seem to be hurting too badly. Why don't you think about it for a few days?"

Meredith and Sam walked down the street to a small park. There weren't many people in the park and so Meredith ignored the 'keep dogs on leash' sign and let Sam run free on the grass. After about a half hour, Sam was panting happily. Meredith hooked his leash back up and took him home. After feeding him, she called Olivetti's office where she thought he would be working. After a few rings, the phone was answered irritably.

"Hello, what do you want?"

"Jack, this is Meredith. Sorry to bother you on a Saturday but you know about what you said about wanting to try the viral vector treatment on a spontaneous animal tumor. I may have one for you. My landlady has a small pug that has just been diagnosed with an osteogenic sarcoma."

"Meredith, I don't know if we are quite ready for this. Besides, I haven't even approached the animal review board people about using animals other than mice and rats, and you know how upset people can get about experimentating on cuddly animals such as dogs and cats."

"Jack, this isn't just an experiment; it's an attempt to cure a sick animal. We didn't give the dog the tumor for research; we are just trying to help it. Besides, I know the owner well and she would appreciate anything we are trying to do. Sooner or later we need to see if this will work on real-world tumors. Why not now? Think about it as getting preliminary data prior to writing a formal protocol."

"Maybe you're right. Tell you what, I need to finish up a few things here right now. How about if I come by and take a look at the dog early this afternoon? Would you talk to your landlady and see if this is OK with her? Give me a call back after you have talked with her."

Meredith hung up, excitedly ran down the stairs, and knocked on Mrs. Gleason's door. Mrs. Gleason opened the door a crack, saw that it was Meredith, and then opened it all the way.

"Meredith, what's the matter? You seem all excited and out of breath."

"Mrs. Gleason, can I come in and talk to you about Butch? I have been talking to my boss and we have an idea for you to consider."

Meredith sat down beside her landlady. Mrs. Gleason leaned forward and listened intently while Meredith explained the basic idea behind the treatment, how it had worked with the mice, and how the next step would be to try it on other animal tumors.

"And so," she concluded, "the only side effects that the mice seemed to experience was a mild case of the flu from the virus itself. They got over this in a couple of days. Of course, there may be long term side effects that we don't know about."

"I don't understand most of what you said, but if you think it might help Butch and won't hurt him, then I would like to try it. Would he be able to come home right after the treatment?"

"Probably. We would need to bring him back and forth to the lab a few times to get the tissue samples we need and to inject the virus, but he should be able to spend most of the time right here with you. My boss, Professor Olivetti, would like to talk with you and examine Butch before he makes a final decision. Would it be OK if I had him come by around 2 o'clock today?"

Mrs. Gleason agreed and Meredith returned to her apartment bounding up the stairs two at a time. After a few deep breaths she called Jack.

"Jack, Mrs. Gleason has said 'OK'. Can you come by at 2 o'clock this afternoon and talk with her and take a look at her dog?"

"I'm having some second thoughts about whether we should do this but I'll be there. Tell me how to get there. I'll come by your apartment first and we can go down together to meet with your landlady."

At 1:30, Jack got into his old green Volvo, whose exterior showed the evidence of several years of benign neglect, and drove to Meredith's apartment building. He checked the tenant directory at the door, found Meredith's name, and then 'buzzed' her apartment number. Immediately he heard her voice over the intercom.

"Hey, Jack, is it you?"

"Yes, buzz me in and I'll come up."

When the buzzer sounded, Jack heard a click in the door lock. He entered the building noticing that the rug leading up the stairs was worn, but very clean. He walked up the stairs and rapped on Meredith's apartment door. It opened and Meredith invited him in.

"You can leave your coat here. Would you like a glass of water or anything?"

"No, I'm fine. Let's go to your landlady's apartment and you can introduce me. What is her name again?"

"It's Mrs. Gleason, and her dog's name is Butch."

The two researchers went down the stairs and Meredith rapped on Mrs. Gleason's apartment door.

"Mrs. Gleason, this is Professor Olivetti. It is his work that I have been telling you about."

"Meredith is too modest," said Jack as he stepped forward and offered his hand to Mrs. Gleason. "She has really played a big part in this whole thing."

"Thank you for coming to take a look at Butch. Do you think you will be able to help him."

"Let me take a look at him before answering. Also, could you show me the paperwork you got from your vet – the pathology report giving the diagnosis?"

"Sure thing." Mrs. Gleason went into the kitchen and returned holding some sheets of paper. Butch hobbled along behind her.

Jack knelt and Butch went over to him to have his ears rubbed. As Jack rubbed his ears with one hand, he ran the other over Butch's body feeling for lumps and gently pushed on his abdomen.

"Mind if I take off this bandage," he asked?

"Not at all. The vet gave me some extras in case Butch chewed it off before it was time to bring him back to the office."

Jack removed the tape and the cotton gauze that had been rolled around the dog's upper leg. The hair had been shaved off a wide area of the leg and in the center was a three centimeter incision held together with four black sutures. The skin next to the incision was slightly red, but the wound did not look infected to Jack's eye. Jack gently palpated the leg and noted a five centimeter hard, rounded mass that was fixed to the femur, or upper bone of the rear leg. The dog acted like the area of the incision itself was slightly tender, but otherwise did not seem to be distressed by the examination.

Jack stood up and asked, "May I take a look at those papers now?"

He took the papers and sat down to read them. He noted that the pathology report stated that bone fragments were present in the specimen and that there were multiple areas of abnormal cells with large, blue-stained nuclei. The final diagnosis was osteosarcoma.

"This all seems consistent," Jack said. "What did your vet tell you about possible treatments for Butch?"

Mrs. Gleason went over the same options that she had discussed with Meredith. "None of these sound very encouraging to me," she said.

"This is a bad-acting tumor and given its size and location, there really aren't any good choices."

"Do you think that your treatment can help him?"

"What do you understand about the treatment?" Jack asked.

"Just what Meredith told me. You have discovered a virus that can kill tumors and that it might work on Butch."

Jack smiled and said, "There is a little more to it than that, but the key thing to keep in mind is that it is in a very early stage of development. It has only been tried on mice and rats, never on dogs or any other animals. There may be some side effects, possibly death, even if the treatment does work on Butch's cancer."

"Oh my. What will happen to Butch if we do nothing?"

"The tumor will probably keep growing; it will eventually cause Butch a lot of pain and may spread to other areas of the body. I can't say how long all this will take but I'm pretty sure that the tumor won't go away on its own."

Mrs. Gleason sighed. "I guess there really isn't any choice. Will you try and treat him?"

"As long as you understand what is involved and want us to try, I am willing. I will need you to sign a couple of papers giving us permission to treat Butch. You will be acknowledging that this treatment is experimental and we can't promise how things will turn out."

Jack pulled a couple of sheets of paper out of his coat pocket and handed them to Mrs. Gleason who scanned them quickly and asked "Where do I sign?"

Jack pointed out the lines for her signature and the date. After Mrs. Gleason had signed, he asked Meredith to sign as a witness.

"When do you want to begin?" asked Mrs. Gleason.

"There is no point in waiting too long as the tumor will just keep growing. Meredith, would you bring Butch in with you when you come to work tomorrow morning? I will go into the lab this afternoon and make sure that everything is ready."

"Sure thing," said Meredith.

"I see by the clinic note that the vet gave Butch some pain medicine. Would you please bring it in with you?"

Jack shook hands with Mrs. Gleason and left. The two women talked for a bit. Meredith told Mrs. Gleason not to feed Butch any breakfast tomorrow morning and she would pick him up at about 7:30 AM.

Chapter 20

The following morning Meredith went down to Mrs. Gleason's apartment, picked up Butch and carried him to her car. She drove to the parking lot by the stadium and then carried Butch to the rear entrance of the medical center building to avoid bringing him through the patient areas. She took the elevator up to the laboratory and found Jack already there, pacing back and forth as he awaited their arrival. Jack carried Butch to the laboratory table.

"Do you know if he has eaten anything this morning?"

"No, according to Mrs. Gleason, the last time she fed him was at bedtime last night."

"Good. Let's get him on the scales and find out how much he weighs. Then I will give him a mild sedative to relax him while we get some tissue from the tumor."

Butch tried to scramble off when Meredith put him on the laboratory scales. But she held him, talked gently, and he soon settled down enough for her to determine his weight.

"Eleven point five kilograms," said Meredith. "Butch is getting a little chunky."

Jack then looked up the appropriate dose of lorazepam and cut it by a third given Butch's age. He got an ampul from the

105

locked laboratory stores and signed out the lorazepam. The he then drew up the proper amount and diluted it with normal saline solution.

"Meredith, we need to get a small IV started in Butch. He is not going to like it much, but once we get some lorazepam on board, he is going to settle right down. Put this rubber strap around the shaved area on his left front leg and look for a vein. That is probably the area his vet used when he did the biopsy."

Meredith continued to talk quietly to Butch as she placed him on the laboratory stainless steel table. She wrapped the rubber strap around his front leg above the upper joint.

"Ok, I've found a good vein."

"Here, hold him and let me inject some local anesthetic to numb the area where I will be putting in the IV."

Butch whimpered as the area was injected but did not fuss too much. After a couple of minutes, Jack approached him with a small butterfly needle to which was attached a half-liter bag of D5 half normal saline solution, deftly inserted the needle and taped it down. After he had injected about half of the lorazepam solution, Butch's eyes slowly glazed over and he flopped over on the table.

"Perfect. Now let me hang the IV bag. You remove the bandage while I bring over the biopsy tray."

Meredith removed the bandage and Jack prodced a small tray containing sterile surgical instruments. He then carefully measured the tumor and called out *five by five by six centimeters* which Meredith recorded in the lab book along with the date and time. Then she then put on a set of sterile gloves and scrubbed the area around the incision with a betadyne solution, blotting off the excess with sterile gauze pads. In the meantime, Jack had donned a pair of sterile gloves. He picked up a set of small, pointed scissors with one hand and a pair of pickup forceps with the other.

He cut the four sutures and removed them. Then he picked up another syringe that he had previously filled with local anesthetic and injected it around the prior incision site. While Meredith mopped up blood with gauze pads, Jack cut down into the wound and retracted the edges. There was one small artery that pumped blood until Jack clamped it. Then he gave the handles of the clamp to Meredith as he tied it off.

"Not as fancy as in the OR, but we will get what we need for the sample preparation."

With Meredith's assistance, Jack continued to cut through the tissues until he reached the tumor. He incised it and removed several cubic centimeters, which he placed in a container holding a culture fluid. There was some additional bleeding as he did this, but it stopped as he irrigated the wound with sterile saline. Meredith used a small suction device to remove the fluid from the operative field. When the bleeding had stopped, he and Meredith closed the wound in layers finishing with five black ethicon sutures to hold the skin closed. Butch continued to snore gently throughout the procedure. Then Meredith re-bandaged Butch's leg and removed the syringe with the lorazepam from the access point in the IV line. She let just the D5 normal saline run for a few minutes until Butch began to stir.

Jack divided the tissue sample into two portions, the larger of which he left in the culture medium while he placed the smaller one into a formalin solution.

"We'll use the larger section for our analysis and viral preparation, but I want to send the smaller one to Comparative Medicine to have them verify that this is indeed an osteogenic sarcoma before we actually treat Butch."

"Shall I put Butch in one of the larger animal cages while he recovers from the procedure? I'll take him back to Mrs. Gleason at the end of the day since it will be a week or more before we can have his tailored viral vector ready."

"Sure, we want to make sure that our star patient doesn't have any problems. After you get Butch settled in, prepare the tumor specimen for processing in the Illumina sequencer. In the tumor DNA sequences, look for something similar to the control points we have found in the mouse tumors. Perhaps we will get lucky and find something right away. While you are doing the fun things, I'll write up a procedural note on how we got the specimen from Butch. Then I have to teach a class and go to a department meeting."

Meredith got Butch settled into his cage and then emulsified the tumor tissue and ran it through the gene sequencer. It took longer than before, probably because of the mixture of tumor and normal tissue that constituted the specimen. Finally, in the late afternoon, she had the preliminary sequencing completed and took the results to Jack who, by that time, had returned to his desk in the lab.

"I've got a tentative output from the sequencer, but it is very complex. and I'm not sure what to do with it. I've sent the file to you as an E-mail attachment."

Jack immediately turned to his computer, pulled up his E-mail program that was running in background mode, and downloaded the attachment. It was a complex series of base pairs represented by the letters A, T, G, and C. He then queried a search routine, having entered the particular sequence that corresponded to the control element for the mouse tumors.

"The program will have to grind a while," he said. "Why don't you take Butch home now. Tomorrow morning we can review what we have and decide what to do next."

Meredith retrieved Butch from his cage and carried him to her car. On the way to her apartment she stopped at Dick's drive in and purchased a couple of hamburgers – one for herself and one for Butch as neither had eaten all day.

"Here you go guy," she said as she removed the burger from the bun and gave it to Butch. Butch wolfed it down and then watched her with pleading eyes as she ate her own sandwich. At her apartment she put Butch down on the grass to 'do his thing' before turning him over to Mrs. Gleason.

"How did it go?" the landlady asked?

"Pretty well I think. Butch was a great patient. We have the tissue we need and are processing it now. We will know more over the next few days."

In her own apartment Meredith fed Sam and then took him for a walk before settling in for some recreational reading – a mystery novel that she had been trying to get through for several weeks. After a few pages, she lost interest, put it away, and watched TV for a while before going to bed.

Her alarm rang at 6. She dressed and went for a run before having breakfast and going to the lab. Jack was already there when she arrived. He was staring fixedly at two computer screens on his desk. One was his desktop monitor, which displayed the base pair sequences obtained yesterday, and the other was his Powerbook, which was also showing sets of base pair sequences, some of which were highlighted in red.

"Hello Meredith. I think we have four possible candidates for the tumor control gene – here, here, here, and here," he said as he scrolled down the Powerbook screen. "Let's pull out these sequences, amplify them with the PCR process, and generate the corresponding RNA homologs. This will take a couple of days. Then we can use the E. Coli to produce the corresponding proteins."

Several days later Jack and Meredith were looking at protein structure images on a computer screen.

"I think we can eliminate this particular structure," said Meredith. "It doesn't have any features resembling those we identified on the mouse tumor control genes. This leaves us with three other possibilities. Do we try and pick out one or do we try to knock out all three?"

"We should try to knock out all three. Remember, this is a wild-type tumor and we would expect it to be a lot more diversified than a laboratory-prepared tumor."

It took several days but eventually three sets of retrovirus vectors were prepared. The report from the pathologist in Comparative Medicine had confirmed the outside diagnosis of osteogenic sarcoma. When everything was ready to begin treatment, Meredith brought Butch back to the lab for examination. The tumor was measured, and his rectal temperature was taken – normal at 38.1°C. All of the data were entered into a lab notebook labeled *Butch*. Then the dog was then injected with the virus preparations. Following the injections, they put Butch in a cage for observation to make sure that he wouldn't have any untoward anaphylactic reaction to the injections. After a few hours, Meredith took him out. His rectal temperature again was taken and recorded – slightly higher at 38.3°C. She carried him out to her car and drove him home to Mrs. Gleason's apartment.

"Please come in. I was just making some tea. Will you have a cup with me?"

"Certainly. It will give us a chance to talk about what to expect next."

Meredith let Butch down on the floor and he trundled off to his bed in the kitchen. Meredith and Mrs. Gleason took their cups of tea to the living room. Meredith began to speak.

110

"Butch's cancer was more complicated than we expected, and so we had to use more virus than we anticipated. This may make him sicker than expected for the next few days. You know, like when you have the flu – sometimes it is worse than others. Well, Butch will probably have a bad case of the flu. It is important that I keep track of how he is doing, so I will come by at least three times a day, take his temperature and measure the tumor. I wouldn't expect to see any change in the tumor at first, so don't be surprised if nothing seems to be happening right away. It takes time for the virus to multiply and infect the body's cells."

"Can I get sick from Butch?" asked Mrs. Gleason.

"Not likely, but you should still use gloves when cleaning up after him and wash your hands well after touching him. This virus has been genetically altered so that it doesn't spread readily – that is why it needs to be injected directly into the body. Still, it never hurts to be careful as there could be some virus shed in Butch's body wastes."

The two women talked for a while longer and then Meredith left. She went up to her apartment to let Sam out for a few minutes before heading back to the laboratory for the rest of the day. Jack was busy with another grant proposal to the NCI and was summarizing the mouse tumor experiments in the 'preliminary data' section. He was grousing about the work involved in getting the proposal together.

"It seems like you have to write things up at least three times these days: once when you are proposing an experiment and seeking grant funding, again when you do the experiment and are keeping track of the results, and finally when you write up the manuscript for publication. Even if the treatment works on Butch, I don't know whether to include it in the proposal or not. It is a 'one-of-a-kind' experiment and not really controlled. I am going to be busy with this for the next few days, so I'm going to depend on you to keep track of Butch and record the results. Make this your priority and don't worry about keeping regular hours in the lab. Keep me posted on what is happening, OK?"

Meredith agreed and took the rectal thermometer, a handful of finger cots, a tube of lubricant, and the *Butch* notebook home with her when she left the lab.

Chapter 21

At 8 o'clock that evening, she gathered up her stethoscope and the supplies she had brought from the lab and went down to Mrs. Gleason's apartment to examine Butch. Mrs. Gleason met her at the door with a worried look.

"Butch is just lying around in his bed. He didn't eat any of his dinner and it's not like Butch to turn away from food."

She led Meredith into the kitchen where Butch was lying in his dog bed near the cupboard. Meredith knelt down to examine Butch. His nose was hot and dry and he was snuffling a little. His neck seemed a little tender and she felt a few enlarged lymph nodes. She used her stethoscope to listen to Butch's heart and lungs. His lungs were clear, but his heart rate seemed a bit more rapid than usual. His eyes were watering a bit. He clearly didn't feel well and barely protested when she took his rectal temperature, which was now up to 38.9°C. She again measured the tumor on Butch's leg, carefully recording her observations along with the date and time in the *Butch* notebook. The tumor still measured about five centimeters in size but it was harder to measure it accurately with Butch awake and wriggling around.

"Mrs. Gleason, I think it is just the virus working on Butch. He will probably be like this for a couple of days. He needs to drink fluids but don't worry about getting him to eat. He can stand to lose a few pounds anyway. I will be down to check on him in the morning, but you can call me anytime tonight if you are concerned."

Meredith went back to her apartment. To better understand what "normal" would be for dogs as background for keeping track of Butch, she looked at several websites on canine physiology.

The next morning she went back down to the apartment and again examined Butch. If anything, he was even more listless than before. His breathing seemed more labored but his lungs still sounded clear. His temperature was now up to 39.4°C.

"Has he drunk anything," inquired Meredith.

"I don't think so. His water dish still seems full. He didn't want to go outside for his morning pee either."

"I'm afraid he is getting dehydrated. I am going to call Professor Olivetti and run this by him. I'll be back down in a few minutes."

Meredith ran upstairs to her apartment and tried to reach Jack at the lab – no answer. She then tried his apartment. After several rings a sleepy voice answered, "Hello."

"Jack, it's Meredith. I need to talk to you about Butch."

Jack woke up immediately. "Why, what's the matter with him?"

Meredith went over her findings with Jack. She hypothesized that the dog was dehydrated.

"You're probably right. If he doesn't show any improvement by this afternoon, I will see if I can get someone in Comparative Medicine to take a look at him. He may just need some IV fluids until the virus has run its course."

Meredith returned to Mrs. Gleason's apartment and told her what Jack had said. She reassured Mrs. Gleason that Butch would be OK until she returned at 2 pm to take another look at him.

"All right Meredith, if you say so. I will see you at 2 o'clock."

Meredith went into the lab where she talked more with Jack about what might be going on with Butch. Then she went to the medical center library to read more about retroviruses and how they affected people and animals. While Butch's symptoms were not the usual ones, she concluded that they could still be simply due to the virus. If so, they should resolve on their own in a few days. After lunch, Meredith told Jack that she would be leaving to take another look at Butch and then would give him a call.

"Tell you what," said Jack, "I have some free time this afternoon. I'll go with you and we will both take a look at him."

"What will we do if he still isn't drinking?"

"I've called Victor Ligand, the head of Comparative Medicine, and he says that we can bring Butch in and he will take a look at him. Victor had a busy small animal practice before he shifted into academics, and I would trust his judgment on what to do."

Meredith and Jack went down to the back lot where Jack, as a faculty member, had a parking place for his car. The spaces were assigned by rank and as an assistant professor, Jack's space was at the back of the lowest parking level. The rear of the old Volvo wagon was filled with boxes.

Jack noticed Meredith looking at the clutter in the back of the vehicle.

"I was planning to visit the recycling center this weekend, but didn't get around to it," he said by way of explanation to the implied question.

Meredith moved a few magazines and papers off the passenger seat and got in. They went around the ramp, exited the lot, and drove the short distance to her apartment, circling the neighborhood a few times before finding a parking place. They walked to the apartment building which was a few blocks away.

"How do you do it", Jack asked.

"Do what?"

"Find a place to park your car."

"I usually take the bus. Now that I need to go back and forth more often, I do drive in more. Since I generally leave early and return late, it isn't a problem. Being a student, I can't afford a fancier place with an reserved parking space."

Jack laughed, "I remember those days well. Still, being a student was a fun time of my life – learning a lot and not being responsible for anyone but myself."

Meredith and Jack entered the building and rapped on Mrs. Gleason's door. No answer. They rapped again and still the apartment was quiet.

"I'll try calling her on my cell phone," said Meredith. She found Mrs. Gleason's phone number on her contact list and dialed. They could hear the phone ringing in the apartment, but no other sounds.

"She must be out, but I wouldn't have thought she would leave Butch alone. Maybe Butch was feeling better, so she took him out. Funny, but I didn't see them in the little park as we walked by. She never takes him further than that, even when he is feeling fine."

"Leave a note on her door," said Jack. "Tell her that we stopped by and ask her to call you when she returns."

The two returned to the lab and resumed work although both Meredith and Jack kept thinking about Mrs. Gleason and Butch and wondering what had happened. At about 4:45, Meredith's cell phone rang. She had it on her desk to be sure that she wouldn't miss the call and answered quickly. It was Mrs. Gleason.

"Mrs. Gleason, is everything all right? Professor Olivetti and I were worried when we didn't find you at the apartment."

Mrs. Gleason paused before replying. "Butch just seemed so sick that I thought I had better take him to his regular veterinarian, Dr. Dobson. He thought Butch was badly dehydrated and wanted

116

to give him some fluids and watch him overnight. Dr. Dobson wanted to know what had happened, so I told him about the treatment that you and Professor Olivetti had given him. He really got upset saying that you should have checked with him first since Butch was his patient. He wants one of you to call him right away and talk to him about what was done. I hope I didn't do anything wrong."

"Mrs. Gleason, I'm sure that you did what you thought was best for Butch. Professor Olivetti and I also thought that it might be necessary to give Butch IV fluids and had arranged for one of our school veterinarians to see Butch later this afternoon. Do you have Dr. Dobson's phone number?"

"Just a minute while I get my purse. Here it is."

Mrs. Gleason read off the phone number and Meredith copied it down. Then she hung up and told Jack what had happened.

"Damn! While I think this was probably the right thing to do for Butch, we could have handled it ourselves and not had an upset veterinarian to deal with. You know, the Animal Rights Review Board has recently added outside members to put on a better public face to the community, and I think one of them was a veterinarian. Dobson's name isn't familiar but it's a small community. Give me the number; I'd better call him now."

As Meredith handed over the number she asked, "We didn't do anything wrong did we? Butch's tumor occurred on its own and we were just trying to treat him."

"It's a bit of a 'grey zone.' In the case of humans, you have to have an approved protocol for an experimental treatment. Butch's case probably falls under the blanket protocol that Comparative Medicine developed with their colleagues in Pullman, but technically we should have had one of them involved from the beginning."

Jack looked at his watch and noted that it was 5:30. Most likely the vet would still be in his office wrapping things up at the end of his clinic. He placed the call.

"Dr. Dobson," came the voice on the phone.

"Hello Dr. Dobson, this is Jack Olivetti from State University. I understand that you wanted to talk with me about the treatment of Mrs. Gleason's dog, Butch."

"Damn right I do! When I last saw Butch at the time we diagnosed his tumor, he was otherwise doing well. Mrs. Gleason said that he was recovering from the biopsy and eating well. Things went down the crapper after you got involved. When I looked at him, I found that his throat was red and swollen – looks as sore as hell. No wonder he can't eat or drink. What did you guys do to him anyway?"

Jack winced and took a deep breath. He began explaining the line of research that had led to Butch's treatment. Dobson listened without interruption and then restated things in a pithy way.

"So what you are really saying is that you injected this poor animal with a massive load of virus that you hoped would kill the tumor. You knew that this virus was going to multiply and cause a massive infection. And you did all this based upon a couple of mouse tumor studies which we both know may not have much resemblance to what happens with real world tumors? How did this protocol ever get approved anyway?"

"Dr. Dobson, it certainly is true that this is an experimental treatment, and Mrs. Gleason was certainly informed of this when she signed the consent form. Please remember that Butch has an inoperable osteogenic sarcoma for which chemotherapy alone wouldn't be effective. It would also make him very sick."

"Oh, so now you're an expert on dog tumors are you?"

"No, I don't claim to be. I'm an M.D., not a veterinarian. But tumors in mammalian species have a lot of similarities, and Butch was treated on a compassionate use protocol that was developed in concert with the veterinarians in our Department of Comparative Medicine."

"I know this protocol. Dr. Ligand gave a talk at the March meeting of the King County Veterinary Society about the animal research going on at State. He said that new treatments were being developed all the time and could be beneficial to animals during their development phase. Many of the members, myself included, were skeptical that the animals would really benefit and not just be additional data points for the investigators. Ligand reassured us that each clinical situation would be reviewed in detail and no animal would be treated without a veterinarian being involved in the decision process – either someone in Comparative Medicine or the animal's regular vet. I want to talk to the veterinarian who approved this treatment and have him explain his thinking to me. Who was it anyway? I know quite a few of the veterinarians State has on staff. He also said that there would be no charge to the owner for any treatment as it was not the intent of State to go into competition with the community vets."

Jack went silent. He was thinking about how to mollify Dobson once he found out that this particular detail had been overlooked in the rush to get Butch treated.

"Wonder if having the pathology reviewed would count?" he thought to himself. Then he began to speak again, "The pathology was reviewed by a veterinarian pathologist before we treated the dog. I will grab the records and give you the name."

"Yeah, but who was the clinical vet who got the tissue from Butch for you – the one who gave his approval for the treatment?"

Jack gave a sigh. "Sam Frederickson, the one I usually work with, has been on vacation for a month. I can have him call you when he gets back."

"Yeah but the dog was re-operated on about a week ago. Who did the surgery?"

"It was just a simple incisional biopsy, so I did it myself."

"WHAT! You just said that you're an M.D. You're not licensed to take care of animals."

"Like all investigators who use animals, I have been certified by State to perform laboratory research procedures on them. We don't have our veterinary colleagues do every biopsy or necropsy for us."

"I think you took advantage of an old lady's gullibility, and I'm plenty mad about it. I'm going to talk to your boss about it. Who is your department chairman anyway?"

"I'm in the Department of Medicine and my chairman is Dr. Samuel Bremenhoff. Just a minute and I will give you his office phone number."

"Never mind, I can get it myself. And I will tell Mrs. Gleason that your lab will be paying her dog's medical bills for my treating this problem."

Jack was getting irritated and said, "Of course. And I will be wanting a complete set of medical records for my files before I authorize payment."

Dobson sputtered and slammed down the phone. Jack stared at the phone in his hand and then hung up. Meredith looked at him with a worried expression.

"It didn't go well did it?"

"That's an understatement. But it's my fault for cutting a few corners in our hurry to treat Butch. Let that be a lesson to you, Meredith. Even when it doesn't make a lot of sense, always follow the written guidelines. You won't get into trouble that way."

"Yes, but what if that conflicts with doing what you think is best for the patient?"

"There is that issue also, but I'm just telling you how to stay out of trouble with the establishment. Even if things turn out well for the patient, you leave yourself open to a lot of risk if you don't follow the rules."

"What will happen now?

"I don't know for sure but I suspect that I will hear from Bremenhoff tomorrow or the next day and will have to tell him what happened. He will probably ask Ligand to review the case and render an opinion. I will take some heat, but it probably won't be too bad – particularly if the dog recovers without serious side effects. Please keep in close contact with Mrs. Gleason and let me know what is going on."

CHAPTER 22

TWO DAYS LATER SAM BREMENHOFF called Jack into his office. Ever polite, his secretary had inquired if 10 o'clock would be a convenient time for Jack to meet with his chairman and Jack could not find a plausible excuse to delay the meeting. At 9:50 Jack walked into his chairman's office suite and gave his name to the receptionist. She asked him to sit down and offered him coffee or tea saying that Dr. Bremenhoff would be with him in a few minutes.

"Yes, thank you. Black coffee would be great."

The receptionist brought him a cup of coffee and Jack sat down on a comfortable chair in the corner to wait. Aware that Bremenhoff did not keep to his daily calendar, Jack had come prepared with some reading material. At 10:15 Bremenhoff's administrative assistant came and escorted him to his superior's office. Even though he was a long standing chairman, Bremenhoff continued to do some research and his office had the comfortable clutter of a university professor. There were stacks of articles and journals at various strategic locations where they could be readily accessed. Bremenhoff's computer was positioned on a counter behind his desk with the university E-mail program running.

"Please sit down Jack. Sorry that I was running late. I see that you already have some coffee but if you would like a refill, the carafe is on the table in the corner."

The two sat down across from one another and Bremenhoff began.

"I suspect you know why I asked to meet with you. It's about the dog experiment that you did a couple of weeks ago. Yesterday, I got a call from a veterinarian about it, a Dr. Dobson. Dobson stated that your experiment was one that harmed the dog and had no chance of helping it. According to him, it should not have been approved under the generic compassionate use protocol. Why don't you tell me exactly what happened."

Jack sat back in his chair, took a deep breath and began his explanation. He went over his theoretical hypothesis, the work that had been done in learning to determine protein structures for particular genes, and the mouse and rat tumor data that appeared to substantiate the theory.

"The obvious next step was to try the procedure on a naturally-occurring animal tumor, and I had just contacted people in the Veterinary College in Pullman about keeping their eye out for some suitable candidates. Butch then turned up and seemed to be an ideal candidate."

Jack then gave Bremenhoff a detailed description of how Butch had been treated and the side effects that had occurred. "The dog probably had a more severe reaction than we expected because of the heavier viral load required to treat the different genotypes that made up his tumor. We were prepared to give him supportive care ourselves when his owner took him to Dobson."

"Jack, it all sounds quite reasonable, and if one of our veterinarians had been involved from the beginning, there would have been no problem. But none was. You may not know this, but the medical reporter for the *Times*, Pillipitch, has been investigating our animal experimentation policies. He plans to write a series of human interest stories. The dean's office has agreed to cooperate and has invited him to attend the next few meetings of the Animal Use Committee to see how we handle things. Everyone agreed that it was better to cooperate with him since he can get this information anyway under the state *Freedom of Information Act*. If we tried to block his access, he will be sure that we are trying to hide something. He doesn't like the School of Medicine much anyway after the federal billing investigation. He was the one who wrote all those *Times* articles about it and he would like to find something else to go after us about."

Jack sighed. "What happens now?"

"I met yesterday with Vic Ligand, the Chair of Comparative Medicine, and asked him to head a committee to review what happened and to write a report that will go to me and the dean. Since Ligand is a veterinarian, his chairing the committee will give its report more weight. After we review it, it will go to the Animal Use Committee for review and possible action. It will probably take a week or so to get things organized, but we would like to complete this fairly quickly. Please give Ligand's committee your full cooperation."

"Of course."

Jack got up to leave.

"And Jack, no more compassionate use protocol treatments until we get this sorted out. Also, I don't want you or anyone from your lab talking with the dog's owner until the review is completed. I don't want it to look like we were trying to influence the investigation."

CHAPTER 23

LIGAND'S COMMITTEE CONSISTED OF himself and two others, Bob Katterhagen from Pharmacology and Nancy Greenbaum from Medical Ethics. He called the committee together for the first time at 5:30 PM Thursday evening to outline the problem and to define its scope of work.

"Obviously, we need to talk with the two individuals involved from the school, Jack Olivetti and the medical student, Meredith Jones, who was working with him on the project. We need to hear things from their perspective. We'll also need to review the rationale for the protocol treatment. Bob, would you please take care of that? Nancy, you were put on the committee to make sure things are covered from the ethics angle. Would you please talk to the owner and see what she understood at the time her dog was treated?"

"Do we have a phone number for the owner?" asked Greenbaum.

"I'll get it for you and send you an E-mail tomorrow with the particulars."

"I will call her and arrange to meet with her and also see the dog for myself."

Katterhagen then inquired, "What form of report do we need to provide to the dean?"

Ligand replied, "Basically, a written summary of what happened, any extenuating circumstances, recommendations about what sanctions, if any, should be applied to the investigators, and whether there should be any changes in our policies and procedures to keep something like this from happening again."

"Jones is just a medical student," said Greenbaum. "I wouldn't want to see this affect her career."

"I agree," said Katterhagen. "I like Olivetti, and he is generally a very careful investigator. But he is the one who is ultimately responsible for ensuring that proper procedures are followed. I will set up a meeting with him and ask him for a written summary of the experiment to use in our report."

"Sounds good. As a veterinarian, I will write the section on the risk-benefit tradeoffs for the patient – i.e., the dog. I will also get in touch with Dr. Dobson to get his take on this."

The three individuals discussed the matter for a while longer and then the meeting broke up. Over the next several days the committee members went about their assigned tasks. Katterhagan met with both Olivetti and Jones. He interviewed them thoroughly, but played his own cards close to his vest. Neither was able to determine what he was thinking. Privately though, he was aghast at how rapidly Olivetti had proceeded with a live virus treatment outside a laboratory setting. *What if the virus had infected other dogs or even humans?* was his biggest concern. Ligand spoke with Dodson on the phone and got an earful about how State investigators were circumventing the intent of the Compassionate Treatment Protocol. Ligand tried to reassure him that the matter was being thoroughly investigated and that a report would be given to the dean who would take appropriate action.

"I want to make sure that this episode is not whitewashed. I want to be notified when the Animal Review Board takes this matter up and I want to attend the meeting."

"I'm sure that this can be arranged. It will be at least a couple of weeks before the report is ready to be reviewed by the board, but I will let you know when and where the meeting will be held."

Nancy Greenbaum made arrangements to meet with Mrs. Gleason at her apartment. Introducing herself, she opened the conversation with Butch's owner, "As I told you on the phone, I'm part of a group investigating how your dog was treated by Professor Olivetti and his group at State University. Please tell me how you found out about this treatment."

Mrs. Gleason told Greenbaum about her relationship with Meredith Jones and how Meredith had proposed Olivetti's experimental treatment to her after she learned about Butch's cancer.

Greenbaum interrupted. "So this is something that Ms. Jones proposed and not something that your veterinarian, Dr. Dobson brought up."

"Yes, that's right. Dr. Dobson had said that Butch's tumor couldn't be taken out surgically and that it was a type – osteosarcoma I believe he said – that didn't respond well to chemotherapy. He also said that the chemotherapy would most likely make Butch very sick if it were tried."

The discussion continued, with Greenbaum making notes as they went along.

"Tell me about what happened after the treatment."

"Well, after Meredith brought Butch back, he seemed tired and just went to his bed in the kitchen and lay in it. The first few hours he would get up to drink some water from his dish but he soon stopped even doing that. And he wouldn't eat anything at all. Meredith came by and looked at him. She was worried too. She talked to Professor Olivetti and later told me that he planned to come with her to look at Butch and that they had discussed bringing him to State for IV fluids. I didn't know that when I took Butch in to Dr. Dobson but I was worried and wanted him seen before things got worse."

"Perfectly understandable. How long was your dog at Dr. Dobson's clinic?"

"Butch was there for three days. He has been getting better each day. He is eating like his old self again, and I don't think his leg hurts him like it did before. Would you like to see him?"

Greenbaum nodded. Mrs. Gleason went into her kitchen and immediately returned with a brown pug at her heels. The dog started wagging its entire behind when he saw the visitor. Butch went right over to her seeking to have his ears rubbed. The bandage was gone from his back leg, but the area still had only minimal hair growth in the shaved region. Greenbaum petted the dog and then examined the back leg. The biopsy site had healed well and the sutures had been removed. The wound itself had a violaceous, purple-red color and was capped with a line of raised tissue. The dog did not act like it hurt when Greenbaum felt the wound and the underlying lump.

"I think the lump has gotten smaller," said Mrs. Gleason.

"Well, this is the first time I've seen the dog, but let me measure it."

Greenbaum pulled a small ruler out of her handbag and measured the dimensions of the tumor. "I think it is about three centimeters in size."

"Then it is smaller!" exclaimed Mrs. Gleason. "Professor Olivetti said that it was five centimeters when he first came by."

"People often measure poorly-defined things like tumors in different ways. We call this 'inter observer variability.' But I will let Professor Olivetti know that you think it is getting smaller."

"I wonder why neither he nor Meredith has come by. I thought they were really interested in how Butch's treatment turned out."

"I'm sure they are, but State University has asked them not to have any more involvement with your dog until the investigation is completed."

"Investigation! I thought that you just wanted to see how Butch was doing. I don't want to get Meredith or Professor Olivetti into any trouble. All they were trying to do was to help Butch."

"I understand," replied Greenbaum. "It is just that we have procedures in place to make sure that the rights of the animals and their owners are protected, and we need to make sure that our investigators follow them. What did Professor Olivetti and Ms. Jones tell you when they took your dog for treatment?"

"They told me about the treatment and that it was experimental and might not help Butch. They said it had worked on some mice with tumors. They also said that it might make Butch sick."

"With all that, you still wanted to have them treat your dog?"

"Yes I did! I even signed papers giving my permission. It seemed like the treatment might help him and that it wasn't likely to make him as sick as the chemotherapy that Dr. Dobson talked about. I may be old, but I can still understand what people tell me and make a decision."

"I'm sure you can," said Greenbaum hastily. "Here is my card with my phone number on it. If you think of anything else you want to tell me, please call."

As Nancy Greenbaum left the apartment building and walked to her car she thought to herself, *Well, that last part of the conversation pretty well sums it up. Mrs. Gleason was clearly aware of her options and the nature of the treatment when she gave permission for her dog to be treated. She is as sharp as a tack and no one took advantage of her.*

At noon the next day, Ligand called the committee together. Box lunches had been provided, since the meeting would go to at least 1 o'clock. As the three members dug into their lunches, Ligand began. He directed his first question to Katterhagen.

"Well, how did your meeting with Olivetti go?"

"Olivetti went over his hypothesis in detail and answered all my questions. It is an intriguing idea, but there is little supporting data. I know that there has been a lot of progress in using computer modeling to predict protein structures from the linear sequence of the amino acid elements, but to use it to determine a treatment – that's a real stretch. I am also concerned about whether or not there have been proper precautions taken to control the virus he is using as a carrier for the antisense element."

"I thought this was a pretty standard technique," interjected Greenbaum.

Katterhagen responded, "Yes, Nancy, it is. But you need to be sure that the genetic element you are putting into the virus doesn't change it in a way that makes it more virulent. You can certainly check this if you are putting in the same element each time, but Olivetti's treatment is predicated on putting in a different, specifically-tailored segment for each tumor. Hence, each virus is a 'one-of-a-kind' experiment. Just because there hasn't been a problem so far doesn't mean that there won't be one the next time. Vic, apart from this, what do you think about using the technique on the dog?"

"Well, the dog certainly had an inoperable tumor, and our own pathology group confirmed it to be an osteogenic sarcoma. It will certainly kill the animal eventually. If I had been asked to review the case ahead of time, I probablywould have approved the treatment from a humanitarian viewpoint. The problem was that there wasn't any clinical oversight from a veterinarian."

Greenbaum chimed in, "I spoke to the dog's owner, Mrs. Gleason, and she is a pretty sharp cookie. She gave a good layman's description of the procedure and its risks and potential benefits. I don't think either Olivetti or Ms. Jones coerced her in any way."

"OK, let me summarize. Our task is to evaluate whether the animal's well-being was put needlessly at risk. Aside from Bob's concerns about the retrovirus mutating in an unforeseen way, I think if there had been proper veterinary oversight, this experiment would have been within the protocol guidelines. Are we in agreement on this point?"

Greenbaum and Katterhagan nodded in affirmation.

"We need to get a written report to the Animal Review Committee before their next meeting. I would like each of you to write up your findings and send them to me. I will put together a draft for us to review and show it to the dean before sending it to the committee Chair, Jane Prescott. She will want to go over it well in advance of the meeting, particularly since Pillipitch of the *Times* will probably be present. She doesn't like surprises, particularly when they might end up in the newspaper. Can you have this to me by the day after tomorrow? Your write-ups needn't be long, just cover the relevant facts."

"What do you think will happen to Olivetti and Jones?" asked Greenbaum.

"I don't know. I hope Jack will only receive a letter of reprimand in his file and will have additional oversight of his program for a while. I don't think there will be any consequences for Jones. A lot will depend on the spin that Pillipitch puts on the story and whether it catches the attention of State's Board of Regents."

Chapter 24

Two days later, Ligand was staying late in his office to put together the committee report. The myriad responsibilities of a department chairman had prevented him from working on the report during normal office hours. His wife was having dinner with friends that evening, so this was a good time to stay late and get the job done. He started his word processing program and opened the files that had been sent to him by Katterhagen and Greenbaum as well as the write-up of the experiment he had asked Olivetti to provide. He wrote a short introduction outlining what had happened and the charge given to the review committee. He relegated Olivetti's description of the experiment to an appendix which eliminated the need to repeat the experimental details in the body of the report. Ligand then went on to incorporate the material provided by his committee members and finished with his conclusions and recommendations.

While retrospectively it appears that the dog was eligible for treatment under the Compassionate Use Protocol and that the owner was indeed informed about the risks and potential benefits of the treatment, proper procedures were not followed in that there was no licensed veterinarian involved in the experiment. The committee regards this as a significant omission and recommends that steps be taken to inform Professor Olivetti of the seriousness of the breach in protocol. We feel that the responsibility for what transpired is entirely Professor Olivetti's and no blame should be attributed to Ms. Jones, who is only a medical student and working under his supervision. The committee also recommends that Professor Olivetti's laboratory funds be used to pay for any associated expenses incurred by the owner when her pet was cared for by Dr. Dobson.

Ligand then printed out the report for one more reading before sending it to Katterhagen and Greenbaum for their review. It was nearly 8:30 and so he put the print out in his briefcase intending to read it after he had gotten home and had dinner. However, he found that a ballgame was on the sports channel, so he decided to wait until morning for the final reading and revisions. He sent his secretary an E-mail from home letting her know that he would be working at home first thing in the morning and would be late coming to the office.

The next morning, Ligand completed his revisions while drinking his second cup of coffee. In finalizing the report he noted an odd discrepancy. Olivetti's write-up indicated that the dog's tumor was 5 by 5 by 6 centimeters while Greenbaum's notes said the measurements were 2.5 by 3 by 3 centimeters. He decided to call Greenbaum's attention to this in the E-mail transmission of the write-up to her and Katterhagen. He sent off the file and then got ready for work.

By the end of the afternoon, both Greenbaum and Katterhagan had responded with minor edits. Greenbaum's E-mail indicated that she was confident in her measurements and that there was no way the tumor could be as big as Olivetti had stated. Both Greenbaum and Katterhagan liked the way Ligand had framed the report's conclusions. They did not recommend specific penalties for Olivetti, putting them squarely in the court of the dean and Olivetti's home department. After making the final set of edits, Ligand sent copies of the report to Dean Schmitt and Samuel Bremenhoff, asking for their input before sending it on to Jane Prescott. It was two days before he heard back from them. Each complimented him and his committee members on their careful analysis. Bremenhoff asked to meet with him directly, and during the meeting asked specifically about what punishment the committee thought would be appropriate for Olivetti.

"Sam, that is something the committee is going to leave to you and the Animal Review Committee. As the report says, we don't think the dog was treated inappropriately or that the owner was misinformed about the experiment. I think we have a couple of investigators who cut a few corners in their eagerness to try out something new. It wouldn't be the first time this has happened. I know that we both cut a few corners ourselves in our younger days."

Bremenhoff chuckled. "You're right about that. But it's a different world today, and everyone now has to make sure that all the minuscule, procedural details are followed or the federal government will really land hard on us."

"Why don't you just see how the Animal Review Committee meeting goes before making any decisions on this?" replied Ligand.

"Will you be at the committee meeting?"

"Yes. Given that Pillipitch will be present, the dean wants me to be there to answer any additional questions that might come up."

Chapter 25

MEANWHILE, JACK WAS MOPING around his laboratory. This behavior was very unlike his usual demeanor. Ordinarily he alternated between enthusiastically reviewing the latest results of his junior investigators and talking about the next set of studies to be done. His group had commented on this change among themselves. They had heard in general about the ongoing investigation, but neither Meredith nor Jack had told them the specific details. They were afraid that their boss was in real trouble and that this would affect their own careers.

Meredith approached Jack. "Have you heard any news about the review?"

"Only that the Animal Review Committee will be meeting the day after tomorrow and that I need to be present. They are keeping Ligand's report under wraps until the meeting."

"It doesn't seem fair that we don't get a chance to see the report in advance. It could be full of errors."

"Ligand is pretty careful. I doubt that there will be any significant factual errors. What I'm worried about is the interpretation of what happened."

"What is the worst that could happen?"

"My whole research program could be shut down and I would have to leave State," Jack said with a wry expression on his face.

"I don't think that is going to happen, but there probably will be something entered into my file that will affect my tenure hearing later this year. Also, I think we are really making progress, and I would hate to see this line of investigation be interrupted."

"Jack, I'm sorry. It's all my fault for pushing you to treat Mrs. Gleason's dog before everything was ready."

"No, I agreed to treat the dog, so any blame is mine. Besides, Butch was a good candidate for treatment. Have you heard anything about how he is doing – unofficially, of course, since you aren't supposed to be in contact with Mrs. Gleason until this investigation is over?"

"Well, unofficially I do run into Mrs. Gleason in the hallway once in a while. She tells me that Butch is doing well and has recovered completely from the virus. I wish I could examine Butch and measure his tumor, but that would be pushing it. Can I attend the Animal Review Committee meeting with you?"

"I don't see any problem with your coming to the meeting, but I will call the committee chair and ask permission. With Pilipitch of the *Times* being there, it is not like it is going to be a closed meeting."

The following morning Jack called Jane Prescott and obtained permission for Meredith to attend the meeting.

The meeting was held in a sterile conference room. A large central table and freshly-erased white boards lined the front and one of the side walls. The green carpet was well worn in places. Twelve chairs were arranged around the table with an additional six chairs along one of the side walls. Shortly before 5 PM, people started filtering in and took seats around the table. A slender man wearing a tweed coat and tie came in with a notepad and took one of the chairs along the side wall. He had short black hair that was well on its way to turning grey, but was still thick and bristly. When Jack and Meredith arrived, Jane Prescott had already taken her seat at the head of the table with two stacks of paper in front of her. One stack contained the copies of the agenda for the meeting; the other stack contained copies of Ligand's report. Prescott motioned for Meredith and Jack to take seats at the opposite end of the table. The rest of the review committee arrived, took their seats and received copies of the agenda and the report. Samuel Bremenhoff, Jack's department chairman, came in and took a seat along the side wall as far away from the man with the notepad as he could get. Prescott looked at her watch and called the meeting to order. She asked everyone to introduce themselves.

The man with the notepad looked up and said, "Stephen Pillipitch from the *Seattle Times.*"

"So that's Pillipitch," Jack whispered to Meredith. "He surely gave State a hard time with his reporting of the billing investigation. Once he gets into something, he doesn't let go of it. I've always wondered what he looked like."

Prescott began the meeting by summarizing the agenda, which contained two minor items of business followed by the report from Ligand's group. The committee took care of the first two items of business quickly. The report was distributed to everyone and the room got quiet while each person took a few minutes to read over it quickly. Prescott again looked at her watch and began to speak.

"This is the first time you have had a chance to look at the final version of the report from Dr. Ligand's committee. However, I have briefed each of you so you know the background for the report. Some you know Dr. Dobson, the veterinarian who raised the issue of the propriety of the experiment done by Professor Olivetti's group."

Dr. Martin Davis, who was a member of the Department of Comparative Medicine, nodded his head affirmatively. "Dr. Dodson is one of our clinical faculty who helps with our teaching program by giving occasional lectures on animal medicine to our students. He called me about this case early on. I had thought that he was going to be here tonight."

"I thought so too," replied Prescott. "Perhaps he was delayed in finishing his clinic and may still show up. However, we can't wait for him any longer."

The discussion of the report began with each committee member having a comment or two. Mostly the remarks were along the line of "while a veterinarian should have been involved, the treatment of the dog was reasonable, given the circumstances." There was, however, one committee member who felt differently and said so forcefully. This was a lay member from the community, a slender woman named Cristine Yasaki, who spoke eloquently about how animal experimentation needed to be carefully monitored since it often resulted in pain and suffering to the animals involved.

"Animals have been entrusted to our care by God, and we have a responsibility not to abuse them. It seems to me that the protocol which was agreed to and which would have ensured that any experimental treatment would be fair to the animal was not followed. The treatment made the dog very ill and didn't help it at all. I think this committee has to deal severely with those involved."

Pilipitch was furiously taking notes of the conversation looking up occasionally to observe the faces of those around the table. The other committee members squirmed uncomfortably on hearing Yasaki's statement. She had obviously prepared it in advance of the meeting.

Prescott resumed control of the meeting. "Professor Olivetti, do you have anything to add?"

"Just that the animal had a life-threatening cancer that occured on its own. It's not like we deliberately caused the cancer."

"Yes," interjected Yasaki, "like the cancers you give those poor laboratory mice."

"Ms. Yasaki," interrupted Prescott, "the mouse and rat experiments are covered by an entirely different set of protocols which have been properly approved and followed. The matter before this committee is the treatment of the dog under the Compassionate Use Protocol. Let's confine our discussion to this."

Just then the door opened and Dr. Dobson walked in. Everyone, Pillipitch included, looked up expectantly as Prescott welcomed him to the meeting.

"Great," thought Jack to himself. *"Just what I need. He is going to support Yasaki and I'm going to be screwed over."*

Dobson was carrying a folder and an x-ray film jacket. "Sorry I'm late, but I've got some important news to bring before this committee. I wanted to examine Mrs. Gleason's dog one more time so that I could tell the committee the latest about how he was doing. The dog is doing great. Furthermore, the tumor mass on his leg has just about vanished. I can barely feel anything, and these x-rays show only a residual calcification. It's as if the tumor has gone, leaving only a little bone callus formation. I wouldn't have believed it if I hadn't seen it with my own eyes. Here, let me pass around these x-rays. The first one is from when the osteosarcoma was first diagnosed and the second was taken in clinic this afternoon."

Jack and Meredith held up the two films as they were passed to them.

"This looks like almost a complete response, and you say that Butch is none the worse for wear? Can we bring the dog into the lab and look at him ourselves? Perhaps we can get a PET scan to see whether there is any residual tumor activity," Jack said excitedly.

Dobson spoke again. "Butch is scampering around, overeating as usual, and doesn't seem to be in any pain. Whatever you did to him seems to have worked. I'm going to put the word out to my colleagues, and you are going to have all the animal tumors you can handle. I can't wait to see where this goes. I'm sorry that I got so upset at first."

"That's all right," said Jack. "You were just looking out for the dog. I apologize again for not getting you involved in his case from the beginning and won't make that mistake again."

"Professor Olivetti," said Prescott, "the committee needs to consider this new information before it decides what to do. I am going to adjourn the group for the evening. We'll discuss the matter further among ourselves and let you know what we decide."

As the group left the room, Bremenhoff turned to Jack and said, "You were really lucky that Dobson decided to have a last look at the dog and turned out to be a fair man. I want to hear more about your treatment. Maybe you really have something and the Department can give you some resources to move things along faster. I'll have our chief resident give you a call about doing a Grand Rounds presentation in the very near future."

After Bremenhoff left, Jack turned to Meredith and said, "Isn't that just like academic medicine – from scapegoat to a Grand Rounds speaker in thirty minutes. First thing when you get home tonight, stop by Mrs. Gleason's apartment and see if she will let you bring Butch in with you tomorrow? If not, ask her if we can come by her apartment to examine him."

Chapter 26

The next morning Dean Schmitt had his feet up on his desk and was reading the *Seattle Times* over his morning coffee. On the front page of the local section was the article by Pillipitch under the banner heading.

ANIMAL EXPERIMENTS AT STATE: BENEFICIAL FOR BOTH SIDES?

The initial paragraph indicated that this was the first in a series of articles on using animals for medical experiments. Particular attention would be given to what was taking place at State University which was in the readers' backyard. Schmitt skimmed through the article quickly. He saw that its focus was the history and rationale for animal experimentation and how oversight policies had changed over the years in response to public pressures. The closing paragraph was a teaser for tomorrow's article. Purportedly, it would expose of the inner workings of the Animal Review Committee at State and the tensions that existed between the investigators and the community members of the committee.

Schmitt turned to his computer and called up the spreadsheet that listed the members of the multitude of committees that managed the activities of the medical school. He scrolled down to the Animal Review Committee, saw that Jane Prescott was its chairman, and asked his secretary to call her. He wanted some advance warning if Pillipitch's next article was going to be unfavorable to State. He was hosting a dinner for major donors on Saturday evening and knew that the issue of animal experimentation was a "hot button" topic to several of them.

A few minutes later Margo stuck her head in the door. "Prescott's not in the office yet, but I asked her secretary to have her call you when she gets in. She's asking what the call is about."

"Just tell her that I want an update of how the last meeting of the Animal Review Committee went – the one that the reporter, Pillipitch, attended."

Schmitt looked through the rest of the newspaper. He noted the write-up in the business section about progress on the construction of State's new research park and how it would revitalize the Lake Union area. He smiled appreciatively and reminded himself to ask Shalle how the laboratory space allocation was going. From a financial viewpoint, it was important to get the indirect cost dollars flowing back into the project while the other two buildings were being completed.

Just then Margo stuck her head back in the door and said, "Dr. Prescott is calling back. Shall I put her through?"

"Give me a couple of minutes to finish this article on our new research park, and then put her through. I don't want her to think that I can drop everything just to take her call."

A few minutes later the phone on his desk rang. Schmitt picked it up.

"Hello. Dean Schmitt, this is Jane Prescott. I'm returning your call. My secretary said you wanted to speak with me about what happened at the last meeting of the Animal Review Committee. I'm flattered that you are paying attention to a small committee such as mine."

Schmitt launched into what he termed his 'usual line of B.S.' about how all committees are important and particularly the Animal Review Committee. "As you know, State is a public university, and as such has to be sensitive to how the citizens view us. Pillipitch of the *Seattle Times* is writing a series of articles on the use of animals for medical experimentation, and the first article alluded to tensions among the members of your committee. I just wanted to find out what that was all about."

Prescott responded, "You are probably referring to the discussion which took place when we reviewed the dog experiment that Professor Olivetti's group did. One of our lay members took the opportunity to expound upon the basic immorality of animal experimentation, which is her personal pet peeve."

"How did such a person get on the committee, anyway?"

"Like the majority of medical schools, we expanded our Animal Review Committee to include community members in response to pressure from the animal rights groups. Christine Yasaki was the nominee of our local group. Anyway, I think by the end of the meeting she was mollified, and Pillipitch left with a good impression of how we do things at State."

Prescott then described Olivetti's experiment and the questions that had been raised about it. She concluded by saying, "It all turned out well in the end. It appears that Olivetti's treatment actually helped the dog. This made both the veterinarian, Dobson, and Yasaki happy. I think we may get some good press out of this."

Schmitt thanked Prescott for calling back and said, "I think it is important that we cooperate with Pillipitch. I'd like you to call him and let him know that you would be glad to answer any questions that he might have."

He hung up and began going through his daily routine which for the most part, consisted of signing papers that Margo had placed on his desk and putting them into his outbox. He was periodically interrupted by phone calls which Margo had put on his schedule. He wanted to get everything cleared away before leaving to get ready for the black tie Symphony fund raiser that evening. His "date" was Alice Maxim. Now that the funding arrangement with Blackmont was concluded, he and Alice were again involved in a hot and heavy relationship. Most likely he would spend the night at Alice's apartment and have breakfast with her the next morning. He kept some clothes at her place and would change into appropriate attire before leaving for work the following morning. Alice was getting more possessive about his time, but now was not the time to irritate her by asserting his independence. That would come after the research park was completed and he had received his honoraria from Blackmont and AVARTEC Pharmaceuticals. Before leaving the office, he sent an E-mail to his department chairmen. He alerted them to Pillipitch's continuing interest and asked them to let their investigators know that Pillipitch might be contacting them. Any interviews were to be coordinated through Tela Morgan, the head of the School of Medicine's Public Relations Department. As luck would have it, Bremenhoff was away at a meeting and so this request was not passed on to the Internal Medicine faculty, of which Jack Olivetti was a member.

CHAPTER 27

JACK AND MEREDITH WERE carefully evaluating Butch, who was sitting on a stainless steel table in the lab with a resigned expression on his face. They listened to his heart and lungs, prodded his abdomen, looked at the mucosal lining of his mouth and throat, and, most importantly, examined his rear leg in the area where the tumor had occurred.

"Everything seems pretty normal," said Jack. "I can barely feel a residual lump in the leg and probably would miss it if I weren't looking specifically for it. It is hard to believe that this was one sick puppy just a few short weeks ago."

"It's also hard to believe how much trouble we almost got into simply by treating him. He really seems to be doing well now. Dobson had said that his throat was raw and inflamed from the virus; that was why he wasn't eating. If we had given him IV fluids until it got better, he probably wouldn't have gotten so dehydrated and sick."

"I think you're right about that. We will keep the next large animals we treat in the lab and watch out specifically for this. I just wish I knew what that residual lump is. It could be just some residual bone formation produced by the tumor, but it also could be the tumor waiting to grow back."

"How would we find out which it is?"

"Well, ultimately by waiting and seeing what happens. But I would like to get a PET scan if Mrs. Gleason will let us."

"I don't know. If we inject Butch with the radioactive PET isotope, then we'll have to keep him overnight to manage his urine and feces until the isotope decays. Mrs. Gleason won't like that."

"Yes, but if it is viable tumor and we find out about it while it is still small, perhaps it could be taken care of surgically."

"Good point. If you put it that way, it would make sense to get the scan now."

Jack called Mrs. Gleason and explained the situation to her. While she wasn't happy about having Butch stay overnight in the lab, she could see how knowing the results of the PET scan could be beneficial to him. Jack then called down to the PET facility and arranged for the test to be done the next day. He then told Meredith to take Butch home with her that night and then bring him back in the morning. Then the phone rang. It was Stephen Pillipitch.

"Professor Olivetti, this is Stephen Pillipitch from the *Seattle Times*. We met a few days ago at the meeting of the Animal Review Committee. I'm doing a series of articles on the use of animals for medical experiments and would like to talk to you – you know, hear things from the perspective of one of the investigators. Would you have some time this afternoon or tomorrow to talk with me?"

Jack looked at his calendar and replied, "How about if we meet at 4 PM tomorrow? Come to my lab and I will show you around while we talk. You can meet some of the other investigators. You can also see the dog that was the subject of all the discussion at the meeting."

Meredith took Butch to Mrs. Gleason's for the night and picked him up the next morning. Butch enjoyed riding in a car and by now had come to associate Meredith with an enjoyable outing. He wriggled his behind when he saw her and readily accompanied her down the stairs to her car. Meredith took him directly to the animal imaging facility and stayed with him while he was injected with the FDG isotope. Being curious, she elected to hang around and watch the scanning process. Butch was sedated and immobilized on the CT-PET table. The CT scan was performed with the scanner head, in its housing, spun around the table as the table moved continuously forward. This was known as a spiral CT scan. The name came from the pattern the x-ray head formed with respect to the patient. Then the table was returned to its starting position and the PET images taken. Several sequences of PET images were taken at different times as specified by the imaging protocols. Meredith asked about this, and was told that the uptake and washout kinetics of the isotope determined the appropriate times for getting the best images. The CT scan gave the most detailed images of the bones and soft tissue. This was registered with the PET images, which mapped metabolic activity. The combined process was what was known as a CT-PET scan. It was used routinely use in cancer diagnosis and management. This particular scanner had been manufactured by Phillips Industries, and was dedicated to research rather than patient care.

The scanner computer quickly reconstructed the images. Meredith collored one of the diagnostic radiology investigators, Dr. Champeaux, and asked her to explain the images. Dr. Champeaux enjoyed teaching medical students and residents, and happily acquiesced.

"By convention, the transverse scans, the ones showing the cross sections, are oriented with the observer standing at the patient's feet. This is the dog's left side and this is his right side," Champeaux explained as she pointed with a pencil. "We'll first look at the CT scan for orientation and go through the images from bottom to top. Look at this area of callus bone in the dog's right femur; it almost looks like he broke it at one time and it didn't heal in perfect alignment. Seems solid enough though. I don't see anything else of concern. Now let me call up the PET images and superimpose them on the CT images."

Champeaux used the keyboard and mouse to instruct the computer on how to align the images. She and Meredith looked at the finished results.

"What are these bright red areas?" asked Meredith.

"These are areas where there is an increased amount of the FDG tracer. See, here is the brain, which uses a lot of glucose, here are the kidneys, which show up since the isotope is eliminated in the urine. The important thing is to look for areas of unexpected uptake, and I don't see any of these. Finally, we'll reconstruct the data to get a set of coronal or upright images. In that mode we look at the dog from front to back rather than in cross section. These will be more like the conventional x rays most people are familiar with."

After looking at this last set of images, Meredith asked "Do you see any increased uptake in the dog's left hind leg? That is where the tumor was originally."

"No, the area of abnormal bone is 'cold,' just as you would expect from an old, healed fracture. Doesn't look like any living tumor there now."

Meredith asked for copies of the images. Champeaux laughed and said, "With all these images, we don't print them out on film anymore. Let me give you the file name and you can call them up on any computer. Here is the password for Olivetti's research archive."

Meredith thanked her. Butch was waking up, and so she took him back to Jack's lab and put him into the corner cage with a small pan of water. Food would come later, after he had completely recovered from the sedation. Then she went to Jack's office where he was working on his talk for the upcoming ASCO meeting. Their abstract on shutting off the tumor control gene had been accepted for the session on late-breaking research. Jack had been allotted fifteen minutes to present their work.

"Jack, I just came back from the Animal Imaging Facility. Dr. Champeaux went over Butch's images with me and she doesn't see any sign of tumor. Here is the image file name, you can look yourself."

Jack turned to his desktop computer and called up the archived images. He looked quickly at the transverse images and then spent more time looking at the coronal images, which were more useful to non-radiologists. He looked up and said, "You're right. I don't see anything that looks like active tumor. That's good news for Butch and Mrs. Gleason. Is he back in my lab or still down in the imaging suite?"

"I brought him back and put him in the corner cage as usual."

"Good. I will be by to look at him later today. Right now I want to get this talk finished before I have to leave to teach my class and I want to put in a couple of slides about Butch."

"I thought you said that what happened in treating only one animal or person wasn't really science, but just an anecdote."

Jack laughed and said, "Your memory is too good. But you're right. By itself, Butch's outcome wouldn't really tell us much, but in the context of the theory and the three sets of mouse and rat studies, it's additional supportive data. Now, go back to the lab and think about what should be the next series of experiments for us to do. By the way, remember the reporter from the *Times* who was at the Animal Review Board meeting last week? He called yesterday and asked to talk to me and my group about our view of why animal experiments are necessary to make progress in medicine. He is coming by the lab this afternoon at 4 o'clock. Why don't you make sure that you are here so that he can talk to you as well?"

A little before 4 PM Pillipitch arrived at Jack's laboratory and announced his presence to the junior investigators and techs working on the lab benches.

One of the techs took him to Jack's office where Meredith was also waiting.

Pillipitch held out his hand. "Professor Olivetti, thank you for seeing me."

"Happy to oblige you. Let me introduce Meredith Jones, the medical student who worked with me on the dog experiment. I thought it might be good for you to also hear from someone just starting out in her research career."

Pillipitch and Meredith shook hands and then Pillipitch sat down and pulled out his well-worn notebook. He asked Jack and Meredith about their backgrounds and how they got into research, making notes as they talked. Then he turned to the primary reason for the meeting. "Tell me about the research that you are doing and how it involves animals," he said.

Jack began with the work of Bryon Heymond on the new drug from AVARTEC and the study results that were going to be presented at ASCO. He emphasized how important the mouse studies were in determining the effectiveness of the new agent, *Compound 10*. Careful not to air dirty linen in public, he skirted the issue of how much of the data would be presented due to the objections raised by the review committee.

"Do you think its proper for a public institution like State to be helping the pharmaceutical industry increase its profits?"

"Actually, if things are done properly, it's a win-win situation for both sides since State's investigators get funding to carry out their work, and if a new, more effective drug is found, the patients are going to benefit."

Pillipitch turned a few pages in his notebook and then asked a more leading question.

"So why do we need to do animal experiments, anyway? With today's computer modeling can't you predict what will happen without the animal experiments? In last month's *Nature* there was an article about how far things had progressed."

Clearly Pillipitch had been doing his homework, but this was an area familiar to Jack and Meredith as well.

"I assume you're referring to the article by Frankenhaven's group in Heidelberg. Computer models have certainly gotten more powerful, but they still can't work with all of the variables that we know about and certainly can't account for variables that we don't know about," said Jack.

"Yes," said Meredith. "That last point was emphasized in the concluding section of Frankenhaven's article. Biological systems are so complex that we just don't know all the relevant variables. We are learning about new variables all the time. The work that our lab has been doing on a fundamental tumor control gene is an example of this."

Pillipitch looked up inquiringly. Jack gave him a quick overview of his hypothesis of a common control gene that controlled tumor growth and what they had been doing to identify it. He explained the results on mice and rats, again emphasizing the importance of studying simpler laboratory animal models before moving to real-world tumors.

"Makes sense, particularly when you're trying a completely different approach, as you are. And you say that experimental protocols involving animal tumors are carefully reviewed and regulated?"

"Yes indeed, that's the case. The review process makes sure that any pain and suffering of the experimental animals is minimized. It also evaluates the study design to make sure that we use only the minimum number of animals necessary to answer the research question."

"What happened in the case of the dog I heard about last week at the review board meeting?"

"That's a different situation. After we have indications that a treatment works on laboratory tumor systems, we need to try it on naturally-occurring tumors, which are more complicated. Often things that work in the laboratory fail miserably in the clinic. With all of the failures, the effective cost of bringing a new drug treatment to market can be in the range of hundreds of millions of dollars – at least that's what big Pharma says. Naturally-occurring animal tumors such as the dog, Butch, had are an intermediate step between the laboratory tumors and trying the treatment in humans. Even so, the treatment must have the potential of benefiting the animal."

"It certainly helped Butch," interjected Meredith.

Again Pillipitch looked up inquiringly. Jack nodded and Meredith explained the results of the examinations and PET/CT studies that had just been performed.

"And you say that the animal is still here in your lab? Would it be OK if I saw him?"

Jack and Meredith opened the door of Butch's cage, and brought the dog out on the table. Happy for the attention, Butch rolled over to have his tummy rubbed. Pillipitch played with him a bit and said, "He certainly seems happy enough now. What happened to him before? Why did he get so sick?"

Jack explained that the carrier virus caused a severe sore throat. "See, that's another thing we learned from the animal experiment – it's important to give the patient IV fluids and supportive care until the virus burns itself out."

"What happens now, that is, what is the next step in the process of testing your new treatment? Will you try it on humans next?"

Jack shook his head. "No, there is a lot more animal work that needs to be done before we can try it in humans."

"But if you can try the treatment in an animal like Butch when there is no other form of treatment, why can't you try it in human beings who are in similar situations?"

"I'm afraid that the regulations are just much stricter for humans. That's a whole other matter."

"This must be frustrating to terminally-ill patients and their families. I think I'll try to talk to some of these people to get their perspective on how medical research is conducted and how long it takes to bring a new treatment to market."

Jack led Pillipitch to the door and said, "I'm sure its frustrating, and patient advocacy groups are always complaining to the NIH and FDA about this. But the first rule of these organizations is "do no harm", even if it means do nothing at all. Meredith, would you please take Mr. Pillipitch to the elevator?"

As Meredith walked Pillipitch to the elevator she said, "I believe that you have really identified a major problem with the way our health research system does things. I see this from both sides. On one hand, as a researcher, I recognize the need to proceed slowly and carefully, one step at a time, to make sure that we really understand things. On the other hand, I have a grandmother with advanced ovarian cancer, and I'm frustrated at not being able to offer this treatment to her."

"That's really an interesting situation and a great human interest story. Do you think your grandmother would be willing to talk to me about this? I would also like to learn more from you."

Meredith shook Pillipitch's hand and said, "I'll talk to my grandmother and let you know."

Pillipitch gave Meredith his business card and said, "Call me at this number."

CHAPTER 28

GABY WAS WILLING TO talk to Pillipitch, so Meredith arranged a leave from her work on Friday so that she could take him to Sequim. At 8 AM Pilipitch pulled up in front of Meredith's apartment. She was waiting outside wearing a Gortex parka to protect herself from a mild drizzle. She hopped into the car and greeted Pillipitch. The car was a new model Toyota 4 Runner with a dog screen between the cargo area and the back seat. A few children's toys were scattered in the back seat.

"Please excuse the way the car looks, but we car pooled one of our children and his friends to a birthday party last night, and they trashed it."

"Don't worry about it. You should see Professor Olivetti's car. It looks like his desk at work only worse."

As they drove to the Edmunds ferry to catch the 9:15 boat to Kingston, they exchanged pleasantries and were soon on a first name basis. On the way from Kingston to Sequim, Pillipitch asked Meredith how she became interested in medicine. She told him about spending summers at Gaby's poking around the beach when she was a young girl. She had moved in with Gaby after her parents died in an accident. Meredith described how her interest had shifted from biology to medicine, after her grandfather was diagnosed with

159

prostate cancer, and she watched his disease progress in spite of several different treatments.

"Is that why you decided to work with Professor Olivetti, because of the cancer research work he is doing?"

"Yes, cancer research is both important and challenging. Most research involves just making small changes to an existing form of treatment and seeing what happens. Professor Olivetti's work takes an entirely new and different approach and may totally change how cancer is treated."

"What will happen to all the drug companies, the medical equipment manufacturers, and the government bureaucrats if their products and services are no longer needed?"

"What do you mean?"

"Well, think about it. If Olivetti's cure really works on all tumors, then chemotherapy drugs won't be needed. That will reduce the income of many drug companies by 40-50 percent. There will be less need for diagnostic equipment and testing to see if a tumor has come back. Besides all this, look at all the organizations that make their living on cancer research, like the 23 NCI designated cancer centers – most of their researchers as well as their support and administrative people.would be out of jobs. It would cause a real shakeup in the health care system and not everyone would be happy – although they wouldn't dare say so out loud."

"I can't believe that people wouldn't be happy if a cure for cancer was found. Almost every family has been affected by this disease in one way or another."

Pillipitch laughed cynically, "Well, just the same, expect some pushback if Olivetti's treatment really works like you hope it will. Besides, there will be a lot of companies wanting to take it over to make money off it."

"I can't believe that Jack would let that happen. He really wants to find a cure for this disease. He isn't motivated by money."

"Well, he might not want it to happen, but he might not have any choice. Anyway, all this is pure speculation since we don't know how good the treatment is. I still don't understand exactly how it works and why it has to be different for each person."

Meredith was happy to talk about the science; she wanted to forget about the unsettling comments Pillipitch had made concerning the possibility that the medical-industrial complex would try to suppress an effective new treatment for cancer. Meredith found Pillipitch's questions very penetrating, and he kept asking them until he had at least a working understanding of the process. The conversation continued until they entered the driveway of Gaby's beachfront home. Gaby had evidently been watching for them, as she opened the door and invited them in before they even had a chance to knock. Gaby and Meredith hugged quickly and then Meredith introduced Pillipitch to her grandmother.

"Delighted to meet you Mrs. Jones. I appreciate your taking the time to talk to me."

"When Meredith called and said you were doing an article on cancer patients and new cancer treatments, I thought it was the least I could do. Maybe your article will help let people know about new treatments that will be coming out, and, you know, give them some hope."

The three sat down in the living room and Gaby brought out some tea and cookies as they began to talk.

"Mrs. Jones, do you mind if I record this to make sure that I get all the facts right?"

Gaby agreed and Pillipitch pulled a small recorder out of his coat pocket and turned it on.

"Why don't you begin by telling me how you found out about your own cancer, ovarian cancer I believe Meredith said."

Gaby began by telling Pillipitch about her breathing problems, the discovery of the lump in her belly, and how it turned out to be ovarian cancer. She spoke of her referral to Dr. Greerson at State Medical Center, and how disheated she felt when Greerson said that he could operate on her, but that he couldn't take out all the tumor."

"What would the point be of having the surgery if he couldn't get out all the tumor? Wouldn't it just grow back?"

"Both Dr. Greerson and Meredith thought it was still the best thing for me." Gaby looked at Meredith to explain things further.

Meredith spoke up. "In the case of ovarian cancer there is a lot of clinical data that shows taking out the bulk of a patient's tumor lets them live longer. That's why Gaby decided to have the surgery. After she healed from the surgery, she had chemotherapy."

"Yes, that really made me sick at first, but there was a medicine that helped with that. Those pills were really expensive too."

Meredith smiled ruefully and said, "She was given odansetron, which was developed especially to reduce nausea from chemotherapy. Only one drug company makes it and it charges quite a bit for the medication. When it comes off patent, then other companies will make it as well and the price will come down."

Pillipitch jotted a few lines on his ever-present notepad and said, "Do you think this treatment helped?"

"Well, my cancer was discovered about 18 months ago and I'm still here. I still go back to State Medical Center for treatments, but they don't seem to be working as well as they did at first."

Pillipitch looked at Meredith and said, "Why do you think that is?"

"No one knows for sure, but people think that cancer cells can change in response to treatment and become more resistant. Chemotherapy drugs like Granner received are pretty non-specific;

162

they just affect the rapidly dividing cells more than they do the other cells. Cancer cells that aren't killed right away can change and adapt – like bacteria can develop a resistance to antibiotics."

"Seems like a situation where the cancer is more likely to win than the patient. Do you think that would be the case with the treatment you and Olivetti have developed?"

"I don't think so since the treatment is designed specifically for one particular cancer. Our method identifies the key control element for each cell type in the cancer and then builds a virus that carries instructions to deactivate that element. For reasons we don't understand right now, it also seems to tell the inactivated cancer cells to die right away and not live out their normal life span."

Gaby looked at Meredith and asked, "Do you think it would work on my cancer?"

"It has never been tried on a human, but I don't see why it wouldn't work, particularly in view of how it worked on a dog with a spontaneous tumor."

Pillipitch asked, "Mrs. Jones, that's a very interesting thought. How would you feel about being the first guinea pig in an experiment?"

Gaby looked Pillipitch right in the eye and said, "If there was nothing else available, I would certainly be willing to try an experimental treatment. It might work on me, but if not, it still might help somebody else."

"How would you feel if bureaucratic regulations prevented you from making this decision?"

"I would be as mad as hell. I think this is something that each patient ought to be able to decide for himself or herself, with good medical advice of course."

"I think I've gotten what I need for my story. Do you mind if I take a couple of pictures of you that our editor might use when the story runs?"

Gaby agreed. "Meredith, how about if I also take a couple of pictures of you and Gaby together? It might make a good side story about a grandmother who is a cancer victum and a granddaughter who is a cancer researcher."

Meredith wasn't so sure about this, but Gaby pulled her close, and Pillipitch took the photograph.

As they were driving back to Seattle, Pillipitch said, "Thanks again for introducing me to your Grandmother. She is a remarkable woman, but I can see that battling her disease has taken a real toll."

"Yes, she is. In spite of everything she has kept a great attitude. She has deteriorated more since I last saw her, and I need to get her back to see Dr. Greerson for another checkup. Changing the subject, when do you think your article will run in the paper?"

"I will work on it tonight and tomorrow; I hope it will run in the Sunday edition. Exactly where it is placed will depend on what news events it is competing with, but I hope it will be on the front page of the local news section."

CHAPTER 29

ALFRED SCHMITT WAS NURSING a hangover when he opened the Sunday paper at Alice Maxim's apartment. The two had been out the night before, and after imbibing heavily, had tumbled into bed. Alice was still asleep when Schmitt awoke, pulled on his pants, and retrieved the paper at the front door. He put beans in the grinder to make some coffee, and grimaced at the noise as the grinder performed its task. When he opened the paper, he saw that the front page was devoted to the probable impending move of the Sonics professional basketball team to Oklahoma and to further production delays for the new Boeing 787 dreamliner. The dean poured his first cup of coffee for the day, went into the living room, and started going through the paper. On the lower left hand portion of the front page were printed the short teasers for articles inside the paper. One of these read

Delays in bringing medical treatments to market and how this impacts patients: Local B1

The Dean turned to page B1. There was the article by Pillipitch headed by a photograph of the pug dog, Butch. The article began with the assertion that animal experimentation is a necessary part of medical research. Certain groups, it said, would like to ban it entirely and rely on computer modeling. However, this was not possible due to the complexities of living organisms. It then talked about the oversight process and the balance between having a robust review system and being able to pursue exciting new research areas. The new work of Olivetti's group was described in simplistic terms for the typical reader. It glossed over the theory and emphasized the specially-designed virus which Olivetti used to shut off cancer cells. Pillipitch dramaticially portrayed Butch's plight and his treatment under a compassionate use protocol. What really got Schmitt's attention was the last paragraph, which was a lead in to a follow-up article in the next day's paper

.... Tomorrow we will look at delays caused by the medical oversight process from the point of view of a terminal cancer patient, Mrs. Gabrielle Jones, and her granddaughter, Meredith Jones, who is a cancer researcher at State University.

This seemed like a sensitive area to the dean. He thought he had better check the content of the story, which presumably had been released through Tela Morgan in Public Relations. He went back into the bedroom where Alice was starting to stir, got his Blackberry from the nightstand, and called Morgan.

"Tela, this is Dean Schmitt. I was just looking at the *Times* and saw the article by Pillipitch on animal experimentation. Looks like it puts us in a pretty good light, but I was curious about what is coming out tomorrow on this Gabrielle Jones who I assume is a patient of ours."

"I just finished reading the article myself and I don't know any more than you do about what is coming next. It is not something that was released through my office. I thought we had agreed that I would be coordinating the information given to Pillipitch like we normally do when dealing with the press."

"Damn it! I explicitly told all of the department chairmen to have their faculty coordinate any communications through you.

You're good at spinning things to put State in a good light. Can you find out more about Jones and exactly who the granddaughter is who is mentioned?"

Alice came out of the bedroom looking somewhat disheveled and gratefully took the coffee that the dean handed her. She then opened the refrigerator and started making breakfast, mildly irritated that Schmitt continued to read through the morning paper instead of offering to help her. However, she did not say anything because at this stage in their relationship she wanted to appear completely accommodating. Besides, Schmitt was a complete klutz in the kitchen. After breakfast the dean finished dressing, bade Alice goodbye and returned to his apartment. His Blackberry buzzed and he answered.

"Hello, Dean Schmitt here."

"Al, this is Tela Morgan. I have a little more information for you about the Pillipitch article. Mrs. Gabrielle Jones is a patient of Ben Greerson with stage IV ovarian cancer and has been admitted several times to our medical center for treatment. I can't find anything about her granddaughter in checking through our faculty lists. I have put a call in to Stephen Pillipitch under the pretext of offering to provide him with additional information. I've also offered to arrange meetings with our faculty for additional interviews, but he hasn't called me back. I thought if I got him talking, I could get some idea of what he was going to write."

Pillipitch eventually called Morgan back. She learned that the granddaughter was not a faculty member but was a medical student working in Olivetti's laboratory. Pillipitch declined going over the next day's article in detail saying that he was still working on it. Morgan offered to help him to check his data and Pillipitch said that if he needed more information, he would call her. She passed this information along to the dean who realized that since Meredith was a medical student, his office had little control over her interactions with the news media.

The dean looked up Bremmenhoff's home phone number. He wanted to ask him why Olivetti had spoken directly with Pillipitch rather than following protocol and going through Morgan. However, all he got was a recorded message: *no one is available to come to the phone right now but to please leave a message.* Schmitt left a terse message asking Bremenhoff to contact him.

On Monday morning Schmitt woke early and stepped out of his apartment to pick up his morning paper. He unfolded it as he walked into his living room and sat down to read it before going in to work. Again Pillipitch's article again was on page 1 of the local news section.

SCIENTIFIC PROCEDURE VS. FAMILY NEEDS: A RESEARCHER'S DILEMMA

The article was primarily devoted to the story of Gaby's battle with ovarian cancer. He quoted her about the patient's right to be the final arbiter in questions of treatment. At the end of the story, Pillipitch described the work that Meredith was doing. He said that although it was a promising form of treatment, it would not be available to treat patients such as Gaby for several years, at best. Both Gaby's and Meredith's frustrations as well as the tension between Meredith's idealism and the bureaucracy of the medical research machine clearly came through in the article. The photograph that Pillipitch had taken of Gaby and Meredith was featured prominently at the top of the page.

No big deal thought Schmitt, as he turned to the sports section. He saw that the Sonics had lost another game and read about impending changes in the State football coaching staff after their disastrous last season. He picked up the automotive section next and read through an evaluation of the newest model Maserati. The review was good and he thought he might head down to the dealership later in the week to check one out. Revenue was starting to flow from the occupied research building and half of his so-called honorarium from the Blackmont deal had been securely deposited in his bank. He was planning to move a substantial portion of it to a new hedge fund his colleagues on the Board were talking about, but he would treat himself to a vehicle upgrade as well. Schmitt felt that first impressions were important and that the car he drove needed to reflect his importance in the Seattle medical community.

CHAPTER 30

AT MEREDITH'S INSISTENCE, GABY had made an appointment with Greerson. Meredith went with her to the outpatient cancer clinic on Eastlake. An abdominal CT scan was taken prior to her appointment. Greerson was his usual brusque self, but took the time to engage Gaby and Meredith in conversation before beginning the examination.

"You two are famous. I saw your picture in this morning's paper. How did Pillipitch find out about you anyway?"

"Meredith brought him out to Sequim to talk with me last week. He sure didn't waste any time writing his article."

Greerson looked inquiringly at Meredith who blushed slightly. Then she quickly explained how she had met Pillipitch when he did a story on animal experimentation. This led to a conversation about moving from research on animals to research on humans and from there to Gaby's situation.

"Very interesting and the story was well done. But here's a word of warning. State doesn't like its faculty to talk to reporters without going through their PR group ,and while this probably doesn't apply directly to you, there may be some fallout for Olivetti."

Greerson pulled up the CT images on the computer monitor in the exam room. He reviewed them, and then examined Gaby.

"I'm afraid that the tumor nodules are growing again and that the amount of ascitic fluid in your abdomen is increasing. There is quite a bit now, probably over a liter. We can continue to administer chemotherapy, but I don't think it will help much at this stage."

Gaby reflected on this and said, "Well, if you don't think it will help, I don't want to do it. No point in getting sick for nothing. I have been having a little trouble breathing, though."

"We can take out some of the fluid, and that should help with your breathing. I can arrange for an overnight stay in the hospital to get this done. If I can find a room for tonight, could you stay over and then go back to Sequim tomorrow?"

Gaby hesitated, but Meredith spoke up, "Granner, why don't you stay over? I will go with you to the hospital, and then tomorrow, can drive you back to Sequim."

Gaby agreed. Greerson called hospital bed control and arranged for Gaby's admission. Meredith drove her from the outpatient clinic to the hospital and sat with her through the admission process which took several hours. She was admitted to Greerson's service by the intern on call, Samuel Hickock. Meredith introduced herself to Hickock and explained that she was a third year medical student at State. Hickock went over Gaby's medical history paying particular attention to any changes that had taken place since her last visit to the medical center. He explained the peritoneal aspiration procedure to her. This involved inserting a catheter connected to a plastic tube into the abdomen and then draining as much fluid as possible into sterile, evacuated containers. Following the proper medical-legal informed consent procedure, he went over the risk factors of bowel perforation and infection with the possibility of emergency surgery being necessary. At the end of his explanation, Gaby looked distinctly uncomfortable and was clearly wondering if she really wanted to do this.

Meredith spoke up. "Granner, he is just doing his job by informing you of all the bad things that could possibly happen. Like you could get hit by a car walking from the parking lot to the hospital entrance. These aren't likely to happen are they, Dr. Hickock?"

"No they're not, Mrs. Jones, but as your granddaughter said, I need to tell you about them."

"I'm still worried. Can Meredith be with me during this?"

"Well, it's not usual to have a family member present during a procedure like this but since she is a medical student and has been on the wards already, it is OK with me if it's OK with her."

Meredith said that she would like to watch. The peritoneal fluid removal would take place in one of the procedure rooms on the sixth floor. Gaby would then spend the night in the hospital for observation and if there were no problems, would go home the following morning.

It was midafternoon before Gaby finally arrived at her room. An IV was started. It was another half hour before she was put in a wheelchair and taken to the procedure room, accompanied by Meredith. In the room she got out of the chair and the nurse helped her onto the procedure table where she lay on her side. Hickock came into the room, put on a mask and a pair of sterile gloves, and told Meredith to put on a mask as well. A sedative, ativan, was injected into the IV tubing. Hickock sterilely prepped Gaby's abdomen with Betadyne and then put sterile drapes over her. Only the midline of the abdomen was exposed. He opened a pericentesis tray that contained a sharp metal trochar and plastic catheter as well as two half-liter vacutainer bottles. Then he injected a small amount of lidocaine solution just below the umbilicus to numb the area. The nurse, having also donned a mask and sterile gloves, handed him the trochar which he inserted into Gaby's belly. The plastic catheter was then threaded through the trochar and the trochar then pulled back leaving only the catheter penetrating the abdominal wall. The other end of the catheter was capped with a valve and large bore needle. With the valve closed, the needle was inserted through the rubber seal capping one of the vacutainer bottles. Hickock opened the valve, and cloudy yellow fluid started running into the bottle, rapidly filling it. When the container was completely full, the valve was closed, the needle withdrawn and then inserted into the second bottle. Again the valve was opened and fluid started draining into the bottle. This time the drainage stopped intermittently, and Hickock would reposition the catheter. Sometimes he turned Gaby in the process, until the fluid started running again. Hickock's bellboy went off twice during this time and finally he asked the nurse to take the bellboy from his belt and answer the page. When the second bottle was about three quarters full and repositioning could not allow more fluid to drain, Hickock removed the catheter.

Just then the nurse came back into the room and said, "There is a stat call from the ER. They have a woman there with an extensive vaginal bleed, and they want you to come right away and take a look at her."

"Tell them that I'm just finishing up a procedure and will be there in a few minutes. I need to get these bottles labeled and sent to pathology."

Meredith asked, "Why do that? There isn't any doubt about Granner's ovarian cancer causing the ascites is there?"

"Not really, but it's protocol, to make sure that nothing is missed. Besides, the fluid will be spun down and the cells saved for future testing in case a new drug comes along and someone wants to see if her tumor might be sensitive to it."

"Well, I know where pathology is. As a medical student, I certainly run a lot of samples down there as part of my scut work.

How about if I take the samples down while the nurse takes Granner back to her room and you see about the woman in the ER?"

"Sounds good to me. The nurse can prepare the labels for the specimen containers and then you can take them down. I'll be back up to check on your grandmother as soon as I can, but it may be a while, depending on whether the woman in the emergency room needs surgery right away."

Hickock put a large bandage on the catheter insertion site, removed his gloves and mask, put on his white coat, and left the room. The nurse came back with the sticky labels, which she affixed to the jars of fluid.

As she was walking down to the lab Meredith thought to herself, *pathology really doesn't need all this fluid, and I would really like to see what the tumor DNA looks like.* Meredith took a long detour via Jack's laboratory. She nodded vaguely to the techs and postdocs who were still hard at work, and then quickly entered the storage area where the specimen freezers were located. She removed the patient label from the partially-full bottle and replaced it with one that said, *Human Ovarian Tumor Cells.* She laid the bottle in a back corner of the freezer. Then she left the lab, retraced her steps to the medical center through the connecting hallways, and left the second bottle in the reception area of the pathology intake room.

Meredith returned to the sixth floor ward and entered Gaby's room. Her grandmother was resting comfortably. Hickock didn't return to see Gaby until 10:30 PM. He was clearly exhausted. He apologized profusely for not getting back sooner. The woman in the ER had a recurrent cervical cancer and it had been difficult to stop the bleeding. Tomorrow she would be seen by Radiation Oncology to see if radiation therapy could be given. Unfortunately, the medical records showed that she had already been treated with radiotherapy once before and he was not optimistic about her chances. Gaby was doing fine with stable vital signs and no pain, so Hickock arranged for her to be discharged in the morning after he had rounded on her. Gaby and Meredith talked until Gaby started nodding off. Meredith excused herself and went back to her apartment.

CHAPTER 31

THE SECOND PHASE OF State's new research park was due to open soon, and Dean Schmitt was making a presentation to the State University Board of Regents at their afternoon meeting. The agenda was full, and he had been allowed only 15 minutes. He quickly reviewed the project scope, the opening of the first building, the number of investigators that had moved into the building, and the number of grant dollars being generated through their work. He shifted his discussion to the update on the second building and its projected opening date in three weeks.

Gary Feinstein, a businessman on the board, asked, "Do you have enough investigators to fill all that laboratory space right away?"

Schmitt replied, "Space allocation was finalized about a month ago and our research faculty are ready and eager to move into their new space."

"What will be done with their old laboratory space? We all know how successful State's research engine is; they must have been working somewhere. If the old space stays empty, then you have just shifted the work into a higher-cost facility."

"The old research space was cramped and it limited the amount of work our people could take on. The old space will be renovated

177

and turned over to more junior people to give them a chance to start projects of their own. You are correct that the new facilities are more expensive than the old, and that is why we have designated the new space for our more senior investigators with good records of grant funding. It is also why the federal government has allowed us an indirect cost rate of 66 percent instead of the 52 percent that they use at our other sites. Recall that this Board approved the concept of using grant revenues from programs located in the new facilities to pay for them. Of course, the business plan shows this is a 15-year payout, but at the end, State will have over twice the medical research space it did before. Some of the new research space is being subleased to AVARTEC, which will provide an additional jumpstart to the revenue stream."

Ever the businessman, Feinstein noted that he was glad that the project debt was structured as being non-recourse, meaning that State was not on the financial hook should the revenue stream not materialize as expected.

Anne Hallmark, the governor's newest board appointee, observed, "Yes, a lot of influential people would stand to lose money if this happened; they would be very unhappy with us all. I'm sure that Dean Schmitt's financial projections will work out. Besides, taking risks is a part of doing business, and the backers of the project stand to make out quite well if the project is successful."

President Emory commented, "Medical research is important to State not only because of the prestige factor from our faculty's work but also because it's something that the people can identify as directly important to them and their families. Basic research in physics and engineering is much tougher to sell to the legislators. By the way, the articles on medical research in the *Times* the last few days came across pretty well. Have you thought about working with that reporter to tell the story of State's expanding medical research program?"

Schmitt replied disingenuously, "We have a good working relationship with Stephen Pillipitch, and I'm sure that we will get some good press when the second research building is opened."

Emory then asked, "Are there any other questions for Dean Schmitt?" As there were none, the dean nodded to the Regents and left the room.

He donned his Burberry coat as he left the building, opened up his umbrella, and strode down the hill to the medical school campus. Passing through the building into the covered parking garage in back, he got into his car. He drove to the AVARTEC building, where he parked his car in one of the visitor spaces, signed in at the security desk, received a badge, and took the elevator up to the CEO's office. Patti greeted him and announced his arrival to Peter Drisco. Schmitt entered Drisco's corner office, where Peter and Arthur Jenkins were waiting.

"Sorry that I'm running late, but the Regent's Board meeting went on a little longer than I anticipated. They had a few questions about the opening of the second phase of the research park."

"That's what we want to talk with you about," began Peter. "We are planning on subleasing 50,000 square feet to accommodate our research program, but I hear that some of your faculty are balking. They don't want to get involved in joint research projects because of the restrictions relating to intellectual property coming out of the collaboration."

"Well, the story that the review board dictated the content of Olivetti's ASCO abstract is pretty widely known, particularly after the issue was raised recently at a MSEC meeting. This may have something to do with it. Nancy Schalle, our vice dean for research, has mentioned that some investigators are reconsidering their move to the new research space. They don't like the requirements imposed by the use of shared resources provided by your company. However, I don't intend to let them change their minds now since we need to get the new building up and running."

"That's another thing; how come I had to learn about this new treatment developed by Olivetti in the *Times* instead of from you? As one of our paid medical consultants, you're supposed to keep us informed about any new discoveries coming out of State that might have commercial application. This sounds like it might."

"Relax, Pete. This was an unusual situation." Schmitt then explained how Pillipitch had gotten involved through the animal experimentation investigation. "Olivetti hasn't written any grant applications relating to the work, so this is still very preliminary. If it looks like it is going anywhere, my office will let you know."

Jenkins then joined the conversation. "AVARTEC was well within its rights to revise Olivetti's abstract since the work was done with our support. It wouldn't have gotten done otherwise. Why can't your faculty understand that this is part of the deal for getting their research funded?"

Peter Drisco answered his subordinate's last question. "Art, it's a matter of perspective. These researchers are just interested in discovery; they don't see what it takes to support their work. When I was younger and just starting out, I thought that way myself, but then I wised up and realized it was better to control the research than to actually do it. I'm sure that Al can quell the incipient rebellion and get the joint research program back on track, right Al?"

"I'll speak to my department chairmen about it and let them know that their faculty have to move as scheduled and make it happen."

"You sound awfully sure. In the past you've told me that being a dean of a medical school is different from being the CEO of a company because of faculty independence, academic freedom, and stuff like that."

"True, but the prospect of better laboratory space will be a big inducement to the faculty."

"I hope so," replied Drisco. Then the meeting broke up.

CHAPTER 32

LATER THAT MONTH, JACK was preparing to go to the meeting of American Society of Clinical Oncology in Boston. The American Society of Clinical Oncology, or ASCO, was the premier organization for medical oncology. It had gotten so large that only a few locations were suitable venues for its annual meeting. According to an unwritten agreement, the meeting site alternated from one coast to the other to accommodate the travel needs of the investigators. As a reward for the work Meredith had been doing in the laboratory, Jack found some travel funds in one of his grants and asked her to come to the meeting as well. She was listed as a co-author on one of the abstracts submitted by the research group and she was excited about attending her first large scientific meeting. She asked Bryon about what to expect at the meeting.

"There will be a lot of speakers, some of whom will contradict each other's results. It is always fun when that happens. There will be what are called plenary sessions where well-known senior investigators give talks summarizing their particular fields. These are probably the most useful to someone just starting out and wanting to learn about a topic. Then there will be short talks on new research results; these are fifteen minutes long. The short time slot forces you to really think about what you want to say and to rehearse well. If you don't get finished with what you want to say, too bad; you just get cut off. Sounds cruel, but there will be close to a thousand of these short talks, and the conference would never get finished if there weren't strict time limits. Nothing is more irritating to other speakers than a session moderator who can't keep things on schedule. There will be ten or more of these research sessions taking place at the same time, so you need to go over the program in advance to pick out what you want to hear. The meeting rooms are scattered throughout the conference center. People spend a lot of time trying to figure out where they want to go next. It's particularly bad early in the week before you get to know where the rooms are located. There will be a huge central area with exhibits by the pharmaceutical companies that make cancer drugs. Both big and small companies will exhibit. You can tell how important the cancer line is to a company by how big its exhibit area is, and there will be lots of free handouts. On one or two evenings there will be buffet receptions sponsored by the drug companies – these are huge, with lots of food and free booze."

"Why do the companies do this? It must cost them a lot of money."

"Getting physicians to prescribe a new drug can be worth hundreds of millions of dollars a year to a drug company. This is a pretty good return. Besides, if one company doesn't do it and its competitors do, it will lose market share. These costs are folded into the companies' advertising and marketing budget, and are one of the reasons why they charge so much for their pharmaceuticals."

"How do you know if they are telling the truth about their products?"

"You do need to listen carefully to what is said and just as importantly, what is not said."

"About what is not said?"

"Yes, about things like the new drug's side effects, study design, and whether there is any real difference in outcome compared to older and cheaper drugs. Things used to be a lot more free wheeling, but now the federal government has rules about how pharmaceutical reps interact with physicians. It is hard to police this, of course, and pharmacy companies are always getting their wrists slapped. One approach the companies use is to sponsor what are called 'satellite symposia,' where they have two or three investigators whose work they have supported give a series of talks about something relating to one of their products. These investigators can make big bucks by being on a so-called speaker's bureau. I know that Jack has been asked to do this, but has always turned them down because he thinks it would be a conflict of interest."

"I can see why he would think that. Why would people want to attend these symposia anyway?"

"The companies make their symposia attractive by combining them with a hosted reception and dinner. Getting a few of these free dinners can really help with your travel budget in an expensive city such as Boston. This is the first conference for you, and you're going to find out that with State's travel policy, you can go in the hole financially when you attend conferences. Besides, sometimes you can learn something useful at these symposia, and it's a good chance to network with other people. I'm going to be doing a lot of networking since I am going to be looking for my first real job next year."

Not being an ASCO member, Meredith hadn't received a copy of the meeting program. She asked Bryon, "Can I take a look at your meeting program?"

Bryon reached in his backpack and handed the program to her. who thanked him. She studied it and saw that Bryon had circled several plenary sessions and individual talks. He had also underlined the notices for the society receptions and several of the company-sponsored symposia. She made a copy of the program and returned the original to Bryon, planning to ask Jack what sessions he would recommend she attend. She walked down the hall to Jack's office and knocked on the partially-opened door. Jack looked up from his desk and invited her in.

"Jack, I borrowed Bryon's ASCO program to look over before the meeting next week and want your advice as to what sessions I should attend. This is my first scientific meeting, and it seems overwhelming."

Jack laughed, "Yes, it can certainly be a little daunting when you are first starting out. There is so much information being presented that it's a little like trying to take a drink from a fire hose. Let me see the program and I'll make some recommendations."

Jack took the program and made a few notations next to some of the sessions. "I see that Bryon has already marked the social events for you. I know a few of the speakers at the plenary sessions who give good talks and I've marked those for you. Nothing is more frustrating than trying to understand an unintelligible speaker, particularly when you are just starting out in the field. I've also marked the sessions where our work will be presented – not just so that you can hear Bryon and me but because these will be the sessions where research similar to ours will be discussed. When will you be arriving at the meeting?"

The meeting starts on a Sunday, so I thought I would fly in on Saturday. Perhaps I could take the same flight as you?"

"Ordinarily that would work and give us a good chance to talk, but this year I need to be in Boston on Wednesday for some meetings on Thursday and Friday ahead of the conference itself. I have been appointed to the organizing committee for next year's ASCO conference, and we need to start planning. The new committee will be meeting with the present committee to learn from them what worked and what didn't work. I am going to be on a task group in charge of approving the satellite symposia that the pharmaceutical companies want to piggyback onto the meeting. Just tell Frances when you want to go to Boston and return. She can arrange things through the travel agent she uses. Have you gotten a hotel room reserved?"

"Got one not too far from the conference center. By the time you told me that our abstract had been accepted for the late-breaking results session, all of the rooms at the main conference hotel had been booked."

"Well, keep checking; sometimes there are cancellations. There will be more going on at the conference hotel itself. When we get back from ASCO, we'll get moving again on the tumor control gene work, perhaps with some new ideas from the meeting. The veterinary group in Pullman is going to send over some tissue specimens from some of their animals. When they arrive, why don't you start the analysis on them and see how many control point genes they have? I would like to pick one with a small number to see if we can avoid some of the side effects we had with Butch."

"Do you trust me to do this on my own or do you want me to ask Bryon to help?"

"I think you can handle things. If you have questions, just talk to me. Bryon is so preoccupied with his ASCO talk that he is pretty much oblivious to everything else."

CHAPTER 33

BOTH JACK AND BRYON were busy with last minute preparations, and Bryon, in particular, was driving the lab techs crazy with demands for rechecking data for his presentation. Meredith was working by herself when the first of the animal tumor samples arrived, frozen in dry ice. She unpacked the specimen, noted that it was a squamous cell tumor that had developed in a dog's tonsil, and started thawing the tissue. As she would be working alone for the next several days, she thought this would be a good opportunity to analyze Gaby's tumor in parallel with the animal specimen. Meredith rationalized this as simply scientific curiosity but deep down she knew she was looking for a possible future treatment when Gaby's health eventually deteriorated. Using her medical center computer identification, she looked up the pathology report on the bottle of ascites fluid that had been sent to the laboratory. It did indeed verify that the fluid contained adenocarcinoma cells of probable ovarian origin. She retrieved the second bottle of ascites fluid from the laboratory freezer and started it thawing. Once the bottle was unfrozen, she divided it into aliquots and passed them through a centrifuge to spin down and concentrate the cells. She carefully collected the cells from each centrifuge tube, and gathered them together. Meredith labeled Gaby's specimen "G - adenocarcinoma" and the dog tumor specimen "DT – squamous cell carcinoma" and started headings for each in her laboratory notebook. She started the concentrated cells from Gaby's tumor through the automated gene sequencer while she began the emulsification process on the dog tumor. The next day the preliminary sequence analysis was done on Gaby's tumor and the analysis on the dog tumor was just beginning. She looked at the sequencer output, and as before, there was a very complex series of the four DNA base pairs represented by the letters A, T, C, and G. Clearly, further computer analysis was required, and she would need to enlist Jack's help without telling him where the specimen actually came from. She had the output written into a data file and sent it to herself and Jack as E-mail attachments. Fortunately, the State University E-mail system was robust enough to handle large attachments, unlike many of the free, commercial E-mail systems that many of their colleagues used. Meredith then knocked on Jack's office door.

"We got a couple of tumor specimens from Pullman, and I've started to analyze them. The DNA sequencing is complete on the first of the specimens and the sequencer is still grinding away on the second specimen. Do you have time to take a look at the first sequence and give me some ideas about where to look for the control point gene?"

Jack replied, "Sure, let me take a look. Did you send me the data as an E-mail attachment as before?"

Meredith nodded in reply.

Jack soon had the gene sequence data displayed on his desktop monitor and was absorbed in going through it. "Looks complicated. What kind of tumor did they say it was, anyway?"

"They sent us a couple of canine carcinomas; this is an adenocarcinoma and the other is a squamous cell tumor."

Jack then started his search routine and told the program where to look for the data file to be analyzed. "I'll start the search using parameters we got from Butch's tumor. If these are close, we should be able to take a look at the output tomorrow; if they aren't close, it will take longer. After we get the results, we will need to put things on hold until after the ASCO meeting since I need to be leaving in a few days. Would you call the Pullman group and let them know we got their specimens and have started working on them?"

Meredith quickly agreed since this would keep Jack from discovering that the Veterinary School had sent only a single specimen. She made the phone call and spoke with a very nice individual who said that the dog squamous cell tumor had come from the tonsil of an elderly Springer Spaniel but that the cancer had now spread throughout the dog's body. He wasn't sure that the owner would be willing to bring the animal to Seattle for treatment, but would talk to the owner again after the analysis was complete. Meredith thanked him and hung up feeling mildly guilty at her deception.

It took two days before Jack's analysis program identified the probable control elements for Gaby's tumor. There were three sequences displayed in red among the otherwise green elements on the screen. Jack pointed these out to Meredith and said, "Looks like these are the candidates. Not as many as we found for Butch, but we still burned through a lot of computer time in finding them. The central regions are similar to what we found for the mouse tumors and for Butch's osteosarcoma, but the peripheral regions are different. Sometimes these search routines get into loops and calculate for a while before getting out of them, and sometimes there is a lot of extraneous DNA to sort through. Do you know what to do next?"

"The next steps are to use PCR to amplify these genes and then to produce the RNA homologs. Since the peripheral regions of the DNA sequences are different, this means that there will be some differences in the control proteins as well. Then I'll use the E Coli to produce the proteins for analysis and determine the key active site against which to prepare the antisense RNA."

"Take it that far and then put things on hold until after ASCO. We need to make sure that the dog will be coming over for treatment before we make the actual retrovirus agents."

This was just what Meredith wanted to hear. She returned to the lab and began to work on the next set of steps in the process. It took several days, in part because of a bad data file she had submitted to the Illinois supercomputer, but eventually she found and corrected the error. She reviewed the images of the two control protein elements on her computer screen. As she moved the mouse cursor and the images tumbled and rotated, she thought to herself, *this is the first time anyone has seen images of the control proteins in a human tumor. They are similar in many ways to those for the animal tumors but yet differ in some key regions. With this information, it would only take a few days to prepare a retrovirus against Gaby's tumor.* Meredith saved the image file and made two backup copies, one of which she put into her briefcase for safekeeping.

CHAPTER 34

FRIDAY EVENING FOUND MEREDITH finishing her packing for the trip to Boston. She had an early Saturday morning United flight with a connection in Chicago, and she planned to be at SeaTac Airport two hours early in order to have plenty of time for checking in and clearing security. Frances had booked the early morning flight in order to obtain a cheaper fare and save Jack's grant some travel money. She had explained that this would make the grant dollars stretch further and allow more people in the group to travel to meetings.

On the plane Meredith got into a conversation with her seatmate, a florid-faced salesman who spent a lot of time flying. She told him that she was going to a scientific meeting and explained about ASCO.

"Cancer research, huh? You don't look old enough to be a doctor."

"I'm still a medical student; I have one more year to go before getting my degree. Then I need to do an internship and residency."

"Cancer must be a depressing specialty with everyone dying. My wife's aunt just died of breast cancer. It spread all over her body. I sure hope that I don't go that way."

The florid-faced man rambled on and on about cancer and the cost of treatment. Meredith remembered that Jack had told her that he never admitted to being a doctor when he was traveling because someone either had a complaint or wanted him to look at a mole on their arm. He just said that he was a university professor and if asked what he taught, he would say *English Literature*. That usually brought back unpleasant memories of high school or college and conversation would cease. He could then read or work. Meredith thought she would try that in the future. The plane finally taxied to the runway and took off. When it reached cruising altitude, Meredith pulled her laptop out of her backpack and pointedly told her seatmate that she need to do some work, but that it had been nice talking with him.

In Chicago, Meredith found that most flights, including the one to Boston, had been delayed due to snow, so her flight was still at its gate. She quickly went from terminal B to terminal C and paused for a moment at the top of the escalator to gaze at the four-story high brachiosaurus skeleton on display. Meredith walked down to gate C25 where boarding still hadn't begun. *Good*, she thought. *There is a better chance of my luggage making it.* The remainder of the trip to Boston proceeded without incident. This time when her seat companion tried to start a conversation, Meredith said she was an English student at State and the conversation soon tapered off. Arriving in Boston, Meredith was pleasantly surprise to find that her luggage had indeed made it; she wheeled it out to the taxi area where she joined a line of people waiting to catch a cab into downtown Boston. Many were carrying handled tubes designed to carry poster presentations. Meredith assumed that these were researchers whose presentations had been slotted for poster rather than oral sessions.

"Where to, lady?" asked the dispatcher managing the line of cabs at curbside when Meredith eventually reached the head of the line.

"I'm going to the Radisson Hotel on Stuart street."

A cab drove up and the portly driver took her suitcase and deposited into the untidy trunk. Meredith took her backpack and laptop with her into the backseat. The driver confirmed the Radisson hotel as her destination. She settled back in the seat as the cab sped away from the airport pickup area. The driver was feeling chatty and pointed out some of the sights as he drove. One item that had caught her attention was the so called "Big Dig" which was a tunnel designed to relieve traffic congestion in downtown Boston and to replace an elevated expressway known locally as the "Green Monster."

The taxi deposited her at the Radisson Hotel, where she plugged in her laptop. In her inbox she found an E-mail from Jack letting her know his hotel and room number as well as some mass mailings to the medical staff and students. Nothing was urgent and so she disconnected, and went to bed. With the three hour time difference, the day would be starting early tomorrow.

Meredith got up at 7 and had a quick breakfast at the hotel. Then she made her way to the registration area at the convention center by taking a conference shuttle bus. The shuttle buses ran on regular schedules from most of the larger hotels where ASCO delegates were housed. The registration area was a madhouse. The lines at the preregistration desks divided according to last name; the one behind the J-L sign seemed to be one of the longest. Meredith identified herself to the pleasant woman behind the desk and received her badge and registration pack. The morning plenary session featured speakers from the federal government who had been invited to address the membership. One was from the Center for Medicare and Medicaid Services speaking on 'Cancer Economics in an Aging Population' and one was from the FDA speaking on 'Shortening the Drug Approval Process without Increasing Patient Risk.' The current president of ASCO made some opening remarks and told the audience to be sure and visit both the poster exhibit areas and the vendor exhibits. She then specifically thanked some of the larger companies for their continued support of the society. The first speaker showed projections indicating a doubling of the number of cancer cases between 2000 and 2050 due to aging demographics alone and trends on expenditure showing an apparent geometric increase over the last decade. Meredith began to understand what Pillipitch had been talking about on their ride back from seeing Gaby.

After the lectures, Meredith followed the majority of the audience into the main exhibit hall where a coffee break was scheduled. The size of the hall was overwhelming. Attention-getting, brightly-colored banners indicated the exhibits of the major pharmaceutical companies. Merck, Pfizer, Bristol Meyers Squib, Sanofi-Adventis, and Medimune were among those that immediately caught her eye. The majority of companies had contributed financially as meeting sponsors and were identified as such on their banners. She walked through the exhibit area to the coffee break area which was strategically located so that the attendees had to run the gauntlet of exhibitors before reaching it. She felt overwhelmed by the material that had been arranged in front of the booths. Attractive young men and women greeted the conference attendees.

As she paused in front of one booth, a young woman approached her. "Doctor, I see by your badge that you are at State University in Seattle. Have you seen the latest results on *Cytomab*? It's our new agent for non-Hodgkin's lymphoma. An *Annals of Internal Medicine* article showed an increase in overall response rate of 10 percent with no additional toxicity. Our company is having a dinner symposium tomorrow night. I can give you an invitation. Dr. Klein, who did the research, has organized a mini-symposium on the work."

Meredith said that she had not heard about this particular work and asked if the company was doing anything in the treatment of ovarian cancer.

"No, we specialize in hematological malignancies, which are easier to approach from an immunologic point of view. In the future, I expect that we will be branching out to solid tumors, but will probably look first at lung and breast cancer because of the larger patient numbers. Can I have one of our detail people come by your office after the meeting and give you some sample medications for your patients? Not *Cytomab*, of course, but some drugs that relieve nausea and stimulate appetite."

Meredith took the proffered invitation, thanked the exhibitor, and continued on to the coffee area. She was careful not to catch the eye of anyone else as she continued on her way. Out of the corner of her eye she could see the exhibitors trying to 'chat up' people going by. They were getting them to register for drawings of various free items ranging from iPhones to tickets to professional sporting events. The registration process consisted of giving out contact information with implied permission for detail people from the companies to contact the registrant. As she drank her second morning cup of coffee and continued to stroll through the exhibit area, she heard a voice call out, "Meredith!"

She looked around and saw Bryon talking with some people at the AVARTEC booth. She walked over and Bryon introduced her to some of the AVARTEC representatives including Arthur Jenkins who was there in his role of Director of Marketing. AVARTEC was in the process of launching *INHIBIT*, and the ASCO meeting was an important venue for the company. The AVARTEC booth displayed the *INHIBIT* logo prominently and there were cycling powerpoint presentations on the product showing on large display monitors in the booth.

"Dr. Jones, it's a pleasure to meet you. Bryon has been updating me on some of the new work on *INHIBIT* and *Compound 10* that has been coming out of your research group at State. Solid work, and I think there may be a place in the company for Bryon when he finishes his postdoc fellowship. This class of compounds is going to be very important in treating cancer patients since it can be combined with chemotherapy agents. He has been telling me a little about the work you and Jack Olivetti have been doing. Sounds interesting; when will we hear more about it?"

"Jack will be presenting some of the initial results at the session on late-breaking discoveries tomorrow."

"I am looking forward to it. This might be something that AVARTEC would be interested in funding as part of our continuing collaboration with State. Our expertise in taking laboratory discoveries to a commercial product dovetails nicely with the research mission of State."

Meredith answered, "I'm sure that Jack would be interested in talking to you about this." However, she privately thought, *after your company put a hold on the Compound 10 work, I doubt Jack will want to do anything that would give you oversight on the control element work.* She excused herself, left the exhibit hall, and headed to the next session marked in her program. There she joined the other attendees in entering the large lecture hall where the plenary session on tumor immunology was being held. Meredith noticed Jack talking to a few people at the back of the room, and joined them. Jack smiled and introduced her to the other members of the group – Sam Wiseman from Harvard, Patricia Gordon who was a Howard Hughes Fellow from Scripps, and Tom French from Penn.

French said, "I read your and Jack's abstract on the tumor control element that you've postulated. Jack says that your computer expertise was what enabled the protein analysis to go so quickly."

"Well, I've always had an knack for programming, but the idea behind the work was Jack's."

Gordon then asked, "How are you enjoying the meeting so far?"

"Well, it's so large, it is hard to know what to take in. This looks like a good session though." Just then Meredith's cell phone rang. She excused herself to answer it. It was Dr. Samuel Hickock, the intern from State Medical Center.

"Hello, Ms. Jones. Sorry to bother you, but I thought you would want to know about your grandmother being admitted to State Medical Center. I got your cell phone number from the registration information she supplied during her last admission."

"Granner, admitted to the hospital? What happened?"

"Her ascites reaccumulated rapidly and made it difficult for her to breathe. It looks like she developed a pneumonia on top of that. She became confused, and her neighbors took her to the Port Angeles Hospital. They transferred her here. We've started antibiotics for the pneumonia and will tap the ascites later today. We also have an MRI of the brain scheduled to make sure that the tumor hasn't spread there. What I want to talk with you about is whether we should put a *DO NOT RESUSCITATE* order on her chart in case she takes a turn for the worse. We are really running out of things to do for her ovarian cancer. There comes a point when it is best for the patient to let things take their natural course. Can you come into the hospital and talk with me about this?"

Meredith grew visibly upset with this news, but took a deep breath to compose herself before answering. "I'm in Boston right now at the ASCO meeting, so I can't come right in. It seems premature at this time to put a *DNR* order on her chart. When I last saw my grandmother, she was still mentally alert. If the tumor hasn't spread to her brain, then she should get better once the pneumonia is treated, don't you think?"

"It's possible, but it is also possible that the pneumonia won't respond to the antibiotics. I just don't think it would be a good idea to call a full code if her heart stops since she has an incurable disease."

"Dr. Hickock, my grandmother is the last close family I have. Please treat her as best you can and don't put the *DNR* order on her chart. I will be back from Boston as soon as I can. OK?"

"Ms. Jones, I understand how you feel, and I will certainly comply with your wishes. Let me give you my pager number so you can get in touch with me at any time."

Meredith wrote down the pager number and entered it into her cell phone directory. Then she went back to where Jack was talking to his friends and told him about her grandmother.

Jack could see how upset she was. "Meredith, I know how close you are to your grandmother. You might want to consider leaving ASCO early and going back to see her. If something bad happens, you will always regret not having gone back, and besides, with this on your mind, you won't be getting much out of the meeting. Call the airline and see what you can do about taking an earlier flight, and don't worry about the extra cost – we can take care of that from the grant. Tell the airline about the medical situation as that will probably help with the rescheduling."

"Thank you. I was really wanting to hear your talk tomorrow and see what the other researchers thought about our work, but you're right. I need to get back to Seattle. Let me know how it goes."

"You'll have other ASCO meetings in the future. Take care of your grandmother now."

Meredith excused herself, went back to her hotel room and contacted United. She explained her situation and after some checking, was told that she could fly standby on a 6 PM flight to Chicago and then have a confirmed reservation from there to Seattle. She thanked the scheduler, packed her bags, and at 3:30 headed for Logan Airport. When she got there she found that a seat had opened up on the flight to O'Hare, so she was able to check her luggage all the way through to Seattle. When she arrived in Seattle late that night, she caught a cab to her apartment where she dropped off her luggage and drove to the medical center.

CHAPTER 35

MEREDITH TOOK THE CASCADIA elevator up to the hospital floor housing the cancer patients. She looked on the white board in front of the nursing station to locate Gaby's room and immediately walked down the hall to 607. Gaby was sharing the room with another patient, so Meredith was careful not to disturb either woman. Gaby's bed was nearest the window and Meredith quickly walked across the room to where the curtains had been drawn around it. Her grandmother was sleeping fitfully. Meredith stood quietly and observed her for a few minutes. The old woman's breathing was labored and consisted mostly of shallow breaths with some deep breaths interspersed. An IV was running; Meredith noted that an empty bag of cefuroxime antibiotic had been piggybacked into the D5/0.5NS solution running in the main line. Meredith leaned over and gently touched her grandmother's forehead, which was hot and dry. Gaby felt the touch and opened her eyes.

"Meredith, what are you doing here? You should still be in Boston, or have I been asleep longer than I think?"

"No Granner, you haven't been asleep that long. I came back from Boston early to check up on you."

"You shouldn't have done that. I know how you were looking forward to having your work presented at the meeting."

"Well, Professor Olivetti is the one actually presenting the paper, and he can do that without my being there. Besides, it's more important that I be with you. Why don't you rest now and I will go out and take a look at your chart?"

Meredith went down to the nursing station after taking her ID badge from her purse and clipping it to her blazer. She located Gaby's chart, took it to a side table, and began to read. The resident's note indicated that on admission Gaby had been confused and in respiratory distress. Examination of her lungs indicated possible pneumonia, which had been confirmed on a chest x ray. No specific bacterial organism had been identified, so cefuroxime, which was a broad-spectrum antibiotic, was chosen. With the treatment, Gaby's breathing had improved and her blood gases were now nearly normal. The MRI of her brain had not indicated any tumor metastases, but her admission physical examination indicated several prominent abdominal masses consistent with tumor. An MRI of the abdomen was scheduled for the next day. Meredith asked the nurse at the station to page the resident on call that night; when he responded, she identified herself and asked for an update on Gaby's condition.

"Your grandmother is doing better with the antibiotics we have been giving her, but this isn't affecting the root cause which is her tumor. We have a consultation request in with the gynecologic oncology service to see if they have any new ideas about treating her tumor. We will be keeping her in the hospital for a few days while we treat her pneumonia and see what else we might do."

Meredith thanked the doctor for his information. She then went back to Gaby's room and found that her grandmother had fallen back to sleep. Meredith knew that the first, second, and third-line treatments for ovarian cancer had already been tried, and from her reading of the literature, she knew that nothing new had come along. There was nothing to lose by taking things into her own hands and trying the new treatment that she had been working on with Jack. She did not want to get him into trouble by involving him in this unauthorized therapy, so she decided to do it without telling him or having him find out about it. She wasn't concerned about getting into trouble herself if what she was doing might help Gaby. Meredith's next step would be to finish constructing the retrovirus vectors to the control points for Gaby's tumor that she had previously identified. Then she would inject them into Gaby before Jack returned from Boston. She was tired from her travels but remembered that she still had a few *Provigil* tablets in her purse from the last set of all-night study sessions she had pulled. She took one before heading to the laboratory. *Provigil* was a drug used by pilots, air traffic controllers, and surgeons who needed to stay alert for long periods of time. It also was used by students as a study aid. Meredith had gotten a supply of the pills from one of her fellow students who got it from an Internet source. She found it to be effective in helping her focus, although it sometimes gave her a mild headache. She reached the lab and unlocked the door with the key that had been issued to her when she joined Jack's research group.

She went to her desk, turned on her computer, and reviewed the data images she had previously obtained for Gaby's tumor. Then she began work on the retrovirus vectors to block the proteins produced by the two control point genes that she had identified with Jack's unwitting help.

CHAPTER 36

IT WAS EARLY TUESDAY morning in Boston, and Jack was making a few last-minute changes in his presentation, which was scheduled for later in the day. He had the Powerpoint slides pulled up on his laptop and was mulling over his summarizing conclusions listed as three bullet points.

CONCLUSIONS

- *Hypothesis of unique tumor control point verified in animal models*
- *Specific retrovirus vectors can be constructed to disable gene that produce control protein*
- *No fundamental reason why approach will not work for human tumors*

Jack wondered if the last statement constituted too much of a leap of faith since the process had as yet not been tried in any human tumor models. Finally, he decided to leave it in since one of the purposes of the new results session was to provoke discussion. He saved the revised talk and copied it to a USB finger drive, which he put into his jacket pocket. There was a breakfast meeting scheduled for next year's conference organizers at one of the hotel meeting rooms. Jack grabbed his backpack and went down to the mezzanine level. He followed the signs to the meeting room and joined those already present. Besides the academic participants, there were representatives from the various pharmaceutical companies helping to sponsor the meeting. After the attendees had helped themselves to the breakfast buffet, the committee chairman, Samuel Hellmeister, from Memorial, called the meeting to order and asked everyone to introduce themselves. Jack knew most of the people from academic institutions but few of the pharmaceutical people. Chicago had already been established as the venue for the next meeting, and the new chairman of the local arrangements committee spoke about the facilities that would be available. The chair of the scientific program committee detailed her plans for recruiting people to review and rank submitted abstracts, proposing a timeline for setting submission dates and notifying authors about acceptance or rejection. The discussion then turned to the proper mix between oral presentations and poster presentations; the later allowed for more papers to be presented at the meeting.

Hellmeister asked, "Will there be special consideration given to first-time submitters? We want to encourage new members to participate in the program."

"Are you suggesting that we use a different set of ranking criteria for them than for established members?" asked the new program chair., The discussion spun off into whether this would allow established investigators to "game the system" by submitting their research abstracts with one of their postdoctoral fellows listed as first author. There were some individuals who routinely used this tactic. The committee ultimately decided to have a special session for the best papers submitted by individuals who were less than three years away from completing training. They would be asked to attest that the submitted work was largely their own. Jack thought this was a good compromise.

One of the pharmaceutical members then requested that the restriction on the number of industry-sponsored satellite symposia be lifted. Other industry representatives chimed in. They argued that these symposia were the best way of communicating in-depth information about company research directions and cancer drugs that would soon be reaching market.

Patricia Gordon from Scripps, who was also on the steering committee, spoke up. "We need to establish some limits on the satellite symposia to make sure that they don't proliferate and take away from the scientific meeting itself. Also, I have concerns that we don't have a good way of reviewing and approving what is presented at the symposia."

Jack then heard the familiar voice of AVARTEC's Art Jenkins. He had entered the room after the introductions had been made, and Jack had not noticed him before. "The main meeting is largely underwritten by donations and stipends from the pharmaceutical industry. We don't try to manage the scientific content of the meeting. We all want ASCO to continue as the premier medical oncology meeting and that won't be the case if we try to manipulate content. The meeting is structured so that new results are presented in short time slots. The symposia are the only way of providing detailed information to the attendees. Conference attendees don't have to come to the symposia if they feel that they aren't valuable, and certainly they are always well attended."

A falsetto voice from the back added, "The free food and booze doesn't hurt the attendance either."

Hellmeister resumed control of the meeting noting that categorical courses also allowed for the presentation of in-depth information on a particular topic. He brought discussion to a close with the stipulation that a separate working group, consisting of representatives from academia and industry, would be established to review the symposia policy guidelines and make recommendations for necessary changes. Hellmeister said that he would think about the make-up of the task force and contact those he wanted on it. The task force was to have its initial work done before the next committee conference call, when the group as a whole would vote on how to proceed.

As the meeting adjourned, Jenkins approached Jack. "Too bad there continues to be this suspicion between academics and industry at most places. Glad we have a better working relationship in Seattle."

Jack nodded. "Good to see you Art. I didn't see you when you came in or I would have said hello. I need to run now as I have to get a copy of my slides put on the conference computer system for a talk that I'm giving later today."

"Yes, I saw the abstract in the program. This was the first I learned about your new work. You know, you probably should have run this by the joint scientific review committee before submitting it so that no one would have been surprised by it."

"Why? This was something that we did without any AVARTEC research funding. It was bootlegged off one of my NCI grants. The NCI gives investigators considerable leeway in following up new ideas as long as we give them credit when we publish."

"Well, don't forget that AVARTEC has given State a lot of research support over the years, including some major equipment purchases. I'd be very surprised if some of our support equipment, for example, the automated genome sequencer, wasn't used in some way. Ask your department chairman for a copy of the latest research agreement when you get back, and look it over. I wouldn't want you to get into any trouble by overlooking something."

Jack's eyes narrowed as he took his leave. He was fuming as he walked to the main conference hall and located the speaker preparation room. He identified himself to one of the attendants, who verified his talk number and the session where it would be given. Jack took a final look at the material on the conference computer. He had learned the hard way to make this final check since the conference computers were typically PCs while he used a Mac in preparing his talks. While the Mac could easily handle presentations developed on a PC, the converse was not necessarily the case. Sometimes formatting adjustments were needed even though Powerpoint software was used on each system.

Ten minutes before his session was to start, Jack entered the conference room. The prior session had just concluded and people were filtering in and out of the room. Jack was the fifth speaker in the session, which was running several minutes behind schedule by the time his talk came up. He quickly climbed the steps to the small stage behind the podium and noted that the technical support person had his title slide displayed on the screen at the front of the room by the time the session moderator had completed his introduction.

Jack began his presentation by stating his hypothesis: All tumors have similar control point genetic elements. If these could be identified, cancer treatments could be individualized and the procedure should work for all varieties of tumors. He went through the procedure by which a combination of experimental analysis and model calculations identified the control elements. It is possible, he said, to focus on the active site of the control point protein and knock it out using a selectively-tailored, antisense element carried by a retrovirus. He described the mouse tumor model work and the treatment of Butch, ending his talk by thanking all those in his lab who had contributed to the work. His concluding slide listed their names and titles and he gave special mention to Meredith's contributions.

At the completion of his talk several members of the audience approached the microphones that were strategically placed throughout the room, to ask questions. A rotund woman at the center microphone began. She was from Mayo Clinic and beagn by acknowledging the work. "Congratulations on a very nice piece of work. However, I don't see how your data support your last concluding statement since you haven't done any human tumor work at this stage."

"You are correct, and certainly in the past, treatments that have worked on mouse tumors have failed miserably when applied to humans," said Jack. "What is different about our approach is that we are not treating tumors as a group. We consider each one individually. We don't need or even want to find simply one effective treatment, such as a chemotherapy agent. We don't need the retrovirus to work on any tumor other than the one for which it was specifically constructed."

A tall, bespectacled man with a grey beard, wearting a tweed jacket asked the next question. "The experiment on the spontaneous dog tumor was especially intriguing to me. Do you think spontaneous tumors will, in general, have more control point elements to knock out than laboratory tumors and, if so, is there a limit to the amount of retrovirus that you can administer?"

"At this point we have only done the one spontaneous dog tumor. However, we have begun work on a second set of dog tumors, and I can say at this point that there were only two control point elements identified. The dog we treated had a severe throat reaction to the virus, and probably the more virus we use, the more supportive care will be required. However, as medical oncologists administering chemotherapy, we are all used to supporting patients as they go through treatment."

The moderator then noted that there was only time for one more question and that others would need to speak with Jack after the session. He pointed to the right side microphone where Art Jenkins was standing. Jenkins asked, "Even if this does work, how would you scale it up to treat the approximately 1.4 million new cases of cancer that occur each year in the United States? This is different from getting a drug that works on a large number of cancers; it's more like developing a new drug for each patient. There simply aren't enough resources to do this."

"At this point, we are simply trying to understand the control point gene and its protein better," said Jack. "That is the first step in developing a better treatment. My own view is that if this works like I think it will, there will be engineering approaches developed to scale up the process to enable the treatment of large numbers of patients. You are correct in that it is not the usual pharmaceutical company, large-scale production model. It is more like nanotechnology models, where many small systems are working in parallel. In terms of looking at the overall cost don't forget that there will be only one intervention as opposed to extended episodes of care and that is a big societal payback."

Jack returned to his seat and listened attentively to the next series of speakers. At the end of the session he was surrounded by questioners pressing him for more details. Eventually, the group around him broke up and Jack went down to the lobby of the convention center for coffee. After getting his coffee, he went to an area called the Cyber Café where ASCO was sponsoring wireless internet access. He started up his laptop and sent Meredith an E-mail telling her about the interest the talk had generated and asking about her grandmother. Then he started going through his accumulated E-mails, most of which he moved to the "trash can" icon after a brief perusal. He took care of those requiring only a few lines to answer and moved those requiring more thought and analysis to a separate folder for later action. At the end of the E-mail string he found one from the current ASCO program committee. It informed him that his presentation had been selected for highlighting in a conference press release titled *Novel Cancer Therapies Announced at ASCO Meeting*. He was asked to come to the press room by 5 PM to review and approve the release.

CHAPTER 37

BACK IN SEATTLE, MEREDITH was in the midst of preparing the viral culture medium when the first of Jack's lab technicians arrived to start work. He was surprised to see her and commented that he thought she had gone to Boston with the rest of the group.

"I was in Boston for a couple of days but came back early because my grandmother was ill. She's resting comfortably now, so I thought I would come down to the lab and do some work to keep my mind occupied."

"Sure thing. Let me know if I can help. With everyone else away, I don't have a lot to do myself."

"Thanks. I'm just mixing some viral culture medium now in preparation for constructing a set of retrovirus vectors for the latest set of dog tumors we got from Pullman. I should be able to do this myself. I could use some help later when I start work on the DNA sequence for the blocking protein to insert in the virus."

"Sure. Just tell me the sequence, and I'll take care of it for you. By the way, keep an eye on the incubator; it's been acting up and the serviceman hasn't come yet."

Meredith completed preparation of the culture medium and then reviewed the amino acid sequences for the two control point proteins she had identified. From the amino acid sequences, she extrapolated the DNA sequences that would produce them. She focused on the key sequences that appeared to be the active sites; from there she determined the antisense element that would disable these sequences. She prepared a computer file and a printout of these antisense elements and gave them to the tech before leaving the laboratory and returning to Gaby's room.

When she arrived, she found that Gaby's bed was empty. Checking at the nursing station, she learned that Gaby had been taken down to Radiology for a total body CT/PET scan to further evaluate her tumor. Meredith went down to CT and found Gaby on a gurney in the waiting area. Her grandmother was awake but looked wane and a little apprehensive. After the study was completed, Meredith decided to hang around for a few minutes and look over the radiologist's shoulder while the images were being reviewed. Gaby was wheeled back to her room for breakfast, and Meredith went to the reading area where she found one of her medical student colleagues sitting at the reading board with an attending physician. The medical student, Angela Kim, had done a pediatric rotation with Meredith, and the two had become casual friends.

"Meredith, what are you doing here? I thought you were working in the laboratory this year."

"Angela! It has been a while since the pediatric rotation. How do you like Radiology?"

"I like the technology and the hours but I miss the direct patient contact. Are you looking for any set of studies in particular?"

"Yes. I'm looking for a total body CT/PET scan on Mrs. Gabrielle Jones who is a patient of Dr. Greerson. The study was just completed; here is her patient ID number to help you find it." To divert the discussion away from the reason she wanted to see this study, Meredith asked how things were going with Angela's latest boyfriend.

"When we were doing Peds, I was dating Paul Johnson, but that didn't work out. Paul was in the middle of his surgical internship and had no free time to spend with me. Now I'm going out with a third year Dermatology resident, who has more regular hours."

Angela retrieved the PACs images. The Radiology attending, who had been amusedly listening to the conversation of the two young women, asked for an update of the patient history which Meredith provided. She scanned through the images, quickly noting that there was no metastatic disease in the brain, but there were new nodules in both lungs, most likely tumor. The tumor masses in the abdomen had enlarged, compared to the previous study and there were small nodules along the underside of the diaphragm. The ascites fluid had also reaccumulated.

Meredith swallowed hard but disguised her distress, thanked Angela and the attending, and went to Gaby's floor. She found Dr. Hickock at the nursing station using a computer to chart in the hospital electronic medical record system. He looked up and saw her.

"Ms. Jones, I see that you came back early from Boston after all. Sorry that I had to call and spoil your conference. The nurses said that you saw your grandmother last night for a while. She's doing better now than when I called you. She had a total body CT/PET scan this morning, but I haven't had a chance to look at it yet."

"I took the liberty of looking at it with one of the radiologists. I hope you don't mind."

"No problem. What did it show?"

Meredith quickly summarized what the Radiology attending had told her. Hickock said, "I'm sorry to hear this, but am not really surprised. You know the limitations of what we can do better than most. Unless Dr. Greerson comes up with something new to try, about all we can do is to keep her comfortable while the cancer runs its course."

Meredith nodded sadly, thanked Hickock for taking care of her grandmother, and went to Gaby's room to spend some time with her. She planned to return to the laboratory in a few hours to see how the work on the retrovirus vectors was progressing. At this stage she really didn't see any reason not to try this on Gaby but she wanted to talk with her about it first.

Meredith forced a smile as she entered Gaby's room, but her grandmother's smile was genuine when she looked up and saw her. Meredith kissed her grandmother on the cheek and sat down on the side of the hospital bed.

"I had a CT scan this morning," Gaby began. "Dr. Hickock hasn't come by yet to tell me what it showed."

"I looked at the scan before coming up to your room. We can talk about it if you like or we can wait for Dr. Hickock."

"Go ahead and tell me what it showed."

Meredith quickly summarized the scan results. As she talked about the cancer having grown, Gaby's face fell.

"Guess this means that the cancer treatment has stopped working."

"I'm afraid so, Granner.

"What happens now?"

"Officially, the recommendation will be for you to be given pain medicine as needed and be referred to Hospice – not right now of course, but in a while. Hospice people will help you take care of yourself at home so you won't have to go into a hospital or nursing home."

"That seems like giving up. Are you sure that there isn't anything else that can be tried?"

Meredith hesitated and then began to speak in a low voice. "Granner, that's what I want to talk with you about. You know the virus treatment that Professor Olivetti and I have been working on?

This is something that might work for you. It would be the first time it has been tried on a person, and I really don't know what will happen. It is something that we could try, but it would have to be 'unofficial' without any formal review or approval by the Medical Center."

"This is the treatment that was used for the dog that reporter talked about when he came over for a visit a while back, isn't it?"

"Yes, it is."

"Well, I guess I really don't have anything to lose by trying. But I don't want you or Professor Olivetti to get into any trouble."

"Granner, don't worry about my getting into trouble. Taking care of you is more important. The treatment itself is pretty simple once the virus has been prepared. I will just bring a syringe up to your room and inject some liquid into your IV line. It shouldn't hurt a bit, but based on what happened to the mice and the dog, you will probably get a hellacious sore throat for a few days. We just won't tell anyone what we are doing until afterwards."

Gaby nodded her head in agreement and then lay back and closed her eyes.

CHAPTER 38

WITH THE HELP OF one of the receptionists at the conference information desk, Jack located the press information room which was situated at the end of a long hallway of small meeting rooms. A woman whose badge identified her as "Kathy", quickly printed out a draft copy of the next day's press release, marked a section, and handed it to Jack.

"What's this?" Jack asked as he took the sheets of paper.

"This is a copy of what we are providing to the news service organizations at 4 o'clock today. I've marked the section relating to your presentation. Look it over and let me know if you have any corrections. Also, please provide local contact information in case any of the press want to get in touch with you for additional details, and give us the name of any of your local papers that we should send this to."

Jack quickly scanned the material and noted that two or three brief paragraphs were devoted to each highlighted research item. These were more like sound bites than detailed information. The section on Jack's work read as follows

Unique Cancer Treatment Identified and Presented at ASCO

Professor Jack Olivetti from State University in Seattle, Washington, has identified a new control element that he says is common to all types of

221

cancer. Not only has he found this new element, but he has also developed a way of putting it out of commission and destroying the ability of the cancer cells to proliferate. At the Boston ASCO meeting he presented work on several mouse tumors and a dog tumor which were all very different from each other. The treatment worked in all cases.

Unlike conventional therapies where a single drug is used to treat all tumors, Professor Olivetti makes a specific and unique virus for each individual tumor. Professor Olivetti acknowledges that making this virus available for large numbers of cancer patients would require different production methods than those pharmaceutical corporations currently use, but he doesn't see any reason why this can't be done.

Jack added a sentence to the first paragraph stating, *This treatment has not yet been tried on human beings*, and crossed out the last item, *but he doesn't see any reason why this can't be done.* Having made these changes, he handed it back to the conference aid.

"Why did ASCO decide to highlight my work anyway?"

"The PR committee always has people listening to the papers in the late breaking session since that is where new and exciting research results come out. I guess someone thought that your work qualified. ASCO feels it is important to get research news out so that Congress can feel good about how the NCI spends its money. Also, we want to let the voters know about the progress we are making. They need to urge their legislators to continue to support cancer research. On the last page, you didn't indicate any particular local newspapers to which you wanted this released. Your institution would probably like some local publicity of this type."

Jack thought a minute, but the only one he knew who might be interested was Stephen Pillipitch of the *Seattle Times.* He wrote down Pillipitch's name and also indicated the names of the three local television stations.

There were no sessions that Jack wanted to attend for the next hour, so he decided to wander through the exhibit area. He showed his conference registration badge to the door attendant and entered the hall. It seemed like acres of space filled with eye-catching booths and displays. There were colorful banners with the names of various pharmaceutical companies. Interspersed among these were smaller exhibits sponsored by cancer patient advocacy groups and publishing companies displaying cancer journals and textbooks. Jack couldn't help but think of the bad pun that people often made about cancer being a growth industry. He talked with some people staffing the advocacy booth to see what activities they were sponsoring in Washington State and was directed to the State Oncology Societies booth. He found that in the next two months a trip to the state legislature in Olympia was being planned. Coordinated with the Washington State Medical Society, it was to lobby for increased Medicaid funding. In addition, it would educate the legislators about factoring in the complexity of medical cases when establishing payment rates. He also saw that there was going to be a trip to D.C., the other Washington. Its purpose was to talk to the state's congressional delegation about getting CMS to approve payment for the newest oncology drugs rather than restricting payment to a formulary of more established and less costly agents. The transportation costs for this trip would be underwritten by the Pharmaceutical Vendors Association, and participation would be limited to the first twenty five people who signed up. The advocacy staff told Jack that he really ought to consider going. Participants would be housed at the L'Enfant Plaza Hotel near the Capitol. On the first day of the meeting, they would be briefed on the Washington political scene and there would be sessions on how to communicate effectively with legislators and their staff. Jack thought it might be interesting to learn more about how government really worked. He promised to check his schedule and get back to them.

Jack felt a tap on his shoulder and looked around. It was Art Jenkins and an attractive young Asian woman, both wearing *EXHIBITOR* identification badges showing their names and affiliation with AVARTEC.

Jenkins said, "Jack, I saw you over here and came over to introduce you to Barbara Misaki who joined AVARTEC a little while ago. Barbara will be heading the West Coast side of the marketing program for *INHIBIT*."

Barbara extended her hand and Jack shook it, noting her strong grip. He wondered if she played a lot of tennis.

I have suggested to Barbara that she talk with you and some of the other researchers at State and put together a scientific advisory speaker's panel to get the word out about the effectiveness of *INHIBIT* and clinical indications for its use. She also needs to learn more about *Compound 10*, which may replace *INHIBIT* in the future. We pay our scientific advisors generous honoraria and travel expenses for attending meetings and giving talks at sponsored CME educational sessions for physicians."

Barbara commented, "I'm just getting grounded now and I'm trying to better understand the politics in our local medical community. I hope that you will find the time to talk with me about it and give me the benefit of your advice."

Jack was nonplussed by her intense gaze, and muttered, "Sure. Why don't you give me a call after ASCO is over and we're back in Seattle?"

"I have to visit the FDA right after ASCO to talk with them about additional clinical indications that we will likely be submitting for *INHIBIT* and about our animal work on *Compound 10*. It would really be a big help to me if we could talk before then. Would you have any time to meet here at ASCO? Over dinner perhaps? You do have to eat some time and this would be a way of killing two birds with one stone," Misaki replied.

Jenkins interjected, "That's a great idea. Let's the three of us go out tonight. I'll make reservations for us at *Sel De La Terre* for 7:30. What hotel are you staying at? Barbara and I will meet you in the lobby at 7:15 and we can get a cab to the restaurant."

Jack couldn't see any way of gracefully declining the offer; besides, he didn't have anything else going on that evening. He said, "That would be nice. I'm staying at the Langham. See you at 7:15."

CHAPTER 39

Entering the laboratory, Meredith immediately approached the tech who had volunteered to help her prepare the retrovirus vectors for Gaby's tumor. He was, of course, under the mistaken assumption that he was working on an animal tumor. The tech, a lanky individual named Keith, looked up.

"How's the preparation coming?" inquired Meredith.

"Pretty well I think. I've made the RNA sequences and have them incubating with the virus in culture media. At the end of the day I'll take out specimens of the virus, verify that some have incorporated the control point RNA antisense elements, and then let these replicate overnight. You should have a usable amount of the virus vector by late tomorrow or the day after, at the latest."

Meredith knew that there was no way of hurrying the process, which was rate-limited by how fast the virus could replicate. She thanked Keith, went over to her desk, turned on her computer, and started going through her E-mails. There were 187 that had accumulated over the two days since she had last checked. She knew from experience that most of them were either irrelevant or of low priority, but the only way to sort these out from the more important ones was to open them and quickly scan the text. The *delete* button on her desktop keyboard would be getting a lot of use. Eventually she came to the E-mail sent by Jack from the Cybercafe.

Dear Meredith:

Hope you got back to Seattle without problems and that your grandmother is doing better. Flying this time of year can sometimes be difficult because of the winter weather in the Midwest and Northeast. I think our talk went over well. There were a lot of questions, most of which involved technical aspects and were easy to answer. Jenkins from AVARTEC asked a different type of question – namely how would one scale up the process to treat the million plus cancer patients per year in the United States, even if it did work. That is something that we will need to think about. Sorry that you had to leave ASCO early, but you will have lots of other meetings in your career.

Jack

Meredith was glad to learn that no technical objections were raised that might cause her to rethink using the procedure on Gaby. At this point, she was much more concerned about her grandmother than about how to apply the procedure to large numbers of patients. She was of the opinion that the first priority was to make something good; later you worried about making it cheap and plentiful. She drafted a brief reply to let Jack know that she had made it back to Seattle without difficulty and that Gaby was feeling better now that her pneumonia had been treated. Unfortunately, her tumor was still growing. She also let him know that she was spending some time in the lab working on the next set of animal tumors in order to have something to do when she wasn't with her grandmother. That way he wouldn't be wondering about this if Keith or someone else in the lab sent him an E-mail about a lab matter and mentioned this in passing. The she then went back to Gaby's room and sat with her for a while. After she caught herself dozing off, she said goodbye to Gaby and went home.

Chapter 40

Jack left the meeting hall and returned to his hotel where he took a shower and stretched out on his bed to watch the 6 o'clock news. He felt that things had gone well with his presentation and the discussion afterwards. At 7 PM he started dressing for his dinner appointment with Jenkins and Misaki. He thought briefly about what to wear, decided that dinner would probably be at a pretty fancy restaurant, given the AVARTEC expense account, so elected to put on a tie instead of just an open collar shirt under his trusty tweed sport coat. He went down to the lobby and after waiting a few minutes Barbara Misaki entered. She was wearing a mink stole over a black cashmere coat and had on high heels. Jack was glad that he had decided to put on a tie.

"Art got tied up in another meeting and sends his apologies. He said that we should just go ahead without him. He will try to join us for dessert."

"Sorry to hear that. Do you think we should just reschedule our meeting?"

"No way! I really need to spend some time with you prior to my FDA meeting and besides, I'm ravenous. We will have a great meal courtesy of AVARTEC." And with that, Misaki took Jack's arm and led him to the revolving door at the hotel entrance. The bellman at the curb summoned a cab, and Misaki gave the driver their destination – *Sel De La Terre* on State Street. It was snowing lightly and the Boston traffic was heavy. The two sat back in their seats and started talking as the driver wended his way along the side streets. After about twenty minutes they pulled up in front of the restaurant. Jack reached in his jacket pocket for his wallet.

Misaki stopped him with a smile and said, "This evening is on AVARTEC." She then paid the driver, adding a generous tip, and asked for a receipt. Jack held the door open for Misaki and the two ducked their heads against the blowing snow and scurried into the restaurant. Misaki gave Jenkins' name to the *maître d'* and told him that the third member of their party would not be joining them until later in the evening. It would be a few minutes before their table was ready, so they headed for the bar.

Misaki ordered a dry vodka martini, specifying Bong vodka from Holland while Jack ordered a Hefeweizen beer, selecting one of the local brews that was on tap. While waiting for their drinks to arrive, Misaki asked Jack how long he had been at State and where he had trained in medicine.

"I've been at State about five years and before that I was at Harvard."

"What made you come to State or for that matter to a university in general rather than to PHARMA or one of the biotech companies?"

"I like the freedom to do the kind of research that interests me rather than being a small part of a big program directed by corporate bigwigs."

Misaki laughed. "It's really not that way at all at AVARTEC. Researchers have a lot of autonomy to pursue good ideas and see where they lead. Also, they don't have to spend half their time writing grants to keep their labs going."

Jack smiled ruefully, "That certainly would be a nice change."

The drinks arrived and Jack and Misaki clinked glasses. After their first sips Jack asked, "How is your martini? I'm afraid that I haven't acquired a taste for them and tend to stick to beer."

"You probably just haven't had a good one yet. Try a taste of mine." Misaki handed Jack her glass and he took a sip.

"Wow, pretty potent stuff!"

The waiter then came over and putting their two drink glasses on a tray, led them over to their table in a corner of the dining room.

The wine steward came over and asked about their dinner selections and their preferences in wines. He finally recommended a lighter red wine such as a Beaujolais nouveau or a pinot noir. He and Misaki then went over the specific choices and settled on something from the Louis Jadot vineyard It turned out to be excellent.

During dinner Misaki and Jack continued the conversation they had started in the bar, found out more about each other's backgrounds, and agreed to call each other by their first names – Barb and Jack. Jack learned that Misaki's parents were born in Japan and had come to the United States fifteen years before when her father had taken a job in Silicon Valley as a software engineer. Misaki learned that Jack had come originally from a small Illinois town not too far from Chicago, and both his parents were school teachers. Misaki then steered the conversation around to Jack's research on *INHIBIT* and *Compound 10*.

"Tell me, do you think *Compound 10* is really a lot better than *INHIBIT* or is it mainly an incremental improvement?" Misaski asked Jack.

Jack replied, "I believe it's the latter. Both drugs have the same target and work by inhibiting tumor blood vessel growth. *Compound 10* is more effective in the mouse models we've tested and there isn't any increase in toxicity. If it's also better in people, then there wouldn't be any reason not to use it instead of *INHIBIT*."

"AVARTEC will still have to do phase II trials in humans to get the dosing regimen established, but we can probably start at the same set of doses as we did in the *INHIBIT* trials. Then we will need to do a phase III study of chemotherapy with and without *Compound 10*."

Always the scientist, Jack wanted to do a more focused study. "What about running a trial with chemotherapy but comparing the addition of *INHIBIT* vs. *Compound 10*? Wouldn't that be the best way of answering the question as to which is the better agent?"

"Well, it might for that one particular chemotherapy regimen, but maybe *INHIBIT* would work better for one tumor and *Compound 10* for another. It would be prohibitively expensive to exhaustively test all possible combinations. Besides, we would like to get both compounds on the market and let the treating physicians do our testing for us. We'll sell more drug that way."

Recognizing what truly motivates the pharmaceutical industry, Jack nodded in agreement.

Misaki continued, "Tell me more about the other research you're doing on individually treating tumors by targeting their specific growth pathways. I didn't hear about this until after you had given your talk, but Art told me about the work."

Jack quickly explained the underlying hypothesis and how he was exploiting the uniqueness of the control elements so that even though the virus would infect normal cells as well as tumor cells, there would be no effect on the normal cells. He had explained this many times this week to various colleagues and it was well rehearsed by now. He concluded with an overview of the experiments to date that provided proof-of-concept.

Misaki was following this closely and asked, "Do you think that the sore throat that the dog developed was caused by the virus? If so, that would mean that it could harm normal cells as well."

"I've thought about that and I think it was because of the particular adenovirus that we used and not due to the genetic element we inserted. We can test this by infecting animals with the unaltered virus and see what happens."

"Jack, this is fascinating work. I think it is the first totally new and different approach to treating cancer in a long time. You need to partner with a company like AVARTEC if you are going to make it anything other than a laboratory curiosity. It would be the perfect partnership between academia and industry, with each bringing to the table what it does best."

"Exactly how would that work? Yes, my lab could certainly use some long-term funding for this project but quite frankly, when the AVARTEC-dominated scientific review board vetoed part of my group's original ASCO abstract, it left a bad taste in my mouth."

"I don't know anything about that but I'll try and find out what happened. That may have been because a specific AVARTEC pharmaceutical, *Compound 10,* was involved. This would be different, and we could probably tailor the agreement to give you sole discretion on the submission of talks and manuscripts on this work. Art told me that the latest set of renewal agreements between AVARTEC and State address this specific point."

"So what's in this agreement for AVARTEC?"

"It's all outlined in the master agreement with State. AVARTEC would have the right of first refusal to market any product arising from research that it supports. This is pretty standard in agreements between PHARMA and universities. Besides, if you want to see this work eventually lead to a new treatment, you are going to have to involve industry at some point. Think about it and let's talk more after we get back to Seattle. I'll have Art's secretary send you a copy of an agreement template as a PDF file for you to look at."

Jack was still skeptical but didn't want to spoil the evening by being disagreeable. He said that he would look at the document after he got back to Seattle.

Misaki leaned across the table, put her hand on his and said, "Jack, having a consulting arrangement with AVARTEC will be a good deal for you personally as well." She held up her wine glass for a toast and said, "To a long and happy arrangement."

In spite of some misgivings, Jack touched glasses with her. It was an excellent vintage. They finished the bottle of wine as they finished their dinners. The waiter cleared away their plates and brought a dessert menu. Misaki chose a creme brulee and Jack a bread pudding with a whiskey sauce. Misaki ordered a Chateau d'Yquem Sauterne to accompany the dessert. By the time the evening was finished, both Misaki and Jack were feeling quite mellow. When the waiter brought their bill, Misaki took it and paid with an AVARTEC company credit card. Jack caught a quick glimpse of the final amount as the waiter took the credit card. Evidently, it had been a very good sauterne. Misaki also asked the waiter to have a cab called to the door.

The snow was still blowing as they left the restaurant and quickly entered the cab. During the ride back, Misaki leaned against Jack in a familiar manner. At this point in the evening, Jack simply enjoyed the sensation of her body pressing against his and leaned back in the seat. Misaki told the driver to take them first to her hotel first. When they arrived at the Four Seasons, Jack opened the cab door and walked Misaki to the hotel entrance. She stumbled a bit and looked up at him. "Whoops," she said. "I may have had a little too much to drink. I'm not walking too well. Be a gentleman and escort me to my room."

Jack quickly returned to the cab and paid the driver. Then he escorted Misaki through the lobby to the elevators, his arm around her for support. Entering the elevator, Misaki pushed the button for the 27th floor. When the elevator door opened, she pointed to her right and the two of them wobbled down the hall and stopped at her room. At this point Jack wasn't sure what to do next; Misaki got the room key card from her purse and handed it to Jack so that he could open the door for her. When he did so, she pulled him into the room with her and shut the door behind them. She dropped her coat on the floor, put her arms around Jack and kissed him passionately. Jack found himself responding. The two of them left a trail of clothing from the entryway to the bed where they pulled back the covers and fell on the sheet together. Other than a few moans of pleasure, no other sounds came from their room until they both eventually fell asleep.

Chapter 41

Late the next morning Jack awoke with a start. He sat up in bed and immediately noted that he had a hell of a headache. He lay back with a groan. Then he realized where he was and that he was alone in the bed. Where was Misaki? He sat up again and this time managed to turn and put his feet on the floor. He looked around and found that instead of a regular room, Misaki had a suite. In the heat of last night's encounter he hadn't noticed this. He thought to himself, *Where is the bathroom anyway?* He got up and saw the door to the bathroom, where he took a long, relieving piss. Remembering training received from prior girlfriends, he lowered the toilet seat before flushing and left the room. He noticed that the closet door was open and the luggage rack was empty. Then he saw a note on the desk.

> *Dear Jack,*
>
> *What a wonderful night! I'm sorry not to be there when you woke up but when I checked my Blackberry this morning, I found an E-mail from the office saying that the FDA meeting has been moved to today. The person in charge of the Compound 10 review will be out for urgent surgery and his replacement will be away next week at a retreat. It was either today or at least a month from now in terms of having the meeting. Since time is money in our business, I booked*

a flight for D.C. and will be on my way when you wake up. Poor dear, you were sleeping so soundly that I didn't want to wake you up to say goodbye. Give me a call on my cell phone this evening so that we can talk about what happens now. I really like you and want to continue seeing you after we get back to Seattle.

Love,

Barbara

P.S. Although I've checked out of the room, I told the desk that someone would be staying in it for a while longer. Take your time and please order breakfast from room service compliments of AVARTEC.

Given his headache, Jack wasn't really hungry but he definitely needed several cups of strong coffee before he would feel human again. He noticed that the hotel room had a small coffee maker that Misaki had used this morning. There was one more package of regular coffee remaining on the tray. Jack rinsed and refilled the coffee maker and turned it on to brew while he took a steaming hot shower. After the shower, he put on the hotel robe that was hanging in the closet, and sat down in an armchair to drink the coffee. Misaki's room was certainly upscale compared to his. He thought about last night and Misaki's note, and wondered what last night really meant. While the sex had been amazing, he wasn't sure how alike the two of them were in terms of their underlying philosophies. It had been a long time since he was in a relationship, so he thought he would just wait and see what developed. He decided that he really didn't understand women. He turned on the big screen TV in the living area and watched CNN while drinking his coffee. Then he dressed, looked around the room to make sure that he wasn't leaving anything, and left for his own hotel. The weather was still very cold, but the snow had ceased falling. The sidewalks were clear, so Jack decided to walk the few blocks to his own hotel rather than take a cab. On the way he stopped at a convenient Starbucks for more caffeine and a breakfast scone.

When she got off the plane at Dulles, Misaki called Art Jenkins to find if there was any last minute information she should have before the FDA meeting.

"Not really," Art told her. "Yesterday we sent them updated post approval data on toxicity from *INHIBIT*, and you should have received a copy of that as an E-mail attachment."

"Got it this morning and reviewed it on the plane ride. The rate of prolonged healing times after injury seems to be creeping up, but it still looks acceptable. I wouldn't want them to put the brakes on *INHIBIT* sales because of something we show them in the *Compound 10* application packet. By the way, what are we going to call this new agent anyway? We can't release it to the market as *Compound 10*."

"Marketing is still working on that. We will do the usual web survey of physicians showing them different marketing material. One of the variables is the brand name of the product and we will see if one name grabs them more than the others. We want something that sticks in the minds of the docs and also isn't too hard to spell when they write their orders."

"OK, I should be able to handle the meeting. I am going to stay in DC for a couple of days to visit friends. I'll be back in Seattle on Sunday. I will send you an E-mail or give you a call to let you know how the meeting went."

"Just make it a phone call. Remember that for all practical purposes E-mails are public documents and you never know who might request material relating to the FDA approval process for *Compound 10* someday. By the way, how did last night's dinner go with Jack Olivetti?"

Misaki smiled to herself, "Outstanding! He is really naïve about the pharmaceutical business, but still very sweet. He may be on to

239

something with this new procedure of his – you know, the work he is doing on regulating the tumor growth control gene. I think that AVARTEC ought to tie this up."

"I agree, but he's suspicious of our intentions – particularly after we held up his postdoc's presentation on *Compound 10*. He knows that I was on the review committee and had a hand in that. He would probably be reluctant to work with me in the near future and we need to tie this up before our competitors start sniffing around."

"I thought the agreement that AVARTEC made with Dean Schmitt gave us the inside track on new discoveries coming out of the State labs."

"Yes and no. Any investigator can apply for grant money from any source. We just made it easier to get it from AVARTEC by expediting the review process. Also, we've gotten the word out to the State faculty that a proposal on a topic that we solicit is pretty well guaranteed to be funded."

"Hmm. Well, Jack and I seem to have hit it off. Let me be the one to interface with him on this. I think I can talk him into it. Oh, looks like my bag just came off the belt. Talk to you later." With that, Misaki picked up her bag, exited the building and caught a cab to the FDA building in Rockville, Maryland.

CHAPTER 42

SINCE THERE WAS NO hurrying the viral replication process, Meredith slept in to recover from the period of prolonged activity brought about by the *Provigil*. The stay-awake drug had done its job, but her body needed to catch up afterwards. She ate breakfast, took Sam for a walk and threw a ball for him to retrieve when they reached the nearby park. Then she showered and prepared to go into the lab. If the virus was ready, she intended to stay as late as necessary to get Gaby treated. Meredith wanted to inject the virus and then erase the trail of what she had done before Jack got back from Boston a few days from now.

When Meredith reached her desk she found a note from Keith waiting for her.

> *Dear Meredith:*
>
> *The viral culture incubator crapped out again and we lost all the retrovirus. I've started the process again but you won't have a usable amount of virus until tomorrow afternoon at the earliest. I stayed late getting the new culture started, so I won't be in until around noon.*
>
> *Sorry,*
> *Keith*

"Damn!" Meredith exclaimed. "Why did the frigging incubator pick now to screw up?"

Two of the other lab techs looked up at this outburst, but did not say anything. Meredith calmed herself down, verified that the incubator seemed to be working properly now, and sat down at her desk to think things through. If she had the virus ready by tomorrow afternoon, she could inject Gaby and still have things cleaned up before Jack got back from Boston.

Following the episode with Misaki, Jack did not feel like attending the final day's sessions at ASCO. He still had a low-grade headache, his stomach was upset from the rich food of the previous evening, and besides, he would rather see Misaki again than listen to more technical lectures. He decided to come back home a day early. Many of the flights were full, so he had to break one of his informal rules about avoiding connecting flights at O'Hare during the winter. His flight was scheduled to leave Boston at 4 PM. He arrived at the airport at about 2:30 and checked in. It was a full flight and so he ended up in a middle seat between a young woman heading to San Francisco and an elderly gentleman who would be visiting family in Chicago. The plane pushed back from the gateway as scheduled but than stopped on the tarmac a short distance away. The pilot's voice came on the intercom.

"Hello folks. Thanks for flying United. It looks like Mother Nature has conspired against us today. There is a late winter snowstorm in the upper midwest and this has slowed traffic in and out of O'Hare. Traffic control has put every flight into O'Hare on a departure hold until things clear up. Feel free to use your cell phones and computers until we start taxiing to the runway. I will let you know when to shut things down. Our flight attendants will take good care of you while we're waiting. Flights out of O'Hare will be delayed also, so there is still a good chance that you will make your connections. If not, we will rebook you on a later flight."

The man sitting in front of Jack reclined his seat to relax taking up most of Jack's work space. No way to use his laptop, but he decided to call the lab on his cell to see what was happening. One of the techs answered.

"Olivetti's lab. This is Joe. How can I help you?"

"Hello Joe, this is Jack. Just wanted to see what has been happening while I've been away."

"Same old, same old. Meredith came back early. She and Keith have been working on the dog tumors from Pullman. The rest of us have been working on the *Compound 10* project."

"Is Meredith there?"

"Yes she is, do you want to talk to her?"

"Please," replied Jack. He waited as the tech called over to Meredith to pick up line two.

"Hi, Jack. What's up?"

"Right now, not much. I'm sitting on the runway at Logan Airport waiting to take off. Thought I would check in at the lab to see what was happening. I also thought I would see how your grandmother is doing."

Meredith started. "You're on a plane? I thought you weren't coming back until tomorrow at the earliest."

"Not much more was happening at the meeting, so I thought I would get out early. May have been a bad idea since weather has slowed things at O'Hare and I'm not sure when we will actually be allowed to leave for there. I got your E-mail about starting work on the new dog tumors. Any surprises there?"

"No, just followed the same procedure as before and have started work on the viral culture. The incubator has been giving us some problems. Wish we could get a new one or at least get this one fixed." Meredith hoped that Jack wouldn't ask too many questions as she did not actually want to lie to him about what she had been doing with Keith.

"That incubator has been a chronic problem for the last few months. I will see what I can do when I get back. Has the dog owner decided to send the animal over for treatment?

"I think he is still waffling on this. I don't see why since there is no out-of-pocket cost to having his pet treated."

"Yes, but there is still the expense of either sending or bringing the dog over as well as the hassle of doing it. If you hadn't already gotten the viral culture started, I would have said to wait until the owner had made a decision to treat the animal. Oh well, I guess it is good practice and it did point out that we need a new incubator."

After hanging up, Jack pulled out a novel from his backpack and began to read, having flagged the attendant for a cup of coffee. Meredith divided her time between anxiously pacing in the lab and sitting in Gaby's room. She hoped that she could get the virus injected and get everything cleaned up before Jack got back. She didn't want him asking any embarrassing questions and prayed to the weather gods that it would continue to snow like hell in Chicago and further delay Jack's return. Then she took another *Provigil* tablet in anticipation of a long push before the work was done.

Meredith's prayers for bad weather in Chicago were certainly answered. Jack's plane didn't actually take off until three hours after it's scheduled departure; then it had to circle for an additional forty five minutes before entering the landing pattern at O'Hare. His scheduled flight for Seattle had already left. The best that could be arranged with the customer service agent, given the reduced fare ticket the University had purchased, was a red eye to San Francisco and an early morning flight from there to Seattle. With nothing to do but wait, Jack found a wireless access area and went through his accumulated E-mails. Then he browsed the science fiction section of one of the airport bookstores and purchased a book by a new author. He passed the time until the plane left, again two hours later than scheduled, by reading the novel and drinking coffee. His stomach was in real distress by the time the plane actually left the ground.

Meredith did not look at her E-mails any more for the rest of the day and did not know that Jack had indeed been further delayed. She fully expected that he would stop by the lab on the way to his apartment from Sea-Tac, as was his habit. She kept pushing in order to have Gaby's treatment completed before he did arrive. Maybe he wouldn't figure out what she had been up to, at least not right away.

CHAPTER 43

AFTER WHAT SEEMED TO Meredith to be an interminable period of waiting, she finally was ready to draw the purified viral culture up into a syringe. She put the syringe and a couple of alcohol wipes into her backpack, headed over to the Medical Center end of the complex, and took the stairs up to Gaby's room on the cancer floor. Waving at the nurses behind the station desk, she went down the hall and entered the room. Her grandmother looked up.

"Hi Granner. How are you feeling?"

"Tired but ready to get this going. Do you have everything ready?"

"Yes, the syringe is in my backpack. Not too late to change your mind, you know."

"We've been all through this before. There really isn't anything else for me to do at this stage. Even if it doesn't work, I would rather try something than do nothing at all. Whatever happens, I know that you have done your best to take care of me, so don't have any regrets. It's just an injection into my IV line isn't it?"

Meredith nodded and bent down to open her backpack, which she had placed on the floor beside the visitor's chair. Just then a nurse entered the room. Meredith stopped in midreach and looked up.

The nurse spoke directly to Gaby. "My name is Sally and I will be taking care of you this shift." She then spoke to Meredith. "You must be Mrs. Jones's granddaughter – the one who is a medical student?"

"Yes, that's right. How did you know?"

"It was one of the things that I heard at rounds at the start of my shift. We are starting discharge planning for Mrs. Jones. Dr. Greerson hopes to send her home in a couple of days at the latest. Will you be the one taking her home?"

"I should be able to, but do you think she is ready to go home? She doesn't have anyone there to take care of her."

"That's the one thing holding up the discharge – making arrangements for a visiting nurse. We've sent the referral but haven't heard back yet. I need to take Mrs. Jones's vital signs and remove the IV line. It's getting late, so why don't you two say goodbye until tomorrow morning?"

Meredith was in a quandary. What excuse could she use to stay with Gaby a little longer, and how could she get the nurse out of the room so that she could inject the virus? The culture was ready and the treatment needed to be given now so that she could get everything cleaned up in the lab before Jack's return.

"Just give us a couple more minutes" Meredith said. Sally did not leave the room, but bustled around, checking Gaby's vital signs and charting on the in-room computer.

Just then a voice came over the intercom, "Code 199, six southeast, room 6127." Code 199 meant that there was a patient in cardiac arrest and a team of physicians and nurses would be hurrying to the room to try and resuscitate him or her. Room 6127 was just down the hall, and Sally quickly ran from the room to help out with the code.

"Granner, now's our chance. I need to get this injection into your line before the nurse comes back."

"OK," Gaby said,. "Just do it."

Meredith quickly shut the room door. She pulled the syringe and an alcohol wipe from her backpack, quickly swabbed the medication injection point on the IV line with the wipe, and then injected the solution. It was about 10 ml of solution, and in spite of her worry about Sally's return, Meredith injected it slowly taking about a minute to empty the syringe. The she then recapped the syringe and put it back into her backpack.

"How do you feel Granner?" Meredith asked.

"I feel a little hot and flushed now, and I didn't feel this way before the injection."

"Probably a reaction to the proteins in the solution. Does your throat feel tight, or do you have any trouble breathing?"

"No, nothing like that."

"Good. I am just going to stay here as long as I can to make sure that you don't have a bad reaction. Based on what happened with the animals we treated, I expect that you are going to develop a really bad sore throat in the next day or so. We need to find an excuse to delay your discharge until we see whether or not you will be able to swallow on your own."

About 45 minutes later Sally returned to the room. She looked frazzled.

"How did the code go?" Meredith inquired.

"Not so good, we lost the patient. The team had trouble intubating her at first, and after that, she never really responded. It was a real thrash."

"That's too bad. It's not something I'm looking forward to when I become an intern; it has got to be a scary experience."

"You would think so, but some of the interns, particularly those on the surgical service, are too cocky for their own good. It takes losing a patient like this to sober them up. Of course, you see more of this in July and August when the new house staff come onto the ward. All codes where a patient dies are reviewed at the morning conference so that people can learn from their mistakes. Not that there was any mistake this time," she added quickly, looking at Gaby. "Anyway, time for you to go so that I can finish up with Mrs. Jones."

"I understand. Granner, I'll be going home now. I'll just give the nurse my cell phone number in case something comes up and they need to reach me."

Sally dutifully copied down the cell phone number and said that she would post it at the nursing station. Meredith kissed Gaby goodbye, but instead of going directly to her apartment, she returned to Jack's lab where she cleaned the incubator equipment and put things in order. When she got to her apartment, she plugged her cell phone into its charging unit but left it turned on so that it would be ready for any incoming calls. She slept fitfully thinking about her grandmother and all the rules, both written and unwritten, that she had broken that night.

CHAPTER 44

MEREDITH AWAKENED WITH A start, quickly showered and dressed. She ate breakfast, fed Sam, and then took him for a quick walk before driving to the hospital. She anxiously went up the stairs to Gaby's room where she found her grandmother alone and sitting up in bed.

"How do you feel this morning Granner? Any side effects from the treatment?"

Gaby's voice sounded a little raspy when she responded. "My throat feels a little scratchy, and the nurse said that my temperature was up this morning. She says that she will tell the doctors about it and see if they want to keep me in the hospital for an extra day."

"I hope so," said Meredith. "I don't want you out of here until we see how it goes."

She felt Gaby's forehead, which did seem a bit warm; then went to the rack by the door where the chart of her vital signs was kept. Gaby's last temperature reading had been 38.5° C, which, while elevated, wasn't too bad. Her heart rate was also slightly elevated in keeping with the low grade fever. Meredith sat down and kept up a light banter with her grandmother for about an hour. She picked up her backpack and left after Gaby fell asleep.

Meredith picked up a latte at the espresso bar in the medical center lobby and then went down the corridor to the building containing Jack's laboratory. *Funny that he isn't here*, she thought to herself when she found his desk still unoccupied. She fired up her computer and upon checking her E-mails, learned about his flight delays. This would give her time to complete the preliminary computational work on the actual dog tumor so that she would have something to show him when he did arrive.

Jack finally came rolling into the lab mid-afternoon looking tired and irritable. However, he perked up when he saw Meredith at work and came over to talk with her. He filled her in on the remainder of his stay at ASCO, conveniently omitting the evening he had spent with Misaki. He did tell her that AVARTEC was very interested in funding their new work on the tumor control point gene.

"It's your decision of course," commented Meredith, "but do you really want to give a pharmaceutical company, AVARTEC in particular, the rights to this discovery? Aren't you concerned that everything will get bogged down with all of the layers of oversight and review that will be set up. Butch would have been dead long before you could have gotten formal approval to treat him if AVARTEC had been running the study."

"Meredith, we need industry help if we're going to make this into something other than just a laboratory curiosity. It might as well be AVARTEC as any other company. But you're right about the investigators needing to be in charge."

"As I said, it's obviously your decision, but I'm thinking of cancer patients like my grandmother who are running out of options. Anyway, I guess the next step is to do more animal trials regardless of who provides the money. Do you want to take a look at what I've done with the last dog tumor tissue that came over from Pullman?"

"Let me look at it later. One of the E-mails I looked at before getting on the plane this morning was from the vet who sent the tissue. He says that the dog's owner has decided against sending it over for treatment. Still, it was a good exercise for you."

"Too bad; things were just about ready to treat the animal," Meredith said with a bland expression on her face. "Since there is no rush now, if you don't mind, I will take off now and spend some time with my grandmother.

"Sure thing. How is she doing, anyway?"

"So, so. Still an inpatient on Six Southeast but she should be going home soon. I'll need to take some time off and drive her back to Sequim after her discharge."

Jack nodded, "OK." As he started to go through the material that had accumulated on his desk, he found himself thinking about whether or not to apply to AVARTEC for research funding and what that would mean both for his lab and for future opportunities to spend time with Barbara Misaki.

Chapter 45

Meredith spent considerable time in Gaby's hospital room over the next few days. Her grandmother's fever had worsened and her throat had become inflamed to the point where she had problems even swallowing sips of water. Greerson and his house staff couldn't figure out what was going on and had consulted the otolaryngology service for their advice. The otolaryngology resident had taken bacterial and viral cultures. The only thing that showed up was an odd adenovirus that no one could identify. In the meantime, Gaby was kept hydrated with IV fluids and there was talk about putting a PEG feeding tube directly into her stomach for nutritional purposes. Fortunately, Gaby's fever broke before they actually got around to doing this. Her sore throat started resolving immediately after that and she was eating and drinking normally one week after Meredith had injected the virus. She was then discharged and Meredith took her home to Sequim with an appointment to come back to Greerson's clinic in a month. Sam came along for the ride. On the drive the two talked about how the viral treatment had affected Gaby.

"Granner, you're the first lab rat that can talk to the investigator and let her know what the treatment really felt like. Tell me in detail what happened after I injected the virus."

"I'm not sure I like being compared to a rat, Meredith, but I know what you're asking. I really didn't feel anything right after you injected the virus into my IV, but the next day, my throat started feeling scratchy and I felt hot. That was when my temperature started going up. Then I started to ache all over and my throat just kept getting worse and worse. It really hurt when I swallowed. I know what that poor dog must have felt like. Then I just felt tired for a few days while the doctors were scurrying around trying to figure out what was the matter with me. Then I started getting better. The aching went away, my temperature went down, and my throat started getting better. Right now I feel great – no pain, and I'm really hungry. Can we stop for a burger on the way back?"

"Sure thing, and I didn't really mean to compare you to a rat."

"I know," laughed Gaby. "Although I was pretty miserable for a few days, the side effects of the chemotherapy I had before were much worse and lasted longer. If this worked on my cancer, the tradeoff was well worth it. When will we find out whether or not it did?"

"It takes time for tumors to go away even after their cells have been killed. I will go with you to see Greerson when you go for your appointment in a month. In the meantime, let's be hopeful."

It seemed to Meredith that Gaby was moving more easily than before. Rather than just sitting in a chair during the ferry ride, she walked around on the deck, looked at the scenery and pointed things out to Meredith. The two stopped and ate with Meredith saving a portion of her burger for Sam who gratefully wolfed it down. Meredith spent the night at her grandmother's place, and she and Sam returned to Seattle early the following morning. She and Gaby agreed to talk on the phone every day so that Meredith could keep tabs on how her grandmother was doing.

CHAPTER 46

BARBARA MISAKI AND ART Jenkins were talking with Peter Drisco in the informal discussion area in a corner office rather sitting than at the larger conference table. They were giving him an update on Misaki's visit to the FDA regarding the approval process for *Compound 10* and also summarizing some talks on new cancer treatment developments that were presented at the ASCO meeting.

"Pete," said Jenkins, "here is Barbara's report on the FDA meeting." Jenkins handed over a binder marked CONFIDENTIAL. "There are no real problems at this stage. They want at least one large animal toxicity study before releasing it for phase 1 clinical trials. This will give us time to reap the profits from *INHIBIT* before starting to think about marketing its replacement."

"OK. Where will we get the animal work done?"

"I would recommend using Nakurmura Laboratories in Dallas. They are under the radar screen of the animal rights groups and have the reputation of getting toxicity studies carried out without a lot of bureaucratic delays. It would probably take twice as long to get the work done at State or another university since their animal research committees will want to micromanage test protocols."

"Just as long at the work passes the sniff test when it goes to the FDA. Now tell me what was new at ASCO."

Jenkins and Misaki took turns talking about the sessions they had attended and the investigators they had talked with in the exhibit area. The two agreed that the majority of the effort was going into drugs which either targeted tumor vascularization or turned off epidermal growth factor pathways. Then Misaki mentioned the work that Olivetti was doing on identifying a unique genome sequence for tumor growth and then targeting it with a viral vector.

"If this so-called tumor control element is truly unique for each tumor, how does Olivetti identify it?" asked Drisco.

Misaki responded, "Perhaps I misspoke. There are common features in the various control elements that allow Olivetti to make a preliminary determination of the important ones. Then he uses a combination of x-ray diffraction techniques and computer modeling to determine the structure of the protein produced by the gene elements. There apparently are some similarities in the active sites of these proteins, but still they're different enough that an antisense element has to be uniquely tailored to each one. At least that's been the case so far."

"How long does it take him to do this?"

"Olivetti says that it has been going faster as he has gained more experience, but it still takes over a week. Some of it is limited by the computational time for the structural calculations, the amount of time it takes to produce enough protein for analysis, and the time it takes to expand the viral vector."

"And this was Olivetti's own idea?"

"The basic idea and the outline of the procedure are Olivetti's. However, he has been lucky in that there is a medical student with a background in computer science who has joined his group. She has been instrumental in making it actually work. Her name is Meredith Jones. Olivetti says that she is the one who is always pushing to take the research to the next stage."

"And you say that this procedure has worked on rodent tumors and a dog tumor that have nothing in common?"

"Yes. Both 4T1 and 36B10 rodent tumors, which are very different and the dog had a sarcoma."

"Interesting. I wonder how we could make a product out of this. The gene isn't the same for each tumor and therefore we can't patent it in advance. I wonder if we could get an overarching patent for the technique itself?"

At this point, Jenkins re-entered the conversation. "How would you make a commercial product out of this even if it works like Olivett thinks it will? Sounds like you've got to do a week of highly specialized and expensive work to just to take care of one patient."

Drisco responded, "I'm not sure, but I can envision a lot of parallel automated processes with different vectors for thousands of different tumors coming out at the end each week. We could certainly charge enough for each viral treatment to make a boatload of money. It would be expensive, but we could plow the profits from *INHIBIT* into it and probably get government money as well. Certainly there will be a hue and cry from the voting public to have their Aunt Maude's cancer treated this way, and with proper media manipulation, they will put pressure on their senators and representatives."

"Don't get too far ahead of yourself, Pete," laughed Jenkins. "First of all, it has to be shown that this will work in humans. You know damned well that a lot of things that work on animal tumors in the laboratory just don't work in the clinic. Secondly, you've got to find some way of tying up the technology, and Olivetti wasn't very friendly towards us when I spoke with him."

Misaki interjected, "Art, he knows that you're the one who insisted that material be cut from one of his group's ASCO abstracts. We can get him past this. I think we can sign him up as a consultant and bring in his work under a non-disclosure arrangement. It will cost us a little money, but I think the gamble is worth it – particularly if this cure does work. Olivetti and I got along very well, and I could be the one who broaches this with him."

"Timing is everything. Even if this does work, we don't want to bring it along too fast. We will need the revenue from *INHIBIT* in order to take advantage of this new opportunity. It certainly wouldn't do to have one of our competitors, like Merck or Bristol, get hold of this. Right now these companies are doing just what we are – talking about what was new at ASCO and how to make a buck from it. Barbara, why don't you bring Olivetti around to meet with me? In the meantime I will talk with his boss, Dean Schmitt, about how to set up the paperwork. Let's get to work."

As Misaki and Jenkins left the meeting, Drisco yelled to his secretary, "Patti, call Dean Schmitt's office and get me a meeting with him in the next few days. Offer to make it a dinner meeting; that will get his attention. He always likes a good bottle of wine, particularly if someone else is picking up the tab."

CHAPTER 47

DRISCO HAD READ SCHMITT correctly. A dinner meeting at the Columbia Tower Club was set up the day following Patti's phone call to the Dean's secretary, Margo. On the day of the meeting, Drisco left his office, got into his car and drove to the Columbia Tower. On the way he passed the REI building and saw several people on the climbing wall, which was visible from the road. He recalled the days when he had the time to enjoy the outdoor activities of the Pacific Northwest. Not nearly as much money in those days, but it seemed that he had fewer worries, and he and his wife, Evie, got along better too. Now he was rarely home for a family dinner. Instead, he had innumerable dinner meetings like the one that night. He vowed to himself that he would get home on time tomorrow night.

He entered the parking garage from Columbia Street, punched the button on the vending machine at the entrance, and pulled a parking ticket from the machine's slot. He wound his way down the spiraling ramp until he came to a floor with some empty stalls. When he got out of the car, he jotted down the floor and stall number on the ticket and stuck it in his coat pocket to have it validated by the club attendant. He had learned the hard way to note his parking space on the ticket. On occasion, after an evening of dining and drinking, he gotten to the elevator and had no idea where his car was located. Drisco took the first elevator up to the building lobby and then exited for the main elevator bank, which accessed the top floor. There was an intermediate stop with a transfer to another elevator before reaching the seventy fifth floor, where the dining club was located. He gave his name to the attendant and was told that his guest was in the bar. His table would be ready in a few minutes. He went into the lounge where he saw Schmitt seated at the bar with a glass of scotch in front of him.

"Hi, Al. What are you drinking?"

"Hello, Peter. I'm having a MacCallum single malt scotch. Good way to end the day."

Drisco caught the bartender's eye and motioned that he would have the same as Schmitt. When the drink arrived, he touched glasses with Schmitt and said, "Zdorovye."

The dean acknowledged the toast and both men took a sip of their drinks. Just then the waiter arrived and announced that their table was ready. The men took their drinks to a corner table in the dining room. They had a fabulous view overlooking the downtown waterfront area. The waiter handed menus to the men, with the wine list going to Drisco.

After perusing the menus, Drisco looked at the wine. "Al, what are you in the mood for, a red or a white?"

"I'm in the mood for a good steak tonight, so a red would be nice."

"In that case, I will have the lamb shanks, and we'll have a cabernet to go with our dinners."

The wine steward came over to the table and Drisco ordered a 1999 Vineyards 7 Reserve. The wine was opened and there followed the ritual sniffing of the cork and the swirling and tasting of the first glass. Drisco approved; and the two men made small talk about the weather; atrocious even for Seattle, the State basketball team, having a bad run of losses; and the old State football coach being hired to coach at at rival school and doing better than State's current coach. Finally Drisco looked over at the dean and began working his way around to the topic of the evening.

"With the cutbacks in federal funding for health research, this must really be a tough time to be dean of a medical school."

"Pete, you don't know how right you are. Not only is it tougher for our faculty to get grants, but even when they get them, the awards are often cut 20-30 percent. There's no real justification other than that these are 'across the board cuts' to make it possible to fund more grant proposals. The agencies still expect you to do all of the work you proposed, but just with less money. Clinical dollars are also under pressure because the federal government needs to reduce domestic spending in order to reduce the deficit caused by the Iraq war. With all this, a dean still needs to keep everyone from the Board of Regents on down to the lowliest faculty member happy."

Drisco laughed, "Sounds like a hard nut to crack. I can't help you with keeping people happy since I have a hard enough time doing that in my own company, but I might be able to help with some of your research funding problems."

Schmitt picked up his glass of wine and looked over it at Drisco. "Pete, we've worked together for a long time. Why don't you just say what is on your mind and why you wanted to meet with me tonight?"

"Fair enough. One of your faculty in the Department of Medicine, an assistant professor by the name of Jack Olivetti, is doing some interesting work that might lead to a new type of cancer treatment. While it is still too early to know how good it might be, I'm intrigued enough to be willing to put some money into his research."

"We always take money, but why don't you just do this through the usual channels? Why bring me directly into this?"

"Olivetti may not be willing to sign an intellectual property agreement in return for the research funding. Now I don't know this for sure, but wanted to give you a 'heads up' in case there's a problem and we need your help."

"Olivetti, Olivetti. The name is familiar. Isn't he the one who got into some trouble with his animal experimentation a few months ago?"

"Yes, but everything turned out alright. It was about using his new treatment on a dog without going through all the approval channels. Fortunately, the dog lived and it looks like the treatment took care of its cancer. So the matter was dropped."

"What terms are you asking for in the intellectual property agreement?

"Pretty much the usual except that this treatment is more of a process than a product and Olivetti has already described some of this work at a major scientific meeting, ASCO, which was held a few weeks ago."

"So you guys didn't fund this research then. Who did?"

"My people tell me that while there was no specific funding, the work was probably piggybacked onto a research grant from the NCI for some other project."

"That could present a problem. However, we try to make sure that all of our research faculty have some portion of their time not covered by federal grants just so that they can explore areas not covered by their grants, write new proposals, have time for teaching, etc., without getting into trouble accounting for their allowable effort exceeding one hundred percent. I'll bet the same is true for Olivetti, so we could interpret this work as having been paid from the the Medical School. In that case any patents coming out of it would be assigned to State. State in turn could sell the patent rights to your company, assuming that we can agree on the terms of the transfer."

"How does a 75-25 split of any net profits after expenses sound to you? Of course I mean 75 percent going to AVARTEC and 25 percent going to State."

"A fifty-fifty split sounds better, particularly since your company will be loading the expense side of the ledger. Also, this split is what we have agreed to in the past with you and other companies, and it will look better if an audit is ever done."

"Al, a lot of work will need to be done before we know if there is anything worth arguing about. AVARTEC may never see a return on this investment, the indirect cost portion of which will be going to support your administrative overhead. We're taking the risk, so we ought to have an proportionate upside."

The dean thought for a minute. He had been around long enough to know that the overwhelming majority of good research ideas never came to anything worthwhile. Indirect cost return was a "sure thing."

"Would AVARTEC agree to take some more research space in the Lake Union project for this work?" he asked.

Drisco also thought for a minute before replying. He had a hunch that Olivetti's work would turn out to be important, but he hated the thought of Schmitt trying to take advantage of him.

"It's a deal with three provisos. First, we keep the same indirect cost rate of 25 percent that AVARTEC projects have gotten in the past. Second, Olivetti needs to come on board as an AVARTEC consultant so that we can put his work under a confidentiality agreement. Third, we make the split of any future profits from the discovery 70-30 in recognition of the risk I'm taking."

The dean toyed with his glass of wine. "Pete, while I am enjoying the dinner and this wine, I find that I am spending more and more of my time problem solving for AVARTEC. Perhaps we should revisit my own consulting arrangement with your company?"

Drisco could play this game as well as the dean. The real question was what would the Olivetti process be worth if it worked as intended? What would people be willing to pay to be cured of cancer? Given that the cost of a bone marrow transplant was over $150,000 and that transplants were of marginal benefit for most tumors, $200,000 or more for something that really worked would not be unreasonable. It wouldn't take too many patients at that rate to recoup his company's investment. Besides, he needed to control the product rollout in order not to shut off the money stream starting to come in from *INHIBIT*. He decided to act generously since he could revisit his deal with the dean at a later time if the dean's services as a consultant were no longer needed.

"OK, Al. We have been asking a lot more of you lately. Suppose we double your monthly consulting fee, effective immediately? I will have our attorneys prepare an addendum to your consulting contract and send it to you for your signature."

The dean thought this would be a fine arrangement and raised his glass in a toast. "Here's to a long and prosperous relationship on both sides."

Drisco touched his glass to the Schmitt's in return. After coffee and dessert, the two men took the set of elevators down to the parking garage. Drisco pulled out his parking ticket and quickly looked at the stall number he had jotted on the back before punching the elevator button. The dean seemed unsure of exactly where he had parked his car but eventually decided to get out on the same floor as Drisco. Drisco went quickly to his car noting with some satisfaction that Schmitt was wondering around peering at the rows of parked vehicles. *Hope you spend a long time looking for your car you greedy son-of-a-bitch* thought Drisco as he waved to the dean on his way out of the building.

Chapter 48

Jack Olivetti's desk phone rang. It was Barbara Misaki.

"Hello Jack, it's Barbara. Sorry to call you at work, but I didn't have your home number. Am I catching you at at bad time or can you talk?"

"Sure, let me shut the office door. I was hoping I would hear from you."

"Really? Well why didn't you call me yourself? After all, I left my cell number with you in Boston. I hope you aren't mad because I had to leave suddenly, but I had to get down to Washington that day and I didn't want to wake you."

"I guess I wasn't sure what to do, Barb. It was the best evening I have ever had, and I didn't want to do anything to spoil the memory."

"That's sweet. It was special for me as well. I wasn't sure what you would think about my jumping into bed with you before we had really taken the time to know each other. I really don't do that, at least not very often," Misaki twittered with a nervous laugh.

There was an awkward silence and then Jack replied, "Me neither. I hardly date much at all, and this has never come up before."

"Don't tell me you were a virgin," Misaki teased.

Jack turned a fiery scarlet. "No, not that. Just not much experience."

"Honey, you did just fine. In fact, I'd like to give you another try."

Jack continued to blush, and stammered, "I'd like that too. Let me buy dinner this time."

"I've got a better idea. If you're free tonight, why don't I cook dinner for you at my place? It would be quieter than any restaurant and a good place for us to get to know each other better."

Jack quickly agreed, and Misaki gave him the address of her condominium located in an upscale area of Belltown He offered to bring a bottle of wine but Misaki told him to bring sake instead since they would be having Japanese. Jack then called his Japanese friend, Paul Kokubu, for advice as to what would be a good bottle of sake to bring to the dinner. "…and so Paul, this is a special date and I want to impress her with a good vintage. Do you have any recommendations?"

Kokubu laughed, "Talk about stereotyping. Just because I'm Japanese you think I must be an expert on sake. I don't know whether to be flattered or insulted."

"Be flattered. Besides, I know that you drink the stuff because I've heard you talk about it."

"True enough, I was just trying to give you a hard time. First thing you need to know is that sake is a form of wine made from rice. Unlike the grape crop, rice doesn't change from year to year, so there really aren't any vintages like there are in wine. What does matter is how much of the rice grains is milled off before making the wine. The more that is milled off leaving a smaller residual kernel at the heart of the grain, the drier will be the sake. I don't suppose you know what kind of sake your new girlfriend likes?"

"Not the slightest idea; this will be the first time we have had Japanese food together. But she is pretty sophisticated when it comes to wine, so I think she probably knows her sake as well."

"In that case she probably prefers a drier sake. Get a bottle of Kokuryu 500 Mangoku. That's a safe bet."

"Thanks, Paul. I owe you one. I'll swing by the liquor store and pick up a bottle."

"You won't find this stuff at one of the Washington State Liquor stores, but I'll lend you a bottle since this is a special date. You can pay me back later with something else."

Jack left the lab early and stopped by Kokubu's apartment on his way home. As he drove home, he wondered where he could pick up a good bottle of something to pay his friend back. While you could buy wine and beer at supermarkets and convenience stores, hard liquor was only sold at state-run outlets. While some people argued that this was for morally justifiable purposes, it was really about the revenue stream which the state wanted to control. When Jack got home, he took a shower and changed into slacks and a sweater. He left his apartment in the University district about 6:45 anticipating some traffic on his way to Belltown and soon found himself at the entrance to Misaki's condominium. He pushed the button for her apartment on the intercom and announced himself when she answered.

"Jack, you're a little early but come on up. You can listen to some music while I finish getting ready." Misaki buzzed him into the building and he took the elevator up to her floor. He knocked on her door and heard her voice telling him to come in. The door was unlocked. He entered and looked around. The place had a clean, uncluttered look, very unlike his own apartment. The furniture was modern in design with lots of chrome and leather showing. Low classical music was playing in the background and the drapes were open to show the view over the harbor. The dining room table was glass; at one end were two place settings.

"Do you want me to put the sake on ice or do you like it served warm, in the traditional way?" Jack called to Misaki.

"I prefer it warm," came Misaki's voice from down the hall. "Be a dear and light a fire in the fireplace. It's a gas log with the valve below and to the right. Just turn on the gas and it should light itself."

Jack put the sake on the counter between the kitchen and the dining area and then lit the fire. As he was doing so, she came into the living room. She had on black slacks and a red and gold silk top. and Her hair was worn long. Jack thought that she was breathtaking. She came over and kissed him lightly on the lips and then stepped over to the counter and picked up the bottle of sake.

"Kokuryu 500 Mangoku – very nice. It will go well with what we're having – ahi sushi, followed by a traditional tako and seaweed salad, and then udon noodles with chicken and vegetables."

"How did you ever find the time to prepare all this?" he asked. "Did you take off work the rest of the day?"

Misaki laughed, "Well, I did have a little help from a caterer that I use. I'm more of a career girl than the homemaker type."

The two sat in the living room to enjoy a glass of the sake prior to dinner. Misaki explained that by tradition, one always poured the other person's sake and not one's own. She filled a glass for him and Jack in turn filled a glass for her.

Jack decided to begin the conversation on a safe topic. "How did your meeting at the FDA go?"

"Apart from the lousy timing, the meeting went well. The bureaucrats listened for a change and were actually helpful in terms of telling me what we needed to do to get marketing approval for *Compound 10*. But you know, *Compound 10* is actually a pretty traditional drug and the processes are in place in terms of deciding which hoops you need to jump through. Your research doesn't really fall into such a clearly-defined area as it's a process and not a drug or a device. It's something that I could see attorneys arguing over for quite a while."

"I suppose that's something that we can worry about later. We need to do a lot more animal work before we try it in humans. Even if things go without a hitch, it will be years before someone has to worry about FDA approval for marketing it."

Jack leaned back and looked around the apartment. "Quite a place you have here. Have you been in it long?"

"About three months. AVARTEC has connections with several realtors, and one of them found it for me shortly after I came to Seattle. I like the view and the social life of the Belltown area, and I think it will be a good investment as well."

Misaki led Jack over to the window, and they looked out. "When I was in school, I promised myself that I would eventually have a place with a view like this, but I didn't think it would happen so soon. AVARTEC takes good care of its people; that's one of the main reasons I went with them instead of another company."

"It's a lot different at a university like State. Everyone there is pretty much on their own in terms of finding a place to live, and it would be years before their salaries got to the point where they could afford something like this."

"That's why I decided early on not to go into academic medicine. I watched the difference in how my dad was treated when he was a professor compared to when he worked at a computer company in Silicon Valley. Still, there is good money to be made by someone in academic medicine who has the right sort of consulting arrangements. That's something you might want to think about."

Misaki brought out the sushi and the salad and the two sat down at the table. Both chopsticks and the usual silverware were at Jack's place, but since Misaki was using only chopsticks herself, Jack decided to do the same. The sushi was freshly made and with the embellishment of soy sauce mixed with wasabi, it was truly excellent. After the udon noodle dish, Jack helped Misaki clear the table and she made a couple of espressos for them to take back into the living room. Jack sat down on the couch, but instead of sitting beside him, Misaki took a chair facing him across the coffee table.

She looked at him intently and asked, "Jack, what do you see yourself doing five years from now? Are you planning still to be a university professor or do you want to be doing something else?"

What a strange question, Jack thought to himself. *That's the sort of question that you ask someone interviewing for a job. Am I interviewing for the job of boyfriend?* "I really hadn't thought much about it. I like being a professor and having students and postdocs in my lab. I also like the freedom to do pretty much what I want, just as long as I can get funding for it. I guess I see myself staying on at State and rising through the ranks, first to associate professor and then full professor. I don't think I want to be a department chairman though; I don't like all the meetings that they have to attend. How about yourself, what do you want to be doing in five years?"

"I want to be in charge of a product line division at AVARTEC with a lot of stock options that will pay off big if my product line does well. After that, who knows? Whether I stay at AVARTEC or move to a bigger company is something I will decide when the time is right. But enough shop talk for the evening."

With that, MIsaki put down her espresso, walked around the table and stood in front of him. She ran her fingers through his hair; he stood up and kissed her, first gently and then with real passion. She pushed him back on the couch and fell upon him. He timidly caressed her breasts and then hurriedly unbuttoned her blouse. She wasn't wearing a bra. She said in a husky voice, "Not here, take me into the bedroom."

Jack lost track of the details after this. It took a while before the passion of the two was spent, but as they were lying on the bed in a postcoital bliss, with Jack drowsily rubbing her back, Misaki said, "No FDA trip tomorrow morning. Can you stay the night?"

"I'd like that more than anything," whispered Jack. "I'll take you out for breakfast in the morning. Hope you don't have to be at work too early as I think it's going to be a while before we go to sleep."

Jack was right. It was after 3 AM before the two finally drifted off to sleep. Misaki had turned off her alarm clock, and so it was almost 10 o'clock when the two awoke. Misaki grinned at him and said, "Me first for the shower and then you can use it while I get dressed. Where are you going to take me for breakfast?"

"Have you ever been to Julia's up in Wallingford? Great cinnamon rolls and egg dishes. It is one of my favorite weekend breakfast spots."

The two got ready and took separate cars as they planned to go directly to work after breakfast. Misaki followed Jack to Julia's. Since everyone else had pretty well finished breakfast by the time they arrived, they were shown to a table immediately. The waitress poured them each coffee and took their order.

"Barb, we've only known each other for a very short while but I'm crazy about you. I don't want this to end."

"I feel the same way Jack." After more of the inane chitchat of new lovers, Barbara gradually led the conversation around to the viral vector work. "Jack, I like the way you take an idea and pursue it, like the viral vector work you've done. Going from the concept to a workable treatment in less than a year. You're just the sort of person who should be working at AVARTEC, where your abilities would be appreciated and rewarded."

Jack found himself a little uncomfortable with the direction the breakfast conversation was taking but he didn't want to say anything that would upset Misaki. "Well, perhaps you're right, but I would need to think about it more first. It would be a big change from what I planned to be doing, but then again, I guess it would mean spending more time with you."

"I understand. How about starting out as a consultant? That way you could get a chance to know the company better and not cut any ties with State. Besides, the money is pretty good, and I hear that you've just hooked up with a woman with expensive tastes."

Jack laughed weakly at this last remark. "Sounds like a reasonable suggestion. Can you send over a consulting contract; I will run it by my chairman who would need to approve it."

"That won't be a problem, Jack. Both Dr. Bremenhoff and Dean Schmitt have consulting contracts with AVARTEC, so I'm sure that you won't have any trouble getting yours approved."

The two finished breakfast and Jack walked Misaki to her car and gave her a brief kiss before she got into it and drove away. Each was preoccupied with different thoughts. Misaki was thinking that Jack was surprisingly sweet. She found herself really liking him, in spite of his naivete. Her plans to bring Jack into AVERTEC's fold seemed to be going well. Jack, on the otherhand, was wondering why he had just about committed himself to becoming an AVARTEC consultant, something he thought he would never do. He wondered what his colleagues were going to say when they found out, particularly the younger, more idealistic faculty and the members of his research group.

CHAPTER 49

ONE MONTH TO THE day after Gaby was discharged from State Medical Center, her next door neighbor drove her to the Kingston ferry terminal. She walked onto the ferry carrying a small tote bag. Meredith had offered to come over and pick her up but Gaby had been adamant that she just wanted to be picked up at the Edmunds dock. This would save Meredith a lot of driving, and Gaby was tired of being so dependent upon her granddaughter. When the ferry arrived in Edmunds, the foot passengers disembarked prior to the automobile traffic. Gaby walked down the side of the dock and saw Meredith waiting just outside the terminal area. The two women greeted each other fondly and then Meredith took the tote bag as they walked to the nearby lot where Meredith's car was parked. Sam was in the back seat and, wagging his tail, woofed when he saw Gaby.

"I haven't been spending much time with Sam – too busy in the lab I guess, so I thought he would enjoy the ride up to Edmunds. We'll swing by my apartment and drop him off before going into the Cancer Alliance clinic to see Dr. Greerson. Your appointment is at 1:30, isn't it?

Gaby nodded. "Yes, a CT scan at 1:30 and then I see Greerson an hour later."

Just then Sam jumped into her lap. Meredith quickly reached over and tried to move Sam off thinking that he might inadvertently hurt her grandmother.

"It's all right, let him stay where he is. You just want your ears scratched, don't you Sam?"

"Are you sure? I'm afraid that your belly might be tender and that the pressure of his weight might hurt you."

"Actually, all the pain went away a couple of weeks ago. If Sam bothers me too much, I'll just push him off into the back seat."

"You are looking pretty good. I noticed that spring was back in your step when you walked off the boat."

There wasn't much traffic on I5, so the drive back to Meredith's apartment went quickly. Soon the car pulled up to the building entrance and the two women and Sam went inside. Meredith prepared a light lunch of soup and sandwiches.

"Are you sure it's all right for me to eat," asked Gaby? "Sometimes they don't want you to, you know."

"I'm pretty sure it's OK this time since you're not having to drink any contrast agents. Let me look at your appointment slip to be sure." Gaby handed over the piece of paper, which Meredith quickly inspected, "Yes, it doesn't say anything about not eating before the exam."

Gaby quickly finished her soup and sandwich and then accepted a cup of hot tea from her granddaughter.

"Looks like your appetite is back too, Granner," said Meredith as she picked up the dishes and utensils and took them to the dishwasher.

The two women drove to the Cancer Alliance building on Lake Union, parked in the underground garage, and took the garage elevator to the lobby. On the drive from the apartment they talked about everything but the upcoming appointment with Dr. Greerson. Neither wanted to consider what they would do if the tumor had not responded to Meredith's bootlegged treatment. They walked over to the reception desk and had their parking ticket validated before taking the elevator to the clinic floor. The sign at the desk cautioned them that there had been some outbreaks of respiratory syncytial virus, or RSV, during the past week. It also said to be sure to wear a mask if you had a cough and let your doctor know. They walked across the reception area and took a second elevator up to the imaging suite. Gaby checked in and was taken to a changing area in preparation for the study. Meredith pulled out her laptop and logged into the building's wireless network using her network user name and password. After running through her E-mail queue, she navigated to the PUBMED website and did a quick literature search on ovarian cancer. *Nope, nothing new* she thought to herself. She then reviewed the news items on Google and Yahoo, just to occupy her time. Finally, Gaby came out and they took the elevator down to the gynecologic oncology clinic and checked in at the appointment desk. They were told that Dr. Greerson's clinic was running about an hour late, so they sat down to wait. Finally they were escorted into the back area of the clinic where Gaby was weighed and her blood pressure was taken. In the examination room she was told to put on a gown and sit on the exam table. Meredith sat on a chair in a corner of the room. She and her grandmother talked quietly. After a short wait, Dr. Greerson, accompanied by two junior residents, breezed into the room.

"Mrs. Jones, very good to see you again. How have you been doing since your discharge?"

"I've been feeling pretty good. My pain is all gone and I have a lot more energy."

"I'm very glad to hear that. Have you had any more problems breathing?"

"No, I'm breathing just fine too."

"Well, we will just take a look at you. Do you mind if one of these younger doctors also examines you?"

"Of course not, that's how they learn. I know that seeing patients was very important to Meredith here when she was spending time in the clinic."

"OK then. Dr. Kim, suppose you listen to her lungs, examine her for enlarged lymph nodes and feel for abdominal masses? Then tell us what you find."

Dr. Kim, a nervous young Korean resident, quickly pulled a stethoscope out of his coat pocket, and walked behind Gaby. After telling her to breath deeply, he listened to her lung sounds. "Perfectly clear," he said. Then he felt her neck and axillae and asked her to lie back while he felt her groin area and her abdomen, first lightly and then more deeply. "No enlarged lymph nodes, and I don't feel anything in her belly either. I'm surprised since her last set of chart notes say that multiple nodular masses are readily apparent in the lower abdomen."

Greerson frowned and said, "Here, let me do it." He did exactly what Dr. Kim had done, first feeling Gaby's belly lightly and then more deeply. "Any pain when I do this?" he asked.

"It was a little uncomfortable when you pushed really hard that last time, but otherwise nothing."

"Hmm. Sometimes it is easier to feel masses in the pelvic area with a pelvic examination. Would you ask one of the nurses to prepare Mrs. Jones?" Greerson said to his residents. "Ms. Jones, perhaps you should leave the room while the nurse gets your grandmother ready."

"Sure, no problem." Meredith picked up her backpack and left the room.

Soon one of the clinic nurses came into the room and shortly afterwards, stuck her head out of the door and indicated to Greerson that everything was ready. Greerson and the two residents went back into the room. About ten minutes later the three came out, talking among themselves.

"I don't feel anything at all either. She says she had a CT scan today; let's look at it on the clinic PAC unit. Kim, what is her patient number?"

Kim recited Gaby's patient number under which all of the studies were archived, and the other resident logged into the computer system and found her image file. He selected the CT scan that had been done an hour earlier. No report had been dictated as yet, but the images were there. The three men in their white coats peered at the monitor as the images scrolled by.

"I'll be damned," said Greerson. "It looks like the ascitic fluid has pretty much gone away and I don't see any nodules in the pelvis. Are you sure these are Mrs. Jones's images?"

"Here's her name and number at the top. See for yourself."

Greerson did just that. "Let's go up to radiology and get one of the diagnostic guys to go over the studies with us," he said to the two residents. As they were leaving the clinic, he noticed Meredith sitting in a chair and looking anxiously at them. "You can go back into your grandmother's room and help her get dressed. I just want to check out a couple of things with the radiologist, and then I'll come in and talk with the two of you.

The radiologist in the reading room listened to Greerson's story and then pulled up that day's images on one set of monitors and the images from just before Gaby's hospital admission on another set of monitors. She locked the two image sets and scrolled through them in synchrony pointing out the changes on a slice by slice basis.

"Congratulations," said the radiologist. "Looks like your treatment certainly worked."

"That's just it," snapped Greerson. "I didn't treat her with anything between these two studies. Just tapped off some fluid. Is it possible that the images have been mislabeled and don't correspond to the same patient?"

The radiologist snorted. "Impossible! The patient cards are bar-coded and scanned and the tech confirms the patient's identity right before the study is done. Also, look at the T12 vertebrae. There's an old compression fracture due to osteoporosis in each set of images. Still, if you are worried about missing some tumor, you could always get a total body PET scan."

"Good idea. When can I get one scheduled?"

"I'll find out." The radiologist picked up a phone, called the appointment desk, and explained what she wanted. She listened to the response. "You're in luck. We can fit her in tomorrow morning."

"Book the appointment and I'll talk her into having the study." The radiologist handed the request form to Greerson, who in turn handed it to Kim to fill out. Everyone knew the drill. For Gaby's insurance to pay for the study, a formal request had to be made. Greerson and crew then went back down to the clinic.

Greerson entered Gaby's room with a big smile on his face. "Mrs. Jones, I have some good news for you. It looks like your cancer may have gone into remission. Sometimes this happens, not very often, and we don't understand why. There is no way of knowing how long this remission will last. I would like to get one more test to see how complete the remission is, a total body PET scan. You had one of these when we first saw you a couple of years ago, do you remember?"

"Yes, they injected me with something that was radioactive and then I lay on a table and was slid into a big ring. I had to be careful with my pee for a while after that because it got radioactive or something."

"All of the isotope that was made for today's patients is spoken for. But I can get the PET scan done tomorrow morning. Can you stay around for it? It's really important."

Meredith spoke up. "Granner, you can stay overnight with me and then I'll take you back to Sequim tomorrow afternoon. This is the best way of seeing what is going on." Then she turned to Greerson, "Her insurance will pay for the scan, won't it?"

"No problem. This is a follow-up scan in a cancer patient to determine tumor status. I will certify that it is medically necessary."

"OK then," said Gaby. As she and Meredith left the exam room, Dr. Kim handed her an appointment slip with the time and date written on it.

"Mrs. Jones," said Kim, "it will take a few hours to process the images. I'll give you a call tomorrow evening and let you know what the study showed. In the meantime, the news is very good so enjoy the evening and we will see you at 7:30 tomorrow morning."

Once in the elevator, Meredith and Gaby hugged each other excitedly. "See Meredith, I told you I was feeling better. I guess the sore throat was worth it."

"Granner, I'll be honest with you. I didn't think it would work this fast, but YIPPEE! Let's celebrate with a really nice dinner tonight and have a good bottle of wine too. My treat."

The ebullient tone of the ride back to Meredith's apartment and dinner that night was in marked contrast to the somber demeanor of the two women earlier in the day.

The PET scan the next day did not show any areas suspicious for tumor. Meredith used her laptop to log into the PACs system and look at the images so that she and Gaby would not have to wait for Kim's call to learn the results. Meredith considered this a very minor bending of the rules compared to giving Gaby an experimental treatment. Surprisingly, it was Greerson himself and not Kim who made the call to Gaby the next day.

"Mrs. Jones," he began, "I have some very good news for you. The PET scan you had yesterday didn't show any tumor at all. I certainly don't understand why it went away, but it did."

Meredith had coached Gaby not to let Greerson know that she already knew that her tumor was gone, so Gaby played along. "How wonderful! Thank you for calling to let me know. Does this mean I'm cured?"

"Well, miracles do happen sometimes. Say, you weren't taking any old Indian herbal remedy or anything, were you?" Greerson added, only half jokingly. "It might be that your body's immune system was activated in some weird way by the fever you had while you were in the hospital. I've heard stories of things like that happening with other kinds of tumors, but not ovarian cancer."

After talking with Greerson a while longer, Gaby hung up and turned to Meredith. "What's Grand Rounds?" she asked.

"Grand Rounds is a kind of lecture that a professor gives. It is generally a talk that would be interesting to a larger number of people compared to a more focused lecture. Why do you ask?"

"Dr. Greerson said that he is going to talk about my case in a Grand Rounds that he is giving to the oncology service next week. He said he is going to use it as an example of why a doctor shouldn't give up on a patient. He hasn't a clue about what really happened, has he?"

"No and that in itself is a problem. Now that we know that the treatment works in people, we need to make it available to more cancer patients. If I tell Greerson what happened, then word will certainly get out, but I will certainly get into a lot of trouble. Jack probably will also, even though he didn't know what I was doing."

"Meredith, you need to talk to Professor Olivetti. He needs to know that his treatment works. Maybe together the two of you can figure out a way to tell people about this without getting into trouble."

Chapter 50

"YOU DID WHAT?", Jack practically screamed at Meredith when she came into his office and told him what she had done. "How could you try something like this on a patient at this stage in its development? You've broken all kinds of regulations. Why didn't you talk to me first?"

"Would you have agreed to let me treat my grandmother?"

"Most certainly not."

Meredith looked Jack right in the eye and said, "That's why I didn't ask you. My grandmother was dying ,and this was her only hope. Besides, it worked."

"What do you mean it worked? You only treated her a few weeks ago. You know that it takes years to ascertain whether a cancer treatment worked or not. All you really know at this time is that the treatment didn't kill her."

"Jack, if you'll calm down, I'll give you all the details." Meredith explained how she treated her grandmother without anyone knowing about it, about the really sore throat that she had developed in response to treatment, about how good she was feeling now, and about the fact that no tumor had been found by Greerson on his examination, on the abdominal CT scan, or on the total body PET scan. She concluded by saying, "Greerson is so impressed by her 'miraculous' response that he is going to talk about her case at a Grand Rounds either this week or next."

Jack sat back in his chair and stared incredulously at Meredith. "It really worked?" He rolled his chair back from his desk, leaned back, and looked up at the ceiling for a few moments. "Now what do we do? On one hand, they will probably kick you out of medical school and me along with you for not preventing this. On the other hand, if this really works, then we need to make sure that enough people find out about it so that it can't be buried. There are a lot of people who wouldn't want this to get out until they figured out a way to make a buck off of it." Jack thought about the conversations he had had with Misaki concerning the work and the consulting job offer. It was one thing to have that conversation when it was only academic, but now the stakes were much higher.

"Jack, remember what you have always said about putting the patient first and that way you would never go wrong? That's what we need to do now."

"In the long run that is absolutely correct, but that doesn't mean that the system won't get in a few licks in the short run. I have a former classmate who is now in a pretty important position at the NCI. I want to give him a call, lay out what happened, and see what he would advise. Maybe the best thing would be to see if the NCI would take over sponsorship of this project? Let's talk again later today."

Jack immediately picked up the phone and placed a call to his friend, Fred Alexander, who had been named to head the Division of Innovative Cancer Clinical Trials. Fred was a driven but jovial Black American who, in Jack's opinion, was smarter than hell and should have been working in a laboratory rather than holding down a desk as a government bureaucrat. He and Jack had been classmates at Harvard before each had gone their separate ways. Fortunately, Fred was in his office and, after putting Jack on hold for a few minutes, his secretary put the call through.

"Hello Jack," came Fred's baritone voice over the phone. "It has been a long time since we've talked. I didn't have the chance to get away and come down to ASCO this year, and that's where we usually see each other. Are things still going well at State or have you changed your mind about the NCI job I keep offering you?"

"That's what I'm calling you about. I've got a problem and I'm looking for some advice."

Fred's voice turned serious, and he said, "OK, tell me about your problem and what I can do to help you out."

Jack quickly described his research hypothesis, his treatment approach, and the animal work that had been done. Fred interrupted several times with questions.

"Hell Jack, you don't have a problem. This sounds like great stuff, just the sort of thing the NCI is looking for in terms of completely new directions. If you need grant money, apply for an RO1 and have it directed to the Clinical Trials Review Board."

"No, that's not all of it. Here's where the problem comes in." Jack described what Meredith had done and his concern that his research program would be shut down once this came out.

"Well Jack, I guess you do have a real problem after all, or at least your lab assistant does since she was the one who treated the patient. You didn't know anything about it until it was all over."

"I suppose that I could just blame Meredith, but I don't want to do this. She is a superb investigator who has done outstanding work on this project. She did what she did with the best of intentions. Besides, the lab would most likely be shut down during the investigation, which would delay our finding out how good this treatment really is."

Fred went quiet for a minute and then said, "Jack, how solid is this work of yours? I've always respected your ability as a scientist, but I need to know the real scoop before I go out on a limb. The real truth, no bullshit now."

"Fred, it's rock solid, a real breakthrough, and you know that I don't overstate things. Yes, I would have liked to do a lot more animal work and gotten approval for a formal clinical trial, but here we are. Any ideas on what I might do now?"

"Here's a possibility: A lot of cancer patient groups have been hammering on the FDA and the entire cancer research establishment because of the slow pace of bringing out new treatments. My boss has been getting calls from a lot of congressmen because they've been getting calls from their constituents. It isn't common knowledge yet, but we're about to get a mandate to pick out a small number of really novel ideas and quickly find out whether they really work. I might be able to get your program approved as a pilot project. With the NCI backing you and giving its stamp of approval to a compassionate use protocol for terminal cancer patients, you can probably ride this out. And if it really works, then we will look like heroes to Congress and that won't hurt at budget time."

"Sounds good. First, are there any downsides? No bullshit from you either now."

Fred laughed, "Fair enough. There are a couple of caveats. First, the support is going to be limited to $250,000 a year in direct costs for each of the approved pilot programs. This sounds good but the stipulation is that the indirect cost rate can be no more than 25 percent which a lot of institutions aren't going to like. Second, any treatments that come out of this are licensed jointly by the NCI and the investigator's institution. That way we can make sure that the treatments remain affordable to the patient. We would really catch hell if some great treatment came out of this and some drug company set the charges so high that it bankrupted Medicare."

"I can live with that but my chairman and the dean would need to sign off on the reduced indirect cost rate."

"That's your problem, but it's a smaller one than you had before. Your chairman is still Sam Bremenhoff right?"

"Yes, why do you ask?"

"My boss apparently knows him from way back and could possibly put in a call explaining why we need to have the indirect cost rate at 25 percent for this set of projects. He can also point out that this is going to be a high visibility program and there will be a lot of good PR for State if they participate."

"OK, you've convinced me. What do I need to do?"

"Why, put in some paperwork, what else? After all, we are an agency of the federal government. Here's what you need to do." And Fred laid out the details of the submission process. "Send it to me by the first of next week, and I'll it to my boss at the next department meeting. Don't worry, just keep it short and to the point. Don't go into an extensive literature review or have a long justification section. We already know about the justification and if there were a lot of literature already, then it wouldn't really be innovative. If your proposal looks good to us, then we will most likely have you come out to give a presentation to the review committee. After that, we can have an answer back to you in a few days. We are going to have a rapid decision process for proposals that make it to the presentation stage."

"I'll get something off to you in three days. I appreciate what you're doing. You won't be sorry."

The two hung up and Jack immediately paged Meredith, asking her to come to his office. He explained what they were going to do and told her that she needed to write up a summary of her treatment of her grandmother, including the side effects that Gaby had, and the outcome thus far. He would write up the theoretical hypothesis and the supporting animal work. "Get going. I need something back from you by tomorrow afternoon at the latest."

Jack and Meredith put in long hours over the next few days writing and rewriting the proposal. Finally it was put in the Fed Ex box. The two of them felt both relieved that it was done and apprehensive that it might not be approved.

The proposal received initial approval at the NCI and Jack received a call from Fred to set up his visit to give a formal presentation on the work. As luck would have it, the only date in the next two weeks that would work for Fred's boss was the same day that Greerson would be giving Grand Rounds and talking about Gaby's case. Jack and Meredith decided to adopt a "divide and conquer" strategy. Jack would go back to D.C. to make the presentation and Meredith would attend Grand Rounds, where she would take careful notes about what was said both by Greerson and the audience.

CHAPTER 51

IN THE HIERARCHY OF the innumerable conferences that take place at an academic medical center, Grand Rounds ranks near the top. It is generally considered an honor to be asked to give a talk at one, particularly one sponsored by the larger clinical departments. In order to give as many people as possible the opportunity to attend, these conferences are held at ridiculously early hours in the morning, typically starting at 6:30 or 7:00. Coffee and pastries are often provided by drug companies or other vendors of medical products. This helps improve attendance and also gives the vendor's products some exposure to physicians who might prescribe them to patients at some time.

Greerson had worked hard to prepare his material. The title of his talk was *Miraculous Responses in Hopeless Medical Cases*. His talk was to start at 7:00 AM, so he arrived at the auditorium at 6:45 to make sure everything was set up and to load his Powerpoint presentation into the room's AV system. He opened the program and ran through the slides to make sure that everything would project correctly. Then he went out into the hall to have a quick cup of coffee before the seminar started and to talk with those who were filtering into the room. Meredith was one of these, and she went up to Greerson to say hello.

"Ms. Jones, how is your grandmother doing? No changes in the last week or so since I last saw her, I hope."

"No, she is doing just great."

"Good," he said with a wry smile. "I would hate to have to make any last-minute changes in my talk. Excuse me a minute, there is someone over there to whom I need to say hello." And with that, he walked over to where a group of older men were talking.

Meredith looked around to see if there was anyone else that she knew. To her surprise she saw Pillipitch from the *Times* putting some pastries onto a plate. She walked over, picked up a pastry, and started talking to him.

"Mr. Pillipitch. I'm a little surprised to see you here at this early hour. I somehow thought of you as being a late night person, you know – working to get out a story before the morning deadline."

"True," replied Pillipitch. "I'm not sure how awake I really am. I generally keep tabs on the list of scheduled seminars at State Medical Center as I can often pick up an idea for a health care article. Miraculous cures in apparently terminal patients – now that should give me material for more than one article. People love this sort of story."

Meredith and Pillipitch took their coffee and joined the rest of the people entering the auditorium. Like everyone else, they ignored the sign on the door saying *No Food or Drink Inside*. They walked up the aisle and took seats near the back of the room. The moderator introduced Greerson with some laudatory remarks and Greerson started his talk. He noted that he would confine himself to gynecologic tumors, which was his particular area of expertise, and would divide his presentation into three categories: (1) Heroic surgical procedures, (2) Unexpected responses to medical treatment, and (3) Responses without known cause.

He talked first about heroic operations. His example was the surgical resection of a mucinous cystadenocarcinoma of the ovary which had grown to an amazing 72 pounds before the woman came for treatment. An astounding set of photographs showed the resection of the tumor. The patient had been turned on her side to roll the tumor out without rupturing it and spilling cancer cells all through her belly. He ended this section of his talk by saying that the procedure took twelve hours and that over ten units of blood were transfused during the surgery.

In his second category he used as his example a young woman with a germ cell tumor of the ovary. The tumor had spread widely through the abdomen with studding or nodules all along the serosal lining. It had also had spread through the bloodstream to the lungs and liver. He said that this tumor was incurable when he first started practice but now, with effective chemotherapy, even disease like this could be cured in a high percentage of patients. At the end of this part of the talk he showed a picture of the young woman holding a baby saying that today's drugs for this particular cancer allow patients to remain fertile most of the time.

Gaby's case was the example of the third category, a tumor that responded for no known reason. Referring to her as "GJ," he went over her case in great detail including her initial surgery and chemotherapy. He then showed pictures of her scans indicating that the tumor initially responded, then grew back over time, then slowed down with different chemotherapy and then started growing again. By this time Greerson had just about used up all of his allotted speaking time. He closed by saying "and so we were just going to admit her to the hospital one more time to tap off the ascites to make her comfortable and then were planning to send her back home for hospice care. She got sick while in the hospital, had the worst sore throat I've ever seen. We couldn't figure out what caused it, but after a few days she got better, and we sent her home. I never thought I would see her again, but when she came to my clinic a couple of weeks ago, her tumor was all gone on both clinical examination and on PET/CT scans."

Greerson showed some images of the PET/CT scans indicating the large amount of tumor at one time and the total absence of tumor on the last scan. "The thing to remember is that we never actually treated her cancer during this admission. It just got better on its own."

The session moderator walked back up to the front of the room and called for questions. A young Ph.D. from Immunology held up his hand and asked, "Dr. Greerson, do you think this last case could have been due to the patient's immune system being activated somehow and recognizing the tumor? This has been reported before for other kinds of cancer – melanoma and renal cell cancer for example. The fever that GJ had could have been a side effect of that happening."

"It is certainly a possibility, but I don't know how you would prove it much less learn to control it. My point is that if we hadn't kept intervening to keep GJ alive, this wouldn't have had a chance to occur, whatever did happen."

After a few more questions, the Grand Rounds wrapped up. Meredith noticed Pillipitch looking at her strangely.

"A really bad sore throat, huh? Kind of like the one that dog, Butch, had and all the mice you told me about? Curious, isn't it?"

Crap, thought Meredith. *Pillipitch is too damn sharp. Besides myself, he is the only one who knows about the viral vector treatment and would make the connection between the animal work and Granner.* "Why yes, now that you mention it. I wonder if our viral treatment somehow stimulated the immune system like that immunologist suggested?"

"Ms. Jones, you would make a good poker player. Speaking hypothetically of course, if someone, unnamed, had given your grandmother an unauthorized treatment as a last ditch effort to save her life, that person would probably have broken a dozen or so regulations that could get her kicked out of medicine, even if the treatment worked. Now this person is in a real pickle since she doesn't want to delay a new cancer treatment that might help a lot of patients, but she doesn't dare talk about a key piece of evidence indicating how well it works."

"Speaking hypothetically, of course, that person would indeed be in real pickle as you have expressed it. Not only that person but probably anyone else connected with the treatment, even peripherally. Would you have any suggestions as to what that person might do?"

"Well, I think the full story would come out sooner or later. A lot would depend on how the public perceives what happened. Do they see it as some cowboy researcher with a blatant disregard for the rules, that are designed to keep things safe for the patient, or do they see it as someone who has helped to develop a brand new cure? That someone needed to use it without approval on a beloved family member because of having no time to go through official channels? Presented that way, that person might be considered a real heroine and get by with only a censoring note in their file, a slap on the wrist as it were. You know, a good reporter could help slant the story that way."

"And why would the reporter want to do that?"

"Ms. Jones, it would be a great human interest story, and there also would be follow-up stories on the ensuing investigation and whatever finally happens to the hypothetical person and the cancer cure. Why, it could be potential Pulitzer Prize stuff. All the reporter would probably want would be an exclusive on the story as it unfolds."

"I need to go to work, now but good seeing you again Mr. Pillipitch. Perhaps we will talk more another time."

The two shook hands and each embarked on the rest of their day – Meredith went to the lab to await word on how Jack's visit went at the NCI and Pillipitch to write a story based upon Greerson's lecture and to think about the story that he really wanted to write.

CHAPTER 52

AT 7 AM SEATTLE time, when Greerson was giving his talk, it was 10 AM at NCI headquarters in Rockville, Maryland, where Jack was being ushered into a small meeting room in Building 8070. His friend, Fred Alexander, and three other people were already there. Fred introduced them to Jack.

"Jack, this is Tom Burnet, my boss. These other two are Sonja Penchala and Eben Fiebelman. We have all read your proposal outline and are interested in learning more. As you know, this is a rapid decision program and so we have deliberately kept the review committee small."

Jack shook everyone's hands. He was happy, he said, to have gotten the chance to present his proposal. Fred asked Jack for his presentation, which he loaded onto a laptop computer connected to a projector. Jack spent about thirty minutes reviewing his underlying hypothesis. He explained the procedure by which the critical tumor control point was identified using a combination of measurements and theoretical calculations, the construction of the viral vector, and the experimental work done to date. He concluded with a description of Meredith's treatment of her grandmother. When he was finished, he called for questions.

Burnet spoke first. "So you're saying that each particular cancer may have a slightly different version of the regulatory control point and you need to construct a unique treatment for each person."

"Yes, that seems to be the situation. Based on the work we have done thus far, while there may be some similarities, a vector constructed for one tumor has only limited effectiveness when applied to another tumor. We all talk about 'individualized cancer treatment'; well this is it."

Penchala then asked, "How long did you say it takes to construct a viral vector once you have a tumor sample?"

"Right now it takes one to two weeks depending on the size of the control protein complex."

"How then would you be able to treat everyone with cancer rather than a select few?" she continued.

"When I first started out, I hadn't given that question much thought, but now I think it might work in the following way: With the right facility, you can work on many tumors at the same time by doing the procedures in parallel. I envision setting up regional centers run under contract to the federal government that would process tumors shipped to them, prepare the viral vectors, and then ship the vectors back to the patient's doctor."

Fiebelman then chimed in, "Let's just take it a step at a time. So at this point what you want from us is funding for a pilot study to treat an additional ten advanced-stage patients who have failed conventional treatment."

"Yes, but depending on the results for these pilot study patients, I would then like support to scale up the process so that we could do a good phase II trial with between fifty and one hundred patients. That's more virus than my lab can really handle, so this will mean setting up a larger facility for the amplification process."

"You could probably handle the first ten patients for the $250,000 which this program could award, but you'll need to apply for a larger grant for scaling up the process. This would best be done by collaborating with a commercial pharmaceutical company familiar with making a product under GMP conditions. Got anyone in mind?"

"The only one I have had any contact with is AVARTEC, which is based in Seattle. They might be interested." Jack thought that he could talk to Barbara Misaki about this.

There were several more questions of a technical nature about the modeling calculations, and then Fred asked Jack to leave the room while the committee talked among themselves. Jack went out into the reception area and sat down to wait anxiously. Even if his proposal was accepted, he still had to negotiate the award process gauntlet at State and finesse any IRB questions relating to Meredith's unapproved treatment of her grandmother.

Finally Fred came out and said to Jack, "So far no show stoppers, but Fiebelman wants to wait until tomorrow before voting on the proposal. He is concerned about the computing resources that would be required to do the modeling for a large number of cancer patients. Each calculation uses up several hours of supercomputer CPU time. By the way, you neglected to mention the cost of this if we moved into a hundred patient pilot study."

"Actually, I haven't been thinking so much about costs as about understanding the problem. Do you think the committee is going to approve the initial ten patient study?"

"Probably. But we won't know for sure until after the vote tomorrow. When is your flight back?"

"Tonight, but I can delay it if you want me to."

"No need. I think we have the information we need and can always get you on the phone if new questions come up. I will let you know as soon as a decision is made."

CHAPTER 53

THE NEXT SEVERAL WEEKS were a blur of activity for Jack and Meredith. The NCI had voted to approve funding for the ten-patient feasibility study and had given it their highest priority. That was good news indeed. However, things took longer to get into place at State. The Dean did not want to approve the grant because of the low indirect cost rate. Jack's department chairman argued vehemently that the dean had previously approved similar low rates for some pharmaceutical-company-sponsored trials. The IRB was concerned about the study going into humans at such an early stage. When told about the treatment of Meredith's grandmother, they had really gone ballistic. They called Jack a "cowboy" who was endangering patients and they demanded an investigation of his entire research program. To counter this, Jack and Meredith met with Pillipitch and turned him loose on the story. He quickly developed a human interest piece built around the discovery of a brand new approach to treating cancer patients. In his series of articles he alluded to the tradition of past great leaders in medicine who had experimented on themselves or their families and used as an example the work of Edward Jenner, who had infected his family with cowpox to protect them against smallpox which was the great scourge of his era. He also talked about the resistance of the medical establishment to radically new ideas and used the more recent example of a bacterium, Helicobacter pylori, which caused stomach ulcers. The conventional wisdom of the day was that ulcers were caused by stress and increased stomach acid output. He mentioned the honors and recognition, including the Nobel prize for medicine in 2005, that the Australian physicians, Warren and Marshall, had received for this after enduring years of ridicule. Following publication of Pillipitch's articles, the School of Medicine information office was inundated with phone calls from cancer patients and their families. All wanted to know how they could receive this new miracle treatment. Mark Emory, the university president, even got a call from the state governor urging him to intervene. Emory in turn called the dean and let him know that this project had attracted the attention of the governor and the legislature due to pressure raised by the voting public. With the budget for State coming up for discussion, there had better not be any screw-ups in getting this project launched. After this phone call the dean acquiesced and had his office sign off on Olivetti's grant. Peter Drisco protested vehemently. He wanted things held up until after he had made a deal with Olivetti. Jack and Meredith then went to the Cancer Consortium IRB, and in a special meeting got its approval for the ten-patient trial pending agreement on the wording in the protocol consent form. The IRB wasn't happy about being told to expedite its review and to eliminate any purely bureaucratic roadblocks. However, the scientific soundness of the project accompanied by the vote of confidence from the NCI persuaded the majority of the members to vote approval. The IRB chair, an elderly pathologist named Lisa Brandon, argued that this approval was premature, but she was outvoted. Jack and Meredith then composed an E-mail notice about the protocol and the type of patient they seeking for the study. They sent it to the clinical investigators treating cancer patients at State, using the Cancer Consortium list server.

Peter Drisco was somewhat mollified when the dean said, "Pete, I don't care if you do fire me as your consultant; I can't hold this project up. President Emory himself has gotten behind it. Rather than yelling and screaming, you need to sweet-talk Olivetti into partnering with your company in the second phase of the study, assuming that the pilot study is successful. I can help you with that."

The floodgates soon opened and more patients were referred for treatment than Jack's laboratory could handle. Jack did not have any clinical service of his own, so he needed to rely on attending physicians from other services to manage the patients on his protocol. He and Meredith decided to try and treat a spectrum of patients having different tumor types. The first patient they accepted was Wallace Jaworski, a long-time smoker with metastatic lung cancer who was currently on the medical oncology service. Jaworski's family had read Pillipitch's articles. They had asked the medical oncology attending physician, an intense, wiry individual named Tom Mellon, to see if Jaworski could be a study candidate.

Jack and Meredith met with Jaworski and then reviewed his case with Mellon. When Jaworski's tumor was discovered in his right lung one year previously, it was treated surgically, followed by chemotherapy. This provided only a short respite and Jaworski's tumor had now spread to his other lung, his liver, and the bones in his back, hips, and legs. This presented a problem since none of these areas was easily accessible, and fresh tumor tissue was needed to construct the virus.

"Dr. Mellon," said Jack, "Mr. Jaworski seems to be a good candidate. He certainly has widespread disease and has failed conventional treatment. It also looks like he will live the two weeks or so it will take to prepare the virus. However, we need a surgeon to go in and get fresh tumor tissue and to get it."

"How much tissue do you need? Your protocol wasn't very clear on this point," responded Mellon.

"At least one cubic centimeter," replied Meredith. "More if you can get it, just to have a cushion."

"Shouldn't be too hard," said Mellon. "Mr. Jaworski has plenty of tumor to spare. I think taking a chunk out of the liver metastases would be the easiest. I will ask Mikani what he thinks. Assuming that he agrees, what's the best way of getting the fresh tissue to you?"

Meredith quickly answered, "I can come to the OR and take the tissue when it is handed off the table. Then I can run it down to the lab and start the preparation."

Mellon paged Mikani and explained the problem to him.

"Tom, I'm in my office now. Give me Jaworski's medical record number and I will pull up his latest abdominal CT and take a look right now."

Mellon did so and listened on the phone to the clicking sound of Mikani's keyboard as he pulled up Jaworski's images. "Shouldn't be a problem. There is a large mass in the anterior part of the right lobe of the liver. We should be able to expose it and resect most of the nodule without difficulty. What's Jaworski's general medical condition?"

"A little emphysema because of his long smoking history and high blood pressure, controlled on medication. Nothing that would make him a high risk surgical candidate."

"OK then. I'm curious about this new treatment of Olivetti's. My part is pretty simple – just take out a chunk of tumor and hand it over. I assume that you and Olivetti will take care of the experimental part of the consent form and all I need to do is consent the patient for the biopsy?"

"That's about it. When do you think you can do the case?"

"I'll have to get back to you on that. A lot of the orthopods are away at one of their meetings this week, so some extra OR time has been freed up. The medical center would be happy to see it used."

Meredith, Jack, and Mellon went back into Jaworski's room and explained the protocol to him in detail, emphasizing its experimental nature and the unknown risks involved. A small surgical procedure would be necessary to get the tissue that was needed.

Wallace Jaworski interrupted, "I've read about this in the paper and at this point I don't have anything else to try. I want to live a while longer to see my grandkids grow up. Let's just get it done. Where do you want me to sign?" He grabbed the consent forms and signed them in duplicate. One copy went into his hospital chart and the second was kept in the investigator file for the protocol.

Jaworksi's surgery was scheduled for two days later. Meredith, wearing a set of surgical scrubs, went to the OR suite. She put on a bonnet, mask, and booties over her shoes before entering the sterile room itself. The OR team hovered about Jaworski who was completely out, courtesy of the anesthesiologist. His belly was open and the assisting resident was just spreading the abdominal wall to expose the liver. Meredith edged up to the table and peered over the shoulder of the resident. Mikani looked up inquiringly.

"Hello Dr. Mikani. I'm Meredith Jones from Professor Olivetti's lab. You probably don't remember me, but I did a surgical clerkship rotation with you a year or so ago."

"Hi Ms. Jones. Actually I do remember you. Have you found out yet when Whipple first reported his pancreatic resection operation? Mikani's phenomenal memory was legendary in the School of Medicine, but Meredith still found it disconcerting that he could recall a question and answer session that had taken place so long ago.

"It was 1935 as I recall."

303

Mikani laughed and said, "Very good Jones. You did learn something during your rotation. Now take a look at our patient here. See these grayish white lumps all through the liver – all tumor. Any particular one you would like us to take?"

"I just need a few cubic centimeters of tissue, so take whichever one is the easiest."

"We'll take this big one here," said Mikani pointing with the suction tip. "Pathology is going to insist on keeping some tissue, part of the Medical Center policy, you know. So we'll take it out and cut it in half; half for them and half for you."

The surgical team got busy and shortly Meredith was handed a chunk of tumor in a small container of saline solution.

"Hope this works," said Mikani as he passed off the tumor.

"I don't know," said the surgical resident. "This could put us cancer surgeons out of business."

"Not for a while," said Mikani. "Besides, there is always work for a good surgeon. The medical oncologists will be injecting the virus and collecting their fee for that. The ones who need to worry are the radiation oncologists, there might not be any need for their expensive technology in a few years."

"Oh well," responded the resident. "They can always retrain and become real doctors if they want."

Meredith quickly left the OR suite clutching the tumor container. She found Jack waiting for her in the lab. Together they removed the specimen, emulsified it, and started the analysis. Both of them were understandably anxious and kept rechecking each other's procedures. It was only a matter of time before the tumor genome was sequenced and probable control points identified. X-ray protein crystallography gave a good starting point and the upgraded computer architecture of *Deep Blue* at the University of Illinois made obtaining the final structure much quicker than before. Still,

Meredith and Jack were exhausted by the time the viral vector was constructed and the amplification process started in the bioreactor. The amplification process took just as long as before, but days later, all was in readiness. The two quickly loaded a syringe, went to the hospital area of the building and entered Jaworski's room. Jaworski was in some pain from the surgery and more than a little cranky. "Just inject the damn virus and let me go back to sleep," was all that he said.

Meredith quickly injected the virus into Jaworski's IV line and Jack noted the event in his medical record. Jack then called the housestaff in charge of Jaworski. He let them know that the virus had been injected.

"If things run true to form," he said, "Jaworski will be complaining of a hell of a sore throat in a few days. Just give him supportive care, and this will run its course."

Jack and Meredith returned to the lab, completed the documentation in their lab books, and then made a list of the requests of patients for entry onto the protocol. Of the eleven applicants, they quickly selected a young mother with advanced, inflammatory breast cancer; a retired military colonel with widely metastatic prostate cancer; and a dot.com executive with inoperable glioblastoma multiforme of the brain. It would take a month to have treatment underway on all three of these patients. Jack and Meredith were becoming acutely aware of the need to streamline the process to avoid delays in treating patients.

"That's enough for today," said Jack. "Tell you what – let me take you out for some Chinese food tonight to celebrate getting our first protocol patient treated."

Feeling the need to unwind and not wanting to cook dinner that evening Meredith quickly agreed. They decided on a restaurant called China Village not too far north of the university and agreed to meet there at 7 o'clock. When Meredith arrived at the restaurant, Jack was already there with a beer in front of him. Meredith sat down at the booth and ordered a beer herself while they perused the menu. They quickly negotiated the order starting with a sizzling rice soup, with chicken and seafood dishes to follow. Conversation was relaxed, with a tacit understanding not to talk too much about work. Each told the other about where they had grown up, their parents, and how they had gotten into medicine. Talk then turned to their hobbies, and they found that they had a lot in common there in terms of staying physically active, Jack with his running and Meredith with her biking.

Finally, Jack asked, "Meredith, what do you want to do now? You've accomplished a lot, particularly for someone who is still in medical school. Somehow I don't see you going back to the usual program of clerkships, internship, and residency."

"I really don't know. I love doing research that helps people. But I know that if I'm going to really do anything with it, I need to complete the work for my MD and be able to treat patients. I want to stay in the cancer field, so thought I would look for a program that combines research and clinical training. Do you have any suggestions?"

"There are some good programs back east – at Harvard and the NCI for example. I know some people there, and I can put in a good word for you. If our work turns out like I think it is going to, you are going to be in high demand. Juggling research and clinical training takes a lot of dedication. You need to get into the right lab, where the leader is supportive of your doing both."

"Jack, what about yourself? Where do you see yourself in five years?"

"I really don't know. If you had asked me that question six months ago, I would have answered here at State, as an associate professor with a bigger lab and more postdocs. Now I'm seriously considering whether it makes sense to move into Pharma. It is possible to get things done a lot faster there, and the bureaucracy here at State is beginning to wear me down. The Pharma pay is better too, but I would like to think that wouldn't be the biggest factor in my decision since I've never really had any desire to acquire things."

"Isn't Pharma research more directed though? Would you still have the opportunity to do something completely new and different like you would at a university?"

"Some companies have 'blue sky' research groups that are pretty much free to do what they want. Of course, this is a small part of their overall research program, which is really directed to turning out new commercial products. Still, this isn't too different from a university. People there work on the same topic for years and years because it is a safe way to keep the funding up for their labs. They only sneak in the 'blue sky' stuff on the side, like we did when we started out with the viral vector work. That's something that has to change if we are really going to make any meaningful progress."

Meredith agreed. When the bill came, she tried to pay half, but Jack refused. This was his treat. When the two left the restaurant, Jack walked Meredith to her car where she impulsively gave him a hug and thanked him for dinner. Jack found himself thinking about the hug as he drove back to his apartment. Meredith was so different from Barbara Misaki. No hidden agenda, unless you counted treating her grandmother on the sly, and he couldn't fault her for that.

CHAPTER 54

DURING THE FOLLOWING WEEKS, Meredith and Jack found themselves evolving into a real research team. Each took on specific parts of the treatment program without a lot of discussion being necessary. Meredith visited Jaworski twice a day, reviewed his medical chart and talked with him. Sure enough, he developed the same horrendous sore throat that her grandmother had experienced, but unlike Gaby, he was quite cantankerous; he complained about it at great length to anyone who came into the room. The medical team kept fluid support going and did cultures to see if anything other than the injected adenovirus was to blame. Now that they knew what to look for, the lab found high titer levels of the viral vector; other than that, only the species of virus and bacteria normally found in the human throat. Jaworski got better and was discharged with instructions to come back to the clinic in one month to get a total body CT/PET scan. It would be paid for by the NCI grant. During the month, the same treatment was given to the three other patients whom Jack and Meredith had selected. On his return Jaworski's CT/PET showed some small, residual masses in the liver that were not metabolically active; everything else had disappeared completely. Mellon was amazed. He couldn't stop talking about Jaworski to the other attendings on the medical oncology service. The treatment also apparently cured the young mother with breast cancer and the retired colonel with prostate cancer, but it had no affect on the dot. com CEO with the brain tumor.

Jack was in continual contact with Fred Alexander back at the NCI. Fred was getting more and more enthused as the results came in. During one of their telephone conversations, Fred said, "Jack, we are all excited about your study. We've had a brainstorming session about why things didn't work on the glioblastoma patient, but did work on an animal model brain tumor. We think it is because of the tumor location. You injected the animal tumor into the mouse's body, and the virus found it. Because of the blood-brain barrier, the virus didn't get into the brain and infect it. That's probably a good thing; otherwise all of your patients would have gotten encephalitis and perhaps some would have died from it. That would have shut down the project."

"But why did it work on metastatic disease in the brain?"

"We thought about that too. Probably because it was a different type of tissue; one that the virus could infect. Also, there is a breakdown of the blood-brain barrier at the junction between the metastasis and the brain."

"This gives me some ideas to work on. Perhaps injecting the virus directly into the brain tumor would work, although that could still cause encephalitis. Perhaps I could use a different type of viral vector."

"Jack, don't get too sidetracked. Even if your treatment doesn't work on primary brain tumors, it still looks like a real home run. You need to complete your pilot study, but don't take on any more primary brain tumor patients. Once we get the larger study up and going, you can go back to thinking about improvements. I don't think you fully appreciate the impact your work is going to have on the field even if you never cure primary brain tumors. View the glass as being 90 percent full and be happy; don't worry about the empty 10 percent."

"OK, but it still bothers me."

The excitement at State kept building, and the remaining six patients authorized on the pilot study were quickly enrolled. It took just over two months to finish the treatments on the ten patients. Jack and Meredith were exhausted from the continuous stress by the time this was completed. Early follow-up results were outstanding with every patient showing essentially complete resolution of their tumor at the four to six week visit. On her second set of follow-up studies, Gaby continued to show no evidence of tumor. Wallace Jaworski's residual nodule showed no change indicating that it was most likely just scar tissue left behind when the tumor cells died. Jack called Fred Alexander and told him the news.

"Fred, looks like your bet on us paid off. Except for the one patient with the primary brain tumor, everyone else has responded to the treatment. We need to talk about next steps."

"Jack, congratulations. Everyone in the division is excited about this. It's unbelievable that the first special project grant paid off like this. Do you have any grant money left?"

"Just about $10,000. The rest went to pay for the hospitalization costs for the patients."

"OK, here's what I want you to do. Prepare a presentation for us on the results and a proposal to do the larger study we talked about. Plan for about a hundred patients. It's time to get a biotech firm involved to streamline the process and prepare the treatments more quickly. I think you had mentioned approaching AVARTEC about this. Do you want to talk to them first or do you want me to?"

Jack thought of Misaki. "I know someone fairly high up in the company. Let me give her a call and see if they're interested."

"Fine. It would be nice to have a specific company identified when you prepare your proposal for phase II. Two other things: You need to write up this material for publication. If I were you, I would try to get it in the New England Journal. Secondly, when you come out, bring your assistant with you. She sounds like a real up and comer and we'd like to get a look at her, maybe talk her into spending some time with us at the NCI when she finishes her degree."

Jack responded, "Meredith is a really sharp young woman all right, and spending some research time at the NCI would be good for her career. I'll ask her to come along."

Jack then placed a call to Barbara Misaki whose secretary answered the phone.

My name is Jack Olivetti of State University and I would like to talk to Dr. Misaki about a possible research agreement with AVARTEC."

"Oh, Professor Olivetti, Dr. Misaki told me that you might be calling her, but that was several weeks ago. Let me page her for you."

It only took a few minutes for Misaki to answer. "Dr. Misaki here."

"Hi Barbara, this is Jack. Do you have a few minutes to talk?"

"Sure. Since I haven't heard from you for a while, I assume this is business and not personal. What can I do for you?"

Jack explained the pilot study that had been funded by the NCI, the excellent results he had obtained for the first ten patients, and the proposed larger phase II study that would involve a larger number of patients. "… and so I would like AVARTEC to make the viral vectors for this phase II study," he concluded.

"Jack, this is going to require some discussion with people higher up in the food chain than I. One thing I know they are going to want to see is the agreement you signed with the NCI for the pilot study, so bring that to the meeting, assuming I can get it set up. Let me make a few calls and get back to you."

"Thanks Barbara. About my not calling you, I'm sorry, but I've been totally immersed in this project. You know how hectic things can get with a big project coming due. Getting the material ready to treat those ten patients has kept me and my lab going full time."

"We can talk about it later," Misaki said hanging up. Jack thought to himself, *I could have called her before this if I really wanted to, but I didn't. Why was that anyway?*

With a sigh, Jack turned to his computer and put his word processing program into outline mode. He started working on a manuscript describing his theory and the protocol study. He took the outline of the first part of the manuscript from the presentation he had given at ASCO, and the discussion of the experimental results from his laboratory notebooks. He decided to ask Meredith to prepare a table summarizing the patient results and then began work on the manuscript itself. When he finally looked up, it was nearly 8 o'clock and everyone else in the lab had gone home for the night. He printed out a copy of his outline and left it on Meredith's desk. An attached note told her to summarize the patient results in the form of a table; he indicated on the outline where it would go. He stopped by the IMA for a short workout and then at the Village Shopping Center for a quick bite before going to his apartment and crashing for the night.

It was late morning the next day before he heard back from Misaki. "Jack, the meeting is for 6 PM the day after tomorrow. I will be there and so will Art Jenkins and Peter Drisco himself. Just come to the AVARTEC building entrance and someone will take you up to the meeting room. See you then and don't forget to bring the NCI agreement with you."

Jack and Meredith worked on the manuscript the rest of the day, but were continually interrupted by phone calls from clinicians wanting to put patients on the pilot study. Some were very upset when told that the pilot study was finished and the phase II study not yet opened. Normally sanguine, Tom Mellon, the medical oncology attending physician, reacted by exclaiming, "What do you mean you can't treat anyone else right now? I've got a patient whose pancreatic cancer is killing him. He can't wait while you and the IRB decide whether or not to treat any more patients right now. I'm going to go to the IRB myself and demand that they let this project continue until the phase II study is ready."

Mellon was true to his work and insisted on a special meeting of the IRB which he, Meredith, and Jack attended. The head of the IRB, Dr. Lisa Brandon, had been appointed to her position because of her anal adherence to regulations. Dr. Brandon's stance was firm – the pilot study allowed for treating ten patients; ten patients had been treated; and that was it until another study was approved. Brandon told the group, "This protocol was rushed through, and we need time to see the results. Dr. Olivetti needs to analyze his data thoroughly to make sure that there aren't any hidden complications that will show up months from now. This board is not going to approve extending it right now."

The entreaties of Mellon and Olivetti were in vain. Meredith was appalled and decided to let Pillipitch know what was going on. She hoped that he would write a story that would pressure the Medical Center to allow patient treatments to continue. Pillipitch did just exactly that, and the next day his article's headline read

BUREAUCRATIC DELAYS DENY CANCER CURE TO PATIENTS.

Dean Schmitt was apoplectic when he read the article. *What was that bitch Brandon thinking of? Didn't she realize how bad this looked in the paper?* Not wanting another conversation with

President Emory, he called Helen Gowan, the chief administrator for Human Subjects Review, and asked her to straighten things out. Brandon backed down after a special committee, which included the chair of pathology, reviewed the matter and concluded that for a dying patient, the risk of continuing the study was less than the risk of not performing the treatment. To make matters worse from Brandon's perspective, Children's Oncology wanted to refer a pediatric patient with very advanced rhabdomyosarcoma that had proven unresponsive to chemotherapy using their own compassionate treatment protocol. The study waiver was granted and patient treatments were allowed to continue. Brandon was not happy and threatened to resign as the IRB Committee chair to the delight of everyone else on the committee. To their chagrin, she didn't actually follow through with this threat. She vowed to file a formal complaint with the NCI about what she felt was a blatant disregard for the rules, but since the NCI was backing the protocol, no one was worried about this.

At the appointed time, Jack drove into the visitor parking lot of the AVARTEC building. Although it was 6 PM, a receptionist was still on duty in the entry area, and after Jack had signed the security log and received a coded visitor's badge, she directed him to the elevator. "Dr. Drisco's office is on the fifth floor. Just turn right and walk down the hall."

Jack followed her directions and entered the reception area for Peter Drisco's office. Patti escorted him into the inner office where he found Misaki, Jenkins, and Peter Drisco himself waiting. Jenkins got up from his chair, walked over to Jack and said, "Good to see you again. You know Barbara, of course, and this is Peter Drisco, the founder of AVARTEC."

Drisco got up, shook Jack's hand and said, "Glad to finally meet you. I've been hearing great things about your work from these two. Would you like coffee or anything?"

Jack replied, "Nice to meet you too. Coffee would be nice if you have it handy. Just black."

Drisco nodded to Patti who quickly poured Jack a cup of steaming coffee from a carafe on a corner table. Everyone took a seat. Drisco leaned forward and began the meeting. "I understand from Barbara that you want AVARTEC to participate in a Phase II trial using a new treatment you've developed."

Jack nodded and quickly summarized his treatment methodology, the animal data, and the results of the ten-patient pilot study. By now he was practiced in giving this spiel concisely. He concluded by saying, "What we need is someone who can make the treatment virus faster so that we can treat a undred patients in a reasonable time. It's a little unusual in that we don't need larger amounts of the same virus, but need a way of rapidly making small amounts of different viruses. This means a facility with a lot of bioreactor tanks to amplify the generated viruses along parallel tracks. My conversations with Barbara lead me to think that your company is uniquely positioned to do this."

"True," said Jenkins. "But it would mean taking some of our other projects off line for a while, and I'm not sure that we want to do that. Some of these projects are close to producing a marketable product."

"Art, we might," interjected Peter Drisco, "if it would give us an advantageous position for future development. Jack, we wouldn't be interested if it just means cooking viruses for you, but if we could get involved in the analysis of the tumor material and the determination of the blocking antisense strands for the tumor control sites, then we might be. Besides, you are going to need some help in this area too."

Jack leaned back in his chair, took a sip of his coffee, and thought a bit. *Peter Drisco is right about that. It would really strain Meredith and himself to analyze the tumor material for a hundred patients. He had thought about recruiting some additional people but it might be easier to have AVARTEC do this.* "I don't see why not, but I would need to talk about this with the people at the NCI."

"Go ahead. I am pretty sure that they want to fast track this based on what you've told me. It's not often that they get such high impact results in such a short time and they will want to push it for all its worth."

Misaki then spoke up. "Speaking of the NCI, did you bring along a copy of your contract agreement with them as I asked."

"Sure enough. It's right here in my case." Jack got it out and handed it over to her. "But I'm not sure why you wanted it since this new work will be under a separate agreement."

Jenkins spoke up, "We just need to be sure we know what we are getting into. Our attorneys insist on that. Tell you what, let me put together a proposal and cost term sheet for doing the work on one hundred patients for you to look at. I'm sure we can agree on something, and you can take it to the NCI when you go back next week. While we are gearing up for the project, we can send some people to your lab to learn how you do the structural analysis and modeling for the control protein and link it back to the gene element which you need to block. Then we can take over the work on that as well, with your oversight, of course. Have you thought any more about that consulting position that Barbara talked with you about? No reason why we can't pay you for doing something that you would be doing anyway."

Jack said he would think about it, and the meeting broke up. Misaki escorted him to the elevator where they said goodbye. Then she returned to Drisco's office and joined the discussion.

Drisco was saying, "Have our attorneys take a look at this agreement and draft our proposal such that we maintain intellectual rights to anything new that we develop in connection with this. Also, when you prepare the cost estimate, pad it with as much overhead as you think we can get away with. The NCI is going to want to fast track this, and we are in a pretty strong bargaining position."

Misaki spoke up, "I don't see how this is really going to benefit AVARTEC. In fact, if it works, it might just put us and a lot of other companies out of business."

Drisco chuckled, "Other companies, yes, us, no. I'm sure we can find a way to twist the process such that we improve it, at least on paper, and then end up with the rights to it. Olivetti has really come up with a new approach, and the data look outstanding. It is going to change how we treat most cancers – truly individualized treatment without any long-term side effects. Instead of cranking out a lot of a drug that is weakly active for a lot of cancers, we are going to set up an assembly line system cranking out individually-designed viruses for each patient. The number of patients we can handle is going to be determined solely by the size of the production plant we build. We are going to probably want several facilities scattered across the country and then across the world. Whoever controls this is going to move to the head of the Forbes list of wealthy companies. Doing well by doing good. I like it! Barbara, it would really help if we could get Olivetti signed on as a consultant – work on that. Art, get a draft of the proposal and term sheet to me by the day after tomorrow. Yes, I know it's a Saturday but just send them to me via E-mail. And with that, the meeting broke up. Each reflected upon the next steps to accomplish.

CHAPTER 55

JACK BLANCHED WHEN HE saw the bottom line on the cost term sheet from Drisco. Five million dollars to prepare viral vectors for a hundred patients! That was $50,000 a patient just for doing something that his lab discovered in the first place. At that rate his lab could have earned $500,000 on the ten pilot study patients, which would have greatly helped his funding situation. Maybe Misaki was right – he was at the wrong end of this business. Jack folded these figures in with the rest of his proposal which mainly consisted of a data management piece to keep track of the patient study information and the cost of CT/PET studies to be performed prior to the treatment and then again at three and twelve months following administration of the virus. Adding in some salary support for himself, Meredith, and some of his laboratory personnel, the net cost of the study was just south of ten million dollars. And that was just for the direct costs. The indirect costs, excluding the subcontract pass-through to AVARTEC brought the total up to $12.5 million. Jack ran the numbers by Bremenhoff as a reality check.

"Jack," said Bremenhoff, "these numbers look OK to me. While they might seem high to you, they really are in keeping with the costs of other clinical trials. That's why it can take hundreds of millions of dollars to bring a new drug to market, counting the costs of all the underlying research before you even get to the clinical trial stage. Your work has cut short a lot of this. The NCI isn't going to balk at these numbers."

Bremenhoff was right. When Jack and Meredith went back to the NCI to present the results of the pilot study with updated patient results and submit a proposal for the phase II study, no one blinked an eye at the numbers. The group convened in the same conference room where Jack had made his original presentation. Jack introduced Meredith to Fred Alexander who in turn introduced her to Tom Burnet, Sonja Penchala and Eben Fiebelman. In his presentation, Jack quickly summarized the updated results for the ten patients on the initial pilot study. Other than the patient with the glioblastoma, who did not respond to the treatment, everyone else was alive and showed no recurrent cancer.

Alexander turned to Meredith and said, "And what about your grandmother, Ms. Jones? Is she doing well too?"

Meredith flushed slightly and replied, "Yes, my grandmother's ovarian cancer has gone away completely and she is as busy as ever."

"It was really gutsy on your part, to treat your grandmother so early in the game. What if it hadn't worked, and she'd had some bad side effects?"

"I would have been sorry of course, but I would have been even sorrier if she had died without my trying to do anything."

"I would have felt the same way in your place," said Alexander. He then turned to his colleagues and asked, "Any questions?"

Sonja Penchala spoke first. "So, including Ms. Jones's grandmother, this has been tried on eleven people and te of these apparently have been cured of their cancer. The only one where there wasn't a response was the man with the primary brain tumor. Looking over the list of diagnoses, this was the only primary brain tumor patient that you treated, correct?"

Jack answered, "Yes, after the treatment failed on him, we chose other types of tumors. It may have been a fluke, but my thoughts are along the same line as yours. This particular virus doesn't get into nerve tissue, and so didn't get into the brain tumor. The treatment did seem to work on metastases in the brain from other types of tumors."

Fiebelman interjected, "The failure in the case of the one brain tumor patient could have been a fluke. We need to treat some more patients with primary brain tumors before we can say for sure whether or not it works on them. You say that your IRB is letting you extend the pilot study while we are gearing up for the larger phase II trial. Why don't you try to include one or two more brain tumor patients just to see what happens? If it doesn't work on them, maybe the answer is to use a different type of virus for them, one that can infect the brain."

Burnet said, "I agree about treating a few more brain tumor patients, but let's don't lose focus here. I don't want Jack fooling around with other types of viruses right now. He needs to concentrate on the one he is using in which everything has been worked out. Still, this would be a good area for future research."

Jack and Meredith were excused from the room while the NCI group discussed things further. They helped themselves to coffee in the anteroom while they waited. After a sip, they both made a face. The coffee had clearly been made a while ago, very unlike the excellent brew Jack had received at AVARTEC, even at the end of the day.

After a while Alexander came out and said, "Burnet is going to put in a formal request for money for the trial. An amount this large needs to be approved by the director. I don't think there is going to be any problem, We will just shift money from some less promising projects. Do you have time for lunch and then a tour of our laboratory before you catch your plane? I would like to show Meredith the lab, and there have been a lot of changes since you were last here, Jack."

Meredith nodded, "Thanks, I would really like to see the lab. I have heard that it is a good place to do postdoctoral studies. I thought I would apply after finishing up at State. Our plane doesn't leave until tomorrow morning, so we have plenty of time."

"That's great. Jack usually catches the evening flight out of Reagan National, and doesn't have time to socialize."

Jack spoke up. "Fred, you know how it is trying to keep a lab going. But this time we decided to fly back from Dulles in order to stop at the Aerospace Museum there. They have the space shuttle Enterprise on exhibit. Have you seen it yet?"

"Can't say that I have. You tourists stay on top of things like this better than we locals do."

"When I was growing up, I wanted to be an astronaut. I still wish I could find a way to take a ride on a shuttle."

Looking curiously at Jack, Meredith asked, "So what happened to change your mind? How did you end up in medicine rather than aeronautical engineering?"

"Partly for practical reasons. My vision and reaction time wouldn't let me be a pilot, and it was becoming clear that the country's commitment to space exploration was waning; the funding was going to other areas, like cancer. Also, I had a very close uncle die of cancer. Funny, I haven't thought about him in a long time, but his death certainly played a part in how I ended up."

As they were talking, Fred led them to another building where his division's laboratories were located. The equipment was pretty much standard, just like back at State, except more extensive in scope. The investigators were happy to take the time to talk to Meredith and Jack and explain what they were doing. In turn they asked Jack and Meredith about their work and followed up with numerous technical questions. Clearly, most of them were aware of their project and its current high priority status.

On the way back to the administration building Fred said to the two of them, "As you can see, there is a great deal of interest in what you are doing. You need to get something written up for publication soon to establish a priority. Meredith, there aren't many people who have a strong background in biology and computer science like you do. I hope that you will stay in research and consider coming here to the NCI for a postdoc after you finish up."

Jack and Meredith caught a cab back to their hotel. Each had brought some running clothes, and they agreed to meet in the lobby and go for a run before dinner. The Washington area weather was cool, so they wore running pants and long sleeved shirts made of one of the newer synthetics that wick sweat away from the body. As they were stretching out, Meredith found herself noticing Jack's well toned body for the first time. The tight running clothes showed it off, unlike the baggy, comfortable clothes he generally wore in the lab. "You look like you stay in shape," was her comment.

"I find that running helps me relax and clears my head. I try to hit the trail at least four times a week when I'm in Seattle. I used to run a lot more when I was in college. How about yourself?"

"I like to exercise too, generally I bike rather than run. When the weather is crappy, like it generally is during the winter, I tend to use the stationary bicycles in State's student athletic facility."

The two started off at an easy pace, turned left at the street, and found their way into an upscale residential neighborhood. The trees were starting to bud and a few birds were chirping in the background. They ran in place while waiting for the traffic to clear at a busy street, and then continued their run on the other side.

"Jack, going back to our conversation this morning, do you ever regret not becoming an astronaut?"

"I do have regrets at times. Mostly I've been satisfied that I chose molecular biology, and I really do like the idea of my research helping people, but still, the glamour and excitement of being an astronaut is seductive." Unconsciously, they had stepped up their pace and both were beginning to pant as they continued to talk. "*Huff, huff,* how about you? Any secret loves besides medicine?"

"*Pant,* Marine biology. I grew up spending summers on the beach with my grandparents and loved turning over rocks to see what would crawl out. My granddad got me a cheap microscope for my nineth birthday, and looking at the algae and diatoms in the water drops really turned me on. Still, I liked the idea of being a doctor and helping people."

"Much of the practice of medicine is routine and boring. Same diseases each day, just different people. Besides, when people think of a doctor, they think about an idealized Marcus Welby type – you know – a family practice doctor who has the luxury of spending enough time with a patient to get to know him, diagnosing complex diseases, and so on. Reality is a different story. Those guys are on a real treadmill these days having to see at least five or six patients per hour just to make office expenses and earn a decent living. Anybody with a complicated medical problem gets referred out to a specialist. At least with the larger group practices these days, they're not on call 24/7."

They ran for about 30 minutes and covered close to four miles according to the jogging map they had obtained at the hotel desk. Then they turned back.

"Most people in my medical school class won't even consider family practice for that very reason. During our first year we get all these lectures stressing the importance of family physicians and how highly ranked the State Family Practice program is, but not too many people bite," said Meredith. "Everyone wants to be either a radiologist, a dermatologist, or a plastic surgeon specializing in boob implants or face lifts."

"Good choices in terms of making a good living and having a decent lifestyle. But still boring as hell in terms of the daily work. That's why I went into research. I was more afraid of being bored than of being broke."

"I think I'm probably like that too. I will probably stay in research, but will want to do some patient care as well."

"It's hard to do both well. Research funding is highly competitive and not something you can do part time, not if you want to keep a lab going. New faculty often start out doing both, but find that after a while they switch to one or the other. Either that or give up any life outside of medicine."

"You've gotten a Ph.D. as well as an M.D. Do you need both to be successful?"

"It certainly helps. While I could do most of what I do with just the Ph.D., I couldn't actually treat patients. Having the M.D. also gets you a better salary, even for the same work as a Ph.D. You've got to be somewhat practical also."

"Your friend, Alexander, hinted strongly that I should apply for a fellowship at the NCI. What do you think about that?"

"It's a good choice. You're learning a lot in my lab, but it's good to see how other people do things. You also could benefit from some mentoring in grantsmanship, and Fred is an expert at that. Fred and his people review a lot of proposals, and you can learn from them what works and what doesn't when it comes to getting funded."

Jack was looking at Meredith when he stepped off the curb, and came down wrong, and twisting his left ankle. He stumbled and swore softly, "Damnit all to hell. That hurts." He began to limp.

"What's wrong?" Meredith inquired.

"Oh, I just turned my ankle. It is my left one and I've had problems with it off and on for years ever since I injured it while on a hike in the Cascades."

"Do you need any help getting back? I can run to the hotel and pick up a cab and come back for you."

"It's not that bad. We are almost back to the hotel anyway."

"Look, let me walk on your left. Put your arm over my shoulder. That way I can give you some support."

Jack hesitated, and Meredith said, "Don't be macho about this. Either let me help you back or wait here until I can get a cab. You know what they say about treating a sports injury like this, RICE.

"RICE – rest, ice, compression, and elevation. Yes, I remember that from my emergency room rotation. I'll start that when I get back to my room. Thanks for the reminder."

Jack put his hand on Meredith's shoulder and leaned on her as they hobbled the remaining blocks to the hotel and turned up the driveway. He noticed that in spite of the run, she had a clean, pleasant odor about her, quite different from that emitted by his locker room cronies after a workout. *Must be a girl thing*, he thought to himself. Meredith helped Jack through the lobby and into the elevator. She deposited him in his room and then went to fill his ice bucket for him. They agreed to meet at 7 for dinner in the lobby unless Jack felt that he needed more rest for his ankle. Jack took a couple of ibuprofen tablets, used a plastic bag from his room's wastebasket to hold the ice against his ankle, and propped his leg up on an ottoman in the corner of the room. He stayed like this until almost 6:30 when he got up to get ready for dinner. His ankle was still tender, but at least he was moving better.

A little before 7 o'clock, Jack heard a knock on his door and hobbled over to open it. Meredith was holding an ACE compression bandage in her hand. "The C in RICE," she said holding it up. I asked the desk clerk if there was a drug store nearby, and it turned out that there was one only a few blocks away – in the opposite direction from the route we ran."

Jack sat down in the chair and propped his foot up on the ottoman while Meredith expertly wrapped his ankle and foot. He had to admit that it felt better with the wrapping. "Many thanks," Jack said. "In return for your kind ministrations, dinner is on me. Hotel restaurant OK? I don't think I'm up to much walking right now."

The two went down the hall to the elevators with Meredith adjusting her pace to accommodate Jack's. The menu was surprisingly good featuring Chesapeake Bay crab cakes as the special of the day. Both chose the crab cakes preceded by a salad. Each declined the wine in favor of a beer, a Hefeweizen brewed locally. Talk over dinner turned to what would happen after they got back to Seattle.

Jack was musing as much to himself as Meredith. "It sounds like the NCI is willing to pay AVARTEC's price for preparing the agent for the phase II study. Boy, it will be a relief not to have to push Bryon and the other techs so hard to make the vectors, but we are still going to have to direct and monitor the work. This is going to be all new to AVARTEC and according to their CEO, they don't have anyone right now with the necessary computer expertise."

"Looks like I have job security then," replied Meredith. "At least I assume that you are going to want me to stay involved with the calculations and analysis."

"Actually, they will probably want to hire you as well as me. They seem fixated on trying to control things through intellectual property agreements. Guess that's the way things are done in the corporate world."

Meredith exclaimed, "I don't think I would like that. You know, being obligated to AVARTEC after what they did in reducing the scope of one of the lab's presentations at ASCO. Can't I just continue to work for your grant?"

"You can if you want, but AVARTEC would probably pay you a lot more."

"That's not a problem. I don't like to talk about it, but I have some money in a trust fund that was set up as part of the settlement after my parents were killed in an accident. Granner and Ed took me in and wouldn't take any money from the fund for raising me. The interest has been mostly accumulating. Unlike most medical students, I won't be in debt when I finish, and I can pick a specialty based on what I really like doing."

"I had no idea you were so well fixed. Brainy, beautiful, and rich to boot."

Meredith flushed and said, "I don't want people thinking about money when they look at me. That's why I don't talk about it. I don't know why I told you tonight."

Jack's face took on a sheepish expression. "Meredith, I apologize for saying what I did. I truly think you are a remarkable person, and your attitude just makes me admire you more. Now let's change the subject. Are you interested in dessert?"

"No, just some decaf coffee, perhaps a mocha if they can do one?"

"Let's find out." Jack called the waiter over and found that they could indeed make espresso drinks. Meredith ordered her mocha and Jack his usual cappuccino made with skim milk. Both chose the unleaded versions because of the lateness of the hour. When walking back to the elevator, Meredith noticed that Jack was limping more than before. When she quizzed him about it, he admitted that it did hurt more than it had on the way down to the restaurant.

"Probably because of sitting with my leg down during dinner. Unless things improve a lot by morning, I probably won't be able to walk around at the Dulles Aerospace Museum, but you certainly should go see it. I will just meet you at the gate."

"No way Jack. Remember, that for me it was marine biology, not astronautics, as an alternative to medicine. I would enjoy it more with you guiding me through the exhibits and explaining things to me. But I agree that you shouldn't do any unnecessary walking right now, so let's just sleep in and catch a later cab to the airport."

Meredith walked Jack back to his room and as she left him at the door she lightly kissed his cheek and said, "Jack, thanks for dinner, and remember about keeping my financial situation quiet."

Unbidden, Jack took hold of Meredith's shoulders and kissed her back. Slowly she responded and then flushed, broke away and said, "Goodnight. See you in the morning. Should we try to catch a cab around 10:30 or 11?"

"Eleven sounds about right. See you in the morning."

Jack entered his hotel room thinking, *I shouldn't have done that. A good way for a professor to get into trouble is to fool around with one of his students. It's one of the few things that can get even a tenured professor fired.*

Meredith quickly walked down the hall to her own room thinking about all the stories she had heard about students and professors getting involved. Such things almost never worked out well. *But Jack is awfully sweet and I enjoyed the kiss,* she thought. *Just don't rush things.*

On the cab ride to the airport the next day and during the flight home, they talked animatedly about many things, but carefully avoided any mention of the kiss the night before. A couple of times Meredith thought that Jack was about to say something about it, but at the last minute he seemed to hesitate, and the conversation went in a different direction.

CHAPTER 56

George Lattimer, the Chairman of Radiation Oncology, also liked to exercise but unlike Jack and Meredith, his thing was swimming. He did this early in the morning at his club before heading into work. A radiation oncologist, unlike a surgeon, didn't have to be at work at a ridiculously early hour. He hated missing his morning swim in order to attend an early meeting set to accommodate the surgery schedule. He changed into his racing suit, draped a towel around his shoulders, and walked towards the outdoor pool. As he left the locker room he noted that the pool temperature was 82°, at least that was what was noted on the white board near the doorway. That was a lot warmer than the air temperature, which was in the high 40s, but seemed even chillier because of the light drizzle. In spite of it being 5:30 AM, someone was already swimming laps in the pool. It was Clyde, a businessman with a similar early morning workout schedule. There was a time when he and Clyde were competing with each other to be first in the pool. Each coveted the lap lane on the south side, which was protected from other swimmers by a string of floats. After they had gotten their arrivals to as early as 4:30 AM, by tacit agreement, they worked their way back to the 5:30 AM time. Besides, since the club didn't open officially until 6 AM, they thought sooner or later one of the attendants would complain about their increasingly early arrivals.

Lattimer liked to reflect on things and plan his day as he swam his laps. He was an experienced swimmer, and his workout was pretty much automatic. Stroke, stroke, stroke, breath, stroke, stroke, stroke, breath – turning his head in alternate directions as he took his breaths. Down to the end of the pool, then a flip turn and back again. Most mornings he ground out 2000 yards before going to work. This morning he was reflecting on a conversation he had had the day before with one of his senior residents. They were seeing a man in his 50s with an inoperable head and neck cancer.

The resident had presented the patient's history and physical findings. Before Lattimer and the resident went back into the room to examine the patient together, Lattimer engaged in the time honored academic practice of *pimping the resident* to see how much she knew about how to treat head and neck cancer. *Pimping* consisted of asking a set of questions starting with the general and then moving to the specific.

"Christine, how would you stage this patient?"

"I would stage him as having a T4N2bM0 squamous cell carcinoma of the oral tongue. His tumor extends into the deep muscles of the tongue, which makes him a T4, and he has neck nodes on both sides of his neck, none of which are greater than six cm in size, which makes him an N2b. His metastatic workup, which consists of a chest CT scan and a cancer panel, was negative which makes him an M0." Christine had played the *pimping* game before and knew how to respond.

"How should he be treated?" asked Lattimer.

"Ideally, you would like to treat advanced head and neck cancer patients using surgery followed by a combination of radiotherapy and chemotherapy, but this patient's tumor is so large that it would mean cutting out his entire tongue leaving him really debilitated. So I would recommend skipping the surgery, and treating with radiotherapy and concurrent cis-platin chemotherapy, perhaps with the addition of cetuximab. The latest phase III trial from the Radiation Therapy Oncology Group showed a benefit when cetuximab was added to radiotherapy and concurrent chemotherapy."

"How large was the benefit?"

"At three years there was an absolute increase in local control from 61 percent to 72 percent which was statistically significant."

"What about survival? Was there also an advantage there?"

"There was, but it was much less. From 45 percent to 50 percent which did not reach statistical significance."

"And why was that?"

"The number of patients on the study was too small for this difference to be significant. The difference could have just been due to random chance. As you know, head and neck cancer patients tend to die from other things even if their tumors are controlled. Things like second cancers, tobacco- and alcohol-related illnesses ... things like that."

"So what should we recommend to him?"

"A few months ago, this would have been easy. I would have recommended radiation with chemotherapy and cetuximab, but now I'm not so sure."

"Oh, and why is that?"

"This patient has heard about Professor Olivetti's new trial and asked about joining that. The trial was mentioned to him by the house staff who were taking care of him in the hospital."

"Olivetti's trial shows considerable promise, but at this stage only about ten patients have been treated on it. It's only open to terminal patients, who don't have any other forms of treatment available to them. This patient certainly doesn't fit into that category; you've said that with a proven treatment, he has a 50 percent chance of being cured of his disease."

"Yes, but with pretty bad side effects, among which are a bad sore throat most likely requiring a feeding tube during treatment, a dry mouth afterward with loss of taste and problems with his teeth for years."

Lattimer and Christine went into the clinic area where they looked at the patient's MRI scan from a few days before. The tumor was indeed a T4 and extended well across the midline of the tongue base. Surgery would indeed require removing almost all of the tongue. They entered the room where the patient waited, and Christine introduced Lattimer as her attending. Lattimer sat down and asked the patient a few questions. He already knew most of the answers because of Christine's presentation but did this to establish a rapport with the patient as much as anything else. He then examined the man, concentrating on the head and neck. When he put on a glove and felt the tongue, he found a rock hard mass at the back extending deeper down than his finger would reach. He disposed of his gloves and sat down on a stool to talk to the patient. He went over his findings and possible treatments, omitting mention of Olivetti's study. He concluded by recommending radiotherapy with chemotherapy and cetuximab and cited the statistical data that he and Christine had discussed.

The patient then asked, "What about this new virus treatment that I've been hearing about? I've heard it works great and it doesn't have nearly the side effects that you told me about."

"That treatment is really experimental right now. Yes, it's promising, but it's way too early to give it to someone like you who has a pretty good chance of being cured with something that has a much longer track record. I don't think you would be eligible anyway for that very reason."

"Couldn't you tell them that you can't treat me and that I need this virus treatment?"

"I could, but that wouldn't be true. It's just not something I can recommend right now. Maybe in a few years it will be a different story, but your tumor is here now. You can't wait a few years to see what happens with this new treatment."

The patient eventually agreed, and Christine set up the appointment for a dental consult and a simulation where the tumor would be localized for treatment. Afterwards, Lattimer and Christine talked some more.

Christine said, "I understand why you said what you did, and of course, you're right. Right now Olivetti's treatment protocol is only for terminal patients. However, the phase II trial that he is developing will soon be open to patients like this. What would you say then?"

"Christine, you know I always support putting patients on research trials. That's how we learn things. I would give the patient the basic information just like we did today, and then let him or her choose."

"And if the Olivetti treatment works like everyone hopes it will, what then? I don't think there will be nearly as many patients receiving radiation therapy as before. What will happen to our specialty? We keep pushing for more advanced and more sophisticated technology to deliver the radiation, just like that proton beam center that you're helping the university build. Could be a lot of money wasted if people can be cured without radiotherapy."

Lattimer had laughed and said that as long as there was cancer, there would always be a need for radiation. But now, swimming his laps and thinking more about it, he wasn't so sure. Right now radiation therapy was one of the big moneymakers for the hospital along with surgery and imaging. Based on this, Lattimer had successfully petitioned State for a major upgrade of his department with all new equipment – about a twelve million dollar commitment. The remodel was just starting and if the administration decided to wait and see what happened with Olivetti's new treatment, they might well put this project on hold. What a mess it would be trying to operate out of a torn-up clinic while the administrators scratched themselves and tried to figure out what to do. Longer term, Lattimer had been lobbying for a proton radiotherapy center and that was something that would involve real money, about 200 million dollars, according to the latest set of numbers. Proton radiotherapy used high energy physics technology to accelerate protons to over 230 million electron volts or about two thirds the speed of light. It used sophisticated computer control systems to paint the radiation dose onto tumors, with little damage to normal tissues. Fortunately, this project wasn't so far along that it couldn't be postponed for a year or so while things shook down. A disruptive technology like Olivetti's treatment wouldn't just affect cancer programs, but everything else the profits from cancer treatments supported. Hospital administrators tended to think in terms of service lines, and for State Medical Center, the service line with the biggest profit margin was 'heart,' with 'cancer' and 'stroke' being numbers two and three. If most of 'cancer' were to go away, many hospitals, State Medical Center included, would go deeply into the red. Lattimer thought to himself that he didn't know whether to hope that this new treatment would be a success or a failure. He was nearing retirement age but had a son in college and a daughter at a private high school; so he needed to work for a few more years. It might be touch and go as to whether he would be able to work as long as he wanted to. And what about the younger people just starting out in radiation oncology who had huge debts incurred during medical school and residency? What about the new graduating physicians choosing careers? You could just see the training pipeline drying up and his specialty withering.

Lattimer finished his 2000 yards and then quickly exited the pool and entered the clubhouse for a short sauna and shower. Then he returned to his nearby home where he had breakfast, dressed, and went to work. He resolved to keep a close eye on Olivetti's protocol during the months ahead.

Chapter 57

Dean Schmitt was also thinking about the possible ramifications of Olivetti's new cancer treatment. His latest conversation with Peter Drisco had not gone well. Drisco wanted to hire Olivetti formally as a consultant, and Olivetti was refusing to sign on. The contract with the NCI was clear. Work which it supported would be in the public domain. Any agreements with private industry would have to be non-exclusive. This was not what Drisco wanted. From conversations with his staff Schmitt knew of the growing excitement in the Medical Center about Olivetti's new treatment. The excitement was not just limited to the Medical Center. Pillipitch was in the middle of a series of articles in the *Times* about how well the treatment was working on supposedly hopeless cancer cases, and this was drawing national attention. The dean thought that it was time to learn more about it.

"Margo," he yelled through his office door, "Call Jack Olivetti and tell him that I want to meet with him at 2 o'clock today in my office. Say that I want to learn more about this new cancer therapy he has developed."

Margo rolled her eyes. At one time she had tried to train the dean to walk over to her desk and make requests like this in a normal speaking voice; at long last she had given up. She made the call first to Jack's office and, when there was no answer, to his laboratory. She asked to speak to Professor Olivetti, and when he came over to the phone she said, "This is Margo from Dean Schmitt's office. The dean would like to meet with you in his office at 2 PM today. Can you make this work?"

Jack replied, "It's kind of short notice, and I'm in the middle of an experiment. Could we have the meeting tomorrow or on another day?"

"Professor Olivetti, the dean is a very busy man and this opening just came up on his schedule. He would really appreciate your seeing him today."

"OK then. I guess my techs can handle things while I'm gone. Do you know what the dean wants to talk about?"

"Yes, he wants to learn more about your new cancer treatment process. I think the urgency for the meeting is because of some ongoing discussions with Peter Drisco of AVARTEC. Be here a little before 2 o'clock." Margo then called the administrative assistant in the Department of Medicine and asked that Olivetti's academic file be sent over for the dean to review prior to the meeting.

Jack arrived at the dean's office a little before 2 o'clock as instructed, but Margo did not actually show him into the office proper until 20 minutes after the hour. The Dean got up from his desk and met Jack as he entered the room.

"Professor Olivetti, thanks for meeting with me on short notice. I've been hearing about you and your work and thought it was time that we met in person." Schmitt gestured to a folder on the center of his otherwise clean desk, "I've been looking over your file. You've done some impressive work since coming to State. Well-funded too. I like that. Sit down and tell me about this new procedure of yours."

Jack and the Dean repaired to the corner table. The dean poured himself a cup of coffee from a carafe on a tray and motioned for

Jack to do the same. Then the dean sat back in his chair and waited expectantly. Jack quickly launched into his spiel, which was well rehearsed by now. The dean listened carefully, but did not ask any questions until near the end.

"Interesting. I'm an internist, not a cancer doctor, but I can see that this is a totally different approach from the usual way of treating a disease. It is a process, isn't it, and not a drug?"

"That's a good way of describing it."

"And if it works like you think it will, it will make a lot of cancer drugs obsolete, won't it? Of course, some companies are going to have to get involved in the production of the virus, but the real key is going to be controlling the process for making the modified virus for each individual patient. That's something that State could probably patent and then lease out."

"Dean Schmitt, don't forget that the NCI has been supporting this work. Won't it belong to the federal government?"

"Have you ever heard of the Bayh-Dole act?"

"Vaguely. It has something to do with technology transfer doesn't it?"

"The Bayh-Dole act was passed in 1980. It allows universities to patent inventions stemming from federally-funded research. If the university makes a patent claim, it can develop it in connection with a private firm, which then pays royalties both to the university and the professor who invented it. Most of the money goes to the university, but you could get a fair bit of change out of this also if you play your cards right."

"I don't know. It sounds good, and I would like to see State get money for research, but I'm pretty sure that the NCI people told me that under this new rapid development program, any discoveries had to stay in the public domain and not be exclusively licensed to any one company."

Hmmm, the dean thought to himself, *so that's why Drisco is so upset about not getting his hooks into Olivetti. He is afraid that I won't be able to turn the patent over to him in the usual way.*

"Jack," replied the dean, "let me have our technology transfer people meet with you and take a good look at what you and the university agreed to when you took this NCI money. Now let's talk about you and your future at State. This work could be very big, and there is a lot more research to do on it – finding a virus that will allow this to work on brain tumors, for example. With the right financial support, I can see you moving into a much larger lab, one located in our new research complex on east Lake Union. I can tell you from personal experience, the view of the lake is great from one of the upper floors and very conducive to contemplative thinking. Also, your faculty jacket indicates that you are coming up for promotion later this year. I don't think you are going to have any problems at all, particularly with guaranteed funding from AVARTEC."

"Dr. Bremenhoff says that the A&P Committee will be reviewing me at their next meeting, although I'm not supposed to know this."

"Jack, let me give you some advice. There are some on the A&P Committee who don't like some of the corner cutting you've done on this project. They will be looking for reasons to deny you the promotion. Take the research support from AVARTEC and move into the new research space. This will benefit both you and State. Work with AVARTEC and I'll provide a letter guaranteeing you the new lab space, which should override any concerns that might be raised in your review. Otherwise, I don't know what will happen. Think about it. Now I've got another meeting coming up, so we are going to have to finish our conversation for now. Give me a call when you've decided about AVARTEC so that I can get the letter ready for the A&P review."

Jack left the dean's office and returned to his laboratory. He sat down with Meredith and reviewed the study results to date. Apart from the man with the glioblastoma of the brain, everyone else's tumor, even the rhabdomyosarcoma of the pediatric patient, seemed to have gone away completely. Children's Oncology was clamoring to have more of their patients treated, and the waiting list continued to grow. There had been innumerable delays, which Jack could not understand, but at long last AVARTEC was ready to start gearing up to produce the viral vectors in the required amounts. When he had asked Misaki about this, she had told him that the company attorneys were worried about one point or another in the three-way contract with State and the NCI. Jack filled Meredith in about his meeting with the dean and told her about the dean's offer to put in a good word with the A&P Committee, provided that he had secure, long-term funding from AVARTEC.

"So what are you going to do?" asked Meredith. "Sounds like the dean has made a not-so-veiled threat. Wonder why it's so important to him that you start working with AVARTEC."

"Speaking of AVARTEC, I would like you to go over to their lab tomorrow with the data for the next patient we want to treat and get them started on making the virus. You will need to guide them through the first few cases. Barbara Misaki has been assigned to work with us on this, so give her a call and find out when and where to show up. I have her phone number here."

Jack opened his brief case, pulled out a small notebook and read off a phone number to Meredith.

Meredith read it back to him and asked, "Are you sure this is the number? It is a different area code from Seattle's."

Jack looked again. "Oh, I've given you her cell phone number. Here is her office number." And he read off another number, this one starting with a 206 prefix. "Before I make a decision about AVARTEC's offer, I'm going to talk to Bremenhoff and ask his advice. As chair of medicine, he has put a lot of people up for promotion. He should be able to tell me how I stack up. I also want to know if the dean has ever overridden the A&P Committee's recommendation on promotion."

He took the paper that he and Meredith had prepared for the New England Journal and put it in his briefcase. He planned to take it home for one last reading before sending it electronically to the journal. He wanted to be able to list this publication as *submitted* on the updated CV he would be sending to the A&P Committee. He had an early dinner, read and reread the article making minor wording changes, and then set his alarm for 6 AM before retiring.

CHAPTER 58

BARBARA MISAKI HAD TOLD Meredith to come over to AVARTEC at 10 AM and to ask the receptionist to page her. Meredith did so and soon a striking Asian woman dressed in an expensive-looking pants suit appeared. The woman walked over, held out her hand, and introduced herself, "Hi, I'm Barbara Misaki. You must be Meredith Jones. You look exactly the way I pictured you from Jack's description."

Wondering exactly what Misaki meant by that remark, Meredith acknowledged the greeting and the women shook hands, each noting the other's firm handshake. Misaki led the way to the elevator. As they walked, Meredith noted that even though she was wearing heels, Misaki was about 6 inches shorter than she. Meredith was dressed for the lab in a sweatshirt, jeans, and athletic shoes and felt a little self conscious next to Misaki's haute couture apparel.

Misaki continued the conversation, "Peter Drisco has assigned me to be the liaison with your group until we get this project up and running. I'm not a technical person anymore; I'm on the business side of the operation. Think of me as a facilitator if any problems come up. The person with whom you will be working directly is Dr. Tony Beckwith. I will take you to his office now, and the three of us can talk."

When they entered Beckwith's office, Meredith was relieved to find that, like her, he was dressed in jeans and a sweatshirt. He looked like someone who actually did work in a lab, and not someone out of a fashion magazine. Misaki made the introductions and the three sat down at a small table. Beckwith had little interest in exchanging pleasantries and quickly turned the conversation to the treatment itself. He was particularly interested in how a combination of experimental measurements and theoretical calculations was used to identify the genomic sections controlling for abnormal cell growth and how different these were for the various types of tumors.

Meredith explained the analysis process in detail. She told Beckwith that she and Jack would be doing the calculations and bringing the sequence information about the antisense element to Beckwith's group, who would then prepare the viral vectors.

"Yes, yes, of course. But I still want to understand how things are done. Maybe I can come up with some improvements. I want to work with the code itself. That seems to be the real key to things."

Meredith responded, "My understanding is that you and your group don't have any particular expertise in computer science, so I don't understand how you can help us there. Besides, much of this code was developed by Professor Reherson's group in the Physics Department, and they might want to patent it eventually. I couldn't give copies away without his permission."

Beckwith's eyes narrowed. "I don't understand your attitude. I was told to drop what I was doing and give my full attention to this. Now you tell me that I'm more or less a glorified lab tech following instructions."

Misaki intervened, "Tony, this is a very important project for AVARTEC. Right now our job is to prepare the virus needed for the phase II trial we've discussed. As we are doing this, of course, we want to learn all we can about the process itself. I'll speak with

Professor Olivetti about our getting access to the computer code. Let me leave you two to talk shop for a while. Meredith, when you are finished here, stop by my office on the fifth floor – just ask one of the secretaries for directions after you get off the elevator."

Meredith opened her backpack and pulled out her notepad and Powerbook which she slid in front of Beckwith. "I can answer some of your questions if you can give me access to your internet server."

Beckwith logged Meredith into the AVARTEC network using a guest account and then pushed the Powerbook back over to her. Meredith pulled up files for the next two patients who were to be treated and showed the reconstructions of the active control sites for each. One person's tumor had two control elements and the other had five. Meredith rotated the images and pointed out the variations among them.

Beckwith was impressed. "While there are some basic similarities, these are different enough that a blocking sequence tailored for one probably wouldn't have much effect on the others. You say that you need to knock out all of these control points to kill the tumors?"

"Yes, that's right."

"No wonder we have been having only limited success with the broad activity agents like *INHIBIT* that we have been using. What do the antisense elements look like for these?"

Meredith pulled up another set of files. These contained the complex sequences of A, T, G, and C corresponding to the required nucleic acid sequences. "Obviously, there is a lot of information here. Why don't you give me your E-mail address and I will send you the files. You can format them for your own RNA sequence production."

Beckwith agreed. The two parted after arranging to meet again in a week and to keep in contact by telephone and the internet in the interim.

Meredith took the elevator up to Misaki's floor and was directed to her office. Misaki's secretary soon escorted her through the door. By any standards the office's polished wooden desk, walnut bookcases, leather furniture, and finely woven wool carpet were plush. Meredith couldn't help but compare it to Jack's office with its metal desk strewn with papers, its linoleum floor, and the metal bookracks bolted to the concrete walls.

Misaki led Meredith over to a sitting area with a view over the lake and offered her coffee, which she gratefully accepted. Misaki then asked, "How did it go? Tony can be brusque at times, but he is really one of our best people. Came here directly from the University of Chicago and was one of the first investigators hired when Peter Drisco founded the company."

"We had a good talk. When I get back to the University, I'll send him the data files for the virus preparation for the next two patients we want to treat. He got a little huffy when I told him that Jack and I wanted to check the sequencing on the virus he made to make sure that it was correct before giving it to patients."

"Sounds like Tony all right. Doesn't like to have his work questioned. Do you think this checking is really necessary?"

"Yes, for the first few batches at least. Just to make sure there are no slipups in the manufacturing process."

"What's Jack up to now? I haven't seen him since we completed negotiations on our contract."

"Jack just got a manuscript sent off to the New England Journal describing the work. He is coming up for promotion soon and wanted to get this submitted before his review. Dr. Misaki, may I ask you a question?"

"Call me Barbara, and yes, you may?"

"It seems like the University is pressuring Jack to take funding from AVARTEC. Why is that?"

348

"AVARTEC has been a big supporter of research at State, and this support has become more and more important with the decline in federal research dollars. I think the University just wants its researchers to have long-term predictable funding for their laboratories. Grant dollars are what keeps the system going. I've had several talks with Jack about joining AVARTEC as a consultant, but he seems reluctant. That's probably why the dean had a talk with him."

I didn't say anything about the dean being the one bringing pressure on Jack. Wonder how she knew this, Meredith thought to herself. Then she responded, "Jack values his independence. That's why he doesn't want to get involved with private industry. He would prefer to stick with the NCI for his funding."

"Oh come on, Meredith. That attitude just doesn't work anymore. Besides, I know Jack pretty well and know that he is seriously considering joining us. We've made him a pretty attractive offer."

"We've worked together for over a year and we've talked a lot about career choice. My bet is that he is going to stay at State, at least I hope so."

"We'll see. Jack and I have spent some time together too and there is a part of him that would enjoy the lifestyle that working for AVARTEC would allow. Besides, he may not have many options if his tenure is denied. Once you have been designated a loser in the academic community, it can be hard to get another tenure-track job. No other school wants to admit that someone who wasn't good enough for State is good enough for them."

Meredith left the office thinking, *That Misaki is a real bitch! Still, she acts like she is pretty close to Jack. He has never mentioned her other than in connection with AVARTEC. Wonder what the real story is and why he has her personal cell phone number.*

After Meredith left her office, Misaki did some thinking as well. *That sanctimonious broad. She seems too possessive toward Jack for their relationship to be just that of a professor and student. Wonder if they've got something going on and if that's the reason why Jack hasn't shown any interest in me lately. Well, I'll just have to get Jack back to my apartment and remind him of what he has been missing. Then I'll get him to sign up with AVARTEC. That will show her and also show Pete that I can do whatever it takes to get the job done.*

CHAPTER 59

GEORGE LATIMER WAS IN his second year as Chair of the Appointments and Promotions Committee, or the A&P Committee as it was more commonly known. Naively, he had thought at the beginning of his term that things would get easier with time, but the internal politics had, if anything, gotten harder to negotiate. The School of Medicine was set up like a series of autonomous fiefdoms with each department more or less setting its own criteria for advancement to the next level on the ranking ladder. To compound the problem, many departments had multiple faculty tracks: regular academic, research, clinician-scientist, clinician-educator, and clinical. Faculty would often start out in one track and then switch to another. Most often that happened when the demands of their clinical workload prevented them from obtaining research grant funding or writing a sufficient number of peer-reviewed manuscripts to allow them to advance on one of the more traditional academic tracks. The dean kept saying that he considered clinical practice equivalent academically to other activities – hence the establishment of the pure clinical pathway. Most people, Latimer included, thought this was only a ploy to justify an ever-increasing clinical practice needed to fuel the growth of the Medical Center. The sum total of the clinical revenue was currently about twice that generated by State's research engine. That required a large number of clinical faculty who needed to be rewarded and promoted for their activities. Latimer was one of the old-time clinician scientists. He had an active research program until he took over as chairman of Radiation Oncology and became overburdened with administrative tasks. He could not understand why anyone would want to come to a medical school solely to do clinical work without taking advantage of the academic perks. The split between the old guard and the young Turks made for interesting discussions at the A&P Committee meetings when someone's contribution to the academic mission was being reviewed.

The A&P Committee was scheduled to meet the following day, and Latimer was reviewing the application packets compiled by the committee's administrative support person, Tabatha Peters. Peters had worked with the faculty promotion process for many years. She was well versed in the arcane rules in the faculty code covering this aspect of academic life. She also made sure that refreshments were available, which helped to ensure that a quorum of the voting members was present. Most of the applications were fairly straightforward and would not require a lot of discussion. About the only time discussion spun out of control was when the primary and secondary reviewers for a given application had differing opinions. In such a case, the discussion would seem to go on forever until Latimer asserted control as chairman. He would establish a list of issues and questions and have Peters call in the faculty member's department chairperson. Then the committee members would ask their questions in an orchestrated forum. The chairs were put on notice to be available whenever one of their department members was going to be reviewed by the committee. Most often these questions related to the teaching activities of the faculty member and whether or not he or she had a truly national reputation. In the case of the more clinically active faculty with CV's a little light in the publications area, questions often related to the quality and impact of what had been published. Eventually, Latimer would close off the discussion, dismiss the department chairperson, and insist that a vote be taken. Professorial rank was the coin of the realm and most people took their roles on the A&P committee very seriously. Like most prestigious institutions, State had a mandatory up or out policy for promotion from assistant professor to associate professor after six years. Decisions by the A&P Committee could greatly affect people's lives. Before a candidate even made it to the A&P Committee, his or her own department did a separate review and had a vote by all faculty who were senior in rank to the candidate. If the vote went against promotion, the department chairman had the option of putting the candidate up for promotion anyway. He would then explain his interpretation as to why the department vote was negative and why this did not truly reflect the candidate's accomplishments. This rarely happened.

In looking through the packets, Latimer could see only two potential problem packets. One was Dr. Serena Egger, who was an associate professor in Rehabilitative Medicine. She was being considered for a non-mandatory review for promotion to full professor. Egger's CV showed little evidence of academic productivity. In fact, she had written no papers during the past two years. The supporting letter from her department chair noted her heavy clinical load. It stated that she had almost single-handedly staffed one of the outpatient clinics at State's affiliated county hospital during a period when her department was short staffed and one of her colleagues was out on maternity leave. Bringing her up for promotion at this time seemed like a payback from her chair. The department faculty vote only included one negative ballot. It would be interesting to see how the discussion played out on her. The other was Dr. Jack Olivetti, who had a golden CV in terms of research support and publications, but whose department vote, albeit favorable overall, did include a significant number of negative votes. The Department of Medicine was notorious for having a small number of curmudgeons who voted negatively on every candidate, but there was more going on here. Still, it could be that if you discounted the curmudgeon vote, there might not be all that many additional negative votes. He decided that he would ask Peters to review the voting records for the last ten promotional candidates from Medicine and tabulate the number of negative votes for each. Bremenhoff's chair's letter alluded to the discussion at the senior faculty meeting where the issue of Olivetti's cutting corners in his research was raised. Some of the senior faculty were clearly aware of the discussions at the Animal Review Board and the Human Subjects Committee. They were concerned that Olivetti's failure to follow the rules would eventually get him into a lot of trouble. They were also concerned that this would eventually taint the Department of Medicine and the School itself. Latimer could see that Bremenhoff would be asked to appear before the committee on this one.

While Latimer had no problem getting up early for his daily swim, he hated going into his office early. He often worked for an hour or two at home in the quiet of his study. When people tried to get him to attend an early morning meeting, he would almost always decline saying that there was a reason he became a radiation oncologist rather than a surgeon. He did not get into his office until shortly after 9:30 as a general rule. When he arrived that morning, he found two notes from his assistant on his desk. They indicated that Dean Schmitt had called and wanted to speak with him about an urgent matter. *Wonder what Schmitt's all excited about now*, he thought as he dialed the number. The more recent note had what appeared to be a cell phone number, at least it wasn't the medical school exchange, so that was the one he tried first. Schmitt answered immediately.

"Hello, this is Dean Schmitt."

"Hello Al, this is George Latimer. I'm returning your call. What can I do for you?"

"George, this won't take too long. I want to talk with you about one of the appointment packages your committee is reviewing today. Ordinarily, I don't get involved unless there is a complaint but I have some concerns about one of the candidates."

"Which candidate is that?" inquired Latimer innocently, thinking that he could probably make a pretty good guess. Word about the dean's interest in Olivetti's research had quickly gotten around the school.

"Jack Olivetti. Sometimes appointment packets don't tell the full story and I want to make sure that you and your committee know about some problems that Olivetti has caused us."

"Go ahead."

"Well, I'm sure you know about Olivetti's new research: trying to put all you cancer docs out of business, heh, heh. What you may not know is that he almost killed a dog when he first tried it and got one of the town veterinarians all upset. He had talked the dog's owner, an old lady who didn't know any better, into giving permission."

"Yes, I know about it. But wasn't this a case where the dog was going to die if nothing was done, and didn't the veterinarian withdraw his complaint? It turned out that there was a compassionate treatment protocol for animals that covered the situation and eventually the Animal Review Committee agreed that things had been done correctly. At least, that's what Bill Bremenhoff's letter says."

"Well, maybe. But it's for damn sure that Olivetti didn't know about all this when the dog was treated. He just got lucky. Had things gone otherwise, the school would have gotten a lot of bad publicity out of it. Also, do you know about one of Olivetti's lab techs treating a patient before a protocol was even written? A clear violation of all our policies."

"According to Bremenhoff, it was a medical student working in Olivetti's lab. She treated her grandmother, who was terminally ill. Greerson was the grandmother's doctor, and he said that this would also qualify as a compassionate use instance. Besides, the medical student did this without Olivetti's knowledge. In fact, he was at a meeting in Boston when all this happened. This was all in the *Seattle Times* anyway, written by our old friend Pillipitch, I believe."

The dean was getting more and more irritated. Latimer just wasn't picking up on what he wanted done. "You're missing the point, Latimer. It was just more blatant disregard for the rules which were set up to protect both the investigator and the patient. Another thing: you know how damn hard it is to get research dollars now. Did you know that Olivetti has turned down a long-term grant from AVARTEC to support his research work?"

"No, I didn't know that. But Bremenhoff doesn't seem to be too worried about Olivetti's research funding. I'll try to find out more about this before the meeting this afternoon, but I don't think it is really relevant to the committee's decision. Deciding on how much funding is required is really something best left to the faculty and their chairs. Anything else you want to tell me?"

"Just that it wouldn't hurt to postpone Olivetti's promotion for a year to see how he shapes up. This would give us time to see if his idea actually pans out. If his new treatment bombs, he is going to lose his cachet with the NCI pretty quick. He will be a dead weight if his government funding dries up and he doesn't have alternate funding from AVARTEC. Think about it Latimer." The dean hung up.

The more he thought about the dean's call, the angrier Latimer became. The dean was clearly trying to influence the committee decision which went against the basic tenets of academia. Decisions on faculty matters were made by the faculty itself. This was codified in a complex document, the Faculty Code. All appointments and promotions were officially made by the Board of Regents with *recommendations* being made by groups further down the line. The dean had no business trying to influence one of the key elements in the process. Latimer called Peters.

"Tabatha, this is George Latimer. Is everything ready for our committee meeting this afternoon?"

"You know that it is. Otherwise, I would have let you know. Why do you ask?"

"Oh, no good reason I guess. There are a couple of things I would like to talk with you about, though. First, would you tabulate the voting profile for the last ten people that Medicine put up for promotion. We all know that there is group of contrarians in the department that vote 'no' on everything. I would like to know how big this group is on the average."

"Does this have to do with the number of negative department votes on the Olivetti promotion?" Peters clearly had reviewed all the packets and was prepared for the upcoming meting.

"Yes it does. Just want to make sure the committee puts this in perspective. Also, can you clarify for me the role of the A&P Committee? What I mean is can someone, say the dean, direct the committee in its deliberations and decisions?"

Peters snorted. "No. I've known some deans who would have liked to, but the charge to the A&P Committee is to evaluate the candidates in terms of the material in their packet and their department's promotion criteria. You can take other factors into account if you want to. As committee chairman, you have discretion in what factors enter the discussion about a candidate. The committee's decision is then communicated to the MSEC Committee, but as you know, MSEC almost always follows the A&P Committee's recommendation."

"Thanks Tabatha. That's pretty much what I thought. See you this afternoon."

Latimer finished his clinic mid-afternoon, picked up the faculty packets, and headed up the stairs to the surgery conference room on the fifth floor, where today's meeting was to be held. Sure enough, refreshments and Peters were waiting. Latimer greeted Tabatha and helped himself to a diet coke and a big chocolate chip cookie. He sat down to await the arrival of the rest of the committee members.

The first to arrive were Alan Wormsmith, Chairman of Molecular Biology, and Fidel Davis who was a professor in biochemistry. Evidently they had met in the elevator and came up together. They dropped their bundles of review packets on the table and went over to the coffee container. The other committee members filtered in, and Latimer called the meeting to order. There were sixteen promotion reviews scheduled; Latimer had decided to leave the more controversial ones until the end. By then, he hoped that people would be tired and less argumentative. He wanted to end the meeting by 6:30 so that he could join his wife at a parent open house at their daughter's high school. No such luck.

Review for the first group of applications went fairly quickly. Each had been assigned a primary reviewer and a secondary reviewer. The primary reviewer had gone over the application and prepared a one or two page written summary and critique, which he or she read to the other committee members. A discussion was followed by a secret ballot. The ballots were collected by Peters, who tabulated them while the committee moved on to the next candidate. Periodically, she would update Latimer on the running tabulation; unless there was a significant difference of opinion on a candidate, the recommendation was passed on to the MSEC group for action at its next meeting. The process broke down well before the committee had come to Egger or Olivetti. There was an argument between Fidel Davis and Edward Randolf from Neurology about the number of peer-reviewed publications someone on the newer clinician-educator pathway should have in order to be considered seriously for promotion. The basic scientists's CVs tended to have many more publications than those of the assistant professors with clinical practices. Davis was having trouble accepting what he felt was a double standard. Randolf was defending the importance of the clinical faculty and arguing that different standards were not only necessary but also appropriate. Otherwise, he said, clinicians would never get promoted and they would all be forced to leave after six years. "...that would make it impossible to recruit any clinical faculty to State," Randolf said in conclusion.

"So why call them professors at all?" asked Davis. "Oh, never mind. We keep having the same argument over and over. Let's just vote."

Latimer agreed and asked Peters to send around the ballots which the committee members quickly marked and collected. It was nearly 5:30 before Egger came up for review. The primary reviewer was herself a clinician from the Department of Psychiatry. She quickly summarized Egger's academic background and current position. She emphasized her contributions to building the rehab clinical service at County Hospital and recommended approval of her promotion. The secondary reviewer, Donald Raleigh, was an M.D.-Ph.D from the Department of Anesthesia. He stated that Egger had only authored or co-authored a total of twelve publications and none had been written during the last two years. Raleigh argued that since this wasn't a mandatory review and Egger's position wasn't in jeopardy, there was no compelling reason to promote her now. After much spirited debate the committee voted. The seven negative votes meant that the committee needed to hear from Peter Eiffel, the Chairman of Rehabilitation Medicine, regarding the question of why Egger had been put up for promotion at this particular time when nothing significant had changed in her career. Peters called Eiffel, who soon walked into the room. Latimer explained the issues that the committee wanted Eiffel to address. It was pretty much as Latimer had first thought. Egger's proposed promotion was a reward for her being a good soldier when Rehabilitation Medicine needed help at County. There was nothing else to justify her proposed promotion. Latimer thanked Eiffel. Once he had left the conference room, the discussion resumed.

"See," said Raleigh, "it is just like I thought. Egger has been a hard-working clinician, but hasn't done anything academically and doesn't have anything new on the horizon either. I still recommend that she not be promoted at this time."

Paula Mathes, the primary reviewer, stuck to her guns. She argued that a long record of clinical service, coupled with program building and administration, justified the promotion. Finally, Latimer called a halt to the discussion and asked for a vote. This time the committee voted eleven to three to reject the promotion. Latimer himself cast one of the negative votes. After summarizing the votes for the committee, Latimer said that he would give Eiffel a call and let him know their decision. He would point out that just because Egger remained an associate professor didn't mean that Eiffel couldn't give her a pay raise commensurate with her clinical responsibilities.

The committee then turned its attention to the last review of the day, the one for Jack Olivetti. Alan Wormsmith was the primary reviewer and spoke glowingly about Olivetti's research productivity, his ability to break new ground by thinking in novel ways about problems, and his CV, which showed 39 publications, many of which were in very prestigious journals. Wormsmith recommended promotion. The secondary reviewer added information about the number of graduate students and postdocs that Olivetti had trained and their uniformly positive feedback. She too recommended promotion. Latimer then opened the review for discussion thinking that he just might make it to the last part of parent night at his daughter's high school. Mathes quickly focused on the seventeen negative votes by the Department of Medicine's own A&P review committee.

The secondary reviewer countered by quoting from Bremenhoff's supporting letter, which summarized the discussion by the Medicine A&P Committee relating to the alleged procedural shortcuts taken in bringing Olivetti's new treatment forward.

"Yes, but what about the department negative votes? There were eighteen of these. The department faculty are certainly split in this matter," said Mathes. "Some of them felt strongly enough to call me about this – just to make sure that this committee took it into account."

Latimer noted several heads nodding at this. Then he said, "Well, you know the Department of Medicine. There is a group that votes *no* on everything that comes up – just to be ornery, I think. I asked Tabatha to look into this for us. Tabatha, what did you find out?"

"As you requested, Professor Latimer, I looked at the last ten appointments from Medicine that came before this committee. In each case there were negative votes from their faculty. The number of negative votes ranged from eight to eleven with the average being ten."

Latimer continued, "So out of the eighteen negative faculty votes, at least half were most likely from the people that vote *no* on everything anyway – only nine or ten were from people truly concerned about Olivetti's behavior. There are over 400 faculty in the Department of Medicine, so that's a pretty small percentage – about two or three percent if I'm doing the math correctly. This would be like a single negative vote in a department the size of mine. Let's take a straw vote and get the sense of how this committee feels. Then if there are concerns, we can ask Samuel Bremenhoff to join us for further discussion and clarification."

The committee vote was eight to six in favor of promotion, but with this number of negative votes, it was almost obligatory to bring in the department chair. Latimer asked Peters to call Bremenhoff. He got up and poured himself another cup of coffee, his seventh of the day, and took another cookie. He sat down at the table and made idle conversation while waiting for Bremenhoff to arrive. Latimer told the medicine chair about the committee's concerns and asked him to address them.

Bremenhoff basically reiterated what he had put in his letter of recommendation and then said, "Jack Olivetti is one of the brightest and most hard working of all my faculty. Yes, a few corners were cut, but if this new treatment of his works like we all hope it will, then delaying it will cost hundreds, maybe thousands of lives for each day of delay. This is potentially prize-winning stuff. Look how stupid State is going to appear if we turn him down and then he gets the Nobel prize for it and develops a big research program somewhere else."

Raleigh asked, "What about his funding? It has been very good so far, but if this new treatment doesn't pan out, is your department willing to support him? He seems to be giving up other research projects in order to pursue this viral vector treatment of his."

"I think he is a good bet. Besides, our department promotion criteria don't specifically require any particular level of grant funding. I believe he will find other research areas if this one tanks."

Latimer then asked Bremenhoff, "Sam, the committee also has the option of recommending that the decision on promotion be deferred for a year. How would you feel about that?"

Bremenhoff thought for a minute before replying. "Sounds like you've been talking with the dean. This is something he proposed to me, but I don't think it would be the right thing to do, and I told him so. Our department promotion criteria are pretty objective and Olivetti meets them all. Deferring the decision for a year would be like a slap in the face to him after all of the hard work he put in. I stand by my recommendation for promotion."

With that, Bremenhoff got up, left the room, and the committee discussion resumed. Latimer looked at his watch. It was already 7:10. He cut off the discussion and called for a vote. The tally was ten in favor, three opposed, and one abstention. He announced the tally and said that the promotion review was approved, but that he would convey the committee's concerns when the recommendation came up before MSEC. He then closed the meeting with a huge sigh of relief and went directly home. It was too late to join his wife for the parent meeting. Fortunately, she was used to the late hours he kept in the service of the university. He would wait until tomorrow to let the dean know the outcome of the meeting.

CHAPTER 60

SCHMITT WAS REALLY TICKED off when he finished talking to Latimer. He would have to let Peter Drisco know that the lever he needed to force Olivetti to join AVARTEC hadn't materialized. He put in a phone call to Drisco, but found that the latter was temporarily out of the office, getting ready for a vacation trip to Fiji. The dean spoke with Art Jenkins instead. Jenkins said he would let Peter know the results of the A&P vote, but he asked, "what does it really mean?"

"So, is Olivetti's promotion now a done deal, and if so, does this mean that he now has a job for life regardless of what he does in the future?"

"Art, the A&P Committee vote was probably the biggest hurdle, but with the negative votes, the discussion will be revisited at the MSEC meeting. Still, the chairs are generally reluctant to override the committee's decision. Latimer will be the one presenting the discussion, and he is favorably inclined to Olivetti. I have the option of overriding the MSEC vote when I pass things up to the Provost's office. That would really create a stink, and my decision would certainly be reviewed and probably overturned, unless I had really good justification. The appointment is WOT which means without tenure due to funding, but unless his program completely disappears, he will be treated as if he had tenure."

"OK. I will let Pete know what happened. This will certainly spoil his vacation with his wife. He may even decide to come back early to take care of this."

Peter Drisco was really worried about the course things were taking at State Medical Center. Schmitt couldn't seem to control his people, and the articles in the *Times* by that damned Pillipitch on how well Olivetti's procedure was working on 'hopeless' cancer patients were attracting everyone's attention. In fact, he had learned from AVARTEC's media advisor that *60 Minutes* was planning a special on it. The advisor had been contacted by the show's producer because of the plans for AVARTEC to produce viruses for the upcoming clinical trials. And to make matters worse, months ago Drisco's wife had made the arrangements for the two of them to spend a week at a plush resort on a remote island in Fiji. He believed it was called Turtle Island. His wife having made the arrangements, all Drisco had to do was pack his suitcase appropriately. The plane was to leave for Los Angeles at 6:10 that night. From there, they would catch an *Air Pacific* evening flight for Fiji. According to his wife, this would be a very romantic vacation, which their marriage needed. She told him not to bother to bring his Blackberry because there was no service or internet on Turtle Island. He didn't dare tell his wife that he couldn't come; he had seen too many of his friends' marriages end in bitter divorce, and he didn't want to risk that. While Drisco was a driven businessman and things were really critical now, a divorce was a very expensive thing with only the lawyers coming out ahead. His wife, Evonne, or Evie as she liked to be called, was very into working on their relationship right now and it wouldn't do to appear more interested in AVARTEC than in her.

"Patti," he said, "I need you to go out and rent a global cell phone with text messaging for me. It needs to be one that works directly with satellite links since there won't be any cellular towers where I'm going. I need to have it before I leave for Fiji tonight. With all that is going on here, I just can't be out of touch for a week."

"Evie isn't going to like that," replied Patti. "You had better keep it hidden or she will probably throw it into the ocean. Do you have any particular carrier in mind?"

"No, I will leave it to you. Just try to find one that is reliable, and tell Jenkins that I will be checking in with him at odd hours and to be sure and leave his cell phone on."

Drisco worked until 2 o'clock and then went home to finish packing. He tried out the phone Patti had gotten him before putting it in his carry-on bag. The limousine picked them up a little before 4 PM and the driver loaded their bags. Peter had only one medium-sized suitcase, which contained his swimming gear as well as the clothes he anticipated needing for the coming week. Evie had two large suitcases as well as a large carry-on bag. Peter wasn't sure why she felt that she needed all this for a one week stay at a place where the dress code was informal, but he didn't argue with her.

The flight out of Sea Tac was a little bumpy but basically on time. At LAX they passed though security a second time and went to the first class terminal where they passed the time until time to board the flight to Nadi. After dinner was served, Evie took an ambien and went promptly to sleep while Peter imbibed several of the liquors that were offered in first class and tried to get interested in some of the movies that were playing. *Even flying first class didn't guarantee anything worth watching* thought Peter. The flight arrived in Nadi on time, and since the first class passengers deplaned first, the Driscos quickly cleared immigration. After a short wait for their bags, they went through customs and then to the airport office for Turtle Island Resort. It would be a couple of hours until they were taken to a seaplane for the final phase of the journey. Evie decided to look around the airport shopping area. Once she had left the office, Peter quickly retrieved his global phone from his carry-on bag and stepped outside the terminal. It was 11:15 AM Fiji time, which meant it was 4:15 PM Seattle time – only a day earlier. Peter called Art Jenkins.

After a couple of rings, Jenkins picked up the call. "Hello Pete. How was the trip?"

"Long and tedious. Listen, I don't have a lot of time. Evie is out shopping, and I don't want her to know about this phone I brought with me. Fill me in on what happened yesterday."

"Quite a bit has happened. You know that the A&P Committee met yesterday and our source on the committee tells me that in spite of his best efforts to sway the vote, the Committee voted to approve Olivetti's promotion to associate professor. They felt that his work was important enough that the irregularities relating to using the procedure on human subjects could be overlooked. The quote was 'look how foolish we would appear if we let Olivetti go and this turned out to be Nobel prize winning stuff.' It could turn out that way you know. There have been seven patients with different kinds of advanced tumors treated and all have shown complete tumor responses, the best anyone can tell."

"Damnit! I don't see any way our company can get control of this; in a short time *INHIBIT* and its sister drug in our developmental pipeline are going to be worthless. AVARTEC and most other drug companies specializing in cancer are going to be just about worthless in a few years."

"What do you want me to do?"

"I don't know for sure right now, but it did occur to me that if problems were to develop with one or two of Olivetti's patients, things would slow down considerably and we might be able to get control of the process from State during the confusion. Gotta go now, but I will be back in touch."

Drisco put the phone into his coat pocket and walked back to the office where Evie waited. "Where have you been, Pete?" she asked.

"Just out for a little walk to stretch out some of the kinks after the plane ride."

"Well, we will soon be on the island, and we can have a good walk on the beach before dinner."

The Turtle Island Resorts driver loaded their baggage into a small van and drove them to a dock near the airport where a Beaver Sea Plane awaited. Another couple was already at the dock. They had come in to Nadi the day before and spent the night there to recover from the jet lag. They introduced themselves as Tom and Kathy, a young couple from New York who had gotten married the week before. The four made small talk for a while until the pilot had finished fussing around the plane. Their Turtle Island escort gave them an overview of their stay on the island. Turtle Island, which was more properly called Nanuya Levu, was part of the Yasawa Island chain of many small islands located about 50 miles northwest of one of the two main Fiji Islands of Viti Levu. Turtle Island had been purchased in its entirety by an Englishman, who ran the very exclusive resort at which they would be staying. Only guests of the resort were allowed on the island, and many famous people had stayed there over the years. The resort had only 15 individual huts or bures where the guests stayed, and it was 'adults only' during most of the year. Families with children were allowed on the island only for short periods of time during Christmas and Easter. Finally, the pilot proclaimed the plane ready and their luggage was loaded onto it. Not withstanding Turtle Island's reputation of being accommodating to its guests, the pilot made a few remarks about how much Evie was taking as he loaded her baggage onto the plane.

"I just believe in being prepared for changes in the weather and I wanted to enjoy everything that Turtle Island had to offer," was her response. "Besides, I like dressing nicely."

The seaplane taxied out into the bay and rose smoothly into the air. The flight only took about 45 minutes, and Drisco found himself enjoying the scenery in spite of his concerns about what was happening back in Seattle. Life was good and he intended to keep it that way. Arriving at Turtle Island, the seaplane taxied close to shore. As part of the traditional arrival, two burly Fiji men formed a cradle with their arms and carried Evie to shore while Peter had to take off his shoes and step off the pontoon into knee-deep water. There was a dock right next to the landing site and Peter didn't understand why the seaplane hadn't just pulled up to it. He stumbled a little and clutched his travel bag tightly to his chest. It wouldn't do to drop it into the water, ruin the phone, and cut off his link to the outside world. The bures were numbered, and Evie had booked *Bure #1*, which was located on a spit of land with a panoramic view of the water. They chatted with the other guests, a mix of newlyweds and older married couples like themselves. Both Peter and Evie were having trouble keeping the names straight. The other guests, who had arrived a few days, earlier referred to *Bure #1* as the 'big Kauna bure' since it was bigger and better situated than the others. After lunch, their Bure Momma, Aggie, walked them to their hut. As they walked, almost everyone they passed waved and called 'bula,' which was the Fijean form of a greeting. It seemed to suffice for everything from 'hello' to 'have a good day.'

"Just leave your bags dockside," Aggie said. "The boys will bring them up in a few minutes." Peter was willing to leave his suitcase but insisted on holding on to his travel case. They walked up to their bure while Aggie told them about the many things they could do on Turtle: swimming, lunch at any one of seven private beaches, scuba diving, horseback riding, bicycling, deep sea fishing, private meals at their bure if they wished, kayaking, or sailing. All this came with the price of their week's stay and all they had to do was to decide how to spend their time. Peter was looking around as they walked and brushed a few insects away from his face. Evie kept interrupting Aggie with questions. The bure had a thatched roof and polished, hardwood floors. There was a sitting area with a small wet bar and counter. Over a cabinet, was a small refrigerator, stocked with champagne and their favorite wines. There was a small walkie talkie in a charging set on the counter for the occupants to use to call for whatever they wanted. A separate area contained the bed, which Aggie had strewn with flowers, and a Jacuzzi tub was bubbling on the other side of the room. As promised, there were no phones, TVs, or computer connections. Aggie left them and they unpacked. Peter was tired and hot after the trip and looked around for the air conditioner, but found only a small unit over the bed.

"No air conditioning! What kind of a place is this anyway? For the money we're paying, I want to be cool and comfortable."

"Oh Peter," said Evie, "didn't you pay attention while we were at the sea plane dock? The owner wants his guests to experience island life and not the sterile atmosphere of a big resort. There are fans everywhere and the windows let in the ocean breeze. Listen to the surf. Think how romantic it is going to be listening to this as we go to sleep."

"Yes dear," replied Peter. "I'm tired from the trip. I think I will sit in the Jacuzzi and relax and then take a nap before dinner."

As Peter sat back in the Jacuzzi he thought more about the situation in Seattle. Olivetti had employed a virus to package the agent used to shut off the control gene. While using a RNA virus to carry genome information into cells was certainly not new, there was always regulatory concern that the virus would do bad things to the patient. He recalled the situation that had occurred at the University of Pennsylvania a few years before, which turned out badly for both the patients and the investigators. All that needed to happen was for some of the treated patients to develop problems that could be attributed to the virus. What if they were infected with another virus, one not so harmless? *Hmm, this line of thought had some possibilities.* AVARTEC had several different strains of pathogenic viruses in its storage freezer. He would ask Jenkins to have an inventory ready upon his return.

Peter got out of the Jacuzzi, dried off, and lay down on the bed. He looked up and saw a high ceiling, A-frame in shape. He guessed this was to allow the tropical heat to rise, keeping the living floor cooler. The beams were exposed logs and looked like they had been harvested locally. There was a crosshatched mat of palm fronds peeking through the smaller ceiling beams. He noticed the woven decorative fiber and shells on the larger horizontal beams, and then drifted off. A few hours later, Evie shook him awake. They both dressed to go down to dinner. Peter was wearing white linen shorts and a black silk shirt; Evie had on a tropical-looking dress with a flashy necklace and gold bracelet. When they arrived at the dining table, Peter quickly realized that they were overdressed compared to the other guests who were mostly in khaki shorts, polo shirts, and flip flop sandals. Just before the food was served, the four new arrivals were informed that traditionally at the beginning of their stay, one member of the couple intoruduced themselves and told how they had learned about Turtle Island. The other member of the couple would talk about the highlights of their stay at the dinner gathering just before they departed.

When the Driscos's turn came, Evie looked beseechingly at Peter, who sighed and began. "I'm Peter Drisco and this is my wife, Evie. We're from Seattle, Washington. For those of you who are not from the United States, Washington state is the 'other Washington,' located on the west coast. I run a pharmaceutical company specializing in making cancer drugs. I don't know exactly how Evie learned about this place, but anyway, here we are."

"What do you do, Evie?" asked a woman from across the table.

"Oh, I stay home and take care of our two children and make Peter's life work well. Before that, I was a senior buyer for Nordstrom, specializing in jewelry."

Dinner continued with lots of small talk about what was going on at the resort, what famous people had stayed there and what gossip the guests had managed to worm out of the staff about former guests. One story was about the young honeymoon couple who had apparently mistaken Long Beach for Nude Beach and had been inadvertently surprised by the staff. Peter swore to himself that he would be keeping a swimsuit on even at one of the so-called private beaches, and he hoped to God that Evie would as well. After dinner, they returned to their bure and retired for the evening. Peter was feeling amorous and awake after his nap but Evie insisted that she was too tired for sex. Peter would just have to wait until the next day. Once Evie was sound asleep and snoring gently, Peter climbed out of bed, retrieved his phone from his travel bag, and placed a call to the dean's cell phone. It rang several times before it was finally answered.

"Hello. Who the hell is this anyway?"

"It's Pete Drisco. Have you figured out a way to shut down Olivetti's clinical study yet?"

"Pete, it's 3 in the morning. Couldn't this call have waited until later?"

"Sorry," replied Drisco. "I have to wait until Evie isn't around before calling. She made me promise to leave work behind this week. She doesn't know that I brought a satellite phone with me."

"Just a second. Let me splash some water on my face to wake up."

Peter heard a light 'thunk' as the phone receiver was set down and the sound of running water in the distance. Then he heard a rustling noise as the phone was picked up again.

"Pete, I'm back. Olivetti and his crew treated another patient today, one with stage IV pancreatic cancer. It's too soon to tell if the treatment is working, but if it does, I am pretty sure that the cat is out of the bag in terms of shutting this off. With all of the scuttlebutt around the medical center and the articles by the *Times* medical reporter, Pillipitch, this has the attention of President Emory who wants me to brief the Board of Regents next week. Most of the Board members have had a personal experience with cancer involving a close family member, and Emory sees this as an opportunity to justify an increase in university funding from the state legislature. Apparently, no one but me sees how this is going to kill our current research business model. I've got Maxim meeting with our patent attorneys trying to figure out a way for us to make some money off this."

"Just don't try and freeze me out," Drisco said hotly. "AVARTEC supplied a lot of the equipment that Olivetti used and also has supported some of his research."

"Yeah, but this particular project wasn't identified in any of his grant proposals. It is just something that he spun off on his own. He wants to put it into the public domain so that it can be used by anyone."

"Christ! Have you talked to him about financial reality? My company and other companies dealing with cancer will be out of business. Doesn't he care about all the people who will be out of their jobs?" Drisco continued without giving the dean a chance to answer. "I've got an idea but it will require some help from inside the medical center, and that's got to be you. I can't say any more over the phone right now but I'll be in touch with you once I get back in town. Got to go now."

Peter broke the connection and lay back in the rope hammock in front of the bure to look at the stars. However, the mosquitoes quickly found him, and he soon gave up and went back to bed. In the morning, his face and arms were covered with red weals from the bites. He found consolation in that Evie's feet and ankles were covered with small red dots where the sand fleas had gotten her during their walk on the beach after dinner. Maybe next time she would wear socks, like Peter had done.

Chapter 61

AFTER BREAKFAST, EVIE SET up a picnic lunch at one of the island's private beaches. At the appointed time, the Driscos walked down to the main area of the resort where they climbed into an oversized golf cart and were taken to 'Honeymoon Beach.' Aggie came with them, and after the driver unloaded their chairs, she set up the small table in the shelter area. The driver tied a hammock similar to the one in front of their bure to two posts under the shelter and then showed Peter how to operate the small radio that they brought from their bure. Just then, a musical tone came from Peter's bag on the picnic table.

"What's that," asked Evie?

Peter gulped. He had put his satellite phone back in his case after his phone call to the dean and must have forgotten to turn it off. Only his office had the phone's number code; it must be they calling.

Evie was nearer the table and quickly ran up and rummaged through the bag. She held up the cell phone accusingly. "Pete, you promised. No business while we are on this trip and you brought a cell phone with you."

"It's a satellite phone, not a cell phone," Peter answered weakly. "It is just for emergencies. There is a lot going on at work right now, things that could shake the future of our company and take away all that I've worked for. I just couldn't be completely out of touch for an entire week."

Evie glared at Peter and then reared back to throw the phone into the surf.

"Don't do that," yelled Peter.

But it was too late. The phone hit about 30 feet out into the surf. Peter ran in after it and after wading around while screaming at his wife, managed to find it with his feet. He picked it up and brought it to shore. Of course, it didn't work.

"Damnit Evie, why did you do that? That phone cost over a thousand dollars."

"Yeah, well this trip is costing us $3000 a night, and you can damn well leave work behind for a week."

"Well, I'm just going to have to use the resort office phone when I get back. I have to know what is going on."

Evie and Peter ate their lunch in sullen silence. After they got back to their bure, Peter showered and went down to the lodge office where he coaxed the receptionist into letting him make a call on their phone. Peter quickly did the numbers and noted that it was about 8 PM Seattle time. He called Jenkins at his home number. His wife answered.

"Hello, this is Pete Drisco. Is Art around?"

"Yes, just a minute while I get him. Art tells me that you and Evie are having a second honeymoon in Fiji. Are the two of you having a good time?"

"Fantastic," Peter said sarcastically.

Arthur Jenkins then came to the phone. "Hang on Pete, let me step outside on the porch where we can talk in private."

There were a few moments of silence and then Art spoke again. "Pete, I tried to call you earlier today, but couldn't get through. I know that you said not to call unless there was a real problem, but I think this qualifies. Our Board has called a special meeting for next Wednesday to talk about the work of the Olivetti group and how it will impact the future direction of the company. Some of the board members want to cancel the *INHIBIT* rollout or at least delay it until we know more about the impact of this new treatment. What do you want me to do?"

"Shit! I really need to be at that board meeting. I will have to see what I can do about getting an earlier flight home. Here is what I want you to do: First thing in the morning have Patti book Evie and me the next flight out of Nadi to Seattle. I will take care of getting the seaplane from Turtle to Nadi. Have her confirm the flight number via an E-mail to me and I will pick it up from one of the public internet connections when I arrive."

"Sure thing. Sorry to spoil your vacation trip."

"This is more important than a damned vacation. See you in a couple of days."

Peter then told the office manager that there was an emergency back home and that he would have to leave. The manager told him that the resort wouldn't refund his money since they could not rebook the bure at such short notice. Peter grumbled but agreed. Then he went back to the bure and told Evie to pack up as they were leaving the next day on the return seaplane flight to Nadi.

"No, Pete, I'm not going to go back with you. I am going to finish out the week and think about things. Obviously, our marriage is a lower priority to you than it is to me."

"For Christ's sake, Evie," exploded Peter. "This is serious. I have to get back for the emergency board meeting. I can't trust Art or anyone else to represent me at the meeting. There is a lot of money at stake.'

"Pete, just do what you want. I will be back at the end of the week and we can talk about things then."

At dinner Peter let Aggie know that he would be leaving but that Evie would be staying out the week. Aggie looked at him reproachfully but just nodded her head. After breakfast, Peter used the lodge internet connection to find out about his plane flights. Patti had arranged for a flight that evening but because first class was full, he and Evie were booked in economy between Nadi and Los Angeles. She said that she thought it was more important for him to get back as soon as possible than to book a later flight. Peter agreed with that and then paced restlessly until it was time to board the seaplane. At least Evie came down to the dock to wave goodbye to him.

CHAPTER 62

DRISCO KNEW THAT TWO things had to happen to slow things down
and give him a chance to get control of Olivetti's discovery. First,
the process had to be discredited, at least temporarily. He would
talk with Tony Beckwith about ways of making this happen. *Simple
is always better* was his motto, so perhaps making a single change in
the viral construction would make it less effective. It would be hard
to detect the change and even if it were found, the company could
plead a simple error in the manufacturing process, not deliberate
sabotage. Second, something bad had to happen to a few of the early
patients who had been treated, something that would cast suspicion
on the safety of the virus.

The first part was easy. Drisco arranged a private meeting with
Beckwith, and was pleased to learn that the man had no more
morals than Drisco himself. Perhaps the large amount of Drisco
stock in Beckwith's retirement account and the not-so-subtle hint of
a substantial cash bonus were factors as well. Beckwith told Drisco
about his conversation with Jones and her insistence that the Drisco
product be tested for exact compliance with the specifications for
the antisense element.

"But I've got a way around that. I'll just make a small amount
of the correct virus for her to test and then a larger amount of the

mismatched virus to give to the patients. I'll start out just making small changes, but will increase the amount of error if I need to."

"Perfect," said Drisco. "Go ahead and do it."

Drisco wondered how to handle the next topic – causing the severe illness or even death of some of the initial patients treated by Olivetti. The previous conversation with Beckwith had gone well, but this task was much riskier.

"Tony, I've been wondering. Just how safe is this treatment of Olivetti's anyway? Is there any way this virus could get out of hand and, say, kill the patient or spread to the care providers?"

"It's an RNA virus and most of the really deadly and contagious viruses are DNA based. We use RNA viruses in the lab all the time. Still, I suppose it could hybridize with another RNA virus before the body's immune system kills it off and make a deadly strain."

"What if all the virus didn't get killed off after it took care of the tumor, but lay quiescent in the body and then re-activated later?"

"Hmmm. A possibility I suppose, but not very likely. Still, I guess it could pick up some genetic segments from a slow-acting virus like HIV and change into something lethal to the patient."

Now Drisco knew what he had to do. He thanked Beckwith and again told him to make sure that the virus for the phase II study just didn't work like it was supposed to. Drisco had maintained a small laboratory in the company's research building for his own use. It was mainly for show, to impress the investors that the CEO continued to be an active scientist. But he could now use it to make the second modified virus he needed for his plans. He asked his lab tech to retrieve a sample of simian HIV from the freezer storage unit. Then he looked up its genomic structure in the NCI database and picked out the segment that coded for the attachment to the host's white blood cells. With the lab's facilities, it would be a straightforward operation to incorporate this segment into a more rapidly replicating adenovirus similar to the one used by Olivetti, but without the governor on the replication process. It just took some time to prepare, and for the first time in many years, Drisco found himself staying late in the lab. Evie seemed glad that he was interested in research again and didn't object to the long hours. Of course, she had no idea what he was doing or why he was doing it. He still needed some way of getting the killer virus into Olivetti's first few patients and for that he needed the right person. He immediately thought of Blackmont boardmember Adam Martileni, whom he knew from past fundraising ventures. He gave Martileni a call and arranged to meet for lunch.

The two men met at Chandlers Restaurant the next day. After some appropriate small talk, Martileni cut the chitchat. "So why are we really meeting? You didn't ask me to lunch just to talk about your vacation in Fiji or about how well your company is doing. My investors and I see your financial statements anyway. Has something soured? Do you need another cash infusion?"

Drisco replied, "No, we're doing OK financially right now, and I'm just trying to keep it that way. To do so, I need to have a messy problem taken care of by someone who can be trusted to keep it to himself. I thought you might know such a person."

"Exactly how messy is this problem, anyway? Does someone need to have an accident or something like that?"

"Yes, but it needs to be a particular type of accident."

"I think I know someone who might be able to help. You should know that help of this kind can be very expensive, and people who do this sort of problem solving don't like to wait for their money. They will generally want half up front and the other half at the end of the job. They also don't take personal checks. If you're sure that you want to do this, I will have someone get in touch with you. I really don't want to know any of the details."

Two days later, Drisco's cell phone rang. A woman's voice at the other end said, "Mr. Drisco, a mutual friend said that you might have a project for me." The woman had a vaguely East European accent, but Drisco couldn't identify any particular country of origin.

"I was expecting a man to take on this project, but if our mutual friend vouches for you, that's good enough for me."

"It's good that you aren't being chauvinistic. I really don't like people who act that way. I'm very good at what I do," the woman said coldly. "It will cost you $10,000 to meet with me and tell me what you need done. We will meet tomorrow at 4 PM in the Peet's coffee shop near gate 88 in the San Francisco airport. Catch a United flight down from Seattle and you'll end up not too far from this gate."

"I don't know if I can get away tomorrow. Can't we just meet in Seattle?"

"It's better if we meet at a place that isn't home to either of us. That way if something goes wrong later on, there's less chance of anyone connecting us. Our mutual friend said this was of immediate concern to you and, if so, you can find a way to be there tomorrow. If not, then maybe I'm not the right person for you."

"No, no. It's not that. I'll be there. How will I recognize you?"

"You won't, but I'll know you. See you tomorrow." And with that, the woman hung up leaving Drisco to figure out how to extricate himself from work activities tomorrow. Drisco quickly went out to his secretary's desk.

"Patti, something urgent has come up and I need to be in San Francisco tomorrow to meet with some important investors. This meeting is very confidential. I don't want anyone knowing about it. I need to be there about 2 PM."

Patti looked over his calendar, asked about rescheduling a couple of meetings, and then asked if he needed a rental car while he was there.

"No, this meeting is only going to last a few hours and we are going to do it in an airport conference room. Book me on a return flight about 8 PM if you would?"

"OK boss," replied Patti.

Drisco caught a flight leaving Seattle at 10:30 AM in order to allow for the almost inevitable delays associated with post 9/11 commercial air travel. As he was standing in the screening line, he vowed again that he would get a private business jet for the company just as soon as the revenue stream could support it. After the company had taken over Olivetti's treatment and was making money hand over fist, he wouldn't have any trouble selling it to his Board of Directors.

The plane was only 15 minutes late landing, but then there was another 20-minute delay waiting for the arrival gate to clear. Drisco quickly found the Peet's coffee shop near gate 88. As he waited in line to buy a latte, he looked around trying to identify the woman who would be meeting him. He sat down at a table and shortly heard the voice from the phone speaking from behind him.

"Pardon me, may I join you?"

Drisco looked around and saw a stunning blonde who looked to be about 30 years old, gazing at him. The woman was dressed casually in expensive designer jeans, a silk blouse, and a black blazer. Drisco stood up and invited her to sit, noting that she was only an inch or so shorter than he, which would make her about 5 feet 7. She was lithe and moved easily as she sat down.

"How was the flight from Seattle?" she asked with a smile.

"Fine. Only a few minor delays. How was yours?"

"Also fine, but we don't need to get into any specifics. You don't need to know anything about where I came from today. Let's talk about this problem you want me to solve."

Peter quickly sketched out what he wanted her to do without getting into the details of why he wanted her to do it.

"So what you want me to do is to locate the people who received a certain treatment and inoculate them with a virus that will kill them. How about if I just shoot them instead?" the woman asked with a quizzical look.

"No, you weren't listening. Their deaths need to look like they were caused by the virus that was given them for their cancer."

"Just how contagious is this virus anyway? Can I catch it myself, and if I do, is there an antidote?"

"The virus doesn't spread well from person to person and needs to be injected to be sure of infecting someone. Just don't stick yourself with the needle and you will be alright. It's a lot like the AIDS virus."

"How many people do you want me to take care of? You keep talking of two or three people; which is it?"

For some reason Drisco thought that question was funny. "Why, does it really matter if it is two or three?"

The blonde woman gave him a dazzling smile. "Why honey, I need to know how much to charge you. I don't give volume discounts you know. Let's say $150,000 apiece and you tell me if it is two or three."

Peter swallowed. "That's a lot more than I expected."

"Why, have you contracted for killings before in order to have a basis for comparison?"

Peter admitted that he hadn't. The woman then looked directly at him and said, "You need this done in a special way and that takes a special person. You want to get it done more cheaply by some thug who will run them over with a stolen car, then go for it. One hundred fifty thousand apiece is my price. Besides, I've done some background research on you and your company, and I know that you can afford it. Have we a deal?"

Drisco nodded.

"OK then. Tell me more about the virus. Does it need to be kept refrigerated, for example. How much will I need to inject? How fine of a needle can I use? Things like that."

Drisco gave her the answers to these and other questions. Then the woman said, "OK, I know how to make this work. I want you to give me the virus solution in an insulin container. That way it will look like I'm a diabetic and I'll have an excuse to be carrying syringes and needles if anyone gets curious." She gave Drisco a card with the address of a mail drop box in San Francisco printed on it and told him to send the virus and the names and addresses of the people he wanted her to take care of to that address. She also gave him the routing number for a bank account in the Bahamas and told him to wire $75,000 for each name on the list and then be prepared to pay the rest once the job was complete.

"How can you be sure that I will pay the rest after the job is done?" he asked.

The woman looked at him coldly and said, "I guess I can't but remember there are other ways to kill people besides with a virus. People who try to welsh on me don't last very long. If you have any doubts, ask our mutual friend." And with that, she got up and walked off into the terminal. Drisco found himself shivering as he watched her go. *That's one cold-blooded woman,* he thought.

The woman took a shuttle to another terminal. She went into a restroom and, entering a stall, removed her wig revealing black hair. She then changed from her high heels into a set of loafers, and reversed her blazer so that its exterior color was now red rather than the black it was when she went in. She then caught a flight to San Diego whence she had begun her day. With all of the airport video monitors, someone in her profession couldn't be too careful.

CHAPTER 63

DRISCO FINISHED PREPARING THE recombinant virus and, as instructed, packaged it in insulin vials along with a set of syringes and 25-gauge needles. He had some trouble deciding how many of Olivetti's former patients to infect, but decided upon two. One could be overlooked as just an unrelated incident, so he needed at least two. Still, there was no point in going overboard given the price quoted by the woman he'd met in San Francisco. *Which two patients? Now that was the question.* He wanted maximum impact. That meant getting the attention of the news service and that meant Pilipitch. Clearly, Gabrielle Jones needed to be one of the two. That also would have the secondary effect of creating some self doubts in her granddaughter, which would slow down Olivetti's research program. He used his contacts at State to obtain information on the other patients treated by Olivetti in the phase I trial and decided on Colonel James Smathers, who had been treated for prostate cancer. He got the patients' addresses and phone numbers from the Medical Center Database, which he accessed using his privileges as a volunteer faculty member. He included these in the packet of material he sent to the mail drop box in San Francisco. Finally, he transferred $150,000 from his personal funds to the numbered account in the Bahamas and waited to hear from his contractor that the job was completed.

In the meantime, Tony Beckwith had received the viral specifications for the first two patients on the phase II study. As he and Drisco had discussed, he prepared two viral samples for each patient. One was prepared with scrupulous adherence to the provided specifications; the second and larger sample was prepared incorporating a small error in the antisense strand. The correct samples were given to Meredith for verification, and her assays verified their accuracy. Arrangements were then made for the two patients to be admitted to State Medical Center for their treatment, and the altered virus material sent over for administration. Both patients were to be housed on the cancer floor just down the hall from each other. One, Joshua Pettigrove, was a long time smoker with small cell lung cancer who had failed chemotherapy; the other, Clara Oldfield, was a woman with widely-metastatic breast cancer. Both were excited about participating in the trial. Under Jack and Meredith's supervision, aliquots of the viruses were injected into their IV lines and the time of the injection duly noted in their medical records. In the following days, the medical teams monitored the patients and kept careful track of their vital signs and any symptoms. The teams had an air of anticipation as if they were taking part in something really momentous. Meredith cautioned them to be prepared for the severe pharyngitis that seemed to accompany the spread of the virus. Jack and Meredith met with the teams daily and reviewed the patients' charts. Things seemed to go well with neither patient having any problems tolerating the procedure. In this version of the protocol, the first ten patients treated were to be kept hospitalized and monitored for a week after the injection. On the third day Meredith was expecting the two patients to start complaining of sore throats, but their symptoms were quite mild and their body temperartures only rose 0.1-0.2 ºC, which was much less than she anticipated.

"Mr. Pettigrove," asked Meredith, "are you having any trouble swallowing?"

"No, my throat seems fine. Maybe a little scratchy like after being out late in a bar and smoking and drinking a little too much. Nothing that I haven't had before."

Meredith asked Pettigrove to open his mouth and checked the lining of his throat. Only a minimal reddening was present.

It was the same story for Mrs. Oldfield: a slight fever and throat irritation but nothing more. Meredith remarked on this when she got together with Jack later that day, but he was not overly concerned. "We don't know why the first patients got that bad sore throat anyway. It's probably unrelated to the tumor response; we will just have to wait and see. Besides, you checked the virus that AVARTEC laboratories prepared, and found it exactly met our specifications, didn't it?"

Meredith replied that she had, but she was still concerned that she was missing something. The two patients hospital courses were followed closely. Pettigrove's tumors in his neck and armpit could be felt and evaluated, but Oldfield's tumor was confined to her bones and would have to be evaluated with a PET scan. Everyone was anticipating that Pettigrove's cancer would start shrinking after four or five days, but that did not happen. The most optimistic interpretation of the medical records indicated that there was some temporary slowing of the tumor growth, but certainly no regression. Similarly, the pain Oldfield was experiencing did not lessen. Four weeks after the treatment, total body CT/PET scans were used to evaluate both patients. There was definite tumor progression in each case. When they were informed, the patients' reactions were quite different.

Pettigrove was stoic and said, "What the hell, we gave it a good shot." Oldfield was angry and said, "Why me? Nothing ever works for me anyway. I knew this treatment was too good to be true."

Jack and Meredith were disconsolate. They checked and rechecked the procedure used to determine the structure of the retrovirus, and found no errors. They reviewed Meredith's check on the viral samples provided by AVARTEC, and Jack concluded that the provided virus was exactly what was specified. They dutifully recorded their data, and Jack called Fred Alexander at the NCI to let him know the situation.

Alexander listened intently to Jack, with a few interruptions. Finally he said, "Sounds like you've covered all the possibilities. No treatment is 100 percent perfect and counting the 11 patients you treated earlier, you're still 10 for 13 which is pretty damn good considering the advanced tumors you are dealing with. Still, I wish that you had gotten a response in at least one of these first two patients. I would recommend you treat two more people, but make sure that they have the same types of tumors that responded before."

Jack agreed that this was the best thing to do. Of the candidates who had applied for the study, they picked a man with a soft-tissue sarcoma and a woman with ovarian cancer. Tumor tissue was obtained and characterized and the control elements mapped out. Jack and Meredith checked and rechecked each other's work. Finally, Meredith sent the specifications for the antisense elements to Tony Beckwith at AVARTEC. The verification sample checked out perfectly, and the State Pharmacy then asked that the treatment material be sent over. The virus was injected and the same results as ensued, no response at all for either tumor. Jack and Meredith were frantic. No matter how many times they rechecked their work, they could find no errors. Their batting average was now down to 10 for 15.

"What do we do now?" asked Meredith. "I can't think of anything else to check. Why should the treatment have suddenly stopped working?"

Jack thought a bit before replying. "It could be that we just got lucky with the first group of patients. That's why it is important to do well-controlled clinical trials to guard against this happening. Still, I don't think that is the case here. For one or two patients, maybe, but not 10 out of 11. Also we have a reason why it didn't work on the one patient: he had a primary brain tumor and the virus just didn't get into the tumor cells."

"What else?" rejoined Meredith.

"We need to ask ourselves what is different now with this new group of patients. One thing has clearly changed. Instead of our making the virus, AVARTEC is now making it."

"Yes, but I have been checking out their work and you have reviewed and re-reviewed the data. There is nothing wrong with what they are sending over."

"Still, it is the one key thing that has changed. Maybe we are missing something subtle; maybe the virus has the right antisense element but something else has changed and it doesn't infect the tumor cells. Let's make the treatment virus ourselves for the next patient we treat and compare it with what AVARTEC sends over. Even if everything seems identical, let's use our virus to treat the patient and see what happens."

Meredith agreed that this was a reasonable thing to try and that she didn't have any better ideas. They decided to carry out this experiment without letting Tony Beckwith know.

CHAPTER 64

ANGELA FROMM, THE WOMAN whom Peter Drisco met in the San Francisco airport, was notified by her mail service that a package had arrived in her San Francisco drop box. That something was waiting to be picked up was all the messages ever said. She paid the service highly for its prompt attention, total discretion, and complete lack of curiosity. Fromm immediately set about making arrangements to fly to San Francisco to retrieve the package. She called the airline and made a reservation with an open-ended return and booked a room for one night at the Mark Hopkins. Then she knocked on the door of her next-door neighbor in the condominium complex where she lived. A young professional couple lived there. The man was working from home that day; he answered the door and greeted her.

"Hi Angie. What's up?"

"Hello Mark. I have a favor to ask of you and Ellie. I've been called out of town for a few days on an urgent consulting job and I wonder if the two of you could look after my place while I'm gone. You know, pick up the mail, water the plants, feed my cat, and stuff like that."

"Sure, Ellie likes your cat. The only problem is that she always wants to get one herself after she takes care of yours."

"Well, why don't the two of you get one then?"

"It's the litter box. Ellie turns up her nose at cleaning it and I'm not signing on for that job on a regular basis. Usual payment?"

"You're mercenary you know. Yes, I'll bring you back a good bottle of wine for taking care of my cat."

"Going someplace interesting?"

Angela thought quickly before replying. She didn't know how long she would be gone and she might need to call and let them know she would be gone longer than expected. With caller ID, they would know where she was calling from unless she used her cell. "Probably several places, but I will be spending at least some time in Seattle. I'll bring you a bottle of Washington wine. I will be leaving later today. Thanks again for taking care of things while I'm gone."

Angela packed a suitcase and a carry-on bag including two different wigs and a full complement of cosmetics with which to alter her appearance. In her apartment, she kept these items in a securely-locked closet so there was no danger anyone finding the material while she was away and becoming curious. Recalling her conversation with Mark, she emptied the cat's litter box a few days ahead of schedule and quickly watered her plants before walking out the door and catching the shuttle service to the airport. After arriving in San Francisco, she rented a totally nondescript, mid-size Chevy and drove to the mail stop storefront where she used a key to open the locked drop box and retrieve the package. Then she drove to the Mark Hopkins, where she checked in. She opened the box and took out the material it contained. First she unsealed the envelope which listed the names and addresses of the two people selected by Peter Drisco. *Two and not three; being frugal are we?* Angela thought to herself. An old woman named Gabrielle Jones, who lived in a place called Sequim, and a retired army officer named Colonel James Smathers, who lived in Tacoma. Well, she had heard of Tacoma and would check out the location of Sequim on Yahoo in a moment. *First things first. Let's make sure that Drisco has transferred the first half of the money to my account.* Angela pulled out her laptop and took the elevator down to the hotel lobby. She walked a few blocks to an espresso bar offering free WiFi, ordered a double latte, and fired up her laptop. She enabled her encryption routine and accessed her bank in the Bahamas. *Yes, there was a very recent deposit of $150,000 routed through a series of bank transfers. You're being overly cautious, Peter,* she thought. *I already know who you are and where you live.* The she used the Yahoo mapping function to locate Sequim, which, she learned, was a small town on the Olympic Peninsula She used the search engine route finder to plot her drive from Seattle, and stored it on her laptop.

Now, how to approach her victims? As she drank her coffee, she noticed a middle-aged man dictating into a hand held device. *That's it. I'll pretend to be a journalist doing a news story. I'll just call and identify myself as working for Time Magazine, and ask to meet and interview them. That will get me close enough to deliver the virus.* Angela used her laptop to book an Alaska Airlines flight to Seattle for the next day with a planned return a week later. She arranged for a rental car to be picked up at the Sea-Tac airport. Then she returned to her room where she used a prepaid, disposable cell phone to contact Jones and Smathers to set up appointments to 'interview' them.

She tried Jones first, but got no answer. Then she dialed Smathers and he picked up his phone almost immediately.

"Hello, Colonel Smathers. My name is Sandra Towns. I'm a reporter for *Time Magazine* and I'm doing an article on new approaches to treating cancer from the patient's perspective. I understand that you recently took part in a new study at State University and I'd like to interview you about it and maybe take some pictures. Would that be alright with you?"

"I guess so. You know, that treatment at State cured my cancer, and I'd like to help other people find out about it. When do you want to do the interview?"

Angela replied that she was on the west coast right now interviewing other patients for the article and could be in Tacoma the next day if that was OK with him. Colonel Smathers, agreed and Angela arranged to meet him at his house at 2 PM. Angela asked him for his address, which she already knew, and directions to his house, which she didn't really need, and finally said, "Oh, one more thing: Will it be possible for us to do the interview in private? I've found that there are too many interruptions if other people are present. Family members tend to inject their own feelings, and what I really want is how you feel about what happened."

Smathers said that his wife would be out playing bridge with her friends the next day, and that their children were all grown and moved away. It would be just the two of them.

Angela went out and browsed the art galleries along Sutter Street looking for a good piece of art on which to spend part of her fee. She believed in a diversified investment portfolio for her earnings, particularly in things that would not attract the attention of the IRS. Upon her return to her hotel room, she called Jones again. This time Gaby answered after a few rings. Angela told Gaby more or less the same story she had told Colonel Smathers. Gaby was going to be away with some of her women friends the next two days on a short junket to Vancouver, but agreed to meet with the Times reporter on the following Saturday.

When she checked in for her flight, Angela placed the virus in its insulin vials and the accompanying syringes and needles in a clear plastic bag along with some small tubes of makeup and pill containers on top of her coat and shoes. When these went through the X-ray unit, the security screener never gave them a second look or asked her about them. Arriving in Seattle, Angela claimed her checked luggage and then rented a red convertible in keeping with the more flamboyant persona she would be assuming as a reporter for *Time Magazine*. She drove first to the Fairmont Hotel in Seattle, where she checked in, unpacked her bags, and with the help of makeup and a wig, became a striking redhead. She carefully packed a small duffle bag with a camera, notepad, recorder, and of course, her diabetic insulin kit. Then she opened one of her pill bottles marked as containing a "sleeping pill" but really containing rohypnol tablets. Rohypnol was one of the agents known as a "date rape" drug and was illegal in the United States. Angela had obtained her supply in Mexico, where the controls were much laxer. Rohypnol came in the form of a white tablet that quickly dissolved in most liquids; it was tasteless and odorless, and rapid acting. It produced disorientation, drowsiness, and occasional nausea in those who ingested it. Best of all for Angela's purpose, people who took it tended to have significant short term memory loss and couldn't be sure about what had happened to them. It was an ideal agent to give her intended victims. It would make them docile and easy to surreptitiously inject with the virus given her by Drisco. Angela put two rohypnol tablets into the side pocket of her blazer, then went down and picked up her car from the valet parking stand at the entrance to the hotel. She punched Smathers's address into the car's GPS system, turned into traffic, wound her way up the hill to the Madison Street entrance to I5, and headed south to Tacoma.

With the aid of the GPS system, Angela had no difficulty finding Smathers's house. It was on a quiet residential street and since it was mid-afternoon on a working day, few people were around. Angela pulled into the driveway, got out of the car, and shouldered her duffle bag. She marched briskly up to the door and rang the bell. *Act like you have a purpose and know what you're doing and no one will ever question you* was her philosophy, and it had worked well so far. A slender, grey-haired man, who looked to be in his early 60s, came to the door. Angela introduced herself as Sandra Towns, and Smathers invited her into the house.

"So good of you to see me," she said. "Where would be the best place for us to talk?"

Smathers led her into the living room and they sat down. He was carrying a cup of coffee. *Perfect,* thought Angela.

"That coffee smells good," she said. "Would you mind if I had a cup with you while we talk?"

"Sure thing," replied Smathers. "I just made a fresh pot in the kitchen. How do you take it?"

"Just with some milk."

"Same as me. I'll just top off my cup while I'm in there."

While Smathers was getting the coffee, Angela quickly palmed one of the rohypnol tablets. When Smathers came back, Angela was in the process of laying out her reporter paraphernalia – notebook, recorder, and camera – on the coffee table. As Smathers took a seat across from her and placed the coffee cups on the table, Angela leaned over to distract him and asked if he minded her recording the interview. As she picked up the recorder with one hand to turn it on, her other hand moved over Smathers's cup and dropped in the rohypnol. She continued the movement and picked up her own cup, sitting back in her chair as she did so.

"Let's do the interview first," she said, "and then take a few photos. I will take some here in your living room and then some out on the front porch."

"Whatever you want," replied Smathers as he picked up his own coffee cup and took a sip.

First Angela asked Smathers about his family and whether he had any experience with cancer before his own diagnosis. She skillfully steered the conversation to Smathers's own prostate cancer diagnosis, his surgery and the side effects, the tumor's recurrence, the radiation treatments, and finally the tumor showing up in his bones.

"Yes, I was in pretty bad shape at that time. Just about every treatment had failed when I heard about the viral treatment of Professor Olivetti and asked to try it." Smathers began to nod as the rohypnol started to take effect. His speech slurred slightly and he said, "I don't feel so good. Kind of sick to my stomach."

Smathers tried to stand up and weaved back and forth. He was clearly disoriented. Angela stood up and caught him as he began to fall.

"Here, let me help you over to the couch. Just lie down for a few minutes and you will feel better."

Angela got him on the couch and turned him on his side. Then she quickly opened her duffle bag and pulled out the diabetic injection kit. She filled a syringe from one of the vials, loosened the belt on Smathers's pants, and exposed one buttock. She pinched a small amount of tissue between a thumb and forefinger, and injected the solution. It was a 25-gauge needle, so only a tiny mark indicated the implant site. This would soon disappear. Angela placed the vial and syringe back in the kit and put the kit back in the duffle bag. She then picked up the two coffee cups and took them into the kitchen where she washed them thoroughly. She left Smathers's cup in the sink and put her own back into the cupboard. Then she exited the house, got into her car, and returned to the hotel.

When Smathers's wife returned, she found her husband asleep on the couch. It was not like him to sleep in the afternoon, and she shook him awake. "How did the interview go dear?" she asked.

"OK, I guess. I don't remember very much about it. There was a woman reporter and she asked a lot of questions. We had some coffee while we talked and I think she took some pictures. Then I started feeling woozy and needed to lie down."

While Smathers had been asleep, the virus had started its insidious work. It dispersed through his bloodstream, randomly bumping up against the blood cells. Occasionally, there was the pull from a receptor on one of the white blood cells calling it to a binding site on its surface capsid, the binding site which had been engineered from the AIDs virus by Drisco. When that happened, the virus injected its genetic material into the cell and hijacked the cell's replication machinery. It made many thousands of copies of its genetic material, choking off the cell. Then, when the cell was filled to the bursting point, the virus material made protein subunits which it assembled into capsids and repackaged itself. It then burst free of the cell, and the new viruses drifted through Smathers's bloodstream to repeat the process over and over again. The virus bore Smathers no animosity; it was just following its own programming to make more and more copies of itself. It really didn't want to kill its host because then the replication stopped. Unless, of course, it had managed to transfer some of itself into a new host where the replication process would continue.

Smathers got up, helped his wife prepare dinner, and then went to bed early. Two days later he developed a cough and high fever. His wife took him to their family doctor who examined him and noted a petechial rash on his arms and chest. He took some routine blood tests that showed an extremely low white count. A chest x-ray showed a probable pneumonia. Their doctor immediately had him admitted to Tacoma City Hospital, where he died the following day. His wife was overwhelmed by the suddenness of the event. She had him cremated intending to hold a memorial service weeks later. This would give her time to pull herself together and notify his extended family. It was a week before anyone thought to notify the research team at State that one of their research study patients had died.

Chapter 65

THE MEDICINE SERVICE AT the VA hospital affiliated with State University had a patient whom they wished to enter into Jack's trial. However, for financial reasons they wanted the patient treated at the VA, not admitted to State. Jack was agreeable provided that the VA's internal review board approved the protocol being carried out there. Unfortunately, the review board had just met the past week and would not meet again for a month. Amidst much grumbling from the VA administration, the patient was ultimately transferred to State Medical Center for treatment. He was an Iraq War veteran whose non-Hodgkin's lymphoma had failed standard chemotherapy treatment. The alternative at this point was either a bone marrow transplant or Jack's experimental virus treatment. The patient did not want the transplant, and since the cost of the transplant was considerably more than that of the viral treatment, which was largely covered by the protocol, the VA administration was in complete agreement. Before the patient was transferred, the VA surgical team sent over tumor tissue to Jack's lab. Meredith immediately began work on determining the growth elements and their corresponding gene sequences. It turned out to be a fairly complex tumor with three different control point elements. Meredith sent the genetic information for the antisense element over to Beckwith. Then she and

Jack worked together on making their own version of the treatment virus. As might be expected, given the resources the pharmaceutical company had available, Beckwith's virus was ready days before the one prepared by Jack and Meredith. Meredith analyzed the AVARTEC sample and compared its structure to that specified by Jack and herself. Identical as far as she could tell. Nevertheless, she and Jack continued their work and amplified their own virus in their lab's somewhat cranky incubator. They analyzed their own product and found that it was as they had specified and identical to that produced by AVARTEC. The State Medical Center Research Pharmacy then called Beckwith and asked him to send over the actual treatment virus, which, as before, Beckwith had engineered to be subtly different from the test batch. Jack picked up the virus from the pharmacy, ostensibly to give to the patient from the VA, but in reality, destined for the storage freezer in his laboratory. He then took the virus prepared by Meredith and himself up to the patient's room and watched as the medical team injected it into the IV line. Two days later, the patient developed a rip-roaring sore throat. He complained bitterly about it, but Jack and Meredith were relieved. The familiar chain of events was occurring again. The medical team gave the necessary supportive care and, as before, the sore throat eventually resolved. When the patient could eat and drink satisfactorily, he was discharged from the hospital. The two investigators anxiously awaited the results of the CT/PET scan scheduled at the patient's one month follow-up visit.

CHAPTER 66

EARLY SATURDAY MORNING, ANGELA checked out of the Fairmont in her Sandra Towns persona, retrieved her car from the valet, and headed north along I5 to Edmunds, where she took the ferry over to Kingston. After leaving the boat, she punched Gaby's address into her car's GPS system. Although the countryside was beautiful, Angela was oblivious to it as she drove. In her mind she was rehearsing her approach to Gaby and planning her return to San Diego. She still needed to pick up a bottle of wine for her neighbors, but would do this on her return to Seattle.

Shortly she pulled into Gaby's driveway. She retrieved her duffle bag from the trunk, checked to see that the rohypnol tablets were in her blazer pocket, and walked up to the front porch of the house. Gaby must have seen her approach, since she opened the door before Angela had a chance to ring the bell. Angela stuck out her hand and introduced herself as Sandra Towns from *Time Magazine*.

"Do come in," said Gaby. She escorted Angela to the living room and asked her to sit down in a chair at the coffee table. Gaby took a seat opposite her, and as she had done with Smathers, Angela explained her desire to hear about new, experimental forms of cancer treatment from the patient's perspective and her needing to conduct the interview in private to avoid interruptions by family members or friends.

"Except for my cat, I live by myself. But before we begin, I was just making myself a cup of tea when you came to the door. Would you like a cup as we talk?"

Perfect, thought Angela to herself. "Yes please. Whatever you're having will be just fine. I'll just get out my notebook and recorder while you're getting the tea. You don't mind if I record our conversation, do you?"

"Not at all," replied Gaby as she got up and went to the kitchen. Angela took her notebook, recorder, and camera out of her duffle bag and laid them on the table. Then she palmed one of the rohypnol tablets from her pocket. Gaby returned with a tray containing a teapot, two cups, a small jar of honey, and two spoons. She placed the tray on the table, poured the tea into the cups, and handed one to Angela. "Hope you like this variety. It's a favorite of my niece, Meredith." She then picked up her own cup and sat back expectantly in her chair.

"When did you first learn that you had cancer?" began Angela, expertly drawing out Gaby's story, including the role of her granddaughter in providing the treatment which had cured her cancer. "You must be very proud of her," said Angela. So far Gaby had not put down her teacup so Angela had not had a chance to slip the rohypnol into it. She needed to prolong the interview in order to find an opportunity to do so.

"Why don't I take a few photographs now and then we will come back and finish the interview? Your hair is a little mussed up in front. Why don't you comb it while I look around for a good place to shoot?"

Gaby got up and went into the bathroom where she looked at herself in the mirror and concluded that her hair really didn't look that bad after all. As she was running a comb through it, Angela was dissolving the rohypnol into the tea that remained in the pot.

"It's a beautiful day," said Angela, as Gaby came back into the room. "Let's take the pictures with you on the porch swing drinking a cup of tea. That will look pretty natural and will show how well you are doing." Angela quickly picked up the teapot and refilled Gaby's cup before the two of them walked to the front door. Gaby sat down on the porch swing. Angela chattered animatedly as she took the photos, finding reasons to take shots of Gaby sipping her tea. She estimated that Gaby had swallowed about half of the cup before they returned to the living room.

"This tea is cold," Gaby said as they sat back down at the coffee table. She sat her back down on the tray and Angela noted that about two thirds of the tea had been consumed. She hoped that this would be enough to knock Gaby out temporarily. *Now to just keep her talking a little while longer*, Angela thought to herself.

"Have you had any more side effects from the treatment after your discharge from the hospital?" she asked, as she turned the recorder back on.

"No, it's like I told you before. The sore throat was the only real side effect that I had. It was over in a few days and never came back. I was sure a lot sicker with the chemotherapy."

Angela asked a few more questions and then Gaby closed her eyes and said, "I've started to feel a little queasy." She rubbed her hand over her forehead and stood up. "I think I need to lie down for a while. Meredith is coming over this evening to spend part of the weekend with me, and I need to feel better before she arrives. You must have all the information you need right now."

Stalling for time, Angela slowly put her equipment back in the duffle bag deliberately leaving a small notebook on her chair. Then she then walked to the door with Gaby who was wobbly, but was still with it, as far as Angela could tell. She needed to allow more time for the rohypnol to work before injecting the virus. She looked at her watch; it was close to 3 PM. *Probably another half hour would do it*, she thought. She drove slowly to Sequim, got a cup of coffee to get the taste of the tea out of her mouth, and then drove back to Gaby's house. The driveway was empty, which meant that the granddaughter hadn't arrived yet. Angela knocked on the door with the ready explanation that she must have left her notebook and needed to come in and look for it. The virus-loaded insulin syringe was capped, and in her coat pocket. She rang the bell several times, but no one came to the door. She tried the door and found it open. No one in Sequim ever locked their doors during the daylight hours unless they were going away.

Angela stuck her head in the door and loudly called out, "Mrs. Jones, its Sandra Towns. I think I left one of my notebooks in your living rooom." No answer. Angela entered the house and looked around the rooms on the first floor. No Gaby. She quietly went up the stairs to the bedrooms on the second floor. There she found Gaby asleep on her bed. Angela quickly exposed Gaby's shoulder and injected the virus. As she did so, Gaby's eyes opened and then widened as she saw Angela standing over her.

"What ... what are you doing here?', Gaby cried out.

Angela grabbed a pillow from the bed and held it over Gaby's face. The old woman struggled weakly but the rohypnol had sapped her strength. Angela did not want to smother Gaby but merely to knock her out. There would be enough residual confusion due to the rohypnol that Gaby would not really be sure what had happened. Drisco had been quite clear that the reason he was paying her all this money was that the deaths needed to be caused by the virus. Angela quickly left the house and in her rush, left behind the notebook on the living room chair. She didn't realize this error until she was driving around the peninsula to the airport by way of Tacoma. She took this longer route to avoid going through the ferry line on the off chance that Gaby might wake up and call the local police, who might look for her there. As she drove, she removed her red wig and rubbed off her makeup, causing her car to veer slightly across the midline of the road, scaring the hell out of an elderly man and woman returning home from a game of golf at the Sun City links.

The woman turned and looked at the retreating convertible and commented to her husband, "Crazy tourists. Always in a hurry. Too bad I couldn't read her license number; otherwise I would report her to the police. Probably talking on her cell phone while driving, and not paying attention."

Chapter 67

Angela was well on her way to the Sea-Tac airport when Meredith's old Passat took the Sequim exit from Highway 101. As usual, Meredith had her bike in the rack on the back and Sam on the front passenger seat. Meredith quickly negotiated the winding road to her grandmother's home and pulled into the driveway. She got out of her car, stretched, and let Sam out to wander about the yard finding just the right bush against which to relieve himself. Meredith walked up to the front door and rang the bell. No answer. This was not like Gaby who generally came out to greet her before she had a chance to ring the bell.

Meredith entered the house and called out loudly, "Granner. It's me. Is anyone home?" No response. Meredith looked around and saw the tray holding the teapot and cups on the coffee table. The she went up the stairs to Gaby's bedroom where she saw her grandmother on her rather messed up bed which appeared quite. Meredith walked over and gently shook her, "Wake up sleepy head," she said softly. Gaby awoke with a start, looked around in a disoriented manner, but then relaxed when she saw it was Meredith standing there.

"Meredith, I'm so glad it's you. There was this woman reporter whom I talked to. She came into my bedroom, and, I think, tried to smother me with a pillow. I'm so confused. I don't really know what happened."

"Granner, slow down. You're not making any sense. What woman reporter?"

With some stumbling around, Gaby succeeded in telling Meredith the story about the *Time Magazine* reporter. Meredith didn't know whether to believe her or not. Gaby was certainly confused, and Meredith was concerned that she might have suffered a slight stroke.

"Granner, we need to get you checked over. I'm taking you to the Port Angeles emergency room right now."

Meredith shut Sam up in her grandmother's house and then drove Gaby to the hospital in Port Angeles. The doctor on ER duty was having a light day and promptly saw Gaby. He was concerned about her confusion and agreed with Meredith that a small stroke was a real possibility. He quickly arranged for a MRI of the brain. The MRI was negative, but noting that Gaby was still confused, he thought that she ought to be admitted overnight for observation. Meredith agreed and helped Gaby through the hospital admission process. Blood was drawn and sent for routine admission studies. Meredith stayed with her grandmother and as she was helping her into her gown, noticed a small, discolored area on her right shoulder with a pinpoint of dried blood at its center.

"What happened here," asked Meredith. "Did you fall and scrape yourself?"

"I don't think so. But this was the area where I was pinched when that reporter was in my bedroom. I think that is what woke me up."

"It's not like you to be asleep in the middle of the day. Weren't you feeling well?"

"I felt just fine when I woke up this morning. I got up and straightened the house because the reporter was coming, and I didn't have any problems then either. Once the reporter arrived, Sandra, she said her name was Sandra, I made us some tea and we sat in the living room and had a nice talk – all about my cancer and how it was treated. She asked lots of questions, and then we went outside where she took some pictures for the story she was writing."

"Just a minute, Granner. Start at the beginning and tell me more about the reporter and the story."

"Earlier in the week I got a call from this woman who said she was a reporter for *Time Magazine* and was writing a story about new cancer cures from the patient's perspective. She wanted to talk with me about my treatment. She said that she was going to be in the Seattle area and wanted to talk with me and some other patients."

"Did she say who else she was going to talk to?"

"No, but I think she said something about talking to someone in Tacoma. It's all so fuzzy. Anyway, I felt just fine until near the end of the interview when we came back into the house after taking the pictures on the porch. Then I felt sick to my stomach and started getting sleepy – all at the same time. I told her that I wasn't feeling well and needed to lie down for a while. Then she left."

"Did you take any medication? Anything at all from the medicine cabinet?"

"Not that I remember."

"I talked to the nurse and she says Dr. Kim will be taking care of you while you are here. I think I'll ask him to have a drug screen run on your blood just in case you did take something without knowing it. Anyway, you seem to be getting better all the time. Get some rest. I need to get back to your house to let Sam out before he makes a mess on the floor. See you in the morning. You'll probably be ready to go home then."

Meredith kissed Gaby on the cheek and exited the room, being sure to leave her cell phone number at the nurses' station. She also left a post-it note on Gaby's chart for Dr. Kim stating her concerns that her grandmother might have inadvertently taken some narcotic medication left over from her cancer treatments. She suggested that a toxicology screen be performed on some of the blood taken at the ER.

When Meredith got back to the house, she let Sam out. The dog anxiously relieved himself in the front yard without even sniffing his favorite bush. She carried the teapot and cups to the kitchen, washed them, and put them away. She made herself a sandwich and went into the living room to sit down and think. There was something on the chair; she reached around behind her and pulled out the notebook that Angela had left behind. Meredith opened it, and saw some notes that Angela had taken during her interview with Gaby. They were not very organized and seemed amateurish. However, the notebook certainly lent credence to her grandmother's story about a visit from a reporter. The notebook was new and there was no name or other identifying material on it. Meredith placed the notebook on the fireplace mantle and then went up to bed.

The next day she got up early for a bike ride before breakfast and then went to the hospital to see Gaby. Her grandmother seemed to be her old self and couldn't wait to leave. Dr. Kim came by early, and after examining her, pronounced her ready for discharge. As he left, he turned to Meredith and told her that he had gotten her note about the toxicology screen and it certainly wouldn't hurt to check this out on some of the blood which was already in the laboratory. Meredith drove Gaby home where Sam greeted them both at the door. Gaby seemed like her normal self, cheerful and full of energy. The virus that Angela had injected would soon change this happy state of affairs.

Chapter 68

Angela called Peter Drisco from an airport phone shortly before boarding her flight to San Francisco. "Drisco, the job is done. Both of the clients you assigned me have been taken care of. Transfer the rest of my fee right away, will you?"

Drisco had checked Angela's competence with Adam Martileni again. What he had learned gave him a healthy respect for her abilities. She was reportedly a crack shot with a pistol and a rifle and versed in a few of the more esoteric martial arts. She was clearly not someone to be messed with, so Drisco promptly agreed to wire the rest of the money to the same previously used account.

"I do have one question," Peter asked. "When did you take care of the clients? Just so that I will know when to look for the announcements of their deaths and make sure they get the proper attention from the university's Human Subjects Review Board."

"I took care of Smathers five days ago and the old woman just a few hours ago. The old biddy gave me more trouble than he did. But not to worry, there's no way anyone will figure out what actually happened. Send a message to my mailbox if you decide you need anyone else taken care of."

After they had disconnected, Drisco sat back in his chair and contemplated his course of action. *Smathers should already be dead, wonder why I haven't heard about it. The old woman in Sequim has maybe a day or two more to live.* He would just have to make sure that the protocol monitoring board learned about these cases. Life was good and he intended to keep it that way. He yelled out his office door to his secretary, "Patti, get me Al Schmitt on the line, will you."

CHAPTER 69

MEREDITH DROVE BACK TO Seattle on Sunday night and worked happily in the lab the next day. On Monday night she received a call from Gaby.

"Meredith, I hate to bother you, but I feel awful."

"Granner, tell me what's going on. Are you weak and confused like a few days ago?"

"No, this is different. I feel all hot and feverish, and I've started to cough."

"Can you find a thermometer and take your temperature and let me know what it is?"

"I've already done that since I knew that you would ask. It is 103.1°. Seems high to me."

"Seems high to me too," replied Meredith. "Can you get one of your neighbors to take you to the Port Angeles ER? It's probably just a virus, but after what happened a couple of days ago, I want to have you looked at. Have the doctors there give me a call once they have checked you over."

Three hours later Meredith's cell phone went off. It was the emergency room doctor in Port Angeles.

"Ms. Jones, this is Dr. Parks. I'm one of the doctors in the Port Angeles Hospital emergency room and I have your grandmother,

Mrs. Gabrielle Jones, here. She insisted that I call you and let you know what is happening. I understand you have a medical background."

"Well, I'm a third year medical student at State and have been working in Dr. Olivetti's cancer research laboratory, but I'm not actually a physician yet. What's up with my grandmother?"

"It's a very puzzling case. She is running a high fever, close to 103° Fahrenheit, but her white count is extremely low, about 400 polys. She was here only a few days ago and her blood pattern was fine. I don't see what could have knocked out her white cells in such a short time. We can either admit her here and work her up or send her over to State for the hematology experts to look at. She wants you to make the decision."

"May I talk to her please?"

There was a short delay and then Gaby's voice came over the phone. Meredith asked how she was feeling and then after listening to her story said, "Granner, I think we ought to get you right over to State and find out what's going on with you."

"Whatever you thing is best," replied Gaby. "My neighbors can look after my place for a few days. Mrs. Fritz drove me to the hospital and is still here. I'll tell her what is happening and tell her that she needn't wait around any longer."

It was a few more hours before the transfer arrangements could be made and Gaby was in an ambulance on her way to State Medical Center. Meredith was waiting at the ER when she arrived. Gaby was quickly processed and taken up to the eighth floor cancer unit where she was placed on Dr. Mellon's service. He and the housestaff examined her very carefully and found that her lungs were congested, and she was beginning to develop some minute, hemorrhagic spots, or petechiae, on her skin. A chest x-ray showed a pneumonia-like infiltrate. Her heart rate was accelerated and her blood pressure was low. What was surprising was that her white blood count was low – the opposite of what should have been the case with an infection. Because of the unknown nature of Gaby's problem, infection control precautions were taken by the medical staff looking after her. This meant that everyone entering the room had to put on a gown, mask, and gloves which were then removed and placed into an isolation container when they left. Multiple tubes of blood were drawn and sent for bacterial and viral cultures, as were samples of the fluid from Gaby's lungs. A bone marrow biopsy showed that the blood-forming cells were hyperactive, meaning that they were churning out white blood cells as fast as they could. But something was destroying them faster than they could be made. Mellon took Meredith aside and spoke with her.

"I don't know what is happening with your grandmother, but whatever it is, it's happening very fast. It is almost like a fast-acting HIV-like virus is attacking her white blood cells. Has she been around anyone who has been sick like this?"

"Not that I know of. There was a strange woman reporter that interviewed her a few days ago, but my grandmother didn't say anything about her being sick."

"Is it possible that this is a latent side effect from her cancer treatment? Has anything like this occurred in any of the other patients you've treated?"

"I haven't heard of any problems with the other patients, and I'm sure that Professor Olivetti would have said something if he had heard about it. Dr. Mellon, what can we do for my grandmother?"

"I don't know whether it is some outside organism or whether it's her own immune system gone haywire. We will just have to give her fluids and supportive care and see what the cultures show."

"She could die from this, couldn't she?" asked Meredith.

Mellon hesitated a moment before answering. "Yes, Ms. Jones, I'm afraid that she could. Why don't you go in and spend some time with her and then go home and get some rest? You know about the infection precautions, so be sure that you gown up before you go in and wash up afterwards."

Meredith put a hospital gown over her clothes, put on a cap, mask, and gloves, and entered Gaby's room. Her grandmother looked sapped of energy. She lay listlessly on the bed, her eyes half closed. Oxygen was running through a nasal cannula. Meredith sat on the bed and held her hand. Her grandmother hardly stirred.

Meredith spoke in a low, soothing voice. "Granner, I've just spoken with Dr. Mellon. He and his team are great. You couldn't be in better hands. They will soon figure out what is wrong with you and get you feeling like your old self again. I'm going to stay right here with you tonight."

Gaby just smiled weakly and didn't say anything. Her breathing became more and more labored. Finally her heart gave out in the early morning hours. A CODE was called, but Meredith asked that it be halted before Gabby was intubated. Her grandmother had been through so much, and no one had any idea how to treat her underlying disease. It just didn't make sense to try and keep her alive for a few more hours with IV lines and tubes running into every body orifice. Meredith left the room numbly, crying softly. After she had gone, her grandmother's body was taken to the medical center morgue where it was placed in a body bag and then into the cold storage unit. The hospital house-cleaning team thoroughly wiped down the room, and completely changed everything, in preparation for the next patient. Hospital rooms were too valuable a resource to be allowed to lie idle for any extended period of time. In a very short time, the room was ready for its next occupant.

CHAPTER 70

MEREDITH REALLY DIDN'T KNOW what to do with herself. She had just lost the only real family that she had. Yes, there were some distant cousins, but she was not connected to them at all. She went back to her apartment, put Sam on his leash, and took him around the block a couple of times to clear her head. Finally, she decided to return to her apartment and make a list of people to be notified and things to do. Then she went to bed and cried herself to sleep. The question that Mellon had asked her kept running through her mind. *Suppose this was some weird side effect of the viral treatment she had given Gaby? If so, I will never forgive myself. I have to know the answer for my own peace of mind, if nothing else.*

The next thing she knew it was 9:30 AM and Sam was poking at her with his cold, wet nose, wondering why she was still in bed and hadn't gotten up to feed and walk him. Meredith smiled at him; at least one thing in her life remained normal. After she had taken care of him, she called Jack at his laboratory and told him what had happened to Gaby. Jack was sympathetic but really didn't know what to say. He murmured that he was very sorry and told her that she should take care of Gaby's affairs and not worry about coming into the lab. "The techs and I can keep things going while you're away," he said awkwardly.

"Jack, Mellon raised the question of whether this could be a weird side effect of her viral treatment. Has anything like this happened to any of the other patients?"

"Certainly not that I know of. If it had, I would have let you and the monitoring board know. I think this is completely unrelated, so don't beat yourself up about it. Anyway, since your grandmother was treated experimentally, I will let the monitoring board know about her death, just to follow the protocol."

Meredith spent the morning phoning Gaby's neighbors and some of her close friends in her Sequim church group. They promised to let others in their circle know and asked about when funeral plans. Meredith had no answer to that question and said she would let them know. In the early afternoon, Meredith's cell phone rang. It was Dr. Parks from the Port Angeles ER inquiring about Gaby. Meredith told him that she had died shortly after being transferred to State. She thanked him for all his efforts to help her grandmother.

Parks expressed his condolences and then said, "by the way, I think I know why she was all confused when she first came in last week. It wasn't anything to do with the virus at all. She had an unusual sedative-hypnotic agent in her blood stream, rohypnol. I just don't know how she could have gotten hold of any."

"Rohypnol, what's that?"

"It's a drug that puts people to sleep and leaves them confused afterwards. It is one of the so-called date rape drugs used by unscrupulous people in the bar scene to make their conquests easier. It is legal in Mexico and in Europe for other medical purposes, say as a sleeping pill, but not in this country. Any idea where she could have gotten it?"

"Come on. My grandmother was in her 70s and certainly didn't do the bar scene or run with a fast crowd. Are you sure about this?"

"It's what the lab tests say. Just wanted to let you know. I'm required to report this to the police department since it is an illegal drug in this country. Again, I'm sorry to hear about your grandmother's death."

Meredith hung up thoroughly confused. She wondered if one of Gaby's friends might have picked up some of this drug on a trip to Canada or another country to use as a sleeping pill and then given some to Gaby to help her sleep. *That just doesn't make sense,* Meredith thought. *Gaby never had any problem sleeping, and besides, she would never have taken a new medicine without first asking me about it.*

Jack also received a disturbing phone call that afternoon. It was Smathers's family doctor in Tacoma letting him know about the man's death a week earlier. Jack listened carefully to the doctor as he described his patient's symptoms and rapid downhill course.

"I've never seen anything like it. Smathers had a high fever and a pneumonia. You would have thought that would cause his white blood cell count to elevate. That didn't happen though. His white blood cells just bottomed out, for no apparent reason, and then he died. He also had a lot of petechi on his skin as if he had a bleeding problem. We never did figure out what was going on. We were going to transfer him to State, but he died before we could arrange it. I thought I had better let you know since Smathers was one of State's research patients."

"Was there an autopsy?"

No, his wife wanted him cremated and the funeral home took him away right after he died."

"Damn! We just had another case something like this and it might have been helpful if we had known about your patient. Why didn't you call me sooner?"

"I've been away on vacation, and you know how it is with a small practice; I have to do most things myself. Sorry."

Jack asked the doctor to send copies of the hospital records and then hung up. He immediately called his NCI contact, Fred Alexander, to let him know about the two deceased patients.

"That's not good, not good at all," responded Fred. "I had a feeling things were going too smoothly. Have you notified the Protocol Monitoring Board and State's IRB yet?"

"No, I wanted to talk with you first. Besides, Meredith's grandmother just died last night and I only learned about the other patient a few minutes ago. It's not like I've been sitting on this news."

"Look, let them know right away. Make a phone call and follow up with a notice in writing – E-mail will work, but send a copy to yourself to document that you have informed the proper authorities. The IRB will probably want to review everything before allowing the protocol to continue, so be prepared for that."

"I don't see how it could be a result of the protocol treatment, do you?"

"Not really, but the fact remains that it looks like some funny kind of virus caused their deaths, and the only funny virus that we know about which the two people had in common was the one you gave them. It would just be prudent to check things out. You say the first patient was cremated. Can you get an autopsy on the patient who died at State Medical?"

Jack said that he would try, and then contacted the IRB and Monitoring Board, as directed by Fred. Fred was right. The IRB chair told him to stop treating patients on the study until further notice. He also asked him to check on the status of the other patients who had been treated. Jack was eventually able to reach all but three of the patients, who were out of town with their families. He was greatly relieved to learn that no one else had come down with anything suspicious. However, he was also aware that Meredith's grandmother and Smathers were two of the earliest patients treated, so if this was indeed a treatment side effect, it could still occur in the other patients. He called Meredith at her apartment and arranged to stop by and talk with her. It seemed that conveying the news about Smathers and asking her to consider having an autopsy performed on her grandmother were things better done in person than over the telephone.

CHAPTER 71

MEREDITH BUZZED JACK INTO her apartment building when he pushed the button at the entryway. The conversation between the two of them was awkward at first, with Jack trying to find the right words to express his condolences about Gaby's death. Meredith was grateful that he had come over, and told him so, putting him at ease. Jack then asked Meredith if she remembered Colonel Smathers who was one of the first patients that they had treated.

"Yes, I most certainly do. He was an older man with advanced prostate cancer. Lived down in Tacoma, I believe. Why do you ask?"

"I just got a call today from his primary care doc. Apparently, Smathers died about a week or so ago of something that sounds a lot like what your grandmother had – a sudden illness characterized by a fever, low white count, skin petechia, and a pneumonia. They were going to send him up to State, but he died before he could be transferred."

"Oh my God! Do you know if any of our other patients have gotten sick like this?"

"Not as far as I know. I've called all but three of them and everyone I've spoken with is doing fine right now. Here's the problem. I'm having his medical records sent to me, but Smathers was cremated, so we can't do any special studies that might tell us what happened to him. Your grandmother is a different story. Would you be willing to let us do a detailed autopsy on her?"

Meredith thought a minute before answering. "This is really important, isn't it? If there is something wrong with the viral vector treatment, then we need to find out before anyone else is harmed."

"That's pretty much it. I have told the NCI and our monitoring IRB about these two deaths and they have stopped further patient treatments for the time being. We need to know if any of our other patients are at risk. I just don't see how the tame virus we used could have caused this problem, but we need to take all possible precautions."

"It's a real bitch of a situation isn't it? People are dying of cancer; your treatment might help them, but on the other hand, it might also be killing them. I'm responsible for things moving as fast as they did, but Granner would have been dead long before this without the treatment. I'm pretty sure that she would want to help us find out what happened to her. I'll give my permission for her autopsy. I'd like to get it done quickly, so that I can make arrangements for her funeral."

"Thanks. I'll tell pathology about the autopsy, and I'll bring the paperwork by on my way home tonight."

"Don't bother. I'm planning on coming in to the lab tomorrow and I'll sign it then. I need something to do. I'd like to look at Smathers's medical records too. There might be a clue there."

Jack stood up to go. Meredith looked so forlorn that he just naturally walked over and gave her a hug before leaving. It may have been the feeling of emptiness after losing Gaby and the need to connect with someone or it may have been something else, but Meredith clung to him hungrily and then kissed him passionately. Jack knew that it wasn't right to get involved with a student, particularly one in a vulnerable situation, but found that he just didn't care. He too got caught up in the moment and eagerly responded.

There might be regrets later, but this was now. Both Meredith and Jack focused on the moment and she pulled him back onto the couch where they fumbled with each other's clothes until both were completely disrobed. Their lovemaking was quickly consummated and they clung to each other for a while. Jack then picked her up and carried her into the bedroom where a second, much more prolonged encounter took place. Then they fell back and just lay in each other's arms for a while until Meredith fell asleep. Jack quietly disengaged himself, got up, and went back into the living room where he quietly dressed. He didn't leave, but sat down in a chair to ponder what had happened and what he would say to Meredith when she awakened. It was several hours before Meredith emerged from the bedroom wrapped in a robe.

"Jack, I thought you had left. It wasn't a dream was it?"

"If it was, then I had the same dream. You are without a doubt the most wonderful woman I have ever known. On one hand, I worry that I've taken advantage of you, but on the other hand, I'm excited to see where this might lead."

"You didn't take advantage of me. If anything, it was the other way around. I've wanted this to happen ever since our trip to Washington, D.C. Let me get dressed and let's go out and get something to eat and talk about where we go with this."

They went out for Indian food at a restaurant in the university district and held hands while they talked about their feelings for each other. Each was relieved to learn that the other had been romantically interested for some time, but had held off making an advance because of their working situation. They agreed that their new relationship couldn't spill over into the research laboratory, but other than that, to just let things take their natural course. Jack and Meredith then went back to her apartment and spent the rest of the night together.

CHAPTER 72

THE NEXT MORNING, JACK drove to the campus, making a detour to his apartment for a change of clothes. Meredith took Sam out for his morning constitutional before driving in, so the two of them arrived at the lab at nearly the same time. Jack gave Meredith the paperwork, allowing her as next of kin, to approve the autopsy on her grandmother. After she had signed the papers, he took them to the offices of the Division of Anatomical Pathology whose faculty members would be doing the procedure. To help the pathologist know what to look for, Jack summarized the details of Gaby's medical history, including the experimental cancer treatment she had received, and wrote down his cell phone number for the pathologist to call if there were questions. Jack did not want the call going to the lab, where Meredith might be the one to pick up the phone.

While this was happening, Meredith went through the medical records relating to Smathers's terminal admission to the Tacoma hospital. *Interesting, according to Smathers's wife, he also had become disoriented for a short period of time a few days before he got really sick.* Meredith wanted to know more about this. She called Mrs. Smathers and identified herself as one of the researchers who had treated the colonel for his prostate cancer.

"Yes, I remember you," said Mrs. Smathers. Jim was doing so well, and it looked like his cancer was completely gone. He was all excited because a reporter from *Time Magazine* was coming by to interview him, and he couldn't wait to tell everyone about it."

Meredith suddenly became very alert. *A reporter from Time Magazine. Just like with Gaby.* "Mrs. Smathers, what kind of an article was this reporter writing?"

"Oh, one about new cancer cures from the patient's perspective. That's what Jim told me before the interview with her."

"So it was a woman reporter. What was her name?"

"I don't know. I never actually met her because I was away playing bridge when she came to talk to Jim. Why, is it important?"

Meredith didn't actually lie but did dissemble a bit when she replied, "Well, it's just that we like to know when a news story is coming out about our research. We like to work with the reporters to make sure that they get all the facts straight."

"In that case, let me take a look in our appointment calendar." There was a short hiatus while Mrs. Smathers walked to the kitchen, got the calendar, and returned to the phone. "Yes, here it is. The reporter's name was Sandra Towns. She talked to Jim two days before he became sick and went to the hospital."

Meredith continued, "You told the doctors taking care of him that he was confused for a short time a couple of days before he got sick. Was that before or after he talked with the reporter?"

"Why it was right after the interview. When I got home from my bridge group, the reporter had gone and Jim was asleep on the living room couch. When I woke him up, he was very confused. I thought for a minute that he had had a stroke. He was really tired and just went off to bed after we had dinner. The next morning he seemed fine, just like his old self, so I guess it wasn't a stroke after all."

Thinking back to Gaby's emergency room visit prior to her illness, Meredith asked, "Had your husband started taking any new medications that might have had these side effects?"

"No, Jim didn't like to take medicines. Our doctor had a hard time just getting him to take his blood pressure pills."

Meredith then found out more details of the colonel's final illness and death. It was just like what happened with her grandmother. Finally, at the close of the conversation she asked, "Mrs. Smathers, do you mind if I talk to your husband's doctor? Your husband was one of our research study patients, and it is important that we keep careful track of everything that happens to them afterwards."

Mrs. Smathers agreed and gave Meredith permission to call their family doctor. She even looked up his office phone number for her. Meredith thanked her and immediately hung up and dialed the number. After a few rings, a recorded voice came on the line with the familiar boilerplate warning to call 911 if the caller were experiencing a medical emergency. Otherwise, listen to the following menu options. When the selection came to *if you are calling from a physician's office, press 3,* Meredith thought *close enough* and pressed that button on her phone keypad. Almost immediately, a woman answered, "Tacoma Heights Physicians. How can I help you?"

Meredith identified herself as calling from Dr. Olivetti's laboratory at State University and asked to speak to the Smathers's primary care physician, Dr. Lawrence Coldstream.

"He's with a patient now. If this is an emergency, I can interrupt him," responded the receptionist.

"No, it's not an emergency. I want to speak with him about a patient of his who recently died, Colonel James Smathers. Would you ask him to call me at this number?" Meredith gave the number of her desk phone to the receptionist.

"It was tragic the way the colonel died so suddenly, wasn't it? I'll let Dr. Coldstream know that you called. It will probably be around noon before he has a break in his clinic and can call you back."

After Meredith had hung up, she didn't know what to do with herself. She wanted to talk to Jack but could see that he was busy. So she just stuck her head into his office door and asked if he had something for her to do while she waited for Smathers's physician to call her back.

Jack looked up and asked, "Why did you call him? Did you find out something from the medical records that he sent?"

"It's probably nothing, but according to the admission history, Smathers's wife said that he became confused a couple of days before he became ill and also talked to a reporter about that same time. Just like Granner. Granner's blood showed that she had taken a drug called rohypnol, but I have no idea how she could have gotten it. I thought I would see if anyone had done a drug screen on Smathers, just out of curiosity."

"Rohypnol, what's that? I've never heard of it."

Meredith explained to Jack what she had learned about the drug. Jack looked perplexed and said, "Most unusual. I don't see how your grandmother could have gotten into it. Let me know if anything turns up with Smathers. Why were the two of them talking to a reporter anyway?"

Meredith told Jack the story that the reporter had given Smathers and her grandmother, namely that *Time Magazine* was doing a story on new kinds of cancer therapy from the viewpoint of patients and wanted to talk with them because of the treatment they had received at State.

"That's funny," said Jack. "Usually a reporter goes through our News and Information Services group first, and the faculty member whose work is featured in the story is notified. I didn't hear anything about this story. Do you know the reporter's name?"

"According to Mrs. Smathers, it's Sandra Towns."

Jack jotted down the reporter's name and said, "In the meantime, you're looking for something to do. Do you remember that refractory lymphoma patient from the VA whom we treated using our own virus and not the one from AVARTEC? Well, I just got word from the VA that when he came back for his one month evaluation, it looked like he was in complete remission. I'm still waiting to hear about the patient we treated after him. Looks like the treatment is working again. Why don't you take another look at the viral vector that AVARTEC sent over for his treatment and see if there is anything subtly different about it, something that we might have missed when we did the check on the verification sample?"

Meredith thought that sounded like a good plan, and it would certainly keep her mind occupied while she waited to hear back from Dr. Coldstream. She retrieved the virus container from the laboratory freezer and began work. She decided to treat the specimen as if it were just prepared and completely new, or *de novo* as it was termed in the language of the medical professional. This meant both determining its genetic sequence and then testing the blocking protein that the virus would produce in the infected cell. This was now something that she could do by rote. The first step was to sequence the virus which required using reverse transcriptase to generate the corresponding DNA strand to be fed into the automated sequencer. Simple enough to do, just a little tedious.

Meredith lost track of the time until the phone on her desk rang. It was Dr. Coldstream. He sounded like an amicable man, and readily answered her questions about Smathers.

"No, a toxicology screen had not been done on his blood because we didn't think it was important," he said. "Smathers had a fever and a funny blood count and didn't act as if he were under the influence of any drugs or agents."

Meredith quickly reassured him that she understood his reasoning. "However, I'm wondering about the episode of confusion he had a few days before he became ill."

"Sorry, but I didn't see him for that. In fact, I didn't even know about it until days after it had occurred. Sounds like it might have been a mini-stroke that resolved on its own. I would have worked it up with an MRI later if Smathers had lived. What are you looking for anyway?"

Meredith told him about Gaby's case and how her clinical course resembled that of Smathers, starting with the episode of confusion a few days before her terminal illness and the drug that was found in her bloodstream.

"So, are you wondering about some sort of a funny drug reaction with the experimental cancer treatment the two of them received? I can see why you would be concerned. I'm pretty sure that there are a couple of tubes of blood still in the hospital laboratory from his admission. How about if I have them sent to you for testing. Remember, they weren't drawn until a couple of days after he had that stroke-like event and so even if he had taken a drug, you might not be able to find it."

Meredith thought it best to let Coldstream draw his own conclusions about why she wanted the blood tested. "That's great," she said. "Please put it on ice and send to to this address. We will pay the shipping charges." Meredith gave Coldstream the address of Jack's laboratory and hung up. Then she turned back to the virus analysis. She would tell Jack about this later when she and Jack got together after work, at least she assumed that they would be getting together.

The virus sample had been placed in the bioreactor earlier that day, and with the use of reverse transcriptase the DNA counterpart to the viral RNA genetic code had been constructed. Meredith then loaded the DNA into the sequencer and set the controls to send the output data file to her E-mail account. Then she went away to let the machine do its work.

CHAPTER 73

DEAN SCHMITT CALLED THE head of the IRB review board shortly after he received the phone call from Peter Drisco. He let the IRB chair, Lisa Brandon, know that he had heard rumors of problems with Olivetti's protocol and to please check into it. "Wouldn't want any bad publicity for State for not keeping track of our investigators, you know," he said at the end of the phone call.

Brandon, who was still chafing at being forced into approving the continuation of Olivetti's protocol, said that she would certainly look into it. Her being alerted in advance of Jack's communication enabled the IRB to come to a rapid decision to stop the protocol. Given the high profile nature of the protocol, the IRB had, furthermore, decided to hold a meeting and question Jack about what had happened.

Collecting and organizing the information relating to the patient deaths was keeping Jack busy. However, he did find the time to call Tela Morgan, the head of the School of Medicine's Public Relations Department, and ask her about the *Time Magazine* article. Morgan said that she was not aware of any such article, but would check into it. It was several hours later when she called back.

"Professor Olivetti, this is Tela Morgan. I just wanted to get back to you on that *Time Magazine* thing. I called one of the associate editors at *Time* whom I know and asked her about it. She checked into it and said that there is no such article underway. However, she thought it sounded like a good idea for a future article, and said she might be getting back to us. One more thing, they don't have any reporter on their staff named Sandra Towns and have never worked with any freelancers with that name either."

Jack thanked her for the information and quickly went over to Meredith's desk to let her know what he had found out.

"Jack, what the hell is going on? I know that Sandra Towns was the name of thte person that interviewed Colonel Smathers and Granner told me that the first name of the person that talked to her was Sandra. Smathers's wife never saw her, but Granner said that she had red hair and drove a flashy convertible. Both people said that she was a reporter from *Time*."

The two agreed to have dinner and talk more about it then. Meredith thought about Gaby's body and the autopsy. Picturing the sequence of events, based upon the few autopsies she had witnessed, made her feel queasy. She decided that she needed to quit thinking about the autopsy and focus instead on something else like the viral sequencing project that she was in the midst of. She decided to check on the work being done by the gene sequencer. Only a few hours more until it would complete the determination of the sequence and send the data to her internet account. She went back to poring over Smathers's medical data, but didn't learn anything new. Finally, she gave up, told Jack that she was going back to her apartment to take Sam for a walk and then have a run herself to think about things other than Gaby. Jack was preoccupied with preparing his summary for the IRB meeting, but stood up, squeezed her hand discreetly, and said he would be by about 6:30 if that was OK with her. It was.

"I really don't feel like going anywhere. Let's just stay at my place for dinner. I'll pick up some things before I go home," said Meredith.

Jack agreed and watched Meredith leave his office. *Poor kid*, he thought. *She seems strong on the surface, but underneath she's really taking this hard. Can't say as I can fault her for that.*

Meredith quickly picked up a few things at the University Village QFC store and went home. Sam greeted her enthusiastically. After taking him for a walk and having a run herself, it was nearly 6 o'clock. Just time for a quick shower before starting dinner. Dinner wouldn't take much preparation time, just some chicken breasts to bake and some steamed vegetables. She would get the chicken started since it would take a while, but not do anything with the vegetables until Jack actually arrived. Knowing how engrossed he got in his work, she fully expected him to be late, but reflected that she found this somehow reassuring rather than irritating. Sure enough, 6:30 came and no Jack. Meredith opened a bottle of wine, a good but inexpensive syrah, and opened up her laptop to pass the time. She logged into her State net account to see if the gene sequencer had completed its work. *Yep, it has*, she thought. There was the data file waiting for her. She downloaded it. Then she logged remotely into the much faster laboratory computer and set it comparing the data file with the initial specification file. As she scrolled through the comparison, several sequences were displayed in red and jumped out at her. These were elements that were different in the two data sets. *Strange*, thought Meredith. She was sure that the first comparison she and Jack had made with the verification sample virus sent by AVARTEC exactly matched the specification data. Just to be sure, she retrieved the data file for the test sample and confirmed this.

Just then she heard the buzzer at the building entrance ring. Looking at her watch, she noted that Jack was only a half hour late.

She hit the button to let him into the building. Jack quickly bounded up the stairs and she met him at the door.

"Sorry I'm late," he began, but then stopped when Meredith grabbed his hand and tugged him over to the table where her laptop was set up.

Hurriedly, she explained what she had found, then asked, "What do you think this means?"

"So the sample from the freezer was different from the test sample that we used to verify accuracy of the virus fabricated by AVARTEC's labs. Do you have any idea where this segment of the viral genome operates?

"I don't know for sure but I think it is in the area that needed to be blocked to control the tumor growth control element. I can check this for sure when I get to the lab tomorrow."

"Assuming that you're right about this, that would mean that the virus provided by AVARTEC wouldn't have worked on the patient. Boy, it's a good thing that we treated that last patient from the VA with the virus we made ourselves rather than using the one AVARTEC sent over. That reminds me, I need to check with the VA to see how he is doing." Jack scribbled himself a note and stuck it in his shirt pocket.

"Jack, remember what you said when we were trying to figure out why the treatment suddenly stopped working? You were listing all of the things that were different; one thing that had changed was that the treatment viruses were coming from AVARTEC and not ones that we were making ourselves."

"Yes, but we checked them out before using them on patients."

"Well, we checked this last one out too and on the first go round it matched our specifications. What if the same thing was true for the other ones and we injected those patients with a faulty virus?"

"Are you thinking that maybe AVARTEC made the test sample and the actual treatment virus in two different batches and the manufacturing processes are not identical? If they are doing that, it would invalidate the entire testing philosophy that was specified by the FDA in the protocol."

"I wouldn't put it past Tony Beckwith to take a short cut like this if he thought he could get away with it. Too bad that we don't have a way of checking on those other batches of virus."

"One thing is for sure: once we get this protocol operating again, we are going to check the actual virus going into the patients as well as the verification sample that is sent over first. It may cause a day's delay but I don't see how we can avoid it."

Meredith agreed and then she and Jack got up to finish preparing dinner. They attempted to talk about things other than work during dinner and afterwards but the conversation kept coming back to the question of who was this Sandra Towns person and what did she really want with Gaby and Colonel Smathers. Meredith certainly planned to have Smathers's blood sent to toxicology when it arrived the next day. *What if it too contained traces of rohypnol*, she thought. It was another piece to a very curious puzzle.

CHAPTER 74

JACK SPENT THE NIGHT with Meredith, and both arose very contentedly the following morning. They had breakfast together and, as before, Meredith went directly to the laboratory while Jack went back to his apartment for a change of clothes. Later that morning, Smathers's blood sample arrived. Meredith took it to the hospital laboratory and filled out the paperwork for a toxicology screen. She asked the lab particularly to check for the presence of rohypnol. In the meantime, Jack got a call from Pathology giving him a preliminary report on Gaby's autopsy.

"Dr. Olivetti, this is Dr. Bloom. I'm the pathology attending who was in charge of Mrs. Jones's autopsy. It was a most interesting case. The bone marrow was hyperactive but the circulating white cell count was next to zero. The ultimate cause of death was a widespread infection. Her immune system had shut down. I can tell you how the various organ systems were affected if you like but this will all be in the written report."

"What could have caused her immune system to shut down this way and so rapidly too?"

"We thought this was very unusual ourselves. The only situation in which we've seen something like this is in the end stage AIDS patient, but this takes years to develop. However, we sent tissue samples to Microbiology for viral cultures, and they found something very unusual. There was an adenovirus that they hadn't seen before. Micro did a genetic screen on it and ran a comparison to entries in the NIH database. It turned out that while most of the gene looked like one of the common adenoviruses, there was a section that looked like a portion of the HIV genome. It's the part that codes for a protein that allows the virus to attach to the host white blood cells. However, the rest of the virus didn't look anything at all like the HIV virus. Micro sent a sample off to the CDC in Atlanta for them to look at. It will be interesting to see what they think. Also, I understand from her medical records that you treated her ovarian cancer using some sort of virus-based gene transfer."

"Yes, that's right. But the virus we used had controls on its replication sequence and wasn't related at all to the HIV virus."

"I understand that, but as another check, would you send me a sample of the virus used to treat Jones so that I can do a comparison?"

"We always store a reference batch of the virus for each patient in the freezer as an archival sample. I can give you some of that. Anything else come up in the autopsy?"

"Just a bruise on her right upper arm. We looked at it in detail and found a minor penetration near its center like an injection site. I suppose this could have been due to an injection of some sort that she received during one of her recent hospital admissions. No big deal."

Jack thanked Bloom for the phone call and then asked one of his lab techs to pull out of the freezer a sample of the viral vector used to treat Gaby and take it to Dr. Bloom in Pathology. Then he asked Meredith to come into his office where he told her about the autopsy findings for her grandmother.

"You don't think it was our virus that did this, do you?" were the first words out of Meredith's mouth.

Jack hastened to reassure her. "Meredith, I don't see how it could have been. We used a pretty standard transfer virus with safeguards on its replication sequence. The special antisense element that we put in against the tumor growth control points looked nothing like the HIV segment that the lab found. Also, just to be doubly sure, I've sent a sample of the virus that was used to treat your grandmother to our pathology laboratory for them to run a detailed comparison."

"Let me know just as soon as you've heard something back, will you? I need to know for my own peace of mind that I didn't do something that may have caused Granner's death."

"I certainly will, but while we're waiting, are you up to doing something to help me get ready for the IRB review next week?"

Meredith smiled and said, "Actually, I would be glad to have something to do. What is it?"

"I've been thinking about what you found out concerning the virus that AVARTEC sent over for the VA patient. I wonder if there was a similar screw-up in the other batches they sent over. Why don't you recheck the archival specimens from the freezer for the other patients and see what you find?"

Meredith agreed and started work. By now this was a very familiar process. It only took about a half day per specimen as long as she didn't try to computationally model the protein structure coded for by the virus. At the end of the day, she had determined the sequence for the patient, Pettigrove, who was the first patient treated using the AVARTEC-produced virus. She couldn't believe her eyes, there was another mismatch in the area of the genome that contained the antisense coding element. Meredith then started work on the treatment virus for Oldfield, who was the next patient in the series. Jack came by and she told him what she had found.

"My God," he said. "We need to check for the rest of the patients that we treated. Here, let me take the next one."

Meredith and Jack worked through the night, and when they were finished had established that a mismatch error was present in all the viruses that were prepared by AVARTEC. The mismatches were different in each case, but were always in the critical region.

"I don't see how this kind of error could have occurred," said Meredith.

"Neither do I," replied Jack. "It would have taken some sophisticated engineering for all of these different types of errors to fortuitously occur in the critical element of the viral genome and not in non-critical regions, which make up the great majority of the genome."

He looked at his watch. It was about 4 AM. "I'm going to give Beckwith a call when he gets into his lab later today and ask him about this." He then stretched and yawned. "Let's call it a night and try to get a few hours sleep."

Meredith agreed, so they buttoned things down and left Jack's laboratory.

CHAPTER 75

When Jack and Meredith awakened later that morning, Jack immediately pulled out his cell phone, called the main number at AVARTEC ,and asked to speak with Tony Beckwith. It was a minute or two before Beckwith came on the line. Jack identified himself and quickly got to the point, laying out the work that he and Meredith had done which showed discrepancies between the specified viral genome and what had been administered to the patients.

Jack asked, "Have you been using two different processes to produce the viral vectors based on our specifications? Otherwise, I can't understand how the pre-screening test batches could be OK but the treatment batches could be wrong."

Beckwith was flustered and stalled for time while he thought. Neither he nor Drisco had anticipated that Olivetti would have preserved a patient's archival samples, which could be tested later. "No, just like it says in the protocol, we use the same process throughout. Your lab checked out the sample specimens before we went ahead and made the larger aliquots used to treat the patients. If something was wrong and you missed it, I don't see how that's my fault."

"Look Beckwith, I just told you there was a difference between the test batches we checked out and the second batch you sent over to treat the patients. The treatment stopped working when we used your viral vectors on four patients, but then started working again when we used our own virus. We have both the test sample and the treatment virus for the last patient, and are going to check both out today. What do you think we're going to find when we do?"

"How would I know? Maybe your testing is all screwed up. Just don't accuse me of sending you the wrong virus. You accuse me of something you can't prove and I'll sue you for slander." Beckwith was growing more and more agitated as the conversation continued. He could see his career shattered if people thought that his lab had made a mistake like that and, even worse, he could go to jail if it was ever discovered that he had deliberately sabotaged a cancer patient's treatment.

Jack also was getting more and more angry as the call continued. He had just wanted to alert Beckwith to the problem to give him a chance to think about what might have gone wrong. Now the jerk was trying to cover his own tail. There was no point in continuing the conversation. "Beckwith, we're not getting anywhere. I'm going to write up what we've found, send it to the NCI, and ask them to look into it. All of the changes have been different but still located in the viral area critical for the treatment to work. I just don't see how this could have happened if your company did what it was supposed to do."

After the phone call, Beckwith raced to Peter Drisco's office. Drisco was in a meeting, but Beckwith demanded to see him just as soon as it was finished. Drisco's secretary, Patti, was used to dealing with high strung, science types, and so told Beckwith that as soon as Mr. Drisco's meeting was finished, she would let him know that Beckwith needed to see him urgently, and she would squeeze in a few minutes on his schedule. Beckwith took her proffered cup of coffee, but was unable to sit down and drink it. He got up continually and paced back and forth until the door to the inner office finally opened and several people filed out. Just as soon as the office was clear, Beckwith rushed in and shut the door behind him.

"Drisco, we're in trouble with this Olivetti thing," were the first words out of his mouth.

Peter Drisco looked up in surprise, clearly needing to change mental gears from the preceding meeting, which had been about marketing. "Tony, slow down. Tell me what's going on."

Beckwith reprised his phone conversation with Olivetti and concluded with, "I had no idea that Olivetti would be keeping samples of the treatment virus and would go back and recheck them. The NCI is going to be all over us once Olivetti's report reaches them. You need to do something because if their investigation leads to me, it is just a short step to you as well."

Stupid bastard, thought Drisco. *Why did he have to get cute and make different changes for each patient?* Drisco asked that question and was told that it made for a more stable virus, as if that were important.

"OK," said Drisco. "Calm down. We will just have to make sure that the evidence turns up missing and the report doesn't get sent out."

"How are you going to do that?" asked Beckwith.

"Don't concern yourself about that," Drisco replied. He would simply have to find the right people and have them take care of the problem. Besides getting rid of the evidence, he needed to eliminate Olivetti and his assistant, Jones. They were the only two besides Beckwith and himself who had any inkling as to the game that Drisco was playing. Afterwards, he would magnanimously step in and offer to take over the process to see if AVARTEC could make it work in the clinic. After six months or so of work, Drisco would announce that his company had found a fatal flaw in the procedure and would be working to bring it back to the clinic. Of course, it would be his company's intellectual property by that time. He thought about using the woman from San Francisco again, but he had no way to contact her rapidly. Besides, he thought that she was ridiculously expensive. He decided to call Martileni and get another reference. Beckwith was also a liability and needed to be eliminated as well. Drisco reflected that he was becoming quite good at making decisions of this type; presumably one got better with practice.

Drisco escorted Beckwith from his office and after he had left the reception area, turned to his secretary and said, "Patti, I need to talk to Adam Martileni as soon as possible. Try his office first, will you?" It was several minutes before Patti announced that she had Martileni on the line.

Drisco picked up the phone and said, "Adam, this is Pete Drisco. I need a referral for someone to do another special job for me."

Pete, I'm out of the office and speaking to you on my cell phone so be circumspect in what you say. It is always possible for someone to pick up our conversation."

"Understood." Drisco found himself getting excited rather than anxious about the intrigue, and quickly got into his role. "You know the job I had done earlier? I need another similar job done."

"Do you want to use the same agent as before?"

"No, the job turned out fine, but the agent was damn expensive and this job doesn't require the same degree of sophistication. It's more of a direct application of the usual techniques, so more routine workers would suffice. Also, it's something that needs to be taken care of in a hurry, and it takes a while to contact the other agent and get things set up to her satisfaction."

"Pete, no matter whom you hire, this kind of work isn't going to be cheap, but probably not as expensive as if you used the first agent again. Then again, you get what you pay for, even in this business. I'll make a few phone calls and have someone get in touch with you. You can make the arrangements directly with them. Just make sure that my investors' interests are protected."

Martileni hung up and Drisco tried to get back to work, but he was unable to. He kept thinking about how to position the company once Olivetti's process belonged to him. He would have to take his time about rolling it out, as if the company was really investigating the process and correcting its flaws. It wouldn't do to have this appear too easy.

It was late in the day before Drisco received the phone call he had been waiting for. He arranged to meet the individual on the line at Jake O'Shaughnessy's pub near the Seattle Center at 8 PM. The man on the phone told him to have a drink at the bar. Someone would meet him there. Drisco got to O'Shaughnessy's just before 8 and found a space at the bar. It seemed quite crowded for a Thursday night. He ordered his usual, an Absolut vodka martini, and watched the bar TV as he nursed his drink. After a while, a short, swarthy man wearing a sweater and slacks elbowed in beside him and asked the bartender for a Jack Daniels on the rocks. When his drink arrived, he turned and said, "Mr. Drisco, my friend and I have a table over there. Why don't you join us?"

Drisco picked up his drink and followed the swarthy man to a corner table where they joined a tall, slender man with blond hair who was nervously twirling his drink on a bar napkin. The two sat down and Drisco looked at each in turn. The tension in the blond-haired man was evident. The swarthy man spoke. "Call me Rocco and him Eric. Adam Martileni said that you had a job for us."

"There are two people who are in a position to cause my company and me a lot of trouble. They are not the sort of people who can be reasoned with – you know – persuaded to do what is in their own best interest. I need to have them removed from the scene."

"Temporarily or permanently?" asked Eric who spoke with a Slavic accent.

"Permanently," responded Drisco.

"Exactly who are these people?" asked Rocco.

"Jack Olivetti and Meredith Jones. Olivetti is a professor at State and Jones works in his laboratory."

"A couple of scientists, huh? What did they do to you that you want them out of the picture?"

"Let's just say they have found out something that could be embarrassing to me."

"Fair enough. How do we find them and how soon do you need the job done?"

Drisco handed over an envelope that contained pictures of Olivetti and Jones taken from the State University web site, their addresses, car descriptions, and license numbers which he had obtained elsewhere. "Everything you need to find them is in this envelope."

Rocco took the envelope, opened it, and quickly perused the contents. "Everything except our fee. Did Martileni tell you about that?"

"No, he just set up this contact. I guess he assumed that was something that we would work out between us."

"A couple of questions first. Does this need to look like an accident and how soon do you need to have the job done?

"Looking like an accident would be best. What is more important is that the job be done in the next few days before these two let more people know about my problem."

"Sometimes it can take a while to set up a believable accident. Are these two involved with each other? What about making it look like a love affair gone bad with a murder-suicide? This would give the police something to look at without pointing to any outside people." Rocco was looking at Drisco when he said this and took his silence for a tacit agreement.

Then he looked at Eric, who nodded. Eric said, "Fifty thousand for the pair, half now and the other half when the job is done."

"How do you want the money transferred?" asked Drisco, thinking of the deal he had made with the woman in the San Francisco airport.

"Transfer, what transfer? This is a cash deal," said Rocco. "Do we look like regular businessmen to you? Cash leaves no trail that can complicate our tax returns. We'll start planning and do the job as soon as you get us the first half of the money."

"How will I come up with that much cash without people asking some awkward questions?" asked Drisco.

"That's your problem," said Eric. "You might talk with Martileni about it. He is good at coming up with solutions to problems like this. Just don't take too long if the job is as rush as you say it is. Call this number when the money is ready." Eric then handed Drisco a card with a telephone number scrawled on it.

Drisco downed the rest of his drink and took his leave. When he got to his car, he called Martileni's cell phone. "Martileni here," came the voice on the phone. Drisco quickly explained his problem in circumspect terms, recalling Martileni's earlier admonition. Martileni laughed and said that he might be able to help Drisco out. The two set up a meeting for the next day to discuss the details.

CHAPTER 76

DRISCO AND MARTILENI MET for breakfast at the 5 Spot Restaurant in upper Queen Anne. After the waitress had taken their order, Drisco began filling in the details of what he needed.

"So why can't you just come up with the money? I know that you are worth a hell of a lot more than 50 grand."

"I told you last night. It's not the amount, but getting it in cash on short notice that's the problem. I pretty well tapped out my ready cash in paying for the last job. Your contractor from San Francisco was more expensive than I anticipated. Most of my other actual cash is in a joint account with Evie right now, and I don't want to have to explain to her where it went. Right now she's acting funny enough without my giving her something else to think about."

Martileni said, "I have some business colleagues who are in the loan business. I'll have to talk with them but should be able to get you $50 thousand in cash by noon tomorrow. I looked at the price of AVARTEC stock this morning and it has been running about $8 per share. Suppose you give me 10,000 of your founder's shares to hold as a guarantee?"

"The loan is only for $50,000; that's only about 6,500 shares. Why do you want so many?"

"There's interest on the loan of course. I told you that my friends are businessmen. They aren't doing this out of the kindness of their hearts. I think I can get you their best rate of 4.5 percent."

"That sounds like a pretty good rate. Maybe I should be using your friends instead of my bank in the future."

Martileni just smiled. "That's 4.5 percent per month, compounded. The extra shares just guarantee the first few months' interest."

"That's highway robbery!" sputtered Drisco.

"Actually, the technical term is loan sharking," rejoined Martileni with the same smile on his face. "Part of what you're paying for is that the money is untraceable. Now, do you want the money or not?"

Drisco quickly realized that he had no choice and agreed to the terms. The two men arranged to meet the following day for the money transfer. Drisco left the table before his order arrived pleading pressing business. Inwardly he was seething at being taken advantage of. He threw a $20 bill down on the table as he left saying, "At these interest rates, I wouldn't want to owe you for breakfast too." Martileni just shrugged and picked up his fork.

Drisco delayed going to his office until after his bank had opened. Then he retrieved the necessary stock certificates from his safe deposit box and put them into his attaché case. He put the case into his desk drawer and locked it. Then he called Dean Schmitt, ostensively to complain about the allegations that Olivetti and Jones were making about AVRTEC's quality of work, but really to engineer a way to bring them to a controlled location for the hit.

"This is defamatory," said Drisco. "My attorneys are advising me to sue not only Olivetti and Jones but also State for not managing its faculty better. However, based upon the long relationship between my company and State, I would like to make one more try to resolve this out of court."

"Right. No need to be hasty," said Schmitt, thinking of the bad publicity such a lawsuit would engender. "Tell me more about the situation."

After listening to Drisco's spin on the story and thinking about the importance of the AVARTEC commitment to the Lake Union research venture, Schmitt asked, "What do you want me to do?"

"For starters, just get Olivetti and Jones to meet with me to discuss things. I'm sure that if they do, I can convince them that my company made the virus exactly as they specified and that their own checks confirmed this. It is absolutely ridiculous to think that we deliberately sabotaged the study. To accuse us of doing so is slander based upon no evidence at all. If this gets out in the press, I will have no choice but to sue for defamation in order to protect AVARTEC."

"Pete, I am sure that I can get Olivetti to meet with you. I'll give him a call right now and tell him that your office is going to call to set up a meeting and that he damn well better be there."

The dean was as good as his word. As soon as he and Drisco had hung up, he had his secretary call Olivetti's laboratory. The technician who answered the phone told her that Olivetti hadn't come into work yet.

"Well then page him," roared the dean. It was several minutes before Olivetti responded. As he was not responsible for a clinical service just then, Jack did not feel the need to respond immediately to his pages, particularly when he was having a late breakfast with Meredith.

"Yes, Dr. Schmitt?" began Jack after Schmitt's secretary had identified herself and put him through to the inner office phone.

"Olivetti, I just had a very disturbing phone call from Peter Drisco. You know who he is?"

"Yes, he is the president of AVARTEC pharmaceuticals. I've met him a couple of times. Why?"

The dean launched into a summary of what Drisco had told him and then asked for Olivetti's side of the story. Jack told the dean about the faulty virus that AVARTEC had provided. Moreover, he said not only did the therapeutic agent not match the pre-therapy test agent, but the errors were different each time, although all were located in the same critical part of the genome. Schmitt did not understand all the details, but clearly got the message that Jack thought what had happened was incompetent at best and deliberate malfeasance at worst. Thinking back to one of his own conversations with Drisco, the dean began to get an inkling of what might be going on, namely that Drisco was deliberately making the study fail so that he could gain control of the procedure and thus dictate the timing of its release. He didn't share this speculation with Jack.

"Olivetti, that's a very serious accusation," said Schmitt. "Peter Drisco is one of our biggest benefactors, and his company has funded a lot of our research. It may just be an innocent error. Drisco wants to meet directly with you and your collaborator, Jones, to talk about this. I want the two of you to make yourselves available when he calls about setting up the meeting. Afterwards, give me a call and let me know how it went."

Jack was highly skeptical about the error being innocent, but agreed to meet with Drisco. However, he said, "I'm still going to include this information in my protocol status report for the NCI."

"Just don't send it out until after you've met with Drisco and then talked with me. Do you understand?"

Jack muttered something noncommittal and hung up. He told Meredith about the dean's instructions and their upcoming meeting with Peter Drisco.

Meredith snorted in disbelief. "Why is the dean getting involved anyway? I can't believe the influence that some people have just because they contribute big bucks to one of State's programs. What are you going to do about the NCI report?"

"Why, I'm going to finish preparing it anyway," answered Jack. "I'll have it all ready to send off after our meeting with Drisco. If he convinces me that there need to be changes, then I will make them before it goes out the door. But I'm not giving the dean veto power on it."

"Good," said Meredith, as she gave Jack a hug.

Across town Peter Drisco called Martileni and arranged to exchange the stock certificates for the money. Then he called the number on the card that Rocco had given him and said that he would have the money ready the next day, which was a Saturday.

"That didn't take too long, did it?" said Rocco. "When do you want us to take care of your two problems?"

"Here's how I want it to work," said Drisco. "I am going to set up a meeting with Olivetti and Jones at my office Saturday evening when nobody else will be around. I will say that it needs to be late because I need to get ready for a business trip and am going to catch a red-eye flight after the meeting. I want you two to come to the meeting with me. You can be a couple of legal advisors. I need to talk to Olivetti and Jones before I turn them over to you to make sure that I know what evidence they have, so that I can get rid of it. After that, they're all yours. You'll need to take them somewhere else to get rid of them, but I'll leave that to you."

"OK by me. Just so we don't act surprised and give things away too soon, what names do you want us to use?"

"Let's go with something simple. You can be Mr. Simpson and your friend Eric can be Mr. Brodsky which fits with his accent."

"Eric's sensitive about his English, so don't let him hear you say that. Bring the money to the lobby of the Sorrento at 2 PM so that I can check it over and put it in a safe place before we do the job."

Drisco then placed a call to Olivetti at his laboratory. By this time, Jack and Meredith had made it to work and the technician who answered the phone transferred the call to Jack's office phone. Drisco identified himself, and Jack, remembering the Dean's admonition, told himself to be cordial.

"Yes, Mr. Drisco, I know who you are. Dean Schmitt said that you would be calling about the problems we've had with the viral vectors your company produced for our treatment protocol. Let me summarize what happened."

Jack then told the same story that he had told the dean with Drisco interrupting from time to time with questions. It appeared to Jack that Drisco had a good grasp of the underlying science.

"I don't see how something like this could have happened," said Drisco. "I want to see your analysis for myself before this goes any further."

"I'll send you a copy of my report to the NCI. You'll find all the data in it."

"Jack, let me have a chance to look at the data before you send the report off. I'm not saying that you're necessarily wrong, but let's be sure before you stir up a lot of trouble for my company. If we have screwed up, then I will apologize and put things right. What do you say to that?"

Jack was surprised at the offer and couldn't very well refuse without appearing very rude, which would surely get him in trouble with the dean. "OK, when do you want to meet to look at things?"

Drisco lied readily. "Jack, I have meetings all the rest of the day and my wife and I are having an anniversary dinner tonight. I'm leaving for a business trip with some investment advisors tomorrow evening and need to get ready for the trip. I really want to get this sorted out before I go. It's an imposition, but would you come by my office about 5 o'clock tomorrow afternoon? I'll have some of my legal advisors there, just so that they can hear firsthand about this problem."

"I will be working on some things tomorrow, so that's not a problem."

"Thanks. I will be sure and let Dean Schmitt know how helpful you've been. Oh, would you ask your colleague, Ms. Jones, to be there as well? I understand that she was responsible for the secondary analysis, and I would like to talk to her as well."

"I don't know if she has plans for tomorrow night or not, but I can ask her." Jack knew full well that the only plans Meredith had were with him, but he wanted to give her the chance to opt out of the meeting if she wished."

"It's important to me that I speak with her as well as you," prodded Drisco. "I don't like leaving any loose ends. You probably have the raw data on your laboratory computers, don't you? Too bad you can't bring that with you also. Sometimes the raw data show something that is glossed over in the final report analysis."

"Actually, I have been doing most of the work on the report using my laptop, so I can bring that to the meeting. Of course, the actual analysis of the virus was done using the much faster computers in my lab but I can show you the output data."

"Fine. You remember where my office is, don't you? On the fifth floor of the building. I will tell the security guard at the desk to expect you and to send you up when you arrive."

CHAPTER 77

THE NEXT DAY WAS Saturday. In the morning Drisco first met with Martileni and traded the stock certificates for a briefcase full of cash. Martileni just smiled when Drisco asked if he wanted him to sign a note for the loan. Drisco had a feeling that he had just sold over $80,000 worth of stock for $50,000. He went to his home on Mercer Island where he counted out $25,000 and dumped the remainder of the money into a small duffle bag. Then he stashed the duffle bag in the crawl space under the house where no one, except for the occasional maintenance man, ever went. He took the brief case into his study. It was nearly noon and so Drisco went into the kitchen to fix himself something to eat before going to the Sorrento hotel to meet with Rocco and Eric. Evie had slept late, and was just getting up. She poured herself a cup of coffee and joined her husband at the table. Things had been tense between the them since Peter had left their Fiji vacation early. By tacit agreement they had kept their conversations to a minimum after returning to Seattle. As for sex, forget it. Neither was interested in intimate relations with the other. Peter could see that a divorce was imminent; just one more thing to take care of after getting the current problem resolved. Idly he wondered just what it would cost to add Evie to Rocco and Eric's client list.

Evie, I'm going into the office to take care of some things. Don't plan on my being home for dinner."

"Pete, it's a Saturday. Don't you ever stop working, or are you seeing someone else?"

"It's work, Evie, it's work," replied Peter. "Just some urgent things I need to take care of."

"I'd almost rather it was another woman. I would have a better chance of competing with that than your damned company," Evie said bitterly. "No matter. Just do what you need to do, and don't worry about me."

Peter left the table without saying anything more, went to his study and retrieved the briefcase. Then he drove to the Sorento where he intended to have a drink at the bar before meeting Rocco and Eric. As he drove, he noticed a black car that appeared to be following him. He didn't think too much about it, and after reaching the Sorrento, drove into the front courtyard, and handed the car keys to the parking valet. The black car, a late model Cadillac, drove by on Madison. He carried the briefcase with him and placed it at his feet as he ordered his usual vodka martini. He looked up when a portly man wearing a sport coat entered the room and took a booth. He didn't know the man, so he turned back to his drink.

Rocco and Eric came in shortly thereafter and took a booth along a side wall. Drisco took his drink and walked over to join them. The two were talking about the portly man.

"Wonder what Jamison is doing here?" mused Rocko.

"Probably watching for someone's spouse having a tête à tête with a lover. Most of his business involves divorce cases. Wouldn't want that work myself. He has been clobbered by an irate husband more than once when he was caught peeping in." replied Eric.

"Who, that fat guy in a sport coat sitting, over there?" asked Drisco.

"Yeah, that's him," said Eric.

A light bulb suddenly switched on in Drisco's brain. "By any chance do you know what kind of car he drives?" he asked.

"Something black. A Caddy I think," said Rocco.

"Yeah, that's right. One of those smaller model Caddys," confirmed Eric.

"Well guys, I think he may be following me. My wife thinks I've been having an affair, and may have hired him to follow me. We need to do something about him so that he doesn't mess up our business with Jones and Olivetti."

Eric looked at Rocco and said, "I'll take care of Jamison. You check out the briefcase Drisco is carrying." Eric then walked over to Jamison's booth and sat down. Eric leaned over and spoke to low for Drisco to hear exactly what he said but Jamison's face flushed and he hurriedly got up, leaving his unfinished drink on the table, and exited the bar. Eric then walked back and rejoined Rocco and Drisco. In the meantime, Rocco had placed the briefcase beside him in the bar booth and verified that it contained money, a substantial amount of money.

"I'm not going to count it here but I'm sure that you wouldn't try to shortchange us. It wouldn't be a good idea to do that," said Rocco.

Drisco nodded and then turned to Eric. "Well, what did you find out?"

Eric smirked and said, "Good guess, Drisco. He was tailing you. I just explained to him that we had some business together that didn't concern him and that it would be healthier for him to find something else to do for a while. He didn't like it, but he got the message. You better watch your back; your wife will probably just hire someone else."

"We'll see about that," said Drisco. "Now let's get ready for Olivetti and Jones. "I'll show you the building, including a back way out, which won't take you past the guard at the front desk."

Chapter 78

Jack and Meredith were discussing their upcoming meeting with Drisco. Given the dean's admonishment about not upsetting Drisco further, they decided to simply give Drisco a copy of the protocol report to the NCI and give him a chance to respond to it. They would then send the report off on Monday morning unless Drisco had convinced them otherwise. Meredith told Jack that he could take her out to dinner after the meeting in return for talking with Drisco and keeping him out of trouble with the dean. They talked about where they would go during the drive to the AVARTEC building.

Jack parked the car and they walked up to the entrance. Jack was carrying his backpack, which held his laptop computer and two copies of the latest draft of the NCI report. The entryway was locked, so Meredith pushed the call button. A disembodied voice asked them to identify themselves and they did so stating that they had an appointment with Mr. Drisco. A sleepy-looking guard came to the door and let them in.

"Don't bother to sign in," said the guard. "Mr. Drisco himself has cleared your visit." The guard walked them over to the bank of elevators and swiped a card in the reader. "Elevator access is controlled in the evenings and on weekends. They don't work without a security card. Mr. Drisco will need to activate the elevator card reader for you after your meeting is finished. Either that or he can call me and I will escort you down."

The guard motioned for them to enter the elevator, leaned inside, pushed the fifth floor button, and backed out the door before it closed. When the elevator stopped at the fifth floor, Jack and Meredith exited and Jack led the way to Drisco's office. Both the outside door and the door to the inner office were open. Jack announced himself and Meredith as they entered.

"Come on in," came a voice from the inner office. Drisco was sitting at a table in the corner along with two other men. He got up, escorted them to seats between the two men, and then took a seat directly across from them. "Professor Olivetti and Ms. Jones, these are a couple of my legal and business advisors, Mr. Simpson and Mr. Brodsky." He gestured, respectively, to Rocco and Eric. "I want them to hear your story too."

Jack put his briefcase on his lap, pulled out the two copies of the report and his laptop computer. Rocco and Eric tensed visibly as he did. *Odd behavior,* thought Jack as he began his story by summarizing the background and rationale for the protocol study.

"Yes, yes," said Drisco. "I know all that. Skip the preliminary stuff and tell me about the problem you say you found with the viruses we provided."

"Sure," said Jack, and he quickly told the story, concluding with "the actual treatment virus specimens just didn't match the test verification samples that were sent over for checking. Your man, Beckwith, got very upset when I tried to talk to him about it, particularly when I asked whether the exact same procedure was used to make both batches."

"No wonder he got upset. Of course we use the same procedure each time. The agreement with the NCI and the FDA requires this.

How do you know that the virus you tested was the same one that you injected therapeutically? From what you told me, you didn't recheck before injecting. We didn't want any delays in patient treatment which was why we specified the pre-testing in the first place."

"But I told you; we kept a sample of the virus that was actually injected in each case. Meredith went back and checked each one last week and they all showed errors in the genome segment coding for the antisense blocking factor for the tumor growth control points. We think it's very strange that the rest of the viral genome checks out OK except for this one critical element."

Drisco was leafing through the NCI report as Jack was speaking. The other two men at the table hadn't said a word, but were just watching Jack and Meredith intently, like snakes eyeing their prey before striking.

Drisco turned to Meredith and said, "So you're the one who did the actual testing? You're just a student, I understand. Probably not well versed in laboratory procedure at all. How do we know that you didn't make a procedural mistake, or for that matter, test the wrong virus?"

Meredith bristled and spoke up before Jack could come to her defense. "I fully understand laboratory procedures and have done the genetic analysis on as many specimens as Jack here. My lab notebook clearly shows what I've done. The virus specimens were labeled with a protocol number corresponding to the intended patient and stored in the corner freezer. Everything is logged in and out of that freezer, and there has been no loss of control. Just like maintaining the chain of evidence in a criminal investigation."

"Your lab notebook, did you bring that with you?" asked Drisco, eyeing Jack's backpack while speaking to Meredith.

"No I didn't think it was necessary. Besides, our policy is that the notebooks stay in the laboratory at all times. Mine is on my desk and is clearly labeled as being mine."

"How about you, Professor? Is your notebook on your desk too?"

"It most certainly is," answered Jack. "I follow the same policies as my staff."

"Just one more thing," said Drisco. "Show me the data files you used in Ms. Jones's analysis."

Jack obediently started up his laptop, entering his password at the prompt, and opened one of the patient data files. "The files are complex," he said. "The problem is easier to see graphically. Look at this genome segment. The correct genome segment is shown in green and the bad section shown in red. Just above the red section is a yellow sequence showing what should have been there."

Drisco took the laptop from Jack and looked at its screen. He nodded. "OK. Has anyone else besides you two seen this report yet?"

"No," replied Jack. "I just printed it out before coming here."

"Very good," said Drisco as he shut the laptop's screen and put it down on the floor beside his chair.

"What do you think you're doing with my computer?" inquired Jack who was quite possessive about his equipment.

Rocco spoke for the first time since Jack and Meredith had entered the room. "Just take it easy," he said. Eric placed his hand inside his coat and left it there while he watched Jack and Meredith intently with an unblinking gaze.

Drisco looked at the two of them and said, "I can't let you send out this report to the NCI. It could start things unraveling and get me and my company into a lot of trouble."

"Taking Jack's computer isn't going to stop us from sending out the report, you know," sputtered Meredith. "We'll just write another one. In fact, I've got several drafts on my own computer."

"You don't understand me. This report would ruin me financially. I really can't let you send it out – ever. My associates here are going

470

to make sure of that. It would ruin me financially. Olivetti, turn out your pockets and give me the keys to your lab."

Jack just looked defiantly at Drisco and made no move to comply. Eric took his hand out of his coat and it came out holding a gun. Then he said, "This is a 9 mm Glock. It will make a hell of a mess of your head. Quit stalling and give Drisco your keys."

Jack felt his stomach churn and he broke out into a sweat. What had they gotten themselves into? He slowly took out his keys and put them on the table in front of Drisco.

"Now give us your car keys too," said Rocco.

Jack took out this set of keys as well and put them on the table.

Why are you doing this?" asked Meredith. "Yes, your company screwed up and some patients got hurt. But that wouldn't put you in jail like threatening Jack and me with a gun will."

"I've got too much at stake to quit now," replied Drisco. "Besides, no one is ever going to find out. These guys are pros. They will make it look like an accident just like I did with those two patients of yours who died suddenly."

Meredith went cold. "What are you talking about? Do you mean you had my grandmother and Colonel Smathers killed? I don't believe that. They died of a virus, which wrecked their immune system. They weren't shot or anything like that."

"How do you think they got the virus?" Drisco asked smugly. "I made it right here in my own laboratory and paid someone to inject it into them."

Suddenly everything that had happened came together for Meredith. This was the missing link to the mysterious *Time Magazine* reporter who had contacted her grandmother and Smathers shortly before they died. Infuriated, Meredith blurted out, "You bastard!" and leaped across the table, attacking Drisco, and knocking his chair backwards. While she had some training in Tae Kwan Do, she was too angry to think about using it. She just punched him repeatedly in the face. Rocco pulled out a gun of his own and used it to strike Meredith on the back of her head, knocking her off Drisco. Before Jack could come to Meredith's aid, Eric stood up and pointed his gun in his face.

Drisco got up with a bloody nose and some bruises starting to form around his mouth. He pulled out a handkerchief and held it against his nose. "Get them out of here," he said in a shaking voice. Having someone physically attack him was a new experience. The battles he fought in the boardrooms, while just as vicious, had never escalated to a physical level. He went over to the bar sink and turned on the water to wash up.

"Olivetti, make it easy on yourself," said Eric. "If you don't, you and your girlfriend are going to suffer a lot before you die. I want you to get up slowly and walk out of the office in front of me."

With a grunt, Rocco picked Meredith up, put her body over his shoulder, and followed Eric out of the office into the hallway. As he did so, he reached into the side pocket of his coat and pulled out the elevator key card that Drisco had given him earlier. He activated the elevator call button. When the door opened, he entered, followed by Jack and Eric, who was still holding a gun to Jack's back. Eric pushed Jack to one side and pushed the button for the second floor. *So much for getting help from the bloody building guard,* thought Jack.

CHAPTER 79

THE ELEVATOR DOOR OPENED and Eric peered out to make sure that no one was around. The floor had been completely deserted when Drisco had shown them the back way out earlier in the afternoon, but it never hurt to check. Eric then motioned with his gun for Jack to leave the elevator and start down the hall ahead of the group. Rocco brought up the rear, with Meredith still slung over his shoulder. They turned right at a hallway junction, passing between rows of laboratories. Suddenly there was a yell from Rocco and Eric turned quickly to see what was happening. Rocko was standing under an emergency decontamination shower, soaking wet. Meredith had pulled the shower handle as they walked under it, and had squirmed out of the startled Rocco's grasp. Taking advantage of the confusion, Jack stepped behind Eric and kicked him in the crotch. Eric groaned and doubled up in pain, but did not drop his gun.

"Run!" yelled Meredith. She grabbed Jack's arm as she sped by him, urging him into action. The two ran down the hall and ducked into a corridor on the left just as they heard a 'pop.' Eric's shot that whizzed by them on the right. The hallway came to a dead end. Acting quickly, Jack tried a door which had a biohazard sign on it. It was locked.

"Now what?" he asked.

Meredith didn't answer but stepped in front of him and kicked the door open. The two rushed into a large biochemistry laboratory. One wall was lined with isolation hoods containing culture media. The center of the laboratory had several benches with chemical apparatus common to such laboratories – glassware on stands connected by glass and rubber tubing, containers of various chemical reagents, and scattered notebooks. There were no obvious hiding places. Jack and Meredith scrunched down behind a bench just as their two pursuers burst through the door, Rocco still dripping wet from his unexpected shower. The setting sun was streaming in the western windows readily illuminating the contents of the room. Meredith and Jack could not move without being seen.

"I'll stay here by the door and you search the room," said Eric.

Rocco moved slowly into the room, his position marked by the squishing noise his wet shoes made on the floor. Meredith looked at Jack with panic on her face. "What are we going to do?" she whispered.

Instead of answering, Jack stealthily opened a sliding door of the bench and searched through the bottles stored there. He pulled out a bottle containing concentrated sulfuric acid and said to Meredith, "There's a large beaker on the table just above your head. See if you can get it without those two seeing you."

Meredith slowly reached up and lifted the beaker off the bench. She passed it over to Jack who poured it half full of the acid. Unfortunately, Rocco had caught the motion out of the corner of his eye and yelled to Eric, "I've got them. They're over in the back of the room. You move over to your left to cut them off and I'll go down this aisle. Remember, we don't want to kill them here unless we have no choice."

Jack handed the beaker to Meredith and whispered, "They don't want to shoot us here. We can take advantage of that. Stay behind me and when the fat guy comes around, I am going to stand up in front of you with my hands in the air. Follow my lead and when I jump aside, throw the acid in his face. Then run like hell through the side door behind him before the blond guy can get over to us."

As Rocco tiptoed around the end of the laboratory bench, he saw Jack and Meredith crouched down about fifteen feet away. He smiled and said, "Game's over. Stand up and come with me or I'll just shoot you right now and worry about cleaning up the mess later."

Jack stood up slowly in front of Meredith and put his hands in the air. Meredith, blocked from Rocco's view, stood up behind Jack, holding the beaker of acid in front of her.

Rocco called out to Eric. "I've got them. Come on over."

Eric started to walk across the room, still slightly hunched over from the kick Jack had given him. He definitely intended to make Jack suffer for that before finally killing him. No crap about this being *just business*; that kick had hurt. He brushed against the corner of a lab bench as he went by, knocking over a glass flask, which shattered on the concrete floor. Rocco looked over at the sound and Jack leaped to his left shouting, "Now Meredith."

Meredith threw the acid at Rocco's face. There was a low hissing noise as the acid hit. Rocco yelled and put his hands up to his eyes screaming, "God damn it! I can't see anything!"

Jack pushed Rocco to one side and ran by him with Meredith right behind. They ran to the opposite side of the laboratory, and opened the side door just as Eric fired another shot. The bullet hit the wall beside the door. The two turned to their right and ran down the hall, took a quick left at a corridor intersection, and ran right into three men holding guns. Two of the men crouched down and pointed their guns at Jack and Meredith. The third stood upright, also pointing a gun at them.

"FBI!" said the standing man. "Stop right where you are and put your hands behind your head."

Meredith and Jack slid to a stop and looked at each other. "Crap," said Meredith. "More of these gangster characters."

"Hands behind your head right now or I'll shoot," yelled one of the crouching men.

Meredith and Jack were out of places to run, so they slowly put their hands behind their heads. They did not notice that Eric had turned the corridor behind them. Seeing the two of them in front of him, he quickly fired a shot which hit Jack in the back of his right leg, knocking him to the floor.

"Get down!" yelled the standing man, and as Meredith hit the floor beside Jack, the three opened up, with several bullets hitting Eric. Eric fell backwards dropping his gun. Two of the men ran past Jack and Meredith to where he was lying. "Dead'" said one of the men after feeling for a pulse.

The man who appeared to be in charge walked up and knelt beside Jack who was bleeding profusely from a leg wound. "I'm Agent Wilkins," he said. "You must be Olivetti and Jones. Looks like we got here just in time. Would have been here sooner, but it took some time to get a warrant for entering the building. Let's get some pressure on this leg and call an ambulance."

"Are you really FBI agents?" asked Meredith.

"Yes Miss," answered Wilkins. "It's a long story, but we have had this guy, Martileni, under surveillance for some time because of suspicion that he is involved with organized crime. He has been doing extensive money laundering for them. We've had a tap on his phone. We picked up a conversations between him and the head of this company, Peter Drisco, setting up what sounded like a hit. We investigated further and discovered that you two were the lucky ones that Drisco wanted to take out. We have been discreetly monitoring things but couldn't let you know what was going on before we had the evidence we needed on Martileni and Drisco."

"There's another one of these gunmen in a laboratory back there. He's probably stumbling around and not seeing much of anything since I threw some acid in his face."

Seeing the look on Wilkins's face, Meredith quickly added, "I had to. He was going to shoot us."

Wilkins called down to one of his men, "Dave and Mort, come back here and put some pressure on this guy's leg and call 911 to get an ambulance here right away. Miss, you show me where this other gunman is."

Dave came back and held a folded handkerchief against Jack's leg while Mort called 911. Meredith led Wilkins back to the laboratory from which she and Jack had recently escaped. Rocco was nowhere to be found, but there was the shattered beaker and foam where the acid splashes had eaten into the concrete floor. Wilkins quickly called for backup and told Meredith to wait while he searched the lab. Meredith stood quietly as Wilknns walked up and down the rows between the laboratory benches holding his gun in both hands. When he had completed his search, he stood up and said, "No sign of him. He probably got out the other door. We'll search the building when the rest of my men arrive. You go back and wait with Olivetti."

"Don't forget about that damn Drisco. He may still be in his office upstairs."

"No, we checked there first. No one around."

"Then check our lab at the university. Drisco was going to go there to get rid of the evidence showing that he had his company deliberately mess up the production of a cancer treatment virus we had him make. He screwed over a lot of people and we can prove it."

Wilkins quickly made another phone call and sent a security team to Jack's laboratory. The subsequent search of AVARTEC failed to turn up the second gunman. Meredith rode with Jack in the ambulance to the emergency room of State Medical Center, where he was quickly admitted and prepped for surgical repair of the gunshot wound.

CHAPTER 80

THE SECOND TEAM OF FBI officers quickly arrived at the university and joined up with the building security team. The security officers led the way to Olivetti's laboratory. The door was locked but the men could see that the lights were on. Using a master key card, the security officers opened the door, and with guns drawn, the FBI officers led the way into the room. They found Drisco and Beckwith taking samples out of the freezer. The desks had frozen slides and flasks scattered over them and several laboratory notebooks were stacked on a table, ready to be removed when the two intruders left.

"What is the meaning of this?" sputtered Drisco as the officers took him into custody.

"Peter Drisco, you're under arrest for attempted murder. We have a team at your company and we've stopped the men you hired to kill Jones and Olivetti," said one of the officers who then read him the Miranda act.

"Murder?" questioned Beckwith, whose face had turned a pasty color. "I had nothing to do with that. I'm only here to retrieve some viral samples that I made earlier. Drisco told me to make some changes in them and that's all I did."

"Shut up," cried Drisco. "Just keep your damn mouth shut until my attorney gets here."

"Your attorney can meet us downtown," said one of the officers. Then he turned to Beckwith. "I don't know who you are and what part you've had in all this, but I'd advise you to be completely candid with us. It will go much easier on you if you do. Right now we only have you for unlawful entry and theft, but if you lie to us, it will also be obstruction of justice." Then he read the Miranda act to Beckwith as well.

The officers took Drisco and Beckwith downtown in separate cars and booked them separately. Both men wanted to talk with their attorneys before saying anything further to the agents. Beckwith's attorney listened to his client's story. Then he quickly cut a deal with the authorities that would preclude any prosecution for criminal activity relating to the deliberate mistreatment of the cancer patients who had received the mal-engineered treatment virus. In return, Beckwith told the whole story about the scheme to discredit Olivetti's work and gain control of the process for AVARTEC. This resulted in additional charges against Drisco. While the FBI wanted to nail Drisco for all that he had done, they wanted Martileni even more since he was their entrée into a much larger criminal operation. They needed Drisco's testimony for that. The Feds decided it was time to play "let's make a deal," and Drisco's attorney took full advantage of this. A few weeks later, the body of a heavy-set, swarthy man was found in the southern part of Puget Sound. The body had facial burn scars and a bullet hole in the head. The Seattle police asked Jack and Meredith to view the body and they identified it as one of the two men who had tried to kill them in the AVARTEC building. This left Peter Drisco as the only one who could link Martilini to the attempted murder. The Feds emphasized his vulnerability to secure his cooperation.

Chapter 81

(Epilogue)

THE SURGERY ON JACK'S wounded leg went well, but it took a while to re-establish mobility to nearly the same level as before. It took months longer before he could enjoy a run again. Drisco's testimony had implicated the dean and Pillipitch used his connections with Meredith and Jack to develop a pipeline into the case. He had a field day writing a series of articles which described in detail the scheme and the part played by Dean Schmitt. Schmitt was quickly terminated by the Board of Regents as an embarrassment to the University. He made feeble noises about 'due process' and the 'faculty code' but this came to naught. It became known that Blackmont had paid the dean for his help in placing the investment bonds for the new research space. For falsifying the agreement letter and concealing the true nature of the transaction, Alice Maxim lost her job as well. Her parting with Schmitt was acrimonious, to say the least. The dean's office was in total disarray for several months as attorneys for State poured through all the records to see what other misdeeds the dean might have committed. The members of the Blackmont directors voted to remove Martilini from their advisory board. He had been indicted for his role in helping to arrange the murders of Jack and Meredith and for using his financial contacts to launder money. AVARTEC common stock bottomed out as investors unloaded it as fast as they could. The common stock of other pharmaceutical and life sciences companies dealing primarily with oncology also fell sharply as investors learned about the radical new form of treatment that Olivetti's lab had developed. State University's overall research effort had only a brief hiccup. Then it recovered because of the influx of funds by various pharmaceutical companies. They wanted to establish a strategic position in terms of developing and marketing Olivetti's treatment. Several also thought that the technique of antisense blocking of key genomic elements could be applied to diseases other than cancer. Much to the relief of State and the Blackmont Investment Group, the new research complex on Eastlake Union remained financially viable.

With the guidance of his high priced attorney, Adam Martilini continued to stonewall the authorities. A great many people were anticipating Drisco's arraignment and wondering what he would say in court. Martilini's associates decided to take their own precautions, and on the day before the arraignment, Angela Fromm entered a building across the street from the main entrance to the courthouse and took up residence in an empty room overlooking the street. There she set up a .308 sniper rifle with a high-power telescopic sight on a tripod. She stood far enough back from the window that nothing was visible from below. Knowing that it would be difficult to target Drisco because of the precautions the Feds were taking, Angela's assignment was Martilini whom his bosses had instructed to be present when Drisco testified. The supposed idea was to intimidate Drisco, who would then be more circumspect in what he said in court. The courthouse entrance was only 150 yards from Angela's position, an easy shot for someone of her skill. She targeted Martilini as he was entering the building with his attorney. As she was squeezing the trigger, Angela smiled and thought briefly of one of her conversations with Drisco when he told her about the elaborate way he wanted the two cancer patients taken care of. *There's more than one way to kill someone and simpler is always better.* The right side of Martilini's head exploded as the bullet struck it and expanded. Angela then quickly disassembled her rifle, put the components into a nondescript carrying bag, and left the building through an entrance on the side away from the courthouse. Scared witless by Martilini's murder, Drisco told everything he knew in court. But without Martillini, the FBI's organized crime investigation quickly came to a dead end.

After completing her MD at State, Meredith took a research fellowship position at the NCI. However, she never stopped thinking about her grandmother's death and wondering whether her murderer would ever be caught. Jack was courted intensively by both academic centers and PHARMA. Eventually, he accepted a position at Harvard, in part because this afforded him an easy commute to Bethesda to spend time with Meredith during her fellowship. After that, who knew what the future would bring?

About The Author

George Laramore holds both a Ph.D. in physics and a M.D. He is a professor at the University of Washington with a career in cancer medicine spanning 36 years. He has been named to numerous "Top Doctor" lists and is the author of over 240 technical papers and book chapters. He enjoys foreign travel with his wife, Shelley. Other interests include running, skiing, and scuba diving. He lives in Seattle, Washington, and has four grown children.

www.ingramcontent.com/pod-product-compliance
Lightning Source LLC
Chambersburg PA
CBHW060756030726
47503CB00002B/274